PRAISE FOR *OURS IS A TALE OF MURDER*

"*Ours Is a Tale of Murder* is a brilliant puzzle of seemingly unrelated stories, intricately and expertly woven together into a satisfying, tense, and unexpected thriller. Congratulations to Nora Murphy for creating a gripping and moody world filled with danger and misdirection that entertains from beginning to end."

—Darby Kane, #1
international bestselling
author of *Pretty Little Wife*

"Beautifully creepy. Deliciously dark."

—Iliana Xander, bestselling
author of *Love, Mom*

"Nora Murphy's riveting thriller *Ours Is a Tale of Murder* is not what it seems…in the best possible way. Three seemingly disparate stories, all captivating in their own right, pull the reader toward a shocking collision, made all the more satisfying by Murphy's brilliant twists. The stakes are high, the casualties tragic, the losses profound. Clear your schedule—you won't be putting this down until that last, mesmerizing page."

—Carter Wilson, *USA Today*
and *Publishers Weekly* bestselling
author of *Tell Me What You Did*

"Slick, masterful writing combined with sleek, serpentine twists add up to a first-rate domestic suspense. Murphy weaves together seemingly disconnected stories in delicious, frightening, and satisfying ways, creating a tale that quietly and cunningly asks a timeless question: How well can we ever truly know our neighbors?"

—Ashley Winstead, *USA Today* bestselling author of *This Book Will Bury Me*

ALSO BY NORA MURPHY

The Favor

The New Mother

OURS IS A TALE OF MURDER

OURS IS A TALE OF MURDER

A NOVEL

NORA MURPHY

Cover design by James Iacobelli
Cover images © sharply_done/Getty Images, Marco Bottigelli/
Getty Images, Karl Hendon/Getty Images
Internal design by Laura Boren/Sourcebooks

Sourcebooks and the colophon are registered trademarks of Sourcebooks.

Published by Sourcebooks Landmark, an imprint of Sourcebooks
1935 Brookdale RD, Naperville, IL 60563-2773
(630) 961-3900
sourcebooks.com

Cataloging-in-Publication Data is on file with the Library of Congress.

Printed and bound in the United States of America.
KP 10 9 8 7 6 5 4 3 2 1

For my sons.
My love for you is
the biggest thing in the world.

Part I

THE STORY

It might seem, as you read, that ours is a story of love.

It's not.

Ours is a tale of murder.

But that's to come. First, there was love. Or something like it. Something that looked like love, that wore its scent like a spritz of perfume.

Something that sounded right, that felt true.

Something that was always, actually very, very wrong.

1

When I see you for the first time, it's clear that you have already seen me.

You stare from across the room, unabashedly, exhibiting no consideration for the possibility that your attention might not be welcome. I don't like it. *How rude,* I think. *How entitled.* Even while a thrill disloyal to my feminist and self-protective principles rips down my spine.

You were scanning the sea of black and charcoal and navy, of tired faces tugged by artificial smiles, and your eye caught on me like I was a sparkle, a reflection from the face of a watch or an engagement ring trailing across the ceiling of the room. Your eye caught, and it held.

Heather, my coworker, an associate two years my junior and who accompanied me to the event, orders a red wine from the man working the open bar. He passes it to her, along with an impractically small paper napkin. She takes a sip, and it coats her teeth like she's a vampire who's been disturbed mid-meal. She's my closest friend at work these days, driven and sarcastic and shrewd. But she'll probably make partner before I do, and that will drive a wedge. We'll grow distant. I'll invite someone else to these dreaded networking events.

The bartender blinks at me, eyes smiling, starbursts of wrinkles at the corners. "What would you like?"

"White, please," I say, still thinking of Heather's teeth. White, please, but nothing more specific than that, because choices are few at a low-budget event like this: red or white or beer.

I take my plastic cup of wine and taste it. Unwillingly, my eyes find yours. I knew you would still be looking, and you are. You stand in a little group with two other men—one youngish, like you, and one much older. I draw my brows down in distaste, as if to communicate to you that I don't like your staring. It makes me feel unsettled, not flattered. But you're grinning, practically gleeful, by this point. It is already too late. You believe that I'm seeking your gaze for a different reason, for the same reason you are seeking mine. That is the sort of person you are, I think—assured, self-possessed. I don't know you, but I know this about you immediately.

"This is shit," says Heather. She wrinkles her nose and tips her cup of wine toward me. "Smell it. I think it's sour."

I lean forward but only pretend to smell it. Even when it's freshly opened, even when it hasn't turned, red wine smells to me like wet leather, like the water that collects in the bottom of the trash bin that's sat out in the rain all day.

"Because they're cheap," I say. "It was probably from a bottle with a screw-on lid. It was probably left over from last month's event."

Heather grimaces, but she takes another sip. "Well," she says, straightening a bit, pulling herself taller, "should we mingle?"

I scan the room, which is packed tightly with lawyers, some in cheap suits, some in expensive ones. Most old, but some young—the people *and* the suits. Some are *youngish*, like Heather and me. I've just surpassed my ten-year anniversary in the workforce, and it's been a long time since I've felt *young*. The grind of private practice takes its toll. The sea of faces, pale and tired, and the suits, navy and black, blend together indeterminably, interminably. Still, I find you easily. This time, you aren't looking. Is that disappointment that flickers to life in my gut?

"I suppose," I say to Heather. "Show face. Kiss a couple of asses. Then get the hell out."

"Stop somewhere decent afterward?" Heather asks. "For something to eat and a real glass of wine?"

"Mmm," I murmur noncommittally. I don't want to stop somewhere decent afterward. I'm tired, and I want to go home and go to sleep. I mentally scroll through my calendar. A deposition the next morning. I need to get up early and review my outline. I don't want to, of course. I would prefer to sleep in, take a spin class, shower leisurely and use that unopened foot scrub that has been resting on the corner shelf for the last month, stop for a pumpkin spice latte on my way to the office. But I can't do any of that. Instead, I must prepare. Because I must make partner. I am thirty-five. It should have happened by now, at a firm the size of mine. It's practically shameful that I—a career-focused, unmarried, and childless woman in her mid-thirties—still have the title of *Associate* on my business cards and in my email signature.

"Are they not serving food here?" I ask Heather, looking around the room again, presumably for servers hefting silvery platters or buffet-style tables dotted with dishes, but also for you. This time, I can't find you.

"I think they are," she replies. "If you can call it that. I'm sure it's shit."

The room quiets just as she finishes her sentence, and her final word—*shit*—rings out obviously. Heather's cheeks redden and mine redden for her, and for myself because of my proximity to her, my association with her, a person who has unfortunately and accidentally shouted "shit" into the ill-timed silence that fell over the crowd at a bar association event.

Silence fell because of the woman standing by the double doors that lead to the rented room of the restaurant. She'd been tapping on a microphone, trying to get the attention of those gathered inside. "Good evening," she was saying, again and again, looking around hopefully.

"Thank you all so much for coming," she continues, the microphone held crookedly beneath her chin. "I'm Audra Kohn, the president of the Montgomery County Bar Association. Welcome to the fourth-annual Judicial Reception."

I drink my wine while she expresses gratitude to the sponsors who paid for the venue, for the wine that tastes like shit, and for the food that has yet to make an appearance. Audra thanks the members of the association who planned the event, a mixer to show appreciation for and honor the county's judges. The sea of faces is all smiles; they nod. They all know the event is really for flagrant ass-kissing and free wine, even bad free wine.

When she stops talking, I turn to Heather. We'd shown face, hadn't we? Should we just go? It isn't partner-like to leave so early, but I'm not a partner, and I've spotted Christine Fierra standing not five feet away from me. Christine was a year behind me in law school, yet she is a partner at her own law firm, which is even larger than mine. I know this from an update I saw on LinkedIn. We were on *Law Review* together. Friendly, but not friends. I don't want to talk to her, to be looked at with a gaze that is both condescending and kind, to have her ask, "What's partnership track at your firm, Klara? Is it not eight years?" Innocent-sounding, but prim and supercilious, a veiled dig. That is the sort of person I remember Christine to be.

But when I turn, it's no longer Heather to my left. It's you.

You are close, and you are smiling.

"Hi," you say, as if we already know each other.

"Hi."

I think I say it. But a second passes, and I'm not sure if I actually spoke. My ears begin to ring because up close, you are very handsome, albeit a little short. Your dark—almost black—hair, thick and wavy, is coaxed tidily into a side part. Your eyes are light brown, just a shade darker than your tanned skin. Your nose is straight and your cheekbones high, your features symmetrical. All of it makes up for your lack of height, and you are standing quite near. There's a thrumming, a strumming, picking up strength within me, despite my brain screaming for it to stop. We are inches apart, and I see so clearly now that you are, that you will become, precisely what I feared: A distraction. A demise. Of something. Of what, I don't yet know.

You hold out your hand. "I'm Troy," you say. "Troy Weston."

I look at your hand for a full three seconds, maybe more. I stare at it for so long that you laugh. "Are you really going to leave me hanging?" you ask. You laugh, but there's a ripple of disbelief, of shame, of *how dare you*?

It is almost as if I know already, even though I can't possibly know already: *Take your hand, and it's all over*. I should eschew it—rude, but eschew it nevertheless.

My instincts kick in. I don't shake your hand.

2

He jerks his hand back, drops it to his side. He wants to look around to see if anyone witnessed him getting rejected by Klara Martin, but he doesn't. That would only make the whole thing more embarrassing.

He doesn't need her to shake his hand, to introduce herself. He already knows who she is. After all, she is the reason he's here. That doesn't mean he's willing to accept such overt repudiation.

He saw her at the last bar association event, but he didn't speak to her then. He noticed her across the room—her delicate features and wide brown eyes, rimmed with luscious curtains of lashes, her chestnut hair falling, thick and shining, to the middle of her back.

She was petite, but not quite thin enough to be considered thin. She was *cute* more so than beautiful, yet she was the only person at the event who was cute—approaching pretty—and for that reason, she stood out.

He was struck by a piercing desire to know her—a desire too strong, too persistent to be explained away by her attractiveness alone. It was something more than that, and he's felt it prodding at him ever since.

He observed her that night from a distance, watching her chat and drink her piss-like wine. Later, he checked the RSVP list from the event and searched for every female name on it until he found her profile on her law firm's website.

Klara Martin. She was a personal injury attorney with the firm Barron & Briggs in downtown Rockville. Based on the year she'd graduated from law school, he calculated her to be thirty-five years old, assuming she'd not taken any gap years. She looked younger than that.

After he found her online, he sought her out in person. He went to her office, walked past the building, spent some time in the surrounding area. On several occasions he found her, and he enjoyed the feeling of watching her when she had no idea she was being watched, of being close to her when she was completely oblivious to his presence.

Today is his chance—his opportunity to meet her. He came to this event solely with the hope that she would be here. And here she is, refusing to shake his hand, and he's livid. Yet he's never wanted her more than he does in this moment, and he had already wanted her quite a bit.

He can't explain it. There's just something about her. A pull. A draw. Recently, he'd been thinking that at thirty-seven years old, it's past time for him to settle down, get married, *start a family*, as people say. For Troy, it's an expression that is more apropos than cliché. *Start* a family. Something new, something he hasn't ever really had before. Besides, he's grown tired of all the women. The women who made him feel wanted but were too superficial or too young or too desperate, or not desperate enough. The few women whom he'd most wanted to stay had fled. He's ready for someone who fits just right—or someone whom he can make fit.

He'd been thinking about that quite frequently; then he saw her, felt her pull. Two unrelated happenings that became inextricably linked solely because of their coincidental succession. It had to mean something. He would make it mean something, anyway. He had a problem, and there she was: his solution.

At last, he's meeting her. Making contact. And she's embarrassed him in front of his peers.

He rubs a hand through his hair. "Sorry," he says, although he's sorry for nothing. But he's noticed that apologizing when you're not at fault tends to stoke guilt in the other person. "I didn't mean to upset you."

It works.

She smiles. Tightly, but it's there. "No, I'm sorry." She still isn't looking at him, like she's afraid that if she does, she won't be able to look away again.

"It's just, you know..." He tucks his hands into his pockets, sheepish. "I was doing what I was supposed to do here—mingle, network... Get it over with."

She snorts delicately. He'd not known that a snort could be delicate, but hers undeniably is. He feels his resolve renew and solidify.

"I mean, not that talking to you is a chore. Or maybe it is. I don't know you, do I? I'm sure it's not, though. These events are just always so painful. I mean, not that talking to you is painful." He slips a hand from his pocket and rakes it through his hair again.

Actually, he enjoys networking events, but the fact that she does not is written across her face. Perhaps she's shy. A wallflower. No wonder she's still an associate—not yet a partner.

Then again, neither is he.

But he's close. And now's not the time to focus on that.

"I'm really fucking this up, aren't I?" he continues, still sheepish, charming, twisting his face into an expression of concern and shame.

"Just a bit." She smiles again, less tightly. He can already see her resolve unspooling before him, growing thin and malleable, just as his own is crystallizing into something firm and strong that will soon take hold of her as much as it has taken hold of him.

"Could we start this over? Unless you'd like to leave," he adds. "I can't say I'd blame you."

She hesitates. A blink, then two. Fluidly, timidly, she stretches her hand toward him. He can see her horse-faced friend over her right shoulder. She watches them, brows raised. She moves away. *Good girl.*

He reaches out and envelops Klara's hand, small and soft and fragile, within his own. It's dry, her nails neat and unpainted—a lawyer's hand. It's a hand that spends its days turning pages of discovery documents and tapping at a keyboard or cell phone.

"I'm Klara," she says.

I know, he thinks. He smiles down at her gratefully. "Troy. Troy Weston."

"Nice to meet you." Her words sound rote and empty. It won't be that way for long.

Soon, she will mean it.

Soon, he will be everything.

"What do you practice, Klara?" he asks.

"I do PI work," she replies. Personal injury work. He knows this already, of course. She takes a tiny sip of her white wine—a delicate sip. Everything she does is delicate.

"Plaintiffs' work or defense?"

"Plaintiffs'," she says. Nothing more, not reciprocating any of his small talk, but he doesn't care.

"Ah," he replies. "You're one of the good ones, then."

"'Good'?" she asks. She blushes, barely—just the faintest pink creeping across her cheeks.

"Good," he confirms. "Inherently good. I can tell."

The blush freezes in its tracks. Fear and discomfort come to life in her eyes, which shift away from his own. He's gone too far.

"Soulful work," he clarifies. "Not like what I do."

The bait is dangling, and he knows that if she bites, there's still hope. If she doesn't, he's better off extricating himself and trying her another time. At the next event, or perhaps orchestrating a chance encounter, as much as it would pain him to walk away when he's so close.

She does bite, in the form of another tiny and delicate action—a smile.

She hasn't asked what sort of law he does, but he decides to tell her anyway. "I'm a commercial lawyer," he says. "Transactional work. Ninety percent of it would put anyone to sleep."

"But it pays well." She takes another sip of wine.

Is that a dig or a compliment?

Her friend is back, a knowing smile on her lips. Pretending he's been bumped by someone behind him, he takes a step toward Klara, angling his body against hers so that if she glances over her shoulder, she won't see her friend. He can feel her warmth now. He can smell her, her scent of cleanliness. Lemon. Olive oil. Natural, or like high-quality hand soap. He wonders whether her firm also has a no-perfume policy. Margaret, a real estate paralegal with an allegedly deathly allergy to sandalwood, is responsible for the perfume ban in his own office. More than once, he's thought of spritzing some on her desk after she's gone for the day to prove that the allergy is exaggerated, if not fabricated entirely.

"Do you practice mostly here in Montgomery County?" he asks. He keeps the conversation hovering in the realm of professionalism, although he would very much like to steer it toward the personal.

"I practice all over the state. And in DC," she says. Her lack of politeness, by not returning his questions, seems to have gotten to her, for she adds, almost grudgingly, "And you?"

"Our clients are all over," he replies. "We can handle most transactions remotely."

Someone behind him does jostle him then. The room is too crowded; the bar association had clearly rented the smallest-possible space to accommodate the turnout. Too small, in fact. It's warm from all the bodies, and people are packed closely together, having to mutter *excuse me* to get to the bar, the bathrooms, the table where the food is being deposited, revealed, and served.

He had no warning, and he stumbles forward, toward Klara, then against her. He bumps into the hand that holds her plastic cup of wine, and she spills it down her front, the liquid soaking her ivory shell.

"Oh," she says, looking down in surprise. He can see the lace of her bra beneath the damp, now-transparent fabric. She must notice it, too, because she quickly closes her tweed blazer around herself, buttoning the top to cover the spill.

"Klara," he says, "I'm so sorry."

"Not your fault," she replies quickly.

"What can I do?" he asks. "Send me the dry-cleaning bill, of course."

She's already moving toward the door. He follows her.

"Don't be silly," she says over her shoulder. Her words, in her soft and youthful voice, are almost swallowed by the din of small talk and exaggerated laughter. "I'll just throw it in the wash."

She's only being polite. The shirt is silk. Not suitable for the washing machine. It was white wine, but the fabric is still ruined.

"Are you leaving?" he asks, feeling ridiculous because that's clearly what she's doing.

She pauses in the doorway, turning toward him. "You've given me an excuse to get out of here," she says. "And I'm taking it. I didn't feel like being here anyway."

"I'll buy you a drink sometime," he says. "To make up for it." He sounds desperate. He is, but he hates to sound it.

"No need," she says. She turns away again. "You've done me a favor. Nice to meet you."

There's a finality to those words. *Nice to meet you.* What she means is, *Conversation over.*

And just like that, she's gone. Out of the rented room, into the restaurant, then onto the street beyond. He watches her go.

She didn't even say goodbye to her friend or tell her she was leaving. She practically fled.

He stands in the doorway, not sure what to do. Follow her? Not to speak to her again, but just to watch her?

He can't follow her, he decides. If she saw him, she would be furious. Or worse, scared.

He spins around and returns to the too-crowded room. On his way into its depths, he stops at the bar and orders a beer. The bartender passes him a bottle of something cheap. He sips it and grimaces.

He came here for one reason alone. He feels like he's failed.

Perhaps he has. For now. But it won't last. It never does. He will get there in time. In time, he always gets what he wants.

And what he wants is already so clear. It's her. A life together—a suburban house, matching rings, routine, and comfort. Hers and his.

3

Is it the most tired trope in suspense fiction—the reclusive woman observing her neighbors from the comfort of her home? He would know; he reads enough of it. Highsmith is his favorite, although he can't think of when she ever employed that particular trope.

They have one here, in the neighborhood of Hawthorne Heights. She has chestnut hair with the shine of hotel-lobby floors and brows a shade darker. They're often furrowed and disapproving. She's beautiful, but would be even more so if she smiled. Her husband has neatly parted hair and a sensible black sedan. He leaves the house by 8:00 a.m., and he's usually home by seven. On Saturday mornings, they walk through the neighborhood together with waxy, environmentally devastating cups from Starbucks. Henry hasn't yet seen her walk without him, even though she's home far more often. On Sundays, they go grocery shopping, and they unload their purchases from the trunk of the husband's car with the garage door gaping open, reusable totes on full display, as though to advertise that they aren't total assholes—while they might like pumpkin spice lattes in disposable containers, they do, in fact, *care.* They're the sort of couple who discusses adopting a dog but hasn't pulled the trigger. *It's not the right time. Let's wait until the kids get older*, they say, although they don't have kids yet. They pay to have their grass mowed, weeds pulled, and house cleaned on occasion, despite that the woman seems able bodied, relatively young, and theoretically capable of doing much of that work herself.

How does he know all this? Because that's the twist, if you haven't already guessed it. Here in Hawthorne Heights, it's not that she, the recluse, watches everyone else. Henry watches her.

He watches them both. The wife and her husband. The unhappy couple.

Henry has no idea what it's like to be part of a couple like them.

They are beautiful, but it's funny—a little unsettling, honestly—how much they look like they could be brother and sister: twin glossy, brunette heads, features symmetrical and attractive, which Henry can see even from a distance.

Even their house is symmetrical and neat, a brick-front colonial with pale-green shutters. The wife bought pansies for the planters that hang from the eaves of the front porch. A repairman came by on Tuesday to work on the left garage door. But there's a stilted sort of energy about the house, an aura of unease. They're a couple with problems and history. They aren't happy.

Henry assumes they were happy at some point. Aren't all couples happy at some point? Otherwise, how did they end up here, rings glinting on their fingers, living in a suburban house in the enviable and mundane neighborhood of Hawthorne Heights?

Forsythia and azaleas bloom along driveways and sidewalks, and the sky is a cloudless blue. The unhappy couple heads out for a Saturday-morning walk. It's late May. They're still new to the neighborhood; their routine is taking shape.

They walk quickly, as though to discourage any chatter or pleasantries from neighbors who happen to be out. They're enigmatic and aloof, which only makes them more attractive. They don't smile, nor do they speak—not to each other, not to anyone—as they pass the windows of Henry's house.

The husband's hair is lush, and Henry hates him for it. Henry is only twenty-eight, yet his own hair, the color of a muddy puddle of rainwater, is thinning at the crown, not thick enough that he could style it to conceal the wink of his scalp. To compensate, he's recently grown a tidy beard and mustache. He thinks it's an improvement, but his mother doesn't. He catches her staring at him sometimes, her thoughts elsewhere, lips tugging downward in an expression of disappointment, or disbelief, as though she isn't quite sure when or how he came to be old enough to have facial hair at all.

"What are you doing?"

Henry startles, spins around. It's his mom, of course. She's been sneaking up on him for as long as he can remember.

"Nothing," he says. He drops his hand, lets the curtain fall closed. It's linen and scratchy, peppered with dog hair, although the dog died last year and they haven't gotten a new one. His mother should launder them, vacuum them. He doesn't tell her this.

She frowns then, as though he said what he was thinking. But he didn't, and that isn't why she's frowning. She just doesn't like that he's standing here, in front of the window, telling her "Nothing," when it's clearly not nothing.

He doesn't like it any more than she does. It's been *months*. It feels much longer. It feels like he's been here forever, like he never left, like he might never be able to leave.

Maybe he still lives with his parents, but he's no longer a child. Henry steps past his mother. He moves around her as he leaves the living room, staring straight through her as though she does not exist at all.

4

Owen was always a quiet boy. Even when he was a newborn, pink and wrinkled with those glassy onyx eyes, he almost never cried.

"He's such an easy baby," she would always tell Ed, smiling fondly, and Ed would grunt and turn the page of his newspaper.

She was so hopeful then. He was pure gold, her boy. He'd make them happy. They'd have another one, another easy baby. The children would grow, and their eyes would track her wherever she moved, and Ed would look on, thinking what a good mother she was.

She's not sure if he ever thought that, and there never were any more babies. Which was for the best because Ed wasn't a good person. The best thing about him was that Mary loved him, and that was the worst thing about her. The worst thing she'd done.

She was foolish to ever be so hopeful.

And everything that happened after, with Ed and with Owen, certainly wasn't all Ed's fault, but it wasn't hers, either.

Nor was it Owen's. Her quiet boy, pure gold.

Mary's knees creak like the stairs as she ascends. She moves past the pictures that hang on the wall in their thick wooden frames: gray photos of her parents, photos of Owen when he was a baby and then a little boy. There are no pictures of Ed.

She clutches a roll of trash bags as she steps into the bedroom at the end of the hall—the bedroom she never goes into.

It's preserved: the bedroom of a fifteen-year-old boy, which is how old Owen was when he last slept here.

But now she needs to sell the house, so everything must go. She doesn't want to lose it, but money has become tighter than ever, and the house is the most valuable asset she has. She grabs at her throat as though that might help her breathe, because she suddenly can't breathe at all.

She crosses the room and sinks onto the bed, and that creaks, too. The comforter is navy and covered in a fine layer of dust. Her eyes flick around her: To the wallpaper border of baseballs, gloves, and bats she installed herself when Owen was three. To the oak bookshelf stacked with fantasy and science fiction novels she used to vow to read, too, so that she'd have something to discuss with her son. To the closet door, which is closed but still holds T-shirts and jeans and the black suit Owen wore when he was twelve and Mary's parents died four months apart.

Mary unfurls a trash bag from the roll, but she goes no further than that. She's frozen, still sitting on the bed where her son slept for nearly a decade, white plastic dangling from her fingers.

This will, she understands, be even more difficult than she thought.

5

I leave you there in the crowded room. I leave Heather, too, without saying goodbye.

I text her as I stride through the too-chilly-for-October air, into the too-dark parking garage toward my car. I spilled wine down myself so I ducked out. Sorry. See you tomorrow.

She texts back as I'm sliding into the front seat of my car: No worries.

Another text follows immediately: Who was that guy??

I ignore the message and return the phone to my bag.

Who was he indeed.

Troy Weston. I remember your name with irritating ease.

I've never been a fool. I know you were hitting on me. You could have chosen to "network" with any other lawyer in that bustling, busy room. You chose me for a reason. You probably clocked my face, my hair, my bare left ring finger.

She'll do, you thought.

You were self-effacing, charming—but it was a calculated sort of charming. Not natural, not flowing and silken, but forced and sharp-edged. It didn't sit well. It rests, still, uncomfortably in my gut like a heavy meal followed by a rich dessert I should have declined.

I turn on my car and flick my headlights on, then corkscrew my way down the parking structure, toward the exit gate. The meter devours my ticket, I charge the exorbitant parking fee to my credit card, and I race from the city as if I'm driving a getaway car, glancing in the rearview mirror like I'm afraid I'm being followed.

I park in a resident-reserved spot in the garage beneath my building, then ride the elevator up to the seventh floor. In my kitchen, I turn the recessed lighting to glowing, white life. Lynn, the woman who cleans for me, was here earlier in the day. I can smell the citrus-oil soap she uses on the wood floors, and the granite counters and chrome pulls gleam. This place has never felt less like a home.

I slide a pre-made meal out of the freezer, puncture the plastic film more aggressively than is necessary, and toss it into the microwave. The half-drunk bottle of pinot grigio chilling in the door of my fridge is tempting, but I know a second glass of wine will only make me sleep more poorly. Sitting on a stool at the island, my cell phone resting beside my tray of food, I eat with one hand and tap out responses to emails with the other.

Ignoring my shower, the foot scrub, and the soaker tub I've used only a handful of times, I wash my face and change into my silk pajamas. Lynn always makes the bed with alarming precision, and it takes several tugs before I'm able to free the edge of the comforter and slide between the sheets. My laptop propped on my knees, the television on the wall across from me playing last week's episode of *Real Housewives*, I respond to more emails, questions from clients and opposing counsel streaming into my inbox unrelentingly, no matter the day or hour.

"Lonely," I say into the otherwise-empty room as I snap my computer shut and place it on my nightstand. Instantly, I regret saying it aloud. Somehow that's made it more real.

It's real anyway. I'm lonely.

I glance at the other nightstand on the opposite side of the bed. It was never Adam's nightstand, nor was this his bed. He never set foot in this condo, in fact. I purchased it for myself after our relationship ended, and I moved in alone. I bought all-new furniture to fill it. Nevertheless, the presence of the second nightstand, never used, makes me think of him.

My own nightstand is dotted with my things: Lavender-scented hand cream. A squat glass of aging water. A plastic container of earplugs. My black silk eye mask. My laptop. TV remote.

I grab the laptop and crawl to the other side of the bed, placing it on top of the second nightstand. There. Now it's being used. Not superfluous.

Except, it still is, actually, and I don't feel any better.

I'm feeling vulnerable and self-pitying, and I know that nothing good can come of that.

I slide my eye mask onto my forehead and curl onto my side, the remote control in my hand, lying in wait to turn off the screen as sleep begins to take hold. More than likely, I'll doze off with it on. I'll wake in the middle of the night, disoriented by the flickering light and sound.

I try to focus on the show, to block out all thoughts of loneliness and Adam.

It works. For a moment. But then it's you who rushes into my mind. You and a feeling that something is missing. A feeling that I am missing something. Or missing out on something—something that has to do with you.

I fled that restaurant, my guard up, my hackles raised like the fur on a dog's neck as it races through its yard, toward the scream of a fox from the woods beyond the fence. I left you behind.

I *did* miss out on something.

I just don't know yet if it was something good or something bad.

6

A deviation in the routine: On Friday they leave in the husband's sensible black sedan. It's dinnertime, so perhaps they're heading out to a restaurant. Perhaps there's something to celebrate.

Henry has something to celebrate, too. He has the house to himself. His parents have driven up to the suburbs of Philadelphia where his perfect, milestone-meeting sister lives with her perfect husband and perfect baby.

"We're going to sell this place, eventually," his mom likes to say, a warning in her tone. "It's too big for just us. When your dad retires, we're going to move closer to Laurel."

There's so much to unpack there, and Henry has done it.

Too big for just us, by which she means just her and Henry's father. As though Henry's not there. Like he doesn't live there, too.

And of course they're going to move closer to Laurel, to her baby who looks like every other bald, white baby who's ever existed.

I'm sorry I've disappointed you so, Henry sometimes wants to tell her. Maybe if he apologizes, she'll feel bad for her own failings.

And she doesn't even know the real—bullshit, but real—reason he was laid off from his job. The things he's done, she has no idea. If she did, if she knew about his interest in their new neighbors, the unhappy couple, she'd lose her shit.

Henry can see the flash of their faces now, the husband and wife, as the car rolls past his house. It's still light out, the days only getting longer. They look grim, like they're heading to a funeral, but Henry doesn't think that's likely. On a Friday night?

For a long time, Henry sits in the living room and reads, their return giving him something to look for, something to look forward to.

But he must have missed it. Suddenly, it's nearly midnight and he's fighting sleep, having finished four of his dad's craft IPAs. But he never saw the couple return home.

At some point, a gentle rain commenced, a whisper-soft patter that fills Henry with an inexplicable calm. He decides to stop fighting, and he lets himself drift away, there on the sofa, empty can tipped sideways on the floor beside him, if only because his mother isn't there to see it or voice her disapproval.

The next morning, Henry's head and back are aching. He drinks water and coffee and Gatorade and tries to ignore the tenderness in his temples. He spends most of the day searching for jobs and finds a few new ones, to which he applies. But a sense of futility sinks in his gut, heavy like a shipwreck. He might be invited to interview. He might get through to the second round. But it will go no farther than that. They'll press him as to why he's been out of work for so long. They'll want to speak to his references, and when he supplies them—only two, and none from his most recent employment—he will receive a terse but tactful email letting him know the company has decided to move in a different direction.

And it's not fair, because Henry isn't going to make the same mistakes again.

He has no need for a pretty colleague with slate-gray nails, hair that smells like lemons, or mauve lips she is always checking in the compact mirror she keeps in her top desk drawer, beside the tin of cinnamon breath mints and three half-empty bottles of eye drops.

Henry never should have found out the brand of the mauve lipstick. He never should have purchased his own tube to touch and smell, smear across the pads of his fingers to rub together until there was heat. He shouldn't have known about the cinnamon mints, the eye drops. But he did know.

He doesn't completely lack self-awareness. He understands that he crossed lines, that he's come dangerously close to being caught. But he's learned from his mistakes. None of that will happen again. Not with a colleague.

Now he has her—the wife.

She's lonely and she's sad, and Henry feels a connection to her because he feels these same things. He feels a thread pulling between them, and he wishes he could see more of her. He wishes he could get closer. He wishes they could speak.

On Sunday evening, his parents return.

"Do you want to see the pictures of Mason?" Henry's mother asks, approaching him in the kitchen, phone screen already alight.

"Okay," Henry says, although he knows her question was rhetorical.

She settles next to him on the family room sofa, while his dad sits on the worn leather recliner and turns on the Orioles game, indifferent to Henry's presence, his open novel. His mother swipes through photo after photo of the chubby-cheeked baby, now with wisps of blond hair. It could be any baby, and Henry feels nothing as he looks at the pictures, while his mother grins at the screen and tells Henry that the baby giggles now and will start eating solid food soon, and she is planning on steaming, mashing, and freezing sweet potatoes and pears and bringing them up to Laurel's house every few weeks.

"Sounds good," says Henry, because it does. He wishes his parents would visit their grandson every weekend, although Laurel probably doesn't. But maybe she doesn't mind their parents' presence. Perhaps she likes the help, and she and her nondescript husband go to the movies or out to restaurants or take naps. It's his understanding that Laurel hasn't returned to work yet, so she must spend an awful lot of time with the child, which must be boring. It must be lonely, though admittedly, not as lonely as Henry's existence.

Then his mother adds, "Of course, it would be much easier if we could move closer. Dad is getting tired of working, you know."

Henry's father grunts noncommittally—a sound that could mean anything.

"I think we'll start looking at condos soon," his mom continues. She locks her phone screen, and the baby's face disappears. She stands and smiles faintly, then meets Henry's eyes. "Something small and manageable," she suggests tentatively.

Henry wants to laugh. As if he might be offended? Someone would have to pay him to live in a condo with his parents. It's bad enough living with them here, and here he has the basement to himself, with a full bathroom and kitchenette.

But no one would ever pay him to live with his parents. It seems no one will pay him for anything, so if his dad does retire, and they do sell the house, where will that leave him?

Henry no longer feels like laughing. He shuts his book and stands up.

"Oh, that's low," says his dad, and Henry's head snaps toward him. But his dad is staring at the television, talking about a pitch, not his wife's words. He probably didn't even hear what she said. Henry wishes he was so skilled at tuning her out.

7

The question burning in his gut as Troy approaches the high-rise office building sets a thrill tingling in his fingertips and kicks off a fluttering in his chest. How will she react?

This could go only very badly or very well. It's a risk, but one he feels he has no choice but to take. What else could he do? Attend every local bar association event with the hope that she might be there, too? That didn't work for him last time. In fact, it was rather disastrous.

But it has created an opening for what he's about to do.

The gift bag dangles lightly from his right hand. He clutches the rose with the fingertips of his left, its stem smooth, the thorns shaved away by the florist.

Troy arrived at the bar association event hoping to see Klara and prepared with a cover story. He wasn't making a pass at her, wasn't *hitting on her*—he'd always hated that expression. Call it what you want, he was merely networking, mingling, in the most platonic way. He is trying a different tactic now. Courting. Wooing. Christ, is there not a bearable way to describe any of this? The point is, this time, he's making his intentions quite clear. It's time for a Gesture.

Klara's office building is tall and reflective, although somewhat less so than his own building, which is a modern monstrosity in downtown DC. Troy pushes through the revolving door and scans the digital directory for Barron & Briggs. Suite 310, third floor. Typically, he would take the stairs, but nervous sweat already pricks his underarms, and he doesn't want to do anything to encourage its flow nor speed up his already-hammering heart. So he rides the elevator two stories up and steps into the office with *Barron & Briggs* engraved into the wall of glass.

The receptionist is pale and doughy. Her eyes meet his, and Troy smiles, holding both the rose and gift bag where she can see them.

"Can I help you?" she asks uncertainly, as though duly perplexed as to how someone like her could ever be useful to someone like him.

"I'm here to see Klara Martin." Assurance drips, his grin widens.

The nameplate on the desk's ledge reads DAWN REED and, redundantly, beneath her name, RECEPTIONIST.

Dawn squints at her computer screen.

"Sorry," she says softly. "I don't see an appointment on Ms. Martin's calendar right now."

Troy laughs, but patiently, kindly. "That's because it's a surprise." He hefts the flower and gift bag even higher. "Call her, would you?"

Dawn appraises him for several long seconds, during which Troy fears she might refuse simply because someone like her would never be the recipient of a surprise long-stem rose and a carefully wrapped present from someone like him. And the fact that this woman, who looks like a bag of flour dressed in a lavender button-down blouse, could foil his Gesture before it's even really underway makes him want to scream.

But then she lifts her corded phone to her ear. "Name?" she demands.

"Troy," he replies.

She blinks twice, hand hovering over the keypad of her phone.

He widens his eyes as if to say, *That's all you need; she'll know*, but the truth is, that might not *be* the truth. His is not a common name, but still, Klara might not recognize it. It pains him to admit that she might not remember his name at all.

"Weston," he adds reluctantly. "Troy Weston. Thanks, Dawn."

She flushes at the sound of her name and taps at the buttons on the phone.

Relief courses through his veins as Dawn murmurs, "Hi, Klara," into the phone.

She's at her desk. It didn't even occur to Troy that she might be in a meeting or out of the office. As it turns out, he was right not to fret over that possibility.

Yet his anxiety is there. Simmering like a low-grade fever. He's perplexed by his lack of calm confidence, which is usually as reliable as his breathing. He both loves and hates this. He both loves and hates what Klara Martin is doing to him.

"Someone is here to see you," Dawn continues. Then, ducking her head away from Troy, as if that will conceal her words, "Troy Weston. I *know* he doesn't have an appointment."

A pause while Troy's heart pounds and blood thunders in his ears.

"Okay, thanks," says Dawn before hanging up the phone. "She'll be right out," she tells Troy. "You can have a seat." She tips her head toward the row of armchairs arranged in the small waiting area.

Troy thanks her, then strides across the room and drops into one of the chairs, but he's disappointed. He was hoping to go back to Klara's office. He was hoping for privacy.

He waits so long that he can't help but wonder if Klara is

making him wait on purpose, if she's hoping he will give up and leave. The petals of the rose wilt, the stem warming between his fingers.

Finally, once panic has begun to course through his mind, obscuring and inhibiting any clear or rational thought, once Troy has begun to consider that perhaps he should just cut his losses and leave, he hears faint tapping against the shiny tiled floor, silken and creamy, and Klara steps into the reception area.

The source of the tapping reveals itself—a pair of red suede kitten heels. Black ankle pants expose inches of golden foot and the very base of her shins. Her blouse is also black, and a scarf with an abstract print of coral, indigo, and red that matches the shade of her shoes perfectly is tied loosely and jauntily around her neck, for fashion rather than warmth. Her mouth is tight and tense as she approaches; her eyes, which he'd remembered as warm, chocolate, and inviting, are hard and cold, and she brushes a curtain of dark hair away from her face as she comes to a stop in front of him. Troy watches her gaze fall to the rose, the gift bag, and he's disappointed to note that her eyes remain devoid of pleasure or excitement. She has clocked his offerings, yet she isn't happy.

"Let's step outside," Klara says before Troy can speak, and then she's holding the door to the office open for him, and her quick and effortless seizure of control irks him.

Troy is aware of Dawn's amused eyes on him as he slips from the office. He wants to whirl toward her and hiss, "Just wait." He doesn't, of course. He moves several steps down the hall and waits for Klara to join him.

She lets the glass door to Barron & Briggs fall closed with a dull thud. She approaches but keeps her distance, as if he has foul body odor.

"Troy," he says, and he smiles, trying to convey warmth, an

absence of threat. "We met at the bar association event the other night."

"I remember," she says curtly, not elaborating as to whether she remembered his name or whether she only remembered meeting him. How could she have forgotten that? He spilled his drink on her, after all.

Hence the gift bag, which he holds aloft.

"I know you said I couldn't pay for your shirt that I ruined, or pay for it to be cleaned—but, well, I haven't been able to stop feeling bad for what I did, so I had to bring you this."

She seems to lean toward him infinitesimally, but she hesitates, not taking the bag.

"Please take it," he continues. "For my sake. If you toss it into the trash the second I step into those elevators, fine. Just don't tell me. But I had to do something to assuage my guilt. I hope you understand."

There it is then, the softening around her mouth and eyes, the chocolate beginning to melt.

"It's really not necessary," she says, but she takes the bag.

Pressing his luck, or perhaps just reading her correctly, Troy extends the rose. "This is for you as well," he says. His eyes are cast down, unable to meet hers, the very picture of embarrassed admiration, of shy respect.

"Oh," she says as if surprised, as if she hadn't previously noticed the rose, when he is certain that it was the very first thing she noticed.

Troy blows out his breath in apparent relief. "Thank you, Klara," he says. "I already feel so much better." He's grinning at her broadly now, and he can tell that he has her.

"Have a great day," he says, and he turns away from her, still smiling.

"You too," he hears her murmur. She seems rooted to the spot, surprised. Like she was expecting him to say more, and that's exactly what he wants.

Troy strides down the hall and pushes into the stairwell, hurtling down two flights and out of the office building, back to his car.

He knows what will happen next. The surprise will wear off, to be replaced by disappointment. A gift, a rose—that's all? She assumed he was going to ask her out on a date, and when he didn't, she was left feeling arrogant and ashamed and, yes, disappointed.

When she returns to her desk, she'll open the bag. She'll remove a shirt—a new ivory silk shell to replace the one he ruined. It will be too small for her, but she will find this flattering rather than annoying. She will unfold the shirt to inspect it, and a small handwritten card will fall to the ground.

Klara,

I couldn't bear to ask you to your face, lest you reject me to mine. But I also couldn't not ask. Join me for dinner sometime? A lunch, a drink, a coffee? I'd love to get to know you better. No hard feelings either way. I'd just never forgive myself if I didn't take the chance.

—Troy

Beneath his name will be his phone number. She will bite her lip as she drops the note into her purse, feeling relieved and confused. She'll agonize over the note for the rest of the day. She'll agonize over it all night—alone in her home, alone in her bed, alone. The sweetness and humility of the Gesture will become too much for her to resist. She will type that number into her phone and then type out a text. She will agree to see him.

8

She starts with the clothes.

Mary slides a hand into the trash bag, separating the clingy plastic. She tells herself not to look at the clothing. Don't even consider it. Everything must go. She'll donate it all. Owen always wore basic, timeless clothes. He was a peaceful boy, and he wasn't rough on his things. No smears of mud or tears in the knees of his pants. No yellow stains under the arms of his shirts. The clothes are old but in decent shape. Another boy could wear them. All Mary needs to do is grab them from the drawers, tug them from the hangers, and shove them into the bags. She doesn't even need to look at them.

She opens the top dresser drawer. Socks, which makes things easy. Who ever gets nostalgic over socks?

She does. She did. She can remember clutching handfuls of his baby socks, white and balled up like used tissues, and holding them to her chest, crying because he was too big to wear them. She thought that was sadness. She had no idea back then how completely her heart would break.

Mary does not let herself do that now. She moves as quickly as she can, dropping handful after handful into the bag. She moves on to the next drawer, then the next. She breathes quickly, heaving, so close to dry sobs, and her shoulders shake with the effort not to cry.

Once the dresser is empty and two trash bags full of clothes rest on the floor beside her feet, she goes to the closet. She unfurls another bag and begins to pull the clothes from the hangers, ashamed about the roughness with which she's pushing them into the bag, that they're not rolled or folded neatly, but this is all she can manage. Her breathing has evened out, her mind nearly blank, and she's doing fine. She's doing quite well, all things considered.

Until she reaches for the caps on the top shelf of the closet—two Orioles hats, one black and one white, yellowed around the bill—and a piece of paper flutters down with them, lands on the floor, tented and small.

The paper is flimsy and old, and Mary crouches down, knees and hips protesting wildly. She picks it up and stares at the words on the page. It's her own handwriting, her own words.

Owen,

My love for you is the biggest thing in the world. Never forget that.

Love,
Mommy

And beneath that is a little picture she drew of herself. A stick figure with a lopsided smile, black button eyes, strings of hair that curl under around at the height of her shoulders, the way she used to wear it before it became so sparse and gray.

She remembers writing Owen this note. She wrote many such notes for Owen throughout his childhood, yet this one strikes a particular chord of pain.

It was always a balancing act, being Owen's mother. Things

would have been so much easier if that had been her only role. But she was a teacher, too. And she cared about that, about her work. Not as much as she cared about her son, but she did care. And she was Ed's wife. She and Ed had been together since she was sixteen years old. His temper was fiery and Mary's loyalty ardent, which ultimately made for a deadly combination.

But for all the years up until that impossibly horrible night, Mary tried to make Ed think she was on his side sometimes. As a result, there were many times she needed to keep her mouth shut when all she wanted was to defend Owen. This was for Owen's sake, she'd tell herself. It was for his safety. Because there was a line in their family. It was Ed on one side, and Mary and Owen firmly on the other. But Ed couldn't see it that way. She couldn't let him think that his wife was against him.

Mary runs the pad of an index finger across the faded ink. *My love for you is the biggest thing in the world.*

When Owen was ten, Ed wanted him to try out for a summer baseball league. Ed had played baseball all through high school, and Owen was tall and strong. He was left-handed. He'd make a great pitcher, Ed used to say, and Mary would smile because that was as close as Ed ever came to expressing affection toward their son, even if it was only hypothetical—affection for a person Owen might potentially be, rather than for who he was. And who he was was an artsy boy, who preferred heading into the backyard with a sketch pad rather than a ball and glove.

But Owen enjoyed the attention from his father, too. For several months before the tryout, he did go out back with his dad to practice pitching. Mary would stand at the kitchen sink and look through the window above it. Occasionally, she'd hear Ed's voice rising. A few times, Owen stormed into the house, face streaked with tears, leaving Ed to lean against the siding, smoke a cigarette, and mutter angrily to himself. But most evenings, things went fine. They'd come inside together, cheeks flushed, hungry for Mary's cooking.

The morning of the tryout, Mary knew immediately that something was wrong. Owen was slow to rise, and once he finally did, he shut himself in the upstairs bathroom. She lingered in the hall, hearing the toilet flushing, the water running. The sounds ceased; the door remained closed.

Ten minutes before it was time to leave, Ed came upstairs, second cup of coffee in his hand. His mustache was neatly combed, and he was wearing a red cap Mary couldn't remember seeing before.

"Where is he?" he asked Mary, who was still loitering outside the bathroom, hoping to catch Owen, to have a moment with him, before Ed did.

Mary sighed, tipped her head toward the closed door. She tapped on it gently. "Owen, honey, it's almost time to go."

"Come on," Ed called. "You need to eat before we leave. Something hearty, with protein."

"I'm not going," said Owen, words tumbling like they'd been waiting to fall. But only Mary could hear him.

"What?" Ed said. "What did he say?"

There was the tiniest hint of worry in his voice, and for a second, Mary thought it would all be okay.

"I don't want to play baseball," Owen said with a boldness that stunned Mary. "I hate it. I don't want to make the team. I'm not going."

There was a second of silence. Then, in an eerily calm voice Mary had heard many times before, Ed said, "Come out and tell me to my face."

If Mary'd had a moment alone with her son, she might have

pleaded with him to go to the tryout anyway. *Just go and don't pitch very hard. Then you won't make the team, and Dad will accept it better than if you don't even go.*

She wasn't certain that was the truth, but she knew instinctively that refusing to try at all was worse.

"Maybe we should let it go," said Mary. *We*. Like she was on his team.

But too late—the bathroom door swung open, and Owen was there. He stared at his father with a defiance only a child would be naive enough to exhibit.

"All those nights practicing?" Ed said. Each word was clipped and controlled. "Hours and hours of time wasted."

"That was your idea," said Owen. "Not mine."

Fortunately, Ed's coffee wasn't terribly hot. When he flung the cup at the wall, the liquid arced and splattered, more of it soaking Mary than Owen. The mug hit the hardwoods with a dull thud. It didn't even break. Mary watched it roll a few feet down the hall.

"What is the point?" Ed said. "What is the point of you? I might as well not even have a son."

Mary wanted to charge toward him. She wanted to run straight into him and shove him down the stairs. Obviously, years later, she'd wish that she had. That would have been as good a moment as any to end things.

"Oh," she said automatically, weary and not as surprised as she should have been. She sighed, looking at the coffee soaking her dress and pooling on the floor, as though the mess was the worst thing about what had just happened.

Ed thundered down the hall, into the primary bedroom. The door slammed; the house rattled.

Owen's eyes met Mary's briefly, but he said nothing. He knew the routine. He stepped past her, returning to his own bedroom. Mary heard the lock click.

Mary used a spare towel from the linen closet to sop up the coffee. Soon, she'd have to go into the bedroom to talk to Ed. But not yet. He needed some time.

Her tears were hot on her cheeks, and she felt saturated with shame, with sorrow, as though she needed to be wrung out and hung to dry. He deserved better, her boy. Her sweet boy. This was his father. It wasn't fair.

She found a clean dress hanging in the laundry room, so she put that on and dropped her stained one into the machine. She went into the kitchen and started a fresh pot of coffee so she could bring a new cup to Ed. And while it dripped, she thought about leaving him. About collecting some clothes and her boy and driving away. But the truth was, she was scared of what Ed might do if she did that. And wouldn't Ed be entitled to see his son? He'd claim he wanted to, if only to spite her, and then she'd be away from her boy every other weekend, or perhaps even more than that. He'd be with his dad, and Mary wouldn't be there to protect him.

The carafe was nearly full. While the machine steamed and expelled its last gurgles, Mary slipped a piece of scrap paper and pen from the kitchen drawer where they kept such things, and she wrote her son a note. She drew a little picture of herself, as she always did when she left a note for him, although she wasn't sure why and she wasn't a very good artist.

Her throat felt thick; it wasn't nearly enough, but she hoped he understood that it was all she could do at that moment. She carried the paper and a fresh cup of coffee upstairs, and as she passed Owen's room, she slid the note under the door. Then she kept walking, down the hall, to her own bedroom, to her husband. To the man she'd once loved but now despised with a passionate and vehement sort of hatred that could only be love's successor.

Owen had saved the note. It had meant something to him. She could see him lying in his bed, tracing his fingers over the letters she'd written, finding comfort in them.

Mary folds the paper along the familiar creases, then slides it into the pocket of her pants. She's not sure what to do with it, just that it doesn't belong in the trash.

9

I meet you outside the restaurant. I am two minutes late, but only because I lean against the building around the corner, my back pressed against the brick, and I wait for those two minutes to pass.

Nerves pump hotly through me. Why did I come? Why did I agree to go out with you?

It was too many nights alone in my shiny new condo, falling asleep to *Real Housewives* reruns next to that damn empty and superfluous nightstand. It was the absence of Adam; the absence of my father; the deficiencies of my mother, both past and present. It was my best friend, Zoe, settling into life as a new mother, too exhausted, too overwhelmed with meeting the needs of her newborn to even think of helping to meet mine. It was that rose, with its velvety petals, and that blouse, too small for me to wear, and imagining you standing in Ann Taylor, holding it up skeptically, fretting over the style and size. It was the note, with its neat block handwriting, and the fact that you didn't ask me to my face.

The note gave me a chance to think. It allowed me to decline your invitation without having to tell you in person. I could have simply ignored it—tossed the note in the trash, never put your number into my phone. But with that time to think, I realized I didn't want to.

And I didn't want to think. I was tired of thinking.

I haven't dated anyone since Adam. Ever since Adam left,

I've been protecting myself from future heartache. But was my self-protection not helping me at all? Was it hurting me, actually? What have I been missing?

Now, my back against the restaurant wall, I'm thinking again. Regret is setting in. Or is it really just fear wearing regret's lipstick and clothes? Would I really rather be in my empty condo watching a frozen meal spin in the microwave?

It's unseasonably cold, and my breath leaves in puffs of white, fast and ephemeral, but I feel pricks of sweat soaking the fabric of my bra. I open the buttons of my black wool coat, welcoming the chill.

I push myself away from the wall and round the corner of the restaurant before I can think any more about what I'm doing. Before I can change my mind.

There you are. You're looking away, like you expect me to come from the opposite direction. You turn as if you can sense my presence, the way I can feel yours. Sparks and light ignite inside me, and I see that same brightness that I feel in your eyes, too. Sparks, but also relief because I'm here. You were afraid I wouldn't show up. You smile and step toward me, and the sparks catch. We don't touch. Not yet. But we move into the restaurant together, our bodies so close that I can feel your warmth, and something hums in my core. It scares me.

We sit across from each other at a table by the window. A white tablecloth grazes our knees and a white tea candle flickers when waiters rush past. My eyes fall to it every few minutes, checking to see if this surprisingly resilient flame has gone out. Really, I'm just taking a break from your gaze, from what I can see in your eyes.

You ask for a bottle of wine—white, and I'm relieved I don't have to explain my aversion to red. When the server returns with the bottle, you let me test it, a tiny swirl in my glass, which I sniff, then sip.

"I trust your judgment," you say, grinning, even though you don't know me at all.

We order our meals, and you ask the waiter to confirm that yours doesn't have any nuts or sesame seeds.

"I'll make sure, sir," he says before slipping away, and you turn to me, a sheepish smile, as though your allergies are something of which you're ashamed. The vulnerability of you, your open face, tender when your eyes meet mine, in a way it's not when you're looking somewhere else. A blush blooms and my eyes flick away, smile pulling.

We start with safe topics. *Where are you from? Where did you go to law school?* We talk about our jobs. What do we like about them and what do we hate? For me, it's jury trials. You laugh at this, charmed and stunned. "You're a personal injury lawyer," you say. "How can you hate jury trials?"

I tell you that I settle most of my cases. I only try a few cases a year, and I love to settle them. That's what keeps me going.

I tell you I was surprised to learn that you're not a litigator, and my cheeks flush anew because it sounds like an insult. It makes it sound like I don't like you, and I realize with a prickle of surprise that I do. I'm enjoying myself more than feels safe to consider.

But you only laugh and say you had litigated commercial cases for a few years and you did like it, but better growth opportunities within your firm drove you to focus on transactional work instead.

I eat sesame-crusted salmon on a bed of spinach and rice, and you have the seafood pasta.

"Sorry," I tell you, pointing to the sesame seeds with my fork. "You won't have a reaction, will you?"

You shake your head, wave a hand through the air. "Not unless you're having a miserable time and slip me a bite when I'm not aware."

"I would never," I tell you, and I'm astonished by how deeply I mean this.

We eat slowly because we have so much to say. The bottle of wine you ordered gradually diminishes, and when it's gone, you ask me if I want to split another one. One more glass? An after-dinner cocktail?

I do. But I say, "I can't. I have to drive home."

You are quiet then, watching me. I can see the question in your eyes. I can read your thoughts as plainly as if they are tattooed across your forehead. But you don't say what you're thinking because you don't want to be too forward, too aggressive. You don't want to mess things up.

So I say it for you.

"Unless you want to share an Uber after this." My voice is soft, nearly a whisper, the words sounding like a secret.

There are starbursts at the corners of your eyes, a dimple in your left cheek, as you smile. You are so pleased. Yet still, a question remains. Also unspoken.

I answer it anyway.

"We could go back to my condo," I tell you. My voice is even and my tone is breezy. Casual yet bold. More sure than before. Your smile widens, consuming your face, and our eyes lock. A server removes our plates and deposits dessert and drink menus onto the table. She quickly swishes away again, and the candle goes out. The fire burns inside me instead.

It's a longing, this fire. It's excitement, anticipation, and maybe the beginning of love. It is certainly the blush of lust. It's only the beginning, yet already so fierce.

10

Her diamonds glitter and flash in the sunlight. Henry can tell, even from this distance; the glimmer on her hand couldn't be anything else.

Is this the start of Henry's opening? The wife is outside alone, for the second day in a row.

He could change into running apparel. He's not a runner, but who would know? He'd only have to jog up the street until he disappeared from her view; then he could walk, savoring the knowledge that he'd gotten closer to her, and she to him. But the unhappy couple lives directly across the street, so it would be odd for Henry to go straight across, toward their house, rather than simply head to the end of the street and cross over later. He might be able to wave, to call out, *Hello*. But would he dare? Is it time?

The wife has flowers. Earlier in the morning, she went out briefly. She walked uncertainly along the front of the house, lined with patches that once were gardens, now barren and in need of fresh mulch. Her arms were crossed in front, hugging tightly, as though she were cold, but she couldn't have been cold. Just a few seconds later, she was gone.

Scouting a spot, Henry now understands. Now she's back, with a plastic tray of flowers. He doesn't know enough about flowers to know what kind they are, only that they're orange and pink, velvet soft–looking petals, already wilting in the heat. She's digging her hands into the ground. She didn't remove her rings before she started, which Henry finds odd. He recalls that when he was a child, his father lost his wedding band when he was gardening. Years later, either his mom or his dad found the ring while planting annuals in the flower bed in front of their brick walkway. For the first time, Henry wonders whether that story is even true. Was it concocted later to explain away a period of years when marital discord silently burned beneath the surface, when his dad had refused to wear his ring?

Henry stands at the window, his book tucked under his arm. He's picturing himself walking past just as the wife rises, turns away from the garden. He'll lift a hand and wave, and she will, too. Maybe that would be enough for now.

But suddenly, the garage door lifts, and the husband emerges, khaki shorts and a bright-orange shirt with the number five. He's the sort of man Henry's dad could chat with about the Orioles. *What a season! Think they have a chance?*

The husband approaches his wife, but she remains crouched low, squinting up at him and into the sun. They speak for a few seconds.

And she never rises. This feels important. She initiates nothing. She wants him to go. She wants to finish her planting.

The husband bends. He's above her, all over her, meeting her where she stays, as their lips meet so briefly that Henry almost misses it in a blink.

Then the husband turns away again, disappears into the garage. A few seconds later, his black sedan creeps out.

A sweet goodbye kiss. That's what other people, who don't know as much as Henry, might think. But there's something possessive about the gesture. It doesn't convince Henry that he is wrong, that the couple is happy after all. Rather, it tells him that he is exactly right.

He watches the wife a moment longer, then decides against going out. The husband has marred the potentiality for a meeting. He leaves the living room, steps into the kitchen. He wants something to eat and drink, something better than the fare in his basement kitchenette. He wants to graze on his parents' snacks, fragrant honey-mustard pretzels, his favorite, and his mom's. She always gives him a sour, sternly displeased look when she catches him digging into the bag.

He was hoping his mother wouldn't be around, but, of course, she's here, lingering, looking slightly perplexed, as though she came into the kitchen to retrieve something but she can't remember what it was.

"What were you doing?" she asks, tone suspicious, like he's a toddler who has fallen unusually silent for a period.

"Just reading," says Henry, holding up his closed paperback.

"Hmm," she replies, and it's nothing but a sound, but the judgment it holds. His anger flashes like a bulb that's abruptly died.

"What, Mom?" he asks. "Just say it." He's weary. Her disappointment is like a migraine that never goes away, an unrelenting ache in the base of his skull that he occasionally, momentarily, forgets about, until the next interaction with her, until the next surge of pain.

"Well, it's just..." She cuts herself off. "Should you be reading?"

Reading. The word is drenched with chastisement, as though she's asked him if he really should be watching quite so much porn. Which, incidentally, he does. Although he's virtually certain she doesn't know about that.

"As opposed to what?" he asks, sighing.

It's Saturday, late afternoon. She opens a cabinet, begins clattering pots, searching for the one she needs, as though she has a very limited amount of time to start cooking dinner, as though that isn't all she has to do and her typical mealtime isn't still hours away.

"As opposed to applying for jobs, Henry. How are you ever going to find a new job?"

It's a seemingly fair question, but his inability to secure employment isn't due to lack of trying.

"I apply for jobs every day," he says, defensive. This is an exaggeration, but he doubles down. "Every single day. The market is difficult." His tone is gentle now, as though he couldn't possibly expect her to understand anything about the *market*.

"I just don't understand why you've not made any progress. Your grades, they were always so good. You're so smart. But it's been months, Henry. Your dad and I won't be here forever."

He's not sure whether she's referring to their inevitable demise or her continued threats to sell the house and move closer to Laurel and her baby.

"I'm trying, and I don't know what more you think I can do. There are only so many jobs I can apply for. There's not even that many. And I didn't think it was possible for anyone to make me feel worse than I already feel about this situation, but somehow you manage. So thanks."

"I'm sorry, Henry, but it's just... You could work in a restaurant. A store. You could tutor kids. There are tons of part-time options until you find the right one. At least then you could save up a little money while you're searching." She tucks a section of hair behind her left ear. It's silky looking, newly trimmed and dyed. That would explain her glorious absence for several hours the previous afternoon.

Henry laughs mirthlessly, his lips shaking with anger. He has a master's degree. He isn't going to serve overpriced food to people less intelligent and educated than he is. How dare she suggest such a thing?

He's too old to storm away from his mom and slam the door, but he does it anyway.

"Henry," she says, pleading, as he turns away from her.

He stops at the pantry on his way and snatches the bag of pretzels, and his mom gasps as though he pushed her. It's petty, but he experiences a jolt of pleasure. He pulls the basement door shut roughly and descends the stairs.

He wonders whether his mother, who hasn't worked since his older sister was born and is oblivious in so many ways, has caught on to the fact that the *market* isn't the only reason why he's been spinning his wheels.

He never told her about Lacey. About what he did. He only said that his company was laying people off. And that was what they called it, by agreement. There would be no reference for him, even though he'd been a model employee in every respect except one, but he was permitted to say he'd been "laid off," which sounded far more benign than "terminated for cause." There was an NDA, signed by all. It was quite tidy. It was quite unfair.

When he wasn't able to find a new job, he grew anxious about his dwindling savings, the cost of living so high downtown. He had to give up his apartment and ask his parents if he could move back home—he didn't have any friends with whom he was close enough, who might have let him crash on a sofa—and he told them that he'd been laid off, that the company was downsizing and he was unlucky. It wasn't entirely true, but close enough. And he always had felt unlucky, cursed.

His mother had seemed skeptical from the start. For a while, she pressed him on it, asked for more details: *Who else was laid off? Are they expecting to do more? I didn't read anything in the news about your company cutting jobs.* But Henry hasn't broken yet. And he won't. He can't.

A good mother would defend him. She'd believe him, perhaps more blindly than she should. She'd love him unconditionally. She'd be happy to have him home again, maintaining faith that he would get back on his feet in time.

Henry feels like his mother has only ever treated his sister to such unequivocal love. It's almost as though she's borne a grudge against him, for as long as he can remember, and he doesn't know why. She's his mother. How can she resent him, who is cut from her? She made him.

In the basement, Henry tears into the bag of pretzels. They don't taste good at all.

11

Adam wanted kids. I didn't.

Do you? I wonder as I watch you sleep. We haven't discussed it yet, but things have become very serious very fast. I know it will come up soon.

Two weeks ago today, we had our first dinner together. We shared an Uber back to my condo. We stepped into the elevator together, just the two of us, specs of mica in the tiled floors glittering beneath the cool lighting above us, our wavering reflections visible in the silver of the walls. I pressed my spine against the back of the elevator, feeling wine course through me, feeling fuzzy and alive and uncertain. Was this really what I wanted?

You were next to me, warm and obvious and not that much taller than I was, but I was humming and buzzing; I was pulled to you, nevertheless. Suddenly, you turned, and before I could finish my thought, before I could answer my own question, your hand was in my hair and your lips were against mine. You wanted me so badly, and that made me want you, too.

The elevator could have opened at any time, at another floor, to another resident waiting, and I felt so young.

We stumbled into my condo, and you didn't leave until morning, after we had shared coffee and shy, questioning smiles. It had been a highly successful date, but what would come next?

What came next was more dates. We have seen each other

nearly every day over the last two weeks. We've gone to brunch and met for lunch. We've grabbed coffee and held hands as we returned to our cars, shame burning on my face because I'm too old to hold hands with a boy, desire burning in my gut because I don't care. We've slept together in your bed and in mine. In my shower, my hands pressed on the glass, you moving behind me as we both watched the mirror across from us. Even once against the wall in the foyer of your apartment. It was so urgent that time, your skin burning beneath mine.

Last night, in my bed, it was tender. You nudged my hair away from my face and stared down into it. You said nothing, and it's only been two weeks, yet I heard your words anyway: *I love you.*

I watch the rise and fall of your bare chest. I can tell that you shave it, can see the stubble. I study your face, wait for the feelings to swell like the tide, to rush in like waves and foam along the beach. Nothing comes. I don't love you.

I didn't love Adam, either, at the end.

Of course, I didn't know it was the end until he told me. I thought everything was fine. I got along with his mother, and in three weeks I was set to be his plus-one for his college roommate's wedding. Sometimes, when I walked past his dresser or glanced at his nightstand, I would wonder whether he had a ring hidden inside one of those drawers. But I never searched for one.

If I had searched, I wouldn't have found a ring.

We ate linguine one evening, sitting cross-legged on our family room floor, watching *Jeopardy!* When the show was over, Adam turned the TV off and stacked our empty plates.

"You're never going to change your mind, are you?" he asked out of nowhere.

"About what?" I replied, fingering a loose thread at the cuff of my sweater. I was stalling because I knew what he was talking about.

"You will never change your mind about not wanting kids, will you?"

I could feel him looking at me.

"I don't know," I said. "I can't say either way. But how I feel about it now is that, no, I don't want kids."

I wanted to be partner, not a mom. I loved my work. And I didn't feel the need to have both, to *have it all*. I was perfectly satisfied with my career alone, with its predictability, its stability. My career was everything, and it was safer this way. How could I—who still sometimes felt like that little girl, lost and confused, whose mother put on high heels with strings that tied up her calves and disappeared into the night, who disappeared as often as she could—bring a new life into this world?

"I might change my mind," I continued, even though I knew that was doubtful. "But I might not."

Adam shook his head once, tersely. That tiny movement held a foreboding sense of finality.

"That's not good enough."

I could hear him swallow. It was the only sound in the room. Five seconds passed. Ten. Then he added, "I think we should break up."

I wrapped the loose thread around my finger, again and again, and I pulled until it tore free.

Now I let my gaze trace your strong jaw, your thick, dark lashes, which cast shadows against your cheeks.

Your lids begin to flutter, and with a heaving and rather satisfied-sounding breath, you're awake.

You catch me watching you, and you smile knowingly, as if you're unsurprised. Your eyes fall closed again. "Good morning," you murmur. "How did you sleep?"

You always ask me this, with great interest and care, as if something quite important turns on how well I slept the past night.

"Good," I say, even though I've been awake for at least an hour, my legs restless, my thoughts racing, something unpleasant and sour but nondescript, inexplicable, needling at me. "You?"

"I always sleep well when I'm with you," you say. You roll onto your side, resting your face on your pillow, inches from mine.

We blink at each other for several long seconds that stretch and sway.

"Where do you think you will be in five years?" I ask vaguely, skirting the issue, dancing around the thing I really want to know.

"Hmm," you say, the corners of your lips tilting upward. "Maybe we'll be in Tahiti. In an overwater bungalow. I've always wanted to stay in one of those. You'll be partner and I'll be partner, and we'll have senior associates to handle all of our work while we're out, so it will be a relaxing trip. We'll have cocktails on our deck, with our feet in the water, and when we get too hot, we'll jump in."

I smile in spite of myself. You're taking it for granted that we'll be together. Your vision is endearingly optimistic. But you haven't answered the question I didn't really ask.

"Do you think you'll have kids?" I say before I lose the nerve to be so direct.

Your face cracks, the fragile shell of an egg, and you're grinning. "Klara," you say. You snake your arms around my neck, tuck your fingers into my hair. "Are you already asking me if I want to have kids one day?"

I swallow and shift, although I can't move much. You're pressed too close, holding me too tightly. "I guess I am," I say.

"Why?" you ask. "What's made you want to know?"

"I'm not sure," I say, trying to sound blasé. "I just was curious."

You watch me, eyes darting over the features of my face, saying nothing.

"That was why my last relationship ended," I add, breaking the silence. Because what's the point of hiding it? I'm too old for games, for passive-aggressive maneuvers, for subliminal messages. "We were together for a long time. But we wanted different things, and it ended."

You extract a hand from my tangled hair and stroke my cheek with the soft, plush pad of a finger.

"Klara," you say, "I want whatever you want."

You smile into my face, your finger still on my cheek, and I force myself to smile back.

Should your words make me feel happy? Relieved? They don't. There's a prickle in my gut. *Too much, too fast*, it says. *Back up. Something isn't right.*

There's something else, too—another feeling or sense—but I can't quite put my finger on it. Until you speak again.

"I love you, Klara Martin," you add.

No, I think. *No, no, no.*

But you are gazing at me expectantly. You are blissful and simply full. Full of love for me. For this new and bright and hopeful thing that we have.

It never occurred to you that I wouldn't say it back. And it's far too soon, but I don't want to disappoint you. I don't want this to end. I don't want to ruin it. I don't want to ruin what would be such a beautiful and perfect moment, if only what I say next were true: "I love you, too."

12

Troy waits for Klara on the sidewalk outside her office building, his own reflection before him, looking pensive and far less anxious than he feels. He and Klara don't have plans, and she doesn't know he's here. He has no idea when she's planning to leave for the day; he could be waiting here for minutes, for an hour, for more. But there's something quite important that he wants to ask her. It feels rather urgent, and it's something he must ask her in person.

This morning was magic. He told her that he loved her, and she said it back.

The revolving door spins and someone emerges from the building. Troy turns hopefully, but it's not Klara. Just a man—older, gray, nondescript. Troy feels his shoulders drop. He hates that Klara does this to him. He hates that she still wields so much control. No one has ever made him feel so powerless before. No one has ever mattered so much. He needs to gain that control back.

And that is why he's here.

Interestingly, he awoke this morning to find her watching him. It was early, still dark, but he could see the whites of her eyes, warm chocolate centers, something pinching between her brows. He could tell immediately that something was bothering her. Then she asked him if he wants kids one day.

Apparently, she doesn't want kids, and that's why her last

relationship ended. And while he told her that he wants whatever she wants, that isn't true. He does want kids. He wants kids with her. Children are the most permanent link there is. And Troy wants to create the picture-perfect family he's never had. A devoted mother, beauty preserved, who consumes only the most reasonable amount of wine. And he, the hardworking provider, walking through the door each evening to thrilled cries—*Daddy, Daddy!* A man who puts his family first. A faithful man who shares a bed with his wife, who sleeps pressed against her, their children peaceful and content just down the hall.

He isn't worried about this diversion in vision, though, because he will find a way to achieve what he wants. He always does.

The revolving door swishes again, and someone bursts through the opening. This time it's her, curtains of dark hair swinging against her cheeks as she notices him and comes to an abrupt stop.

"Troy," she says, and he can tell she's surprised but not if she's pleased.

He steps toward her, slides a hand into a silken curtain, pulls her face toward his.

When they break apart, she's smiling. Maybe she wasn't entirely happy when she first saw him standing out here waiting for her, but she's happy now.

"Drink?" he asks.

She snags her lower lip in her teeth for a beat. "What are you doing here?"

"I wanted to see you," he replies plainly. "Drink?" he repeats.

She nods, and he holds out a bent arm. She hooks her elbow around his.

They cross the street and walk down a block. They both know where they're going without having to discuss it. A horn blares as they approach the front doors of their favorite restaurant. It's rush hour, and traffic is gridlocked. Everyone is trying to escape the city, frustrated at everyone else for leaving at the same time they did, frustrated at themselves for not leaving earlier.

Troy uses the brass handle to tug the front door open and steps aside so that Klara can enter.

They find themselves a high-top table for two in the bar area and drape their coats over the backs of their chairs before settling down and picking up the menus lying on the table.

"A glass of Riesling, please," says Klara when the server comes by.

Troy orders a beer on draft, and when the server leaves, they smile across the table at each other.

"So," says Klara, "I wasn't expecting to find you standing outside my office building."

Troy shrugs. "I wanted to see you," he says. "How was your day?"

"It was all right. Had a mediation this morning, and I was really hoping the case would settle, but the insurance company won't give us anything to work with. Not yet. It'll probably settle the morning of trial. My client has a strong case. It's just frustrating because I'll have to prep everything, and the trial probably won't move forward."

"I'm sorry," says Troy. "That is frustrating."

He leans back, giving their server, who has returned with their drinks, room to put them on the table.

"Anyway," Klara says, reaching for her wine, "how was your day?"

Troy tells her. He tells her about the commercial lease he spent the day negotiating. As he talks, he watches Klara, memorizing each concrete detail. There's a fleck of mascara beneath her left eye. She tucks her hair behind her ears, revealing emerald studs—probably fake. She's not the type to wear expensive jewelry. Her nails are bare but clean, and filed into perfect ovals.

"Do you think it will fall through?" she asks.

"No," says Troy. "I think they're just playing hardball. They need this space. We'll agree to their demands before we let it fall through."

"So doesn't that mean you're the one playing hardball?" Klara's smile is crooked now.

"Always," says Troy.

He swallows, turns his beer in a tight circle. "The truth is, Klara," he continues, "I didn't just want to see you. I was waiting for you because I wanted to ask you about something, and it just couldn't wait."

"Oh," says Klara, sitting back slightly, looking surprised. "What is it?"

"I had a thought. I know it's early, but we've been seeing a lot of each other, and things are going well." The words they said that morning seem to shimmer between them as they exchange a knowing smile. *Love. I love you.*

"I wanted to see how you felt about possibly moving in together," he continues.

Klara stills, watching him. She's a deer in the woods who has heard something. Will she stay and listen, or will she cut and run?

"I want to be with you, Klara. Every day. I want to get up before you every single morning to make you coffee. I want to hand you your lunch and make sure you have your umbrella before you walk out the door if it's supposed to rain. When I'm thinking about you during the workday, I want to text you and say, *When will you be home?* And I want to mean our home. The place we share our lives. I want to pick out new towels and sheets, and I want to buy impractical throw pillows with you and then complain about having to take them off the bed every night and wonder why we ever got them. I want—" He rubs a hand over his cheek. Klara is watching him, and he's suddenly feeling uncertain because he can detect something behind the small tightness of her smile, and he thinks it might be fear.

"Troy," she says.

He cuts her off. "I want you, Klara. I just want to be around you. And I'm sorry if it's too soon, but I just had to ask you. I know your answer might be no, it's too early—but I just had to ask in case there was any chance you might say yes."

"Troy," she says again. She takes a sip of her wine and squints at something, likely nothing, beyond his right shoulder. "I don't really know what to say. It is a bit soon, isn't it? I mean, I only just met you three weeks ago."

"Yes," he says, "but we've seen each other every day for the last two weeks. We've spent the last five nights together. It feels right."

"Have we?" Klara asks, looking surprised.

"Five," he says, nodding. "And I was expecting tonight would make six, but I might've just ruined it."

"You haven't ruined it," Klara says. "I just don't know. I mean, I only just bought my condo a few months ago. I can't imagine leaving it, and you have your apartment."

"But I don't own it," Troy says. "I'm only renting."

"Yes," says Klara. She's looking at something behind him again, and Troy turns, fearing that she's seen someone she knows. Maybe an ex. Maybe a man who's taller and more attractive than him. But there's no one there. She's not distracted by someone else, only by her own thoughts.

"I understand," says Troy. "I know why you're hesitant, and that's completely fine. No rush. I just thought I'd throw it out there, you know, in case there was, like I said, any chance you might be interested."

Troy lets his shoulders dip as he takes a swig of his beer, his eyes flitting around the room as if checking to see if anyone has noticed his faux pas. He paints himself as the picture of shame, of lovestruck devotion.

"Let me think about it," Klara says, wrapping her small hands, her fragile, delicate fingers, around her stemless wineglass. "It's a big deal."

"It is," he agrees. "That makes sense. Let's think about it."

He says it as if it was his idea, too. But he doesn't need to think, and he's actually not terribly ashamed or bothered by her hesitation. Because he will make her see how much she needs him. Soon, he will find a way to bind them together forever. He's chosen her, and he's already devoted so much. She's the one he's picked to be the family he never had. He won't let her go.

"Do you still mean it?" Troy asks sheepishly, watching Klara, his chin dipped as if he can't stare straight at her, as if she is the sun.

"Mean what?" Her brows furrow in confusion, and he has the urge to lean across the table to press his fingers into the little divot between them, the one that will, as she ages, come to be permanent.

"You said I haven't ruined things. But I have ruined the streak. It stops at five nights in a row?" he asks. "We won't make it six?"

Klara watches him for several seconds that take an eternity to tick by.

"No," she says at last. His stomach drops.

But then she lifts her wineglass and drains the rest of her Riesling, and when she puts it down, she smiles. "No, you haven't ruined it."

13

Finished with the dresser, the closet with its accordion doors, Mary turns to Owen's desk. She has no idea what to do with his computer. She's not even sure it works. It's not been turned on for nearly twenty years. But she doesn't try, doesn't press her finger to the power button or wait for that familiar sigh as the fan whirs to life. That would feel like too much of an intrusion, which doesn't exactly make sense, considering what she's doing to Owen's room and to his things. But the computer was always Owen's alone, a gift for his tenth birthday.

Ed had reluctantly agreed to the gift. "Hopefully, he'll get into coding."

"Yes," said Mary, but she didn't care. She just wanted her boy to be happy, and the things that made him happiest were the games he played on that computer and his art.

Mary sits on the floor, knees bent, legs tucked to the side. She carefully unplugs every cord from the power strip, lets the wires dangle. That's as far as she goes. She'll have to research what she can do with old electronics, but she has a feeling she'll simply put the machine into a box and seal it, bring it to the new apartment. She'll put it in a closet and never use it, and one day she'll die, and it will no longer be her responsibility.

In the top drawer, Mary finds exactly the sorts of things one would expect to find in the top drawer of a desk: paper clips, pencils, binder clips, index cards, pens, and permanent markers. Things Owen would have used for his schoolwork. He always did his homework at this desk. Every day after school, he was here. She never had to ask him. When he was older, and his school let out before the elementary school where she taught, she'd head upstairs to find him sitting in the black office chair, faux-leather seat worn. It groaned when he swiveled it side to side, and the height was once adjustable, but it would only lock in the lowest or highest settings. Ed had brought the chair home from his office one day and given it to Owen, and the gesture nearly made Mary cry. It was one of so few kindnesses he ever showed their son.

After she returned from work, Mary would always find Owen right here, head tipped down as he wrote in a spiral notebook, a browning apple core resting on a plate beside him. She'd kiss the top of his head, and his hair always smelled like sweat and freshly cut grass because he was the sort of boy who'd spend his lunch break at school lying on the ground, staring up at the clouds. If it rained or was too cold, he'd go to the art room. He never had enough friends, just a handful of boys he was friendly with, but he seemed to be excluded from after-school and weekend plans.

Mary opens the drawers at the side of the desk. One of the pulls is missing, another is loose. She finds empty pencil cases, scrap paper, binders, and spiral notebooks from his last year in school. She finds his colored pencils, the set she bought him several months before that night. She was the one who'd put the set in the drawer. She remembers in the weeks after, she'd come into his room. The set was resting on top of his desk then, with an open sketchbook.

That's all she finds there, in the desk. It's almost nothing. Not enough to make him feel real, to conjure his smell and the feel of his skin beneath hers. She doesn't have nearly enough memories of him. She was cheated out of so much. It makes her want to scream.

After a few weeks, she stopped coming into his room. Stopped trailing her hands along the colored pencils, turning the pages of his sketchbooks, pressing her cheek into his pillow. These things only made her feel worse. Everything she had with Owen only made her think of everything she didn't have. All the things they'd missed. So she shut the door and told herself, firmly, *No. No more.* The pain was unimaginable either way. And she never did open the door again. Until today.

The rush of water through pipes pulls Mary from the depths of her fruitless thoughts. The house is aging, and it seems like with each year that passes, the floorboards creak more, the pipes become louder. This time, it's a gentle stream, telltale and brief.

She knows that two floors below her, in the basement, a toilet has flushed.

14

I sit in my car, watching the rain slam against the windshield. It's a hard rain—*torrential* comes to mind. Surely it can't last. Rain like this never lasts for more than a few minutes.

Then I glance at the clock on the dashboard of my car, and I realize I don't have a few minutes. In only ten, my hearing is scheduled to begin, and I still have to unload my evidence bag from my car, walk down the ramp to the courthouse, go through security, and ride the elevator up to the third floor. My choices are get drenched or be late.

I'm appearing before Judge Palmieri, so it's an easy decision. A tardy lawyer is worse than a wet one.

I was certain I had an umbrella on the floor in front of the passenger seat, but it's not there. I searched for it without getting out of my car, as thoroughly as my skirt suit allowed, sliding the seats backward, then forward, checking beneath them, then crawling into the back seat to check the floor.

But I didn't find an umbrella.

You were with me this morning. We woke together in the same bed for the eighth day in a row.

I wanted to look professional today. I used a curling iron to form loose waves in my hair, then pulled half of it back with a tortoiseshell clip and doused my head with spray. Every hair in place, nothing to tug loose, to distract me.

You twirled a gentle finger through one of my manufactured waves.

"You look beautiful," you said.

I moved toward the door, expecting you to follow me.

"I'm going to leave a little later. I have an early call I was planning to take before going into the office," you said. Then you faltered, uncertain. "Is that okay? If you want me to leave, I will."

"Don't be silly," I told you. "Just lock the door behind you."

We blinked at each other for several seconds.

It wasn't moving in together, which we were both still considering, but it was, perhaps, the preceding step.

I opened the middle drawer of the console table in the entryway and removed my spare key.

After I handed it to you, you stared at it with wonder before slipping it onto your key ring. Then you took my face in your hands and kissed me. It felt like you never wanted it to end, as if we might melt together, into one, at any moment.

I left you there, alone in my condo, and I went to work.

It feels like enough of a step for now.

I went to the office feeling buoyant, a balloon bobbing above a toddler's head. The sky was only clouded over then, no rain yet. I reviewed my notes, packed my bag for my afternoon court appearance. During my drive to the courthouse, the rain began suddenly, but still I was unconcerned. Because I knew I had an umbrella.

I was wrong.

I peer out the passenger-side window at the sky, hoping for a break, a beam of sunlight, a brightening. But there's only grayness and more rain.

To say that my hair will be ruined is an understatement.

"Just go," I tell myself.

I move as quickly as I can. I fling my door open, then retrieve my evidence bag from the back seat. I parked as close to the front door as I could, but I still have about fifty yards to go.

My flats splash through puddles, soaking my feet. I run shamelessly, as quickly as I can—which isn't very quickly in this restrictive pencil skirt—to the front door of the courthouse.

When I push inside to the security station, the deputy sheriffs smile at me with sympathy. I heave my evidence bag and purse onto the conveyor belt, then step through the metal detector.

Although I prefer the stairs over the courthouse's creaky, old elevator, my bag is too heavy, so I ride it up to the third floor. I know I'm in courtroom 4, and I know exactly where it is. This courthouse is like my second office, but its familiarity brings little comfort. There remains too much unknown every time I walk through the doors, adrenaline pumping. Did I prepare enough? Was there something my client hid from me that will come out before the judge and make me look like a fool? Will opposing counsel be an asshole? Will I lose or forget my umbrella and enter the building looking like a drowned rat?

I find my client outside the courtroom. Sheila Fritz spins around, then stares at me. "What happened to you?" she asks.

"I forgot my umbrella." I push my wet hair away from my face. "How are you?"

"Better than you." She sniffs disdainfully.

Sheila has never seemed to like me, has always regarded me dubiously. She speaks to me as though I'm a little girl, perhaps a friend of her preteen daughter whom she doesn't particularly like. Showing up with drenched hair and, I'm certain, running makeup has done nothing to assure her of my competence and intelligence, never mind that I have always represented her competently and intelligently.

I take off my coat—a hoodless trench, because of course I

didn't even have enough luck to have worn a coat with a hood—shake the water from it, and drape it over the back of a chair in the hallway.

Opposing counsel sidles up to me then. Jason Sargent has been nothing but professional and pleasant to work with thus far, and I hope he isn't about to do anything to make me reconsider that assessment.

But he merely gives me a sympathetic smile. "Forgot your umbrella?"

I nod as I gather my hair and spin it into a twist, wringing out the water, which falls onto my blazer.

"I just checked in with the law clerk, and Judge Palmieri is finishing up a pendente lite hearing. He won't be ready for us for another thirty minutes or so."

"Oh," I reply. "Thanks."

Jason smiles tightly and turns, wandering back to his client.

There is nothing further for us to discuss. This is a discovery motion—a hearing about a motion for a protective order that I filed on Sheila's behalf. There are no settlement discussions to be had. Jason wants Sheila's medical records—specifically, her psychiatric-treatment records, to be released and admitted into evidence—and I do not. We will make our arguments, and the court will decide whether to quash Jason's subpoena or give him access to the records he seeks. Often, when I arrive for a court appearance, there are last-minute settlement discussions, and sometimes they're fruitful. This is not such a situation.

I turn back to Sheila. "We won't get started for about thirty minutes," I tell her. "The judge's prior hearing is running late. I'm going to the restroom."

"Good idea," Sheila replies. Immediately, her eyes flick away from mine, as if she can't stand to look at me.

In the bathroom, I'm appalled to discover that my appearance is even worse than I'd expected. My hair hangs limply; mascara pools beneath my lower lashes. I search my purse for a hairbrush or comb, but of course I don't have one. That would be far too convenient. All I have is a plastic fork, so I run the tines through my hair. I crouch beneath the hand-dryer and turn it on, again and again, cycle after cycle, until my hair is merely damp. When I check the mirror once more, it's an improvement but is by no means a tidy or professional look.

When I return to the hallway, I remove my outline from my evidence bag and review my notes. Although I practiced my argument several times, I feel ill-prepared and oddly, dizzyingly off-balance. I feel like a child dressed in a lawyer costume. I'm waiting for someone to chuckle at my cuteness and lead me away, back to my mother, away from this courthouse, where I so clearly don't belong. It's an unusual thought because I am thirty-five years old. I don't belong with my mother, either. I never did, and she always made certain that I knew it.

Fittingly, I lose the hearing. Judge Palmieri looks at me with skepticism over the rims of his thick-lensed glasses. When our arguments have been made, he rules from the bench, telling us that the records Jason's client seeks are to be received by him within two weeks. He will issue a written order today. He sweeps from the bench.

"What the fuck?" Sheila murmurs as we return to the ground floor. "Why did we lose?"

"I don't know," I tell her. It's the truth, but it's also a wholly inadequate thing to say to someone who is now going to have her private psychiatric records released to the insurance company of the driver who rear-ended her with his car last May. I genuinely hadn't expected to lose the motion.

"It's frustrating," I say, still dizzy and stunned. "The ruling doesn't make sense."

She merely shakes her head. She has no use for my platitudes.

I want to tell her that it's not the first surprising or nonsensical ruling, one seemingly not grounded in law, that I've received in my career—every lawyer has his or her list of them. In my experience, those lists are longer for relatively young, relatively inexperienced female lawyers. There's a bias—I've felt it countless times. It may be subconscious, but may not be. When a male attorney several decades my senior opposes me in the courtroom, certain judges have automatically awarded him a head start, an extra hundred points, before he even opens his mouth.

Perhaps my rain-washed face and unkempt hair caused a waver in my voice. Perhaps a lack of confidence in my unprofessional appearance seeped into my legal argument, at least into the way it was delivered. Perhaps Judge Palmieri simply decided that a lawyer who couldn't remember to keep an umbrella in her car deserved to be further shamed. Such is the prerogative of a judge. Wrong, unfair, but it happens. That's litigation. That's why I prefer to settle whenever I can.

I suspect voicing these thoughts to Sheila would only make her more likely to fire me.

I stand beneath the covered area outside the courthouse, watching Sheila open her umbrella and step into the deluge. She doesn't suggest that I walk with her. Perhaps she thinks I deserve to get soaked again.

Suddenly, I think of you. I ache for you. It's been an awful day, and you're the one I want to share it with.

And, unbelievably, inexplicably, there you are. You're holding a black umbrella over your head and walking toward me quickly, purposefully. You lower the umbrella once you're beneath the awning and pull me against you. I melt. Although I feel like crying, I don't let myself.

"What's wrong?" you ask, your lips pressed into my hair. "What's wrong, Klara?"

"I forgot my umbrella," I say. "And my client hates me and I lost my hearing." I sound like a brat, I think. These are minor issues in the realm of all that I could be facing. But they matter to me. I care about them, and you do, too.

"It's okay," you tell me, stroking my hair, combing it with your fingertips. "Everything will be okay. I'll walk you to your car."

I nod gratefully. "What are you doing here?" I ask.

"I was dropping off some materials for Magistrate Clancy. She's running the business section bar association meeting next week. Then I had just returned to my car and I looked up, and there you were, leaving the building. I knew your hearing was here today, but I didn't realize you would still be here."

"It started late," I say as you hold the umbrella over both of our heads with your right arm, your left wrapped around me.

I let this go, but your explanation seems off. Delivering physical materials to the magistrate? Why not just email electronic copies?

But I don't press further. I let you walk me to my car and tuck me inside. I let you bend down to kiss me. "Should I come over?" you ask, and I smile weakly and nod. You slam my car door and walk away. I watch you disappear.

And I find myself doing what I promised you I'd do. I consider how badly I had needed to see you and how much better you made me feel. And I think about what it would be like if your parting statement had not been *Should I come over?* but rather *I'll see you at home.*

It's not until later, when we're lying in bed and you're on your side, tracing the whisper-soft pads of your fingers along my clavicle, that it occurs to me that the umbrella you, on your white horse, brought to the courthouse was the exact same one as mine that was missing. And something unsettled blooms within me, like a drop of ink in a glass of water. It swirls and expands until it has turned everything dark.

15

Troy knows that Klara is considering his proposition that she move in with him. He knows that she is leaning toward agreeing. But she is taking far too long.

He pushes through the front doors of Tiffany & Co. in Chevy Chase and is immediately greeted by a salesperson who identifies herself as Elvie. She's plain-looking, with hair that's a sort of noncolor, pale skin, a pear-shaped build, and Troy is immediately skeptical of her sales skills.

"What brings you in today?" Elvie asks.

"I'm looking for an engagement ring," says Troy. Diamonds sparkle and glimmer around them.

"Ah," Elvie says. "Congratulations."

This is a bit premature, Troy thinks, but he merely smiles back at her.

Klara has seemed a bit cold toward him ever since the day last week when he met her outside the courthouse with an umbrella and walked her to her car. True, it was her umbrella. He'd taken it from her car early that morning for the very reason that he could use it to rescue her later. It was an entirely generic umbrella, though—plain black, no insignia or recognizable brand name. She wouldn't have been able to insist that it was hers or that he'd taken it. She would have sounded crazy if she'd tried, and indeed, she did not try.

"Would you like to browse?" Elvie asks. "Or is there a particular design or setting you have in mind?"

"My girlfriend is very elegant," Troy begins. "She likes classic, simple things."

"Perhaps a solitaire, then," Elvie suggests, trailing toward a particular display case. "The Tiffany Setting is the most classic." She unlocks the case and removes a ring. She passes it to Troy. "This is a brilliant-cut diamond on a platinum band."

He accepts the ring and turns it in his hands. The stone is big, probably bigger than he can afford, or at least bigger than he wants to afford. He suspects this is a sales tactic on Elvie's part. Get him to fall in love with something large and expensive so that by the time she's mentioned the price, he's already indelibly imagined it on Klara's graceful left hand.

"That's a two-carat stone," says Elvie. "Of course, you can go bigger or smaller. What sort of budget did you have in mind?"

"I'm not sure," Troy answers honestly. He's distracted because he's picturing Klara's face when he opens the box. It's an impressive ring, kaleidoscopic, its mesmerizing rainbow facets. He knows she would love it. And she is the one. This is the only engagement ring he will ever offer to anyone, and he has chosen her. It's taken him so many years, so many dates to find precisely the right woman at precisely the right time. He's never felt so serious about anyone. Their common history, their absent or distracted parents, and their shared desire for stability have pulled them together so tightly, so quickly. Klara has told him about her mother, that they're not close and never have been. That her mom walked out on Klara and her well-meaning but relatively inept father when Klara was young, nearing the age when she would have most needed her. And Troy, in turn, told Klara about his mother's drinking, his father's infidelity, his parents' volatile arguments. They never seemed to remember that he was just a floor above, trying to sleep, or they never seemed to care. That it was a relief, in some ways, when they died.

Now he and Klara are both looking for something solid. Not merely a box to check, but an actual family. Troy wants Klara to be his family. And that's what this ring means, isn't it? It's not just jewelry; it's a symbol of what she means to him. It is the only engagement ring Klara will ever have in her life. He wants her to have something special.

"How much is this?" he asks.

Elvie consults a tablet that has been discreetly resting on the counter before her. "That particular ring has excellent cut and clarity. It is..." A pause. "Fifty-eight thousand dollars."

"Jesus," Troy says. It's just a whisper. An exhalation.

"We offer financing," Elvie adds quickly. "Interest-free. You can pay for the ring over the course of a year."

Troy sighs. It's a sound of resignation. He wants the ring, and Elvie knows it. He considers his salary, his monthly expenses. He has quite a bit in savings, his bonuses over the last few years. He can make it work, even with the much larger expenses he has planned.

He has to make it work. He suddenly, fiercely understands that he needs this ring. That Klara needs this ring. That it will draw her more securely to him.

She is classy and intelligent, perhaps more traditional and cautious than she, an enlightened and educated young woman, might seem. Once this ring is on her finger, surely she will move in with him. They will marry. They will move to a house with a yard. They will have the baby Klara thinks she doesn't want. This ring is the next step in their perfect life together.

Troy hands the ring back to Elvie. “Perfect,” he says. “I’ll take it.”

16

The interview went well.

Henry is feeling rather buoyant as he drives home. He parks his car at the curb outside his parents' house.

And yes, they did ask for references. "Shoot us a couple of references in an email," they said after he'd firmly shaken their hands, before he walked out the door of the conference room in the high-rise office building downtown. The office space was modern, all glass and clean lines. It's a newer consulting company, looking to expand its IT department, and Henry's hoping they'll be less discerning than an older, more established firm.

"A couple of references" means only two. Usually, people asked for three, and he'd have to dig deep for a third—back to an internship he'd had during his sophomore year of college. And when he sent the names, email addresses, and phone numbers, the interviewer would cross-check them against his résumé, and they'd be puzzled by the fact that he didn't include anyone from his most recent employer, where he'd worked for three years. They'd notice that employment had an end date rather than saying *to present*. Which raised the stark and unavoidable question as to why no reference was provided.

But the two men who interviewed him had seemed genuinely excited about his experience and responses. As a candidate, he has red flags; this is undeniable. Suspicion will almost certainly niggle like a loose tooth. But perhaps he will finally get lucky and they will give him a chance.

Maybe soon he'll be parking outside this house as a visitor rather than an unwelcome resident. His mother makes him feel like a squatter. Her own son.

No, he decides. Once he's able to leave, he won't come back.

Henry shifts his car into park and turns off the engine. He's about to fling the door open when he notes movement to his right. It's her—the wife. She's stepped outside, through her front door, and climbed down the porch steps, a green plastic watering can dangling from her right hand, and he can tell by the lopsided and lurching sort of way she's walking that the can is quite heavy, quite full. She tilts it over the flowers she planted a few weeks earlier. While her back is to him, Henry is free to observe her, the delicate curve of her spine. Her dark hair is gathered in a low ponytail, and under the high summer sun, there's a gold sheen to it, like a stream of coffee as it descends into a cup. There have been other women he has watched, followed, approached, punished, who were more beautiful than her, but he never felt a pull toward them quite as strong as the pull he feels toward the wife.

The watering can is empty now, so she turns, unburdened by its weight, her head still tipped forward. She carries it into the house, back through the front door, which is strange. The garage, he thinks, would be a better, more logical place for it.

As the door closes behind her, Henry notices that her feet are bare.

She didn't spare him or his car even a glance. Sometimes she seems like a prisoner, as though the husband is in the house, waiting. "You have forty seconds," he says. "I want you back in here in forty seconds."

It's almost noon on a Wednesday, yet she's home. She might

be employed, could have a job where she works remotely. He could see her as a graphic designer, something techy and artsy. If he knew her name, he could search for her online. He could look for a professional profile or social media accounts. But he doesn't want to know her name. He doesn't want to slip when he finally meets her, to say something he shouldn't already know. Besides, he knows enough.

He thought his mom might mention their names, the husband and the wife. He knows she met them shortly after they moved in. "We have new neighbors," she told Henry and his dad as though it were breaking news. "Nice young couple." She was looking at Henry. "Reminds me of Laurel and Dan."

Which was ridiculous because his sister looks nothing like the wife. She's not nearly as beautiful. And last time Henry saw Laurel, he was shocked by her sudden softness. She'd become excessively fleshy, skin milk white, since having the baby, like a soft and floured dough version of her former self.

Henry's buoyancy has faded. He feels like a prisoner himself.

He'll send off his references when he gets inside, and they'll raise those familiar red flags. He'll never hear anything back, or he'll receive a curt and tactful rejection email in a couple of weeks.

His mom must have been standing in the foyer, waiting for him.

He can picture her frowning, the parentheses bookmarking her mouth deepening, watching him sit in his front seat and observe the wife. *What's he doing, sitting out there?*

"How did it go?" she asks brightly, frown gone, as he steps inside. She must have put on her Good, Caring Mom mask while he was walking to the door.

"It went great," says Henry, trying to conjure some of the

optimism that had flowed only minutes earlier. But his tone is flat, and his mother smiles a smile that is tight and concerned, because they both know that interviews have been "great" before and they've yielded nothing but disappointment. Henry now fears this one will be no different, and his mother has removed her mask.

"I'll be right back," he murmurs, retreating to the basement. As though she cares. He goes into his bedroom and changes out of his suit, shaking it out, smelling the jacket, before hanging it back up in the closet. His thoughts trail away from his mother, away from the interview, back to the wife. He wonders what she's doing inside her own brick-front colonial, which has more space than she needs. He pictures her padding through her own bedroom, into her own closet, changing out of her sweat-dampened T-shirt, her bare feet slapping against the hardwoods.

She was too far away; Henry couldn't see her toenails, but he's sure they're red.

17

Last night I told you that I needed space.

Rather, last night I needed space. That wasn't what I told you.

"I'm tired," I said on the phone. You had called me when you were leaving work for the day, and I called you back an hour later, having lingered at my desk for longer than I needed to, having stayed to finish something that didn't need to get done. "I am so tired. I just want to put on my oldest sweats and climb into bed and pass out. I wouldn't be any fun. You don't need to see me like that."

"I would love to see you like that," you told me. "I could bring over takeout. You need to eat anyway."

I wanted to scream. *Suffocating. You are suffocating me.*

"It's fine, Troy," I said. "I'll see you tomorrow." Finality in my tone, flashing irritation I couldn't quite hide.

I could sense your hurt, disappointment, or annoyance—perhaps all three—churning. But I hung up, and I drove home.

I softened while I was lying in bed, alone and wearing threadbare lounge pants and a waffle-knit top. I sent you a text: Sorry about wanting to be alone. Love you.

You didn't reply, and perhaps you sense that I'm still not sure that I mean those words.

Now I park my car in the garage beside my office building and climb out, dropping my keys into my bag, belting my trench coat.

I check my phone as I wait for the elevator. Still no response from you.

Things have been moving so quickly, intensely, between us, and something is holding me back. But what?

It's been several weeks since you asked me to move in with you, and I owe you an answer. You are attentive and thoughtful. You are there when I need you. But are you there too much? Sometimes you make me feel like a mother with very young children, overstimulated from having her hair pulled, her face pinched, her clothes tugged, from being needed and needed and needed, all day and every day, until she can't bear it anymore and must sit alone in a dark room to recharge.

I had moved in with Adam, of course. But we were together for more than two years before we rented that town house. We ordered furniture online and browsed showrooms, picking out things we liked. We put some pieces on my credit card and some on his. We intermingled our dishes and utensils and towels. Then, two years after that, we had to split it all up. *Was this mine or yours? You bought that. You take it. Yes, I'm sure.*

It was all so cordial, so stilted, but with simmering antipathy, hurt rolling into a boil, tight lips and nothing left to say.

I don't want to go through that again. I don't want to move in with you unless I believe our relationship will last forever. And the fact is, I'm not certain that I want it to.

You seem so perfect. But are you? I fear you are too good to be true, and are therefore not true. I'm thirty-five, wise enough to be suspicious.

You don't play games. You don't pretend to be busy or behave as though you aren't that interested. You just like me—love me, actually. Is that because of our age? Are we too old for games, our biological clocks counting down, each tick a warning? Or is that just how you are? Confident in what you want. Vulnerable in your simplicity.

The elevator doors glide open, and I step inside, using an index finger to punch the button for the ground floor. The doors close again, and the elevator begins its descent with an unsettling shudder.

My parking garage is just across the street from my office building. The walk sign flashes, and I step into the crosswalk. I see a man standing in front of the building. Tidy, dark hair; long black coat. As I approach the revolving door in the building's face, the man turns, and I see that it's you.

Still a couple of yards away, I freeze.

You're grinning at the sight of me, at my surprise, and you have a coffee in each hand. "You said you'd see me tomorrow," you say, extending one of the coffee cups toward me. "It's tomorrow."

You are always giving me coffee. During the workweek, you place a steaming mug of it on my nightstand before I can even climb out of bed. On the weekends, you run out for Starbucks or Dunkin', treating me to sickly sweet syrups and whipped cream.

And how many times have you done this? It isn't the first time you have been waiting for me outside my office building. There was the time you appeared outside the courthouse, my missing umbrella in your hand. I chalked this up to a mistake or a coincidence. Maybe my umbrella was in my condo and you picked it up one day, needing it and thinking it was a spare. Maybe you thought it was yours. Maybe it was yours. It's not impossible that you had the same one.

I know there have been other times, I just cannot specifically remember them. Memories of you fill these last few months. You fill them, the blur of you.

"Sorry I didn't reply to your message," you say, stepping

closer to me. "I was sulking. I was being petty and bratty, and I missed you."

"It's fine," I say, smiling tightly.

You step closer still, and then you close the gap completely. You kiss me, right there on the sidewalk, like I am your oxygen and without me you cannot survive.

Isn't this what any woman would want? Aren't you? What is wrong with me that I am so unsure?

You are so much more devoted than Adam, than any relationship I ever had. You are more devoted than my parents ever were, my mother gone, living out her glittering freedom, my father tired and inept, bearing more responsibility for me than he'd wanted or expected, until he died. I've relied on myself for forever. I've had to. And here you are, always wanting to love and give, yet I don't welcome it. The dependability of you scares me.

When we break apart, I force myself to smile again, but discomfort and embarrassment twist and tumble in my gut and heat my cheeks. Partnership decisions are being announced in just a few weeks. Kissing one's boyfriend on the sidewalk outside the firm's office building doesn't exactly scream partner material. In fact, it screams the opposite. It screams youth, I think. Unprofessionalism. Distraction.

"Did you—" I swallow, not knowing what I was going to say, what I should say.

You rescue me, answering the question I wasn't certain I was trying to articulate. "I know you need to get in to work. I do, too. I just wanted to drop off your coffee and let you know I was thinking of you."

"You're sweet," I say, wrapping my fingers around the cup. "But no worries. I'm sorry I was being lame last night."

You shake your head. "You're entitled to your space, Klara."

Your words don't land quite right. Why are you telling me what I'm entitled to?

I glance toward the revolving door, and you take the hint.

"I should head to work," you say. "Just couldn't start the day without bringing my beautiful girlfriend her coffee."

I smile, and you kiss me again, lightly, the length of a blink.

"See you tonight," I say before pushing through the door.

I sip the coffee as I wait for the elevator in the lobby. It tastes bitter—you didn't order it quite right. I drink the whole thing anyway.

18

Troy watches Klara disappear through the revolving door in the front of her office building.

He's going to be late for work, but he needed to bring her a coffee. It's important that he not miss a day. Their future together depends on it.

And she tried to foil that, unknowingly, by claiming she was too tired to see him, by requesting to be alone for the night. It was inexplicable. It enraged him. But he can't let her see that.

So instead, he told her he was sorry, even though it was him who was owed the apology. He brought her a coffee with pumpkin spice syrup, skim milk, half a packet of raw sugar, and two packets of Splenda, even though she's certainly already had her caffeine fix for the day.

He knows exactly how she takes her coffee, her complicated, borderline-irritating order. He feels like a fool placing it himself. He has invested so much into this relationship. So much more time than Klara even knows. She has no idea that sometimes, even when he isn't with her, he is watching her. She has no idea how long he's been planning, watching.

Months ago, before she knew of his existence, he listened as she placed her order at a coffee shop. This was after he saw her at that first bar association event, after he'd figured out her name and where she worked. On a few occasions, he enjoyed being able to observe her in close proximity without her noticing. That day, he lingered outside her office building and followed her to a café around the corner. He waited in line behind her, one customer between them. He stood in the corner and waited for his own coffee, large and black, as she slipped from the shop.

Troy can no longer watch her as closely as he wants to when they aren't together. He can still cruise past her condo building and stare up at the windows he knows are hers, glowing golden around the edges. He cannot see her through the shades, but he can know that she is behind them. He did that last night, just to be sure she was really home.

And she was, the glow of her windows a comfort.

Fortunately, most nights he can be much closer. He can be with her. He can hold her and stroke her and be inside her. He can stare at her fluttering eyelids as she sleeps and feel the beating of her heart and the rise and fall of her chest as he lies in bed beside her.

But not if she claims she's too tired to see him. This is why they need to move in together—so that she has nowhere else to go.

Which is why he needs to propose. But he can't do that until he is certain she will say yes.

Yet he can feel her pulling away from him, can sense her displeasure. So perhaps the right move at this point is to give her a little space, which she is so clearly craving. That feels like a setback. But he's not sure what else he can do. If he continues to press, he might lose her. That's happened in the past with the few women whom he could've seen himself marrying. He pressed and pressed until they fled, ungrateful for his gestures, for the way he'd filled their lives. That can't happen with Klara. She's too right for him, and he's devoted so much time and energy and risk into making her his.

Troy wants to watch Klara longer. He wants to follow her into her office and watch until she's finished the entire cup of coffee. But he can't do that, and so he turns away and heads back to where he parked his car, in a metered spot around the corner.

There will be plenty of other times to watch her. There will be forever.

19

It was such a shocking thing for Hawthorne Heights, a quiet neighborhood, a peaceful neighborhood, a family neighborhood. Middle class back then, upper-middle now, two decades later. Home prices have soared and school ratings have improved. It never was the sort of place where a murder might happen.

But domestic disputes, as people refer to them, really do happen everywhere. Mary read something in the news recently, a father shooting his two teenage children and then himself in a town just ten miles away.

People hear the news of such tragedies, and they feel the cool plunge of horror. *How awful. How sad.* But such things make a strange sort of sense. The targeted nature of the deaths makes them somehow less horrible, creates the illusion of distance when there's truly very little of it. It's startlingly easy for people to move on, to still consider Hawthorne Heights a safe and desirable place to live.

Even in this room—this young boy's room, the bedroom of her sweet boy—Mary can feel the terror of that night. She can taste it like something sour and rotten coating her tongue. While outside, in the other brick-front colonials, up and down this tree-lined street, boring and pleasant life moves on. Parents register their children for activities and sports for the fall. People log on to virtual meetings. They take chicken out of the freezer to thaw. They water their flowers and pull weeds. They wave to each other while they retrieve their mail, their thoughts so far from that blood-soaked night twenty years ago, in this particular house, when Mary's life shattered.

"That's right," Mary says to herself as she settles onto the thinning carpet beside Owen's bed. She reaches beneath it to remove the plastic bin—long and low, with small gray wheels. She slides it out and opens the lid.

This was where she stored his art.

This isn't productive. It's not why she's here. But Mary can't stop herself. Not now. She removes paper after paper. She spreads them out across the floor.

Owen favored an abstract style. Ed never understood his work.

Mary studies it now, searching for some hint at the violence that was lurking inside her sweet golden boy. But she sees nothing. The art is *gorgeous*—colorful and urgent and gripping. She wonders whether everyone would think so. Art is subjective, yes, but some garners mass appeal. Would Owen's? Or is Mary the only one who can see its beauty, who could see Owen's potential? Was she always blinded by her motherly love? Was the art really just scribbles and chaos, the work of a child avoidant of physical activity and useful subjects that might one day lead to boring and comfortable financial stability?

She inspects each piece, trying to remember when he did them. Her favorite was completed shortly before that night. It's on a thin, hard canvas. He'd painted it black, then layered colors over it, striking fluorescent slashes. Mary runs her fingers along the bottom of the painting where Owen had painted his initials: OLI.

His art was his escape. It wasn't enough.

She stacks everything back up, fits it tidily into the plastic bin. She'll keep this, too. It will come to the new apartment. Perhaps she'll hang her favorite pieces on the walls. Why hadn't she done that here, she wonders? Why had she kept it hidden away, beneath his bed?

Ed's influence, she assumes. Silent and unrelenting even now, all these years later.

She'd met Ed when she was sixteen years old, and her life became a riddle. Anticipating his moods, his irritations. At first, it was thrilling and endearing. It was brutally dysfunctional.

He was five years older, and she'd tumbled into his life still a girl. But he was a man. He had a job, possessed the promise of a new life; someone who could pull her out of girlhood, which she was in such a rush to leave.

She was a waitress at the local diner, and he was a regular who paid for his meals with cash he seemed to unthinkingly unfold from a thick black wallet. He always dined alone. He was handsome and alarmingly tall, and the other girls whispered about him in the kitchen, argued over who could cover his table. They all wanted him to choose them, and he chose Mary.

When his company transferred him down to the Maryland office, Mary was eighteen, applying for college. She went with him. She took a gap year and settled into domestic life in a two-bedroom rancher. She painted the front door herself, daffodil yellow. She found a new waitressing job and went to college at night. Ed helped her pay her tuition. Eventually, they traded up to a bigger house, then an even bigger one, the one in Hawthorne Heights. Mary became pregnant, and they both followed along the tracks that stretched ahead of them, seemingly predestined.

Her life with Ed had afforded Mary some of the highest of highs, but as the years passed, those became fewer and fewer, the lows spreading, dampening, like sea foam soaking into the sand.

What had once felt like intensity and love was abuse, and by the time she saw that, it was far too late. She had Owen, and from the moment he entered the world, everything she did was for him. She tried her best.

Mary sits there on the floor a moment longer, steeling herself to stand. After so many years working as a teacher, spending hours on her feet, these days she spends too much time sitting. She's traveled from one discomfort to another. Besides, her joints are aging, cartilage thinning. She doesn't take care of herself the way she should.

She reaches for the edge of the bed, preparing to use it to pull herself upward. Then she freezes. There's a gentle creaking from downstairs. She recognizes it, knows the exact board in the kitchen that always makes that sound. He knows it, too, and he's usually sure to avoid it. He must think she's not home. But he's wrong.

He does this on occasion, when she's been silent and still long enough. Sometimes, when he thinks she's out, he ventures up from the basement. He'll look through the kitchen cabinets and the pantry. He'll peruse the fridge. She'll find a few things missing when she goes back downstairs or returns home. He'll help himself to what he wants and needs. She doesn't mind.

Mary thinks about going downstairs—moving as quickly as she can and catching him. But it would hurt to see him. It wouldn't be like she imagines it might be.

So she sits on the floor and waits. Not until she hears the squeal of the basement door's hinges, as it's pulled firmly closed, does Mary move again.

20

I watch you over the rim of my coffee cup. It's Saturday, and we sit in my favorite coffee shop together, working on a crossword puzzle. I told you that I need to go into the office for a couple of hours to review my exhibits for a trial scheduled to begin Monday. You were good about this—you've been good these last few months about giving me space.

Neither of us has brought up your suggestion that we move in together. I never said no, but I never said yes, so that's really the same as no. And yet our relationship has continued. Paradoxically, your pulling back, your offering me space, has brought us even closer. We spend nearly every night together, and every single weekend. We stay in my condo, and when we don't go out to restaurants, I make you dinner. You always compliment my cooking and tell me sheepishly that you're awful at it. You suggest that I teach you sometime, but in a vague way. I don't think you mean it.

The truth is, I received a settlement offer on Friday that my client is going to take. The trial won't move forward on Monday, so there's no need for me to work today. But I don't tell you this. There's something else I must do, and I don't want you to know.

"Bummer that you have to work on the weekend," you said, although you often do so yourself. "If you want to do something afterward, let me know. I might grab lunch with some friends."

This intrigued me. Why have I never met your friends? Why haven't I introduced you to mine? I've talked about you, of course. It took me a month to tell Zoe about you. We went out for drinks, salty margaritas, cloudy with lime juice, and warm tortilla chips that shimmered with oil in a basket on the table between us.

"He sounds perfect," Zoe said. She was happy for me. Her engagement and wedding rings glittered on her hand. She kept it to a single drink because she still wanted to be able to nurse her daughter during her overnight wake. Baby Daphne was only four months old, sleeping better than expected, and Zoe's nanny was a dream. She was blissful and so full of love; your perfection didn't scare her. Rather, it was expected that I would eventually find someone like you, that I would meet "the one" and "settle down." And I always hated those expressions. I still do.

I've filled Zoe in on the progress of our relationship. "I'm so happy for you," she always says as I stare at her, studying her face, searching and pleading that she will read the skepticism on mine, that she will hear the hesitation in my flat tone, in everything I do not say.

What are your friends like, I wonder? For some reason, I can't picture you with other men your age, drinking craft beer and eating food-truck tacos. I can only picture you with me because you've made me feel like your sun, the everything around which you orbit, whether I want to be or not.

"What's three across?" you ask now, your brows creeping together, forehead furrowed.

I glance at the clue, roll my eyes, nudge you playfully. "'Swift,'" I say. "Everyone knows that."

You shrug and fill it in.

I finish my coffee, and my thoughts drift to the blood in my underwear a few weeks back, to the blood that should be there again today but is startlingly absent, to the tenderness of my breasts.

"I should go," I say. "Get my work over with so I can enjoy the rest of my weekend."

I lean across the table so that you can kiss me, and you do. "Have fun," you say. "I'm going to stay here, finish my coffee and this puzzle. But I'll be lost without you."

"I'm sure," I say, and I think we both know that your words aren't a joke. I have become your compass. You've made that clear. Sometimes it's beautiful. Sometimes, still, I cannot breathe.

I leave the coffee shop, and I walk back to my condo building. But I pass it, instead turning the corner and stepping into the CVS a block away. People with baskets, with arms full of things, running Saturday-morning errands, move idly through the store. I move quickly to a section I've never before had occasion to visit.

I buy two tests, knowing that whatever the result, I'll need a second opinion.

I am thirty-five years old. I have been prescribed a birth control pill since I was seventeen, and I've taken the dosage religiously, every single day since. Swallowing that little pill at the same time I brush my teeth in the morning is as automatic to me as breathing. The packet of pills sits next to my toothbrush, a visual reminder I can't miss. I'm too old, too careful, too regimented to become pregnant without trying to.

Yet after I get home, shut myself in my bathroom, tear into the box, and hold the stick beneath me while I pee, two pink lines appear. Once, and again, and urine pools on the bathroom counter, and I stare at it, stomach churning, because this isn't what I want. And you know that. You agreed, insisted that you want what I want.

Don't tell him, I think.

21

It's fate. It's kismet.

Henry is just about to pull his car away from the curb when the unhappy couple's garage glides open. The wife's car emerges. It's a nice car, silver and sleek, a few years old. It's exactly the sort of car he'd expect her to drive, and she so rarely leaves the house in it.

He wasn't headed anywhere important himself. Just to the store to restock his provisions in his kitchenette. He shops for himself in his parents' kitchen as much as he can, but there are some things he likes that they don't stock, and, despite his dwindling savings, there are some things he can't live without.

But that will have to wait because the wife is going out, and Henry must follow her.

He waits until her car has eased to a stop at the sign at the base of the street and begun to turn to the left before he presses his foot against the gas and shifts away from the curb. He sees her idling at the neighborhood's exit, and he lets a car pass before turning to the right, behind her.

He knows how to follow people. He's gotten better at it over the years.

His spins the dial of his air-conditioning, shifts the vent so that it's blowing directly into his face. He bought the car shortly after graduating from his master's program, applying for a loan with his first full-time salary. It's nearly five years old now, and some things don't work as well as they used to—one of them being the air-conditioning system, blowing only tepid air when the temperature outside crests over ninety. But he can't justify the expense of repairs right now.

Ahead of him, the wife merges onto the highway.

Henry keeps a car between them, and he lowers his window, air whipping around his face, mussing his hair. But that doesn't matter, because she won't see him. She can't see him.

After five miles, the wife flicks her turn signal and pulls onto an exit ramp. Henry does, too. She turns cautiously through the secondary streets, and at a stop sign, she pauses for far longer than is necessary. For a second, Henry fears that she's spotted him despite his discreetness, his practice.

Hours of practice, the summer after senior year of high school. It became something of a game, to while away those vacant days until it was time to leave for college. He was working for a computer-repair shop, but that was mostly to pad his résumé. The work was too menial, the hours too few, to adequately amuse him.

Kelly's hair was copper, and it curled around her forehead in the heat. She had catlike eyes that glowed amber in the sun. Henry sometimes caught glimpses of them reflected in her rearview mirror. The way the light hit them, the way they shone.

Her family had moved to the neighborhood at the start of the summer, just after graduation. An unavoidable transfer for her father's work, Henry's mother had told them, always on top of the neighborhood happenings. Kelly's younger brother would be starting his freshman year at the local high school at the end of the summer, and Kelly would be off to the University of Delaware. She'd only be around for a few months. *Perfect*, Henry thought.

It was August, heat waves fluttering up from the pavement, when Henry followed Kelly to the local ice cream stand, a small cottage in a grassy field, with sliding windows and a parking lot that was aging and turning to rubble. She brought her little brother with her, probably because she'd not been able to make any friends in the area. Henry waited in his car. He watched Kelly stand at the window of the gray clapboard hut to pay, tugging a single bill from the back pocket of her cutoffs. He imagined her parents handing it to her before she left the house. Her legs were so pale they were almost fluorescent, loose threads from her shorts grazing her thighs, bare skin dotted with freckles. She wasn't his usual type, but Henry found her beautiful nevertheless.

He'd followed her when she walked through the neighborhood, when she went out to run errands. Once, she'd visited an eye doctor. Another morning, she had gone to Target with her mom. They'd maneuvered a red cart laden with plastic bags through the parking lot, struggling. It'd had a bad wheel and seemed to be tugging toward the left, and they laughed about it, Kelly's giggle a high trill that made Henry smile. Some nights, after darkness had fallen over the neighborhood, he stood in her yard, just beyond the reach of the motion-detecting light affixed to the back of the house. The back gate opened and shut soundlessly, and the family had a dopey blond dog who'd lope up to Henry, welcoming him with a lick—the worst guard dog ever. Henry knew which window was Kelly's; sometimes he could see her silhouette against the curtains in her room.

Henry thought he'd been careful, but that particular August afternoon, Kelly and her brother tossed their empty ice cream cups into the trash, then walked back to their car. Henry was feeling perhaps more confident than he should have, his weeks of success turning him brazen. His window was down, head turned toward them.

The brother climbed into the front passenger seat, but Kelly didn't get in the car. Not yet. She spun around, copper ponytail dragging across her shoulders. She looked at Henry, straight at him. The venom in her eyes was startling. He should have looked away, shifted his car into drive, but he was frozen. There was anger slashed across her face like a scar—*I see you and I know what you're doing*—and there was no fear.

Perhaps that was the first time he felt it. The rage. It was like fingers wrapping around his forearm, knuckles white. Why did she not flush and glance away, smiling knowingly and pleased? Why was his attention so unwelcome? It made him want to turn his wheel sharply, foot to the gas until his car crashed right into her, pinning her.

He didn't. All he did was stare straight back at her until she caved. Her gaze dropped and she got in her car, then backed out of her spot, and Henry wondered whether he'd been wrong, whether he'd imagined the whole thing. But that he hadn't backed down, that he had stared back, felt his anger pumping hotly, so much stronger than hers, came as a comfort to him.

Later that night, in Kelly's yard, he scratched the dog behind the ears. Kelly's curtains were pressed firmly closed, and when he left, he didn't shut the gate behind him. The dog tilted its head, watching, curious, before slipping through the open gate behind him.

Two days after that, Kelly and her brother walked along the neighborhood streets carrying flyers printed with their blond dog's smiling face. They hung them on stop signs and knocked on doors. Henry stood at the living room window and watched as Kelly's eyes met his, as her lips turned down, as she murmured something to her brother, as they skipped Henry's house.

He's pretty sure the dog found its way back home eventually. Henry didn't hurt the dog; that wasn't the point. The point was that he hurt Kelly.

Now Henry is certain that the wife hasn't noticed him—she's just not sure about where she's going. Her turn signal flashes, and she goes left. He follows her, left, then straight through a roundabout. She turns into a sprawling parking lot outside a looming brick building—a medical pavilion, he realizes. There's a white sign out front listing the names of various doctors and medical practices.

He parks his car across the aisle from hers and watches her climb out. She slings her purse over her shoulder and squints at the building, then checks her phone, drops it into her bag. She walks slowly, hesitantly, toward the front doors.

Henry can't risk following her inside, yet how can he not?

He doesn't pause too long to think. How does she know he doesn't just have a doctor's appointment of his own? What a coincidence, that they're both here at the same time. Besides, as much as he hates to admit it, she probably wouldn't even recognize him.

He smooths his hair down as he walks, uses fingers to correct the part, to rake it into place. As he's stepping through the sliding glass doors, she's standing in the lobby area, studying the directory. She runs her hand across her dark ponytail, twirls it slightly at the end. A nervous tick.

She opts for the stairs. Henry studies the directory, too, standing in the exact place she just vacated, until he hears the door to the stairwell click shut.

Her footsteps ascending above his, his breaths coming quickly.

On the third floor, she leaves the stairwell. Henry waits two seconds, three, then pulls the door open. He catches a glimpse of her, the stream of her hair, as she disappears into the first office, across the hall from the stairwell.

Henry pauses just long enough to read the sign outside the door; then he spins around, goes back down the stairs, through those sliding doors, across the steaming blackness of the parking lot. His heart hammers, dread pools. It might not mean anything, but it might mean everything.

Dr. Frances Singh & Associates, read the sign, *Obstetrics and Gynecology*.

22

My secret is like a whisper in my ear.

I'm pregnant. I'm thirty-five and accidentally pregnant.

After the meeting with Grant Wilpers, managing partner at my firm, it becomes a roar.

"I'm sorry to tell you, Klara, but it's not your year," he says.

I stare hard at his receding hairline. My emotions feel uncontrollable, and I have a sudden urge to cry into my palms. Instead, I take a breath, swallow. "Can I ask why?"

"The evaluation committee decided that you didn't have enough trial wins. You were a strong candidate for partner, but not quite strong enough. With a few more trials under your belt, you'll probably get there."

"But I settle my cases," I say, unsure if I sound confident and strong or like a whining toddler. "I avoid a lot of trials because my clients take settlement offers. I negotiate those offers. I negotiate favorable settlements for my clients, which saves the firm time and money. I wouldn't think I'd be punished for that."

"Well," says Grant, "that may be. But sometimes trial is the right move. Certain members of the committee felt that you… you might accept a settlement offer that other lawyers wouldn't, to avoid trial."

There's fire on my face. "Whether to accept a settlement offer is the absolute right of the client," I say, although Grant obviously knows this. "I can't accept a settlement offer if my client doesn't want to."

"No, but you manage their expectations. You sway them. We all do. It's part of our job."

"And I think I do it well."

"Look," says Grant with a gentle finality that makes me want to slap his smug male face, "it was a tough decision. You were close. Think about the feedback. Take some time to digest it, and if you'd like to discuss it further, we can set up a time to chat. How does that sound?"

It sounds like you're ending this argument because you can't win it. It sounds like you're full of shit.

"Sure," I tell him. I stand and leave the glass conference room with its glass walls.

It's only three in the afternoon, but I stop in my office just to turn off my computer and grab my purse. I leave without telling anyone where I'm going or why.

I need to talk to someone, but Zoe is at work. I can no longer turn to Adam. My mother would only make me feel worse. I've never been able to go to her in the face of professional upset, in the face of any upset. My mother would barely be able to hide her glee. *You're not so much better than us after all, are you, Klara?*

But as I flee to the parking garage, I realize that I want you. Only you.

By the time I get to my car, I'm crying. I never call you during work hours. You answer on the first ring.

"Klara," you say. "What is it?"

Thirty minutes later, you use your key to enter my condo. I'm on my bed, still wearing my blouse and pencil skirt, but I've unzipped the back. My stomach feels bloated, and wisps of nausea swirl. I need it to go away, to rid my body of the cells that are making me feel so weak.

"What happened?" you ask. You climb onto the bed beside me and kiss my hair. You lie down, face inches from mine, and use your palms to blot the wetness from my cheeks.

"I didn't make partner," I tell you. Saying the words out loud adds certitude to them, like they're now carved into stone.

"Oh, Klara," you say, tracing a finger along my temple. "I'm sorry."

"Me too," I say. Then: "Sorry." I turn my face, bury it in my pillow. "I'm a mess."

"Never," you whisper. "You're perfect. And you deserved to make partner."

You don't know this, but it's the right thing to say. It makes my heart swell, my shoulders shake.

"What is it?" you ask gently.

"I feel so emotional," I admit. "Like I can't control my emotions." And I am usually, always, so controlled, so poised. It's terrifying to be anything else.

"That makes sense," you tell me, explaining my own feelings away, but this doesn't bother me the way it normally would.

"No," I tell you, even though it does make sense. Because you don't get it. You don't know. "You don't understand," I insist.

I feel your finger on my chin, nudging gently, trying to turn my face. "What is it, then?" you ask. "Help me understand." Your voice is slightly breathless, full of wonder, like you already know.

I vowed to take care of it. I vowed not to tell you at all. But I'm crushed. I'm a mess. I'm not in control.

"I'm pregnant."

You are quiet and still for one beat, then two. Then you pull me into your arms. "Klara," you whisper, and you're holding me so close that I can't breathe. Your cheek finds my neck, and it's damp. You're crying.

"What?" I ask, pulling away from you, feeling your arms release with a reluctance that makes my chest feel tight.

"I'm so happy," you tell me. "I'm just so happy."

Your lashes are long and thick, and I picture them on a baby, on a plump-faced toddler with cheeks as soft as the back of a dog's ear.

So I press my lips together, and I don't tell you about my appointment the following week. My thoughts race, but I try to hold them steady. I let your joy and surprise wash over us both, and I wish that I held it inside me, too.

Your body shifts, hand diving into the pocket of your dress pants, then back out again. In your fingers is a black velvet box. Exactly the shape and size most women my age would be thrilled to see.

"I've had this for months," you say, and your eyes don't leave mine. "Sometimes in my apartment. In my car. In my desk drawer. Today, I put it in my pocket. Isn't that strange? I know it's early, but I know, Klara. I love you more than I've ever loved anything in my life."

You use a thumb to flip the box open. My blackout curtains are still drawn, so there's no light to catch the diamond.

I should feel joy. I should feel relief. I'm thirty-five and pregnant. I'm not a partner. A decade out of law school, married to my career, childless, and still not a partner.

In your hands, you hold a different path. One I'd not wanted to take, but how easy might it be? How comfortable? Just a slight turn of the wheel, and I can veer that way. The path has already been paved. In fact, the decision has been made for me, in some ways. And you love me in a way that no one ever has.

So while something inside me screams *No*, that isn't what I say.

23

By dinnertime, Mary is too tired to do any more. Her knees are aching, a low-grade hum she's used to ignoring. But the sciatica pain spurts white hot. She needs to swallow a pill, to lie down with a heating pad, a book, a cup of tea. But first, she needs to eat.

She has no appetite this evening, and perhaps, if it was just herself to worry about, she wouldn't bother with dinner. A carton of yogurt or a bowl of cereal before bed would be fine. But it's not just her. So she must go through the motions, the effort. She must prepare a real meal for them both, even when they'll each eat it alone.

Mary descends the stairs, one step at a time, feet meeting before she attempts the next step. She's too young to be so stiff isn't she? Sometimes she feels like she's ninety. Too many years spent on her feet. Too much weight on her shoulders—the loss she carries is heavy and unrelenting.

She thawed two chicken breasts that morning, so she doesn't have to think too much. She minces garlic, slices a lemon. She tries, as the knife tugs through the garlic, through the flesh of the fruit, not to be reminded of the way the knife had tugged so easily through flesh all those years ago.

Of course, that was a different knife, from a different set. Once the crime scene tape came down and Mary was permitted to return to the house, she got rid of the rest of those knives. She took the entire block and put it in a trash bag, which she dropped into the can and left at the curb. It probably wasn't the proper way to dispose of them, but she didn't care. She couldn't look at them. She ordered a new set and still has it, the blades dulled now from years of use and hundreds of cycles through the dishwasher when she should have been washing them by hand.

Mary makes a salad, microwaves a packet of rice while the skillet sizzles and oil pops.

Still, the house is too quiet, too still. Mary spins the dial of her radio, volume up. It's her favorite public station, which plays jazz in the evenings. Occasionally, she'll dance to it for a few minutes, the way she used to with Ed, when they were young and she didn't know him all that well. But not tonight.

When the food is ready, she prepares a plate. She carries it to the kitchen table and pours herself a glass of wine from the screw-top bottle in the door of the fridge.

But she doesn't sit down to eat. Not quite yet. She prepares a second plate, first—the other piece of chicken, the rest of the salad and rice. She puts it on a wooden serving tray, then adds a paper napkin, a fork and knife, a bottle of water. She carries the meal to the door that leads to the basement, which she opens. She leans carefully down—knees still smarting, that nerve in her back pinching persistently—and places the tray on the top stair. Then she backs away, listening, waiting.

Mary considers leaving the door open a crack, a silent invitation; he'll see it when he retrieves the food. But she's tried that before, and it's never made a difference.

Soon, everything will change—the house going up for sale. She'll be leaving, so he will have to leave, too. But for now, he's got his head in the sand. It's been there for years. He's hiding, still not ready to see her. He's still not ready to speak.

He can't hide forever.

She shuts the door with a click. She doesn't know what else to do.

24

We decide to elope. The courthouse, I suggest, and your face falls.

"Weddings are about attention," I tell you quickly, my hand tucked into the crevice of your elbow. "They're about everyone else. If we just do this, just the two of us, at the courthouse, it will be about us."

You like this, and you smile slowly, a Cheshire cat grin that stokes the disquieting sensation that's ever present in my gut.

"What about your mother?" you ask. "Won't she want to be there?"

"She'll understand."

A lie. My mom will be livid when she finds out I've excluded her from my wedding. It will prove, in her mind, that she's right about everything she thinks of me. That I'm ashamed of her, of my upbringing. That I'm better than her, with my expensive degrees, my white-collar work, my handsome fiancé with the dimple in his left cheek, with my engagement ring that costs more than every car she's ever owned. She's so skilled at convincing me that our distance is all my fault. As though she wasn't the one who left.

I'll deny her claims. *I don't want a big wedding, Mom. I just want to marry my fiancé, and that's all. It has nothing to do with you.* As if that will be an easier pill to swallow. My mother struggles with comprehending that everything isn't always about her.

"Friends?" I ask you. "Would you want to include any of your friends?"

"I don't care about them." Your left hand finds mine, pinches the diamond, turning my ring side to side.

"Sounds like we're in agreement."

I select a white dress that grazes my shins. I order it online, and of course it doesn't fit exactly right. After it arrives, I meet Zoe for dinner. We go to the tailor first, and she smiles at me, almost shyly, as the seamstress tucks pins into the straps.

"You look beautiful, Klara," she says. It's all so fast. There's a question in her eyes: *Are you sure this is what you want—all of this?*

There's no answer in mine.

What could I say? I'm thirty-five and pregnant, and you love me in a way I've never been loved before. In a way that scares me, that leaves me breathless, that propels me forward down the only path that makes sense. And so how can I, always so prudent, stray from such perfect logic?

Zoe and I leave my dress with the tailor and walk to our favorite Chinese restaurant. We order two entrées to share. Zoe drinks dry white wine.

I wave the server away. "I'm fine with water."

"Really?" Zoe asks lightly after he's disappeared.

"Bit of a headache," I tell her, fingertips to my temples. I don't say anything about the baby. I can't. Even though Zoe is my closest friend, and she has been since we lived in the same dorm room freshman year of college, I'm not ready to tell her about the life growing within me. She knows too much. She knows I've never wanted children. She knows that's why things ended with Adam, the person I thought I'd marry. And now here I am, less than a year later, preparing to marry someone else. She'd press, she'd question, and I'm afraid of what I might say.

The smell of the food, the spice in the sauces, make my persistent nausea swell. I cut chicken and broccoli with the side of my fork and move it around my plate while Zoe watches, brows furrowed.

"Is everything okay, Klara?" she asks before sipping her wine, regarding me over the rim of her glass. "You seem… I don't know. A little down. More down than you should be, considering." She trails off, her gaze falling to my ring.

"Just the headache," I insist, but she presses her lips together and waits for me to continue.

"It's just a little fast, Zoe." I reach for my water, avoiding her face, the unrelenting care in her eyes. "That's all," I insist. "I mean, this time last year, I was living with Adam. And now?"

"Now you've found someone who really seems to love you. He seems so devoted, Klara. But if you feel it's too fast, of course you should slow it down. You don't have some big wedding planned. What's the harm in pushing things off for a few months?"

"You're right," I say, and I force myself to smile. And I pretend that's an option, that a delay wouldn't devastate or anger you.

"You know I'm just so cautious," I tell Zoe. "I can be overly prudent."

"Oh, I know," says Zoe, smiling back at me, and I can tell I've reassured her.

"I'm sure it's just that," I say. "I'm worrying for no reason. I promise."

When I get home, you kiss me like I was gone for weeks.

"How was it?" you ask. "How's Zoe?"

"It was good," I tell you, and I feel like a fool because you're so perfect.

I sit beside you on my bed—our bed now—and eat an entire sleeve of saltines. You rub my feet with the pads of your thumbs, even though my feet aren't sore.

That was it, my way of including my best friend in our wedding. It's not nearly enough, but I don't let my thoughts linger on that for too long. This is happening. We're getting married.

Zoe isn't there when I pick up the dress. I didn't ask her to go with me, and she didn't bring it up. I can't pull her away from her work, her life, her baby to again watch me try on a dress I don't want.

I slip it on, then stand before the array of mirrors, my reflection blurring, a hundred copies of myself, none of them familiar.

"It's perfect," I tell the tailor. "Thank you so much."

I leave with the dress covered in translucent plastic, not sure that I've ever felt so lonely, although I can't quite figure out why.

25

Henry cannot be seen.

Her ponytail brushes against her back, steady, metronomic. She's not moving particularly fast, occasionally speeding up or slowing down, and he has to adjust his own pace to match hers.

Of course, he was hoping it would be the right time to talk to her. He sat in the living room and waited until her front door swung open. She paused on the porch to lock her front door behind her—not everyone in this neighborhood does; people really are too trusting—then started down her driveway. But there was something in her expression, something forbidding. Hostile, even. *Not today*, Henry thought. He knows her so well.

He must tread so carefully; he's chosen poorly in the past. But he's determined that things go differently this time.

He studies the back of her, the swing of her hips. He looks for signs of widening, excess flesh, thinking of the sign outside the doctor's office: *Dr. Frances Singh & Associates, Obstetrics and Gynecology*. But he sees none.

Walking behind her in this way makes him think of Esther.

But Esther was wirier, with birdlike wrists, a sharpness to her clavicle. Her hair held more curl.

Sophomore year of college, Henry took Advanced Computer Science, and the professor insisted on assigned seats. Henry was lucky to be seated next to Esther. Her skin was always cool when he'd brush against her, the scent of cucumber wafting from the tender places behind her ears; he'd apologize even though it never was an accident.

He tried to talk to her nearly every class, but he was always met with tight lips, frigid terseness, her body angled away from him.

She lived on the third floor of a dorm across the quad from Henry's dorm, and all he had to do was sit on a bench in the darkness for a few weekends to notice the pattern, the way she'd stumble home drunkenly, traveling at least a few dozen yards by herself because her friends lived in a different building.

It was nearly two in the morning, the sky so black, the April air too warm for Henry's dark hoodie, its strings cinched tight around his face. Esther's laugh rang out, and she and her friends embraced sloppily on the sidewalk.

"Be safe," called out one of the friends before they parted ways. They left Esther all by herself on the sidewalk, too far from the reach of the security cameras that were perched in the eaves of every school building. There were four friends. They should have stood there and watched Esther to make sure she'd made her way to her building, that she'd climbed the stairs, that she'd gotten inside safely. Or they should have walked her up to the door. That's what good friends would have done.

Henry watched the friends disappear into their own dorm before he moved soundlessly across the path. Esther tripped on a raised stone, and Henry grabbed her. Arms around her chest, palm rising to cover her mouth, to stifle her scream. Her terror ignited him.

Now, although he's been so quiet, the wife's head turns, and Henry's steps falter. His heartbeat seems to pause. But it's a false alarm. She's just glancing toward a neighbor who's walking down her driveway, a Pomeranian straining at its leash. The wife waves to the woman, then looks forward again and picks up her pace.

But he's not so lucky with the dog. The dog sees him approaching and lunges, yapping exuberantly.

The older woman lifts a hand. "Sorry," she calls. "She hates men."

Henry waves a hand as if to say *No problem*. But he doesn't speak. His heart hammers, and his eyes are on the wife. She spares only the briefest glance over her shoulder. She's walking more quickly now, and he's risked enough. To say he's disappointed is an understatement, but he turns anyway and heads toward home. He must remind himself that this project is a marathon. That his plan is still developing and that all good things take time. That she is worth waiting for.

When he reaches his house and steps in the front door, he senses her.

His mother likes to talk about the way her grandson's gaze follows Laurel wherever she goes. The baby's head turns, and he watches Laurel like she's the whole world. She says that the baby can smell his mom, he can smell the milk. It's like that with Henry's mom, yet it's nothing like that. It's a shark detecting the tiniest drop of blood.

Their eyes meet, and the corners of her lips turn down automatically, as though she knows exactly what he was doing. She's sitting in the living room, on the sofa by the front window, a dog-eared paperback resting on her lap. He isn't sure that he's ever seen her sitting there. In fact, it's where he sits when he's reading during the day. It's where he watches the wife.

He waits for her to speak, to soften, to offer him a kindness, a tenderness, to show him that her love, her maternal instincts, still burn for him, not just for his sister. Her lips are pressed whitely, and she smiles the smallest and most tentative of smiles. But she just looks at him, her eyes dark and unsure, and says nothing. She has nothing to say, and it really is true that silence can sometimes feel like the loudest thing in the world.

26

Suddenly, I'm your wife.

The day of our wedding is gorgeous. It's a Friday and brilliantly sunny, in the weeks preceding the stifling and unrelenting humidity that will bathe the area in a soup-like damp heat. It's a day that calls for an outdoor party, bare feet in the grass and sangria full of ripe seasonal fruit.

We say our vows, secular and brief. We sign our names. A courthouse employee looks on. She congratulates us—not curious, only distracted, already looking to the next couple in line.

Afterward, you are giddy. We go to lunch at an expensive steakhouse downtown. French fries are one of the only foods that don't make me feel sick. You laugh while you watch me eat and joke that if I'm not careful, I'll give birth to a fry in eight months. I think secretly, darkly, that I might prefer that to a baby.

I try not to look at the blood pooling on your plate as you slice through your steak. Your hand on mine while we share a wedge of cheesecake—on the house, after you told the server exuberantly that we'd just gotten married. I only eat a bite, and you don't seem to notice.

Early the next morning, we fly to Grand Cayman. You take the middle seat and give me the window. We think that might help with my sickness.

The flight is turbulent, and I vomit into a paper bag, curled toward the window. You rub my back and curl around me, shielding me from our seatmate.

"We'll get you some fries as soon as we get to the hotel," you whisper conspiratorially. "My pregnant wife." There's a smile in your voice, like I am something you own, something you take pride in, something you had orchestrated.

Now the diamonds in my wedding band glitter beneath the high Caribbean sun. My hands have darkened, a deep golden brown, and the stones in my rings look even brighter and more brilliant. It looks like the hand of a stranger.

The sea is still and clear and warm, like nothing I've ever felt. We're reclining on padded lounge chairs together, beneath an umbrella whose shade has shifted, the light touching my legs, forearms, the gentle swell of my belly beneath the black Lycra of my swimsuit.

"Paradise," you say, your face obscured by sunglasses I've never seen you wear before.

"Yes," I agree. "It will be difficult to leave."

I mean it. We took a last-minute vacation from work, rearranging schedules. When we get back we'll have doctor's appointments and arrangements to make. Parental leave and finding a nanny or day care. Selecting a pediatrician and buying baby books. For now, reality feels suspended, life on hold, the bundle of cells in my uterus forever no bigger than a blueberry.

"Not too difficult," you say, your hand finding mine without looking. "We have so much to look forward to when we get home. So much will change."

And it's true. You're right. So I'm not sure why your words feel like a threat.

27

They leave the airport garage, winding downward. Troy pays the exorbitant exit fee—they'd parked in the one closest to the terminal so that they wouldn't have to wait for a shuttle in the predawn darkness the morning they left. Then they're off, turning along the back roads, then easing onto the highway. It takes Klara fifteen minutes to notice they're not heading toward her condo in downtown Rockville.

Troy has been living there, too, the last few weeks, ever since he slid the ring on her finger, but he doesn't think of it as his. It's only Klara's name on the deed—it was hers before she met him, something left over from an earlier life, in which he didn't exist and that he'd rather they both forget. It's something they'll soon be rid of. His wife just doesn't know this yet.

She's exhausted, head tipped sideways, resting against the front passenger window.

"Where are we going?" she asks, voice soft and weary, perhaps still considering the possibility that he's simply taking her back to the condo via a different route than what she's used to.

They are traveling west but veering to the north, not south, hurtling down the highway. He's nervous, pulse fluttering in his neck. That's the Klara effect, still, even now that she's his wife.

"I have a surprise for you," Troy says.

It's early evening. They had a long day of travel. But it's

nearly summer now, one of the longest days of the year, so the sky remains lit.

"Troy," says Klara, still weary, "I'm so tired. I just want to rest. Is that okay?"

"Of course," he tells her, affronted. Of course he knows his pregnant wife, with her first-trimester sickness and fatigue, needs to rest. "That's where I'm taking you. Somewhere you can rest."

"I want to go *home*," she says, tiny and petulant. She sounds thankless, entitled. Anger flashes before Troy's eyes.

"Just trust me," he tells her, his anger injecting a stern father-like finality into his tone.

Klara sighs, but she says nothing more.

It's a shorter drive than it would be to the condo. Only fifteen minutes more, then he's easing onto the brake pedal as his car coasts down the street. He spins the wheel, curving into the driveway. He can barely breathe as he shuts off the motor. He turns his head to study his wife.

"What is this?" she asks, squinting through the windshield. "Where are we?"

"We're home," Troy says. "This is home."

Troy watches her take in the brick-front, the freshly painted door, the covered porch, the two planters overflowing with pansies. The pristine front yard, with no For Sale sign. That's because the house isn't for sale. Not anymore. Troy already closed on it.

Troy watches his wife catalog her observations, watches them click into place. He expects her to smile, gasp, throw her arms around him. Instead, her face crumples.

"What do you mean?" she asks. "I don't understand."

"This is our new home," he tells her patiently. "Come on," he adds, pushing his car door open. "I'll show you."

He has the key to the front door on his key ring already. They leave everything in the car, suitcases and backpacks, and he unlocks the front door, pushes inside. Klara follows him tentatively.

"I think the previous owners had cats," he tells her, because the odor is undeniable. "Maybe that's why I got a good deal."

He didn't. Not really. There was a bidding war for the house, and he ended up paying more than the listing price. He spent an entire day completing forms, securing the mortgage, selling stock, and liquidating part of his retirement account. But he needed the house. He refused to lose it to some other couple. It was the perfect family home, already a cedar playground in the backyard, with dark-green awnings and two yellow swings, babyproof locks on the kitchen cabinets, a two-car garage big enough for the stroller and wagon as well as both of their cars.

"Formal dining room," he tells her, hand gentle on the small of her back. "Living room. This is an office, or it could be a playroom."

Klara's face is impassive, lips pressed into a line.

"The kitchen is nice, right? The Realtor told me it was fully remodeled in the last five years."

She nods slightly, the tiniest acknowledgment of his words. The cabinets are white, the countertops a glimmering ivory veined with gray. The walls, throughout the entire house, are freshly painted—by the sellers, but they did them in a pale dove-gray, classic and inoffensive, so Troy's not expecting they'll need to be changed.

He ignores the powder room, which is perhaps the most dated room in the house, and takes her out back onto the deck. Beneath it is a stone patio, and beyond that the playground, before the yard slopes gently downward.

"It's not fenced," Troy says, "but since two of the neighboring yards are, it won't be too expensive for us to close it in completely."

He's picturing a dog, golden ears flopping, while his gorgeous, dark-haired daughter runs parallel. He's not sure why, but he thinks they'll have a girl. He'll call her *kiddo*, and he'll learn to braid her hair. His girls.

"Huh," says Klara. She turns away before he does, back toward the sliding glass door.

"Upstairs," he tells her—a suggestion, not a command—and she hovers in the hallway for a beat too long, but then she follows.

The hardwoods creak slightly as they climb. He leads her to the three smaller bedrooms first, all of which are empty. "Kids' bathroom," he says, gesturing toward the other full bath on the second floor. "And this is the primary bedroom."

He steps inside the room at the end of the hall, the final part of his surprise. It's the only room that's not empty.

"I told you," he says, "that you could rest."

He spent nearly twenty thousand dollars on this room alone. The bedroom furniture is a stylish and beachy distressed gray, the bedding bright white. He can picture Klara placing the baby in the middle of the comforter, dark hair sliding against her cheeks in curtains as she leans forward to blow raspberries on their daughter's belly.

"This is a Ritz-Carlton mattress and bedding," he explains, trailing his fingers along the fabric. "Apparently, you can order everything on their website. I looked into it after we booked the honeymoon and thought it would always remind us of when we stayed in paradise. The softest bed we've ever felt."

He takes a few steps away from the bed. "And this is a smart bassinet. It senses when there's crying, and it rocks the baby and plays white noise." He'd performed hours of research on his phone before selecting the bassinet.

"Wow," she says, but she's already looking away, eyes darting around the room.

"I bought you a toothbrush and a pair of pajamas," he says. "So you can go to sleep here. Now, if you want. You don't even have to go back to the condo."

"What if I want to go back to the condo?" Klara snaps, suddenly alert, like he's shaken her awake.

Troy flinches at her tone. He waits for her to continue.

"How did you—when did you even do this? How did you do all of this behind my back?" There's a wobble in her voice now, tears imminent.

"I used my savings and I did a three-week close. I ordered the furniture and scheduled it to be delivered and assembled while we were away. I had a cleaning service come in to clean and make up the bed, to open and unload the packages. And they'll come in every week to clean. I've already signed a contract with them. You won't have to worry about that."

"Thank you," she says, and she laughs, the most bitter laugh he's ever heard, a sound so brittle and hateful he'd never thought his beautiful Klara was capable.

"I thought you would be," he says, frowning. "Thanking me, I mean. I thought you'd be happy. I did all of this for you, Klara. For you and our baby. Were you really planning on staying in your condo? On raising the baby there? We have a yard here. There's a preschool and elementary school within walking distance, and they're highly rated."

"Maybe so," Klara says. "Maybe this is empirically a better place to raise a child. But I don't even know where I am right now. You've taken me completely out of it. Don't you get that? I've gotten no say in anything. You've made all the decisions for me."

"Good decisions," says Troy, defensive. "The best decisions. I bought you a fucking house, Klara."

She opens her mouth, closes it again. He's never cursed at her before, and he wishes he hadn't, but he's angry. This was not how he'd expected things to go. He was certain that even if Klara was less than pleased by what he'd done, she'd hide it. He thought that, at best, she'd weep with joy, and at worst, she'd thank him with a tight smile and icy tone, and she'd be cold for a few weeks but she'd come around, to the house, to the life he'd created for their family.

"But this house must be forty-five minutes from my office," Klara says at last. "Much worse in traffic. How will I manage that commute? Especially when I have the baby to manage. When I have to cut into my workday to pump milk and take her to day care and appointments. I can't spend a couple hours in the car every day. And when I have to go even farther out, for court appearances..." She sounds panicked.

"Klara," he says, "haven't I made things clear? You don't have to."

"I don't have to what?" She seems genuinely bewildered.

"You don't have to manage your career, the commute, along with the baby. You can quit your job. Enjoy your pregnancy and rest. Take a few years off, if you want."

She laughs, that bitter sound again.

"You didn't make partner," he reminds her gently. "And I—well, I did."

His final surprise. He studies her face, searching for pride, for relief. All he sees is tightness.

"I found out just before we left."

The truth. He doesn't tell her the way he forced the firm's hand. That he interviewed for a senior associate position with a competing firm, that he secured an offer. That he took the offer back to his firm and demanded that he be included in the next class of partners, or else he'd be gone in two weeks. He doesn't tell her that he fudged the offer a bit—the salary, the title—when he informed his current boss. A risk, yes, but risk is what Troy does. And things tend to work out just the way he wants. He makes sure of it.

"I hope that's not upsetting for you, Klara," he continues. "That I made it and you didn't." He decides to call her on her icy envy. Her utter lack of happiness in the face of her husband's success.

She blinks at him, then glances down. "Of course not," she says stiffly. "Good for you."

"Klara, I'm your husband. I love you so much," he insists. "I did this, all of this, because I love you. Because I want the world for you."

For another moment, she's frozen. And then her shoulders begin to shake, her chin falls to her chest.

"I'm sorry you didn't make partner, and I'm sorry you got pregnant when you didn't want to. But maybe that's the universe telling us that this is what's right for you, for us, right now."

Klara shakes her head, and Troy takes a tentative step toward her. She doesn't back away, and when he stretches an arm across her upper back and leads her to the edge of the bed, she allows it.

He sinks down beside her, arm resting heavily on her shoulders, which are shaking still.

"Let me take care of you," he whispers, pressing his lips into her hair. "That's all I'm trying to do."

28

Mary eats alone at her kitchen table. She always eats alone.

A floor below, he eats alone, too.

Sometimes Mary thinks that it's not unlike being pregnant. When she's home and she feels alone, she's really not. She will never forget that feeling, the alien movement within her—a miniature foot to a rib, a tiny fist against her bladder.

The chicken turned out well. Tender and fragrant, with the lemon just right. She wonders if he likes it.

Mary thinks of Greg on occasion, the man she wishes she had married. Of course, it was too late by the time she met Greg. She'd been married to Ed for so long, and Owen was fourteen. And if she'd met Greg when she was young, before she'd met Ed, she wouldn't have chosen him. It took many years, it took time being married to Ed, for her to recognize Greg as an ideal sort of husband. When she was a teenager, she would have proclaimed him boring. Too short, too bespectacled, too nerdy. He wasn't exciting or handsome like Ed. But he would have been a good father. He wouldn't have broken her heart.

He did reach out to her, after the murder. But she never responded to his message. It wasn't his fault, what happened, yet she couldn't help but blame him. If it hadn't been for him, for the things she felt for him and he for her, everything would have been different.

Mary finishes her dinner and her wine. She rinses her plate and glass, then loads them into the dishwasher. Later, she'll open the basement door to retrieve the rest of the dishes from the top step, but not yet. He won't have put them there yet.

She cleans the counters, a spritz of grapefruit spray and a paper towel. That nerve in her back still pinching, Mary wants desperately to settle onto the sofa for the night, but when she throws the paper towel away, she realizes that the can is far too full. She should have taken it out yesterday, and trash pickup is in the morning.

Mary tugs the bag loose, knots the top, and carries it out to the larger can in the garage. She keeps her eyes cast down as she rolls the can to the end of the driveway. If there are any neighbors out, she doesn't want to see them. They don't greet her pleasantly or genuinely, her neighbors. They don't call out, "Hey, Mary. How are you?" They don't want her here, don't understand why she's stayed all these years. They wish she'd leave. Soon, their wish will come true.

But as she parks the can at the curb, she senses a presence, and she can't help but glance up, peering through the golden light cast by the descending sun. Janet, across the street, is in her own yard, hose aimed over her front garden. Janet smiles tentatively and lifts a hand in the briefest of waves. Mary, relieved, returns it—the smile, the wave—before turning back toward her house. It's something. It's enough. More than any other neighbor would offer. And perhaps more than Mary would want from anyone else. Janet, a mother of grown children, one of whom still lives with her, is possibly the only neighbor who doesn't make Mary feel like she's something shameful, something that doesn't belong.

Mary slides beside her car, back toward the door to the house. She's been putting off cleaning out the garage, knows it will be almost as unpleasant as cleaning out Owen's bedroom. The memories it holds aren't as painful, but the volume and weight of the things stored in here are overwhelming. But she's running out of time. She'll have to tackle it one box at a time.

She scans the array now, the cardboard boxes and heavy plastic containers stacked against the walls, perched on rickety metal shelves Ed had built himself. In the back corner, there's a glint of green, of black rubber, and it causes a stabbing in her chest.

She knows what it is. She should go inside. It's time for a bath, to lie down with her heating pad, a novel that can transport her someplace far away, someplace far happier than here. But she can't help herself. She squeezes between the boxes, steps closer, tugs at the handlebars, and unearths Owen's bike. His first bike, his only bike. Fluorescent-green metal, shot through with white and black accents.

They bought him the bike for his fifth birthday. It rained that morning, the driveway damp and water pooling because they needed to have it repaved, the concrete cracking and dipping in places.

They forgot to buy him a helmet. "I'll run out to the sporting goods store and get one," Mary said, car keys already in her hand.

"He'll be fine," said Ed, and that was when the sick feeling began, trickling into Mary's gut, the knowledge that whatever was to come wouldn't be good.

Mary found her old helmet, the one she used to wear when she was in her early twenties and would ride her bike to the diner where she worked, when Ed wasn't available to drive her. They had gotten rid of the bike during one of their previous moves, but somehow the helmet had made it from house to house.

It was too big for Owen, slipping over his eyes even once she'd tightened the straps as much as she could.

An hour later, Owen was crying, left knee dripping blood that was collecting in his sock.

"Stop crying," Ed hissed. He had a way of speaking to Owen on those rare occasions when they were out front, where neighbors could see him. He had the ability to lace his tone with cruelty even while his face was placid, his body language loose.

"Get back on." Ed flicked a hand toward the bike. "Falling is part of learning."

"I think we can take a break," said Mary. "Get his knee cleaned up."

"He's fine."

Owen, decidedly, was not fine. He was five. Mary's parents were coming later that evening for cake and ice cream, and Owen was gulping wetly, staring at his father with a hatred that Mary understood all too well.

"You're not a baby anymore," said Ed sternly. "If you don't want to get back on the bike, we'll take it back to the store."

Mary's heart was aching.

"I don't care," said Owen. He was looking at his shoes.

If they hadn't been out front, on the driveway, Mary had no idea what Ed might have done. But they were, and Janet, across the street, was outside, too, pulling weeds from the little garden around her mailbox. So while Ed's eyes bulged in a way that made Mary's stomach churn, he said nothing. He spun around and went into the garage. The door slammed, the house rattled, and Mary collected her boy in her arms. His breaths slowed and evened out, and his fingers dug into her back. She held him close, and she didn't tell him she was sorry, although she was. She just couldn't bear to explain precisely why. It was so complicated for a five-year-old. It was more, sometimes, than even she could understand.

Ed never took the bike back to the store like he'd threatened, but he also never offered to teach Owen how to ride it again, and Owen didn't ask.

And here it is, tucked against this back wall all these years, old but perfectly intact. Mary will donate it along with Owen's other possessions. Things from a childhood so auspicious to start, but that had gone so spectacularly wrong.

She closes the garage door, goes back into the house. It's time, at last, to rest.

29

With every day that passes, I hate the house more. Yet I almost never leave it.

The Monday I returned to work after our wedding and honeymoon, I gave my two weeks' notice. Health reasons, I said, which wasn't exactly a lie but wasn't precisely true.

The drive to my office took more than an hour, traffic lurching and halting, which only cemented my decision. I am crushed by fatigue. Sometimes I feel like a slug, melded to cement, sneaking forward millimeter by millimeter. And yet I suspect this is nothing compared to the fatigue I'll feel once the baby is born.

Besides, you want to take care of me. You pleaded, *Let me take care of you.*

Fine, I thought as I left Grant Wilpers's office, his judgmental gaze on my back. *Take care of me. Give me health insurance and pay my expenses. Sell my home. Level my life—you've already done so much. Finish the job.*

It's as though you could hear me. You pay for a service to pack up my condo. My furniture is delivered to the new house—your new house—and arranged here. My bed, nightstands, and dresser are set up in the guest bedroom. I go in there sometimes. I lie on the bed and close my eyes, and I pretend I'm back in my condo.

But soon my condo will no longer be mine. I didn't own it for long, and I'll be lucky to get back what I paid. The market has dipped. I suggested that I hold on to it for a while, to see if things improved, but your Realtor didn't think that was a good idea.

"Things may only get worse," she said, tapping her red nails along my countertops.

"She's not exactly impartial, is she?" I told you later. "Of course she wants me to sell it. She gets a commission whether I lose money or not."

"She has a point," you said. "I'm sure you'll get more than your mortgage. And we could use that money. We could remodel the powder room. We could put in a pool."

I don't care about the powder room, and I don't want a pool. It feels like a safety nightmare for the child growing inside me. But it's easier not to argue. I don't have the energy to disagree. I don't have the energy to try to analyze or understand why I want to.

My last two weeks at the firm, I mostly work from home. The unrelenting nausea, the exhaustion—the drive is too much. I'm sure the partners are irritated with me, but I can't figure out why I should care. Soon, I'll be gone.

I'm not feeling well, I write in email after email. *I'll be working remotely today.*

On a blistering-hot Friday, I do head into the office, but only because I have plans to meet Zoe for lunch in Georgetown, at a restaurant midway between our offices. Inside, the air is too warm, the volume and laughter of the diners too loud, the tables and chairs on the sidewalks going unused.

It's much farther than I'd usually go for lunch, and it will be a much longer break than I usually take, but I have to tell her. I have to explain.

"I can't wait to see your new house," she says, unfurling her napkin and draping it across her lap. "It's all so exciting."

"It's far," I say, reaching for my water glass, taking the tiniest sip. Somehow, water remains one of the most nauseating things I can ingest. I look up, searching for our waiter.

"From what?" Zoe flips her menu open, gaze skimming the pages.

"My office," I tell her. "But I guess that won't matter soon."

Her brows furrow, but before I can say more, our server is beside our table.

"Are we ready?" she asks brightly, and we both nod and order our meals.

"And could I have a lemon?" I ask, gesturing toward my water.

"Of course," she says before taking our menus and ducking away.

I look at Zoe.

"You never get lemon for your water," she says, nose wrinkling.

"Um..." I smooth a wrinkle from the tablecloth, adjust my fork.

A second later, Zoe lifts her hands, cupping her mouth.

"Are you?" she asks, somehow both a whisper and a shout, and I nod.

"Klara," she says, and then she's squealing, reaching across the table for my hands.

I feel myself smiling, the warmth of her fingers gripping mine, her joy contagious like a yawn. I'm smiling, yet I'm also, somehow, trying not to cry.

"But I thought—you and Adam." She releases my hands, rests her forearms on the table, leans toward me.

"It wasn't exactly planned," I admit.

"So that's why," she says, nodding. "The quick wedding. The move…" Her voice trails off.

How can I explain to her that it's not? How can I articulate the tornado of you? The way you've swept me in so completely, making everything seem so obvious and clear?

"Well," I tell her.

The server is back, a wedge of lemon on a tiny plate. I pick it up and squeeze it over my water.

"Things change. I gave notice at work," I add, and her eyes widen. "Maybe I'll find something closer to the new house after the baby comes and I'm feeling more settled," I add hurriedly.

"That makes sense," she says, even though I know that Zoe, who is already thinking about when she'll try to give baby Daphne a sibling, would never dream of leaving her successful career as a business-management consultant. "I probably didn't take enough time off after Daphne. And God, I could've used some more rest while I was pregnant with her."

I nod, staring at the lemon juice descending through my water.

"I just—" Zoe swallows. She scratches at her wrist beneath the band of her watch. "A few months ago, I was helping you move out of the place you shared with Adam. All of a sudden, you're married, living in the suburbs, and expecting a baby. And you've left your job? It's all so wonderful, I think… But, Klara…" Her voice is tentative, eyes searching. "I guess I'm just a little shocked."

My smile is feeble, forced. But there. "I know," I tell her. "I am, too."

"But if you're happy, then I'm happy for you," she continues hopefully.

The words are right there. *I'm not.*

"I get it," she adds, as though reassuring herself. "We're in our mid-thirties now. It's normal."

"Right," I say, and the moment has passed. "Right," I say again, as though I have any idea what she means.

During my remaining working days, I pass off my active cases to other associates, delegate discovery responses to my paralegals, and let my clients know that I'll soon be stepping away from the practice of law but that they'll be in highly competent hands. I quickly discover that if I share my excuse—because of my health—people are far more sympathetic and less irritable about being passed off to a new lawyer.

Two days before my last day of work, I have a settlement conference at the courthouse. I have to wear a suit and style my hair.

"Good luck," you say cheerfully, kissing me on top of the head. You're perfectly content to undertake your hour-long commute to DC each day. You work nine or ten hours, and with the drive, you're out of the house for eleven or twelve hours a day. You're a partner now, and you never complain. You're a martyr, giving your pregnant wife the peaceful suburban life she never asked for or wanted. You're an insult, your success, your achieving my goal when I'd failed to achieve it for myself, like a slap to my cheek.

I stand in our walk-in closet and try on every one of my suits. But I can't button a single pair of pants, and the zipper of every skirt gets stuck. My belly feels swollen and soft, not the pert or firm beginnings of a baby bump, but more like I've just returned from a vacation during which I overindulged in fried food and dessert. Which is true, actually. I did, eating fries and ice cream, slurping frozen virgin daiquiris, the only things I could stomach on our honeymoon.

I finally pull on a navy wrap dress I usually wouldn't wear to court and a gray-plaid blazer that's always been a little big but now fits snugly across my chest. Even my flats feel tight and uncomfortable.

I'm dizzy and unfocused during the conference and can't settle the case. We set a trial date, and I choose something that works for my colleague's schedule. For the first time, I feel a sense of relief, and as I push through the courthouse doors for the final time, I wonder whether this is for the best.

It's over. I should cut and run before complete incompetence sets in, before I become so tired that I commit malpractice and cost my firm millions.

I wave to the deputy sheriffs lingering near the doorway. "See you later, Klara," they tell me. I don't correct them. I step outside.

But on my first jobless Monday, I feel dazed and hollow. I've no email to check, no laptop to open. I drink ginger ale and wander aimlessly from room to room, looking out the windows, until the doorbell rings.

Zoe has taken the day off work to come see the house. She arrives late morning, ten minutes later than she said she'd be here.

"Sorry," she says, reaching for me, pulling me in for a one-armed hug. "Traffic was brutal, even this late."

"No worries," I tell her. "I get it." Somehow this house, which is nearly midway between Baltimore and Washington, DC, only forty-five minutes away from my old condo, feels like a foreign land.

I give her a tour, and the amount of space feels shameful. It's three times bigger than the little bungalow where I was raised. Zoe remarks on the recent renovations, the abundant natural light, the convenient open-floor plan. She doesn't mention the lingering cat odor, although my pregnancy nose often can't detect anything else.

We end up in the kitchen, and I make us coffees in the machine you bought last week. It uses little plastic pods, and I feel guilty every time I toss the brewed ones into the trash, think of them sitting in a landfill for hundreds of years, like the one around the corner from the tiny bungalow in Florida where I grew up, its odor settling thickly into the sticky wetness the air always held. This place, everything about it, couldn't be more different from that house, that neighborhood, and that should be a comfort to me. More so than it is.

I make decaf for myself, as I've already had my allotted caffeine intake for the day, although it's not nearly enough. My mind feels foggy, and I stand before the open fridge for at least fifteen seconds before Zoe reminds me gently, "Creamer?"

"I still can't believe he bought you this house," says Zoe as we settle onto barstools at the island.

"Me either."

"He just brought you home from your honeymoon. Here, to this gorgeous house he'd bought all by himself. It's so…romantic."

I lean back, winded. The way she sees you—sometimes I wish I still saw you like that, too.

"I'm lucky if Garrett buys me a Starbucks on Saturday mornings," she continues. "I get a latte sometimes. You get a house."

"Well," I say, "it's not really my house, is it?"

"What do you mean?"

"I'm not on the deed. He bought it, closed on it, on his own. So it's really his house."

"But you're married." Zoe's eyes fall to my ringed hand.

"He bought it before we were married, so it's a premarital asset."

"Oh," says Zoe, blinking questioningly. "But that only matters if you—if you get a divorce, right?"

"Right," I tell her, and her brows are drawn low, the divot between them more pronounced than I've ever seen it.

I've only been married to you for three weeks. How could I even be considering such a thing?

"Are you...worrying about that?" It's as though she can't bring herself to say the word. *Divorce*.

"Of course not," I tell her hurriedly. "It's just my lawyer brain. I've told Troy I want to be added to the deed, and he agreed that I should."

You did. "That was always my plan," you told me. "After the surprise." Yet each time I've brought it up since, you've sighed. "Sorry, Klara. I didn't have time to get to it today."

Something tells me you never will.

And in truth, the house ownership is far murkier than I'm making things seem to Zoe. You will make the mortgage payments from our marital funds. The house will soon become at least partly marital property. But not completely. It will still always be more yours than mine. It's far away from the job I loved. Never mind that I didn't make partner this year, that I didn't excel at trials. I know I'm a good lawyer—*was* a good lawyer. Better than anyone at securing favorable settlements for my clients. And that job was my purpose. You've never explained your plan, but I can see what you're doing, as though you're setting up plays on a chessboard. You've pulled me away from the only home I've known for the last ten years, into this unfamiliar suburb that feels improbably remote, where I've got nothing else but you. Your plan is growing clearer, while I'm too sick and too tired to come up with a plan of my own. Besides, on paper it's all so perfect. Why would I need a plan at all? Why would I ever want to leave? What's so wrong with me that sometimes leaving is all I can think about?

You want to be my purpose in life. You and our baby. You're making that happen. I'm letting you.

"Anyway, how are you feeling?" Zoe asks. She blows across the top of her mug, and her gaze falls to my abdomen.

"Honestly, I feel like shit," I admit. "I'm nauseated all the time, not just in the mornings. I throw up at least once a day. I can't even think about eating a fruit or a vegetable." I pause, cover my mouth with my palm. Just the words conjure almost unbearable sickness.

"God," says Zoe. She looks horrified. "I never threw up. If only you'd known that would happen." Her face flushes. "Sorry," she adds quickly. "I didn't mean—"

"It's fine," I cut her off. "You know that I wasn't trying to get pregnant. I really don't even know how it happened. I was on the pill."

"I guess nothing is really foolproof," Zoe says sagely. She possesses the luxury of distance when it comes to the subject of life not happening precisely as planned and on schedule.

"I guess." I sigh, raise my mug. Knowing that there's no caffeine, that it won't set my blood buzzing, reduces the appeal. I lower it again.

"How far along are you now?"

"Ten weeks. It's the size of a kumquat, according to the app on my phone. I have never seen a kumquat in my life."

"'It'?" repeats Zoe.

I nod bleakly. "Next week it'll be the size of a fig."

"Ah," says Zoe, nodding. "Are you okay?" she adds tentatively after a beat of silence. "You seem—I don't know. Off."

It's so similar to what she said when we went to dinner, after I'd left my wedding dress with the tailor. It feels like the moment during our Georgetown lunch, when I was so close to telling her everything.

And I want to tell her the truth. That I'm not okay at all. That I am *off*. That I'm so off that I have no idea how I used to feel. That I have no idea who I am. That when I look in the mirror, I'm scared—the fullness of my cheeks, the purplish half-moons beneath my eyes. At night, I lie in bed and my thoughts race. I'm so tired, always so tired, but I can't sleep. You breathe evenly and peacefully beside me, perfectly content. You seem to think everything is perfect. And why shouldn't you? This was your masterpiece. You envisioned it, you created it. I'm your subject, your beautiful unmoving muse. My agency is hurtling away from me, barely a speck on the horizon.

I open my mouth.

On the counter between us, my phone begins to vibrate. *Troy* says the screen. Of course it's you. *Hush, now. Good girl. Keep it together.* Like you knew what I was about to say.

Zoe's eyes fall to the phone, then flick up to meet mine.

"You can get it," she says. "I'm going to use your bathroom."

"Okay," I tell her, and I offer directions to the powder room, the one with the eggplant walls and black-and-white-tiled floor. The room you hate.

Once she disappears down the hall, I tap the red button, declining your call. It gives me the tiniest bit of satisfaction, and it's so sad that this is all I have.

30

Henry still thinks of her sometimes, the woman who ruined his life.

Her Instagram account is gone. Not just private, but gone. He supposes he scared her, that she's become more private since the incident. But her precautions are belated and futile. She never could have stopped him. He's too good at finding what he needs. It was so easy to get into her phone, to find those images—she'd sent them to some tool named *Kent* three weeks earlier. And if that didn't prove that she'd been asking for what she got, then what did?

No Instagram, but she does still maintain her LinkedIn profile. Henry checks it now and sees that she's made a new post.

It's a selfie of Lacey sitting in an office Henry doesn't recognize, before an expansive window, three computer monitors in front of her. She's smiling demurely, mauve lips closed, one elbow propped in front of her keyboard, chin in her palm. He reads the caption.

> It was a difficult year for me at work, but I'm so happy to announce that I've started a new position as Director of IT at LKOP Enterprises! #career #careergoals #girlboss

His stomach drops. He was laid off, still unemployed eight

months later, and she's found a new role. And it's a fucking promotion.

She should be fired for her final hashtag alone. And the reference to a "difficult year"—does that not come perilously close to violating the NDA? He feels a vibration in his chest—his anger, so tightly contained.

He's smarter than she is, and they're the same age, the same experience level. It should have been him who'd landed that role. He's pretty sure it's one he applied for, yet he wasn't even invited to interview. Their old company must have helped her get it, must have given her a glowing review and someone called in a favor.

Of course, even though he was gone, she couldn't stay at their old company. How could she face those people after what they saw?

That picture, flashing on the screen at the beginning of the PowerPoint presentation, the human resources director, Penny, fumbling at the keyboard to make it go away—Lacey's mauve mouth open, breasts bare, fingertips grazing her own skin. The collective gasp of the employees assembled in the conference room. When Penny finally managed to tap a key and the image disappeared, it was replaced by another—Lacey's ass, recognizable only to herself. Her scream rose in that too-crowded, too-warm room. Penny slammed the laptop shut.

She's sure it was you. You've been making her uncomfortable for a while, his boss had said later that week. *She said that she rejected you. That you've followed her. That she's caught you going through her desk.*

Henry should have had excuses prepared.

When she caught him in her office, he'd thought she was gone for the day—he thought everyone was. But it was raining and she'd come back for the umbrella he hadn't noticed was resting on the floor. She caught him sitting in her chair, her top desk drawer open, one of her cinnamon mints dissolving on his tongue and her lipstick tube open between his fingers. He heard the gasp, looked up, and there she was, standing in the doorway, those mauve lips forming a perfect *O*.

"I thought you were gone," he'd said automatically, stupidly.

"My umbrella," she had said, their joint shock apparently forcing civility and honesty. That was when he first detected the patter of rain against the windows. That was when the anger flickered across her face.

"Why are you in my office?" she had asked, voice icy, arms crossing tightly against her chest.

"I was looking for a flash drive," he'd said. "We're out. Greg said you might have one." They weren't out, and Henry hadn't asked Greg. It was such a flimsy excuse.

He'd stood, then ducked past her, slunk into his own office, knowing he was already on thin ice with her, ever since she'd so frigidly rejected his invitation for drinks.

He should have denied everything to his boss. That he'd ever propositioned her. That he'd ever followed her.

But it didn't matter. He didn't stand a chance. They laid out their terms, and it all seemed so swift and neat; how could he not agree?

Still, the unfairness of it—the stupid hypocritical bitch could have a public Instagram account, could post photos of herself in a yellow bikini, could send nude pictures to fucking *Kent*, yet he could still get fired for opening her desk drawers, for eating her cinnamon mints, for inspecting her mauve lipstick, for lingering nearby while she made her coffee, for following her to the bathroom and then pushing into the men's room at the last second, for touching her forearm toward the end of a company happy hour and inviting her to leave with him to another bar.

The pictures on the screen at the meeting—no one could prove it was him. That was what Henry said to his boss. *You can't prove it was me.* But that was the wrong thing to say. His boss's eyes hardened, and Henry realized too late that he shouldn't have mentioned proof at all.

Anyway, if he was better looking, Lacey might have said *yes*; she might have gone to that other bar with him, she might have touched his arm while she laughed, and he'd still be working there. He'd still have his apartment. He'd be interacting with his parents a normal amount, rather than living in their basement.

They're not home now, so at least he has that. His mother went out for lunch. His father is at work. Despite all his mother's threats that his dad will soon retire and they'll sell the house and move closer to his sister, Henry can't imagine how his father could retire. If he does, he'll have to be with Henry's mom all the time. And there's no way she'll let him spend his days in his recliner with crossword puzzles and baseball games on the TV. She'll write *to-do* lists, things she's capable of doing herself.

Henry closes Lacey's LinkedIn page, rage still simmering. It makes sense now. She was probably offered a payout, and help securing a better job. That was why she signed the NDA. And he's expected to be grateful that it wasn't worse for him.

He wishes for a moment that he knew the wife's name, that he could look at her LinkedIn page or her Instagram account. Yet he suspects she doesn't have one. She wouldn't. Not her. She wouldn't share photos of herself in a bikini or her avocado toast. She has probably never even had avocado toast. He loves that about her. She's not trendy. She's classic. She's perfection—this beautiful and lonely soul. This deeply unhappy wife.

And it's as though he's summoned her with his thoughts. There she is.

She's been coming out more lately. Not just her Saturday-morning walks with her possessive husband, but walks by herself, during the week, while her husband and his black sedan are at work. Once so sporadic, they've become more predictable, something he can track. She wears a white baseball cap, and her dark hair cascades from the hole in the back like a waterfall. Henry took a photo of her when she passed his house. He zoomed in as much as he could and snapped, then studied the blurred image, confirming what he'd thought—there were no headphones, no earbuds, no AirPods. And she doesn't run, never runs. She walks and she does not smile, listening to nothing but her own thoughts.

She's not heading out for a walk now. Just into the garden, where the mulch has grown sparse, the flowers she planted weeks ago turning parched, obscured by creeping and wiry weeds. Someone needs to pull them, to replenish the mulch, to water everything.

Inexplicably, Henry tastes something sour and hopeless. He swallows, rubs at his throat. He feels stuck, just the same as he has felt for months now.

At least there's her. Stuck, too, he thinks. He can't be sure, not until he meets her. But there's that connection, that thread tugging between them.

The wife crosses her arms over her chest, looks down at her front garden. She leans forward, inspecting something more closely, her left leg lifting slightly, as though for balance.

Henry tucks his novel under his arm. He's feeling reckless, like that day he went into Lacey's office. It wasn't the first time he went, although it was the first time he got caught.

Once, he found a long, dark hair on the headrest of her desk chair. He wound it around his index finger until the tip turned blue while he crunched down on two of her cinnamon mints.

Now he has less to lose. And he'll never meet the wife if all he ever does is sit in the living room, looking out the front windows with his book on his lap. He's here alone.

It's time to make his move.

The first move. Who's to say what's to come? But for now, this.

Paperback still beneath his arm, Henry steps outside onto the front porch. The wife isn't looking at him. She's still inspecting her garden. She bends to pluck a weed. But Henry pretends that she is watching him. He strolls down the driveway, glances both ways, then crosses the street. He's looking ahead, up the sidewalk, but he hesitates, eyes catching on the wife, the weed dangling from her left hand.

He glances away, then back again. *Ah, well*, he thinks, feigning a lack of premeditation for no one's benefit but his own. *Why not say hello?*

He takes a few steps closer, onto her driveway.

"Hey there," he says. He can hear the tremor in his voice, but he hopes she can't. "I don't think we've met."

He's smiling. She turns.

31

My new life in this unfamiliar suburb is taking shape. My barren days, my aimless routines, the inconsequential minutiae of my precious moments, the sense that I'm waiting for something to happen, the dread growing heavier like a deepening pit.

I've had to familiarize myself with the area: Which grocery store do I like best? Which coffee shop makes the best iced lattes? We need things, so many things, for the house, and I order what I can online, preferring to stay in when I can, leaning in to my newfound seclusion.

I had to find a new gynecological practice, too—my former doctor, the one I'd seen since I was in law school, is too far away for the appointments that will gradually increase in frequency until they're weekly, at least. And I needed to find a doctor with privileges at the hospital closest to our house. When this baby comes, I won't want to be an hour from the hospital where I plan to deliver.

When I arrived for my first appointment with my new doctor, a cheerful nurse walked me back to the exam rooms. I wrote my name on the side of a plastic cup, then peed into it, wiped drops from the rim, washed my hands.

My heart fluttered, and I sat on the edge of the exam bed, feet kicking like a little girl's. The doctor bustled in, blue-and-white dress swirling around her calves. She confirmed that I am, in fact, pregnant, and she was smiling, but she didn't congratulate me. There was a tiny part of me that felt relieved, another part disappointed—a dichotomy that dizzied me, head spinning, as she asked me if I had any questions and whether I'd been feeling okay.

I told her I wasn't, not really—the nausea, the vomiting (usually when I'm trying to brush my teeth), the crushing fatigue (a physical weight that flattens me even as my thoughts race, wired and troubling).

She offered suggestions to help me deal with the nausea, but nothing I hadn't tried, and my stomach sank.

I used to be so alert, productive, polished. Now, every day, I feel like a melted-wax version of that shiny and poised woman I once was.

I left with instructions to have my blood work and genetic testing done, and an appointment scheduled for the following week. I left the building, sliding doors gliding crisply open, numbness burgeoning, a sort of distance, like I was hovering in the wings, observing a stranger proceed through her life. As I walked back to my car, I placed a palm against my abdomen, testing it out. I felt silly. I felt nothing.

Now, a week later, it's time to see our baby.

"I'm so sorry, Klara," you told me when I shared the appointment date and time with you. "I have a closing that morning. I wish I could move it, but I can't."

"It's fine," I told you. "There will be plenty more appointments."

I'm surprised that I'm disappointed that you won't be there. I want you to see the baby. I want you to see what you've done.

I'm ten weeks and three days pregnant as I sit in the waiting room, hands tucked beneath my thighs. I'm nervous, a little ashamed to be here alone. Everyone else in the room is here with a partner. A little girl with dark pigtails plays on the floor nearby while her parents look on, each of them with a palm resting on the mother's belly.

A nurse appears in the doorway, pink scrubs, welcoming smile. "Klara Martin?" she calls out.

I stand and move toward her.

"Right this way," she says, but she's looking over my shoulder.

I turn, and there you are. Hair mussed as though you sprinted all the way here from DC, but your blazer is immaculate, stiff shirt collar peeking open.

"Sorry," you say, stepping forward, a hand to my lower back. "I was afraid I wouldn't make it."

I blink into your face, and you're grinning. "I got someone to cover my closing. I couldn't miss this."

The relief crushes me, and I know that's what you wanted. That's why you did it. There probably was no closing. You probably got here when I did, waiting in the parking lot until the time of my appointment. You wanted me to think you couldn't be here, but you knew all along that you would. It's like the day you rescued me with my own umbrella. You look like a hero, don't you? I'm starting to know better.

The nurse asks me to remove my shorts and underwear, and I slide onto the chair.

"First baby?" she asks conversationally as she squirts gel onto a probe.

"First baby," you confirm, speaking before I can. You're beaming.

"This may be a little cold," she tells me, pushing the probe inside. She squints at her screen, flips a switch, and black, white, and gray swirls to life on the screen across from us. The thumping whoosh of a heartbeat. You grip my hand.

"There it is," she says. "There's the heart."

I watch the flicker on the screen, and I feel something. Warm and heavy and irrevocable. I feel changed, and I try to push it away. *No*, I think. *Not yet.*

You're laughing, giddy, your grip tightening. "She looks like a baby squirrel," you say.

"A frog," I insist, and suddenly, I'm laughing, too. I can't help it.

"Congratulations," says the nurse. She seems relieved by the departure of my frigid aura, by our now-shared joy. "I'll print some pictures for you."

She clicks her mouse, presses her keys, taking measurements, snapping photos. She prints a glossy roll of them, and you take them, holding them against your chest.

We are moved to an exam room, where we wait for the doctor.

"I can't believe it," you say, holding the roll of pictures close to your face. "Can you believe it?"

I shake my head, my mirth, the surprising happiness, beginning to drain away. This is real. This is happening, and I'm still stunned. How did this happen?

The doctor knocks sharply on the door, then sweeps into the room.

"Everything looks great," she says, settling onto the stool in front of her computer. "And I have the results of your genetic tests. There were no abnormalities, and I've released them to your chart, so you can review them in the app if you choose. But they do reveal the sex of the baby. So if you don't want to know, I suggest that you don't open them."

I hear the inhale of your breath, see your mouth open.

"No," I say firmly, cutting you off. "I don't want to know."

You look at me, an expression I know so well, but you don't argue. You won't with the doctor here. But I can tell that you want to know.

This is mine, something inside my body. Something I can control. I don't want to know. And how could you deny me this choice?

"Anything else?" the doctor asks, eyes volleying between us.

"Nothing," I tell her, every question I've had over the past week forgotten, unreachable. "Thank you."

We leave the exam room, those pictures trailing from your right hand, your left pressed into the small of my back, just a little more firmly than feels right.

32

Mary showers quickly, water scalding. Something sticky from the side of the trash can had brushed against her leg, and she could sense the dust from Owen's room that had collected on his things, layering her skin.

When she's finished, she towels her aching limbs and her back dry, then squeezes water from her hair. She dresses in her pajamas—silky but not real silk, seams pulling loose—and tosses her dirty clothes into the hamper. It's full now, so she hefts it upward and empties it into the machine in her walk-in closet.

Ed had the foresight to have a set installed in their bedroom. He was so proud of the house, so much grander than anywhere either of them had ever lived. Anytime he had an especially successful year, drew in more commissions, he wanted to use the extra money on the house. New hardware in the bathrooms, lighting in the dining room, a shed in the backyard for his tools, a washer and dryer in the primary closet, and custom shelving, even though there was already a laundry room in the basement.

The projects were endless, and Mary never cared about them. Ed earned so much more than she did, and he seemed to think that entitled him to sole financial decision-making power. Mary had wanted a playground out back, then more deposits into Owen's college fund.

The house hasn't been as well cared for these past twenty years.

Mary couldn't afford much, and she's feeling the age of it. It seems brittle, wheezy. It will be so hard, yet she knows it's time to go.

She tosses a detergent pod into the machine, then turns it on. There's so little laundry to do these days, just for herself. Sometimes she'll wear the same shorts or pants for three days. It can take weeks for enough for a full load to build up.

She remembers how, in the months after Owen was born, laundry felt like an interminable chore. How, when he was a newborn, he'd soil three pairs of footie pajamas a day. She would wash them every morning, a pour of Dreft into the machine, her baby draped over her shoulder. The way he clung to her back then. Like Velcro. Like the cord was still attached. Like he was part of her still, and always would be.

Mary closes her eyes, feels the sadness swell, the memories cresting, tall and unavoidable. It makes sense, after the way she spent the day. Cleaning out his room. It's only natural that this day would be more difficult than most.

She just misses him. That's all. Even those bone-deep-exhausted days as a new mother. Even those sticky, shrieking whirls of toddlerhood.

She will never forget the way his face looked just before he fell asleep. The particular fullness of it, the specific perfection. She loved holding him while he slept. Even when he was nearly three, that summer before he started preschool, when he would resist his afternoon nap. She'd rock him and sing to him and wish she could still feed him from her breasts. She'd coax him into sleep, then rest beneath his warm weight. It soothed her.

When Ed was home and walked by the doorway, he'd grunt disapprovingly. "He's not a baby anymore, Mary." Jealousy and irritation flashing in his voice. She knew Ed thought that her devoted attention and care should be returning to him.

But Mary would smile at her husband, pleading. *Let me have this.* She'd shrug sheepishly, then smooth her finger across Owen's faint brows. And Ed would say nothing more, indulging her in a way he so rarely did, ever since those first few intense and lustful years. Then, when Ed was gone, Mary would curve toward her son. She would press a kiss to his forehead and breathe in his heat, his lavender smell. "My most perfect boy," she'd whisper.

He always was.

33

"I haven't talked to you in ages" is the first thing she says when I answer the phone, and I nearly hang up.

I breathe as slowly, as deeply as I can before I speak. "Hi, Mom."

"Well, don't sound too happy to hear from me. My ego might get too big."

I press my lips together, glance out the window. The street outside is still, no movement. The flowers I'd halfheartedly planted in the front garden last week are already wilted, petals clinging to the sparse mulch. Turns out, I have a black thumb. And my planting them had pleased you, so maybe that's why I let them die.

I'm using a finger to hold the living room curtains to the side. When we first moved into the house, I would pass through each room every morning, throwing curtains open, tugging blinds upward, until natural light touched everything, as though the sun could warm the coolness rising within me. But as the summer heat has intensified, I've been trying to limit the amount of sunlight that streams in, to keep things cooler, and I do sometimes wonder whether the darkness is making me the tiniest bit more depressed than I otherwise would be.

"I'm surprised you answered."

Me too.

"How's everything?" I ask, trying to sound cheery. I try to sound like I care.

"Things are fine. It's been hot as hell. Thank God for the pool here, and the beach."

"It's been hot here, too." I've reached the edge of the living room, so I turn and start toward the opposite end. I've always paced while I talk on the phone. I used to wear the commercial-grade carpeting in my 150-square-foot office thin, from one wall to the next, phone to my ear, negotiating settlement deals worth hundreds of thousands of dollars.

"You should take a vacation," my mom suggests. "Come down and visit."

"I don't know if we're going to be able to get away this summer. Things are busy."

"You work too hard." She somehow manages to make it sound like an insult, her voice devoid of pride.

"I enjoy it." The lies flow easily when it comes to my mom.

"I'd love to meet my new son-in-law, you know."

There's a pause. My mother inhales wetly while I swallow acid.

"I know that, Mom. We'll make time soon." She's still upset with me for excluding her from the wedding that, I have repeatedly insisted to her, wasn't even really a wedding. And she knows nothing of the baby, of my abrupt unemployment. I fear that if I tell her about the baby, she'll be on a plane. I won't be able to stop her. Visiting, purportedly, to help, but I can picture her sharing stories about taking care of me when I was a newborn, her own tales of new motherhood, ignoring the unignorable fact that she'd left it all behind. She'd tell me about her customers at the salon and her friends, chatting with forced pleasantness as I tried to nap, asking with obvious impatience when I planned on making dinner.

"I know I'm too *Florida* for you," my mom says suddenly, voice shrill. "My lawyer daughter with her fancy and expensive degrees. But I am still your mom, whether you like it or not."

I squeeze my eyes shut, reach up to pinch the bridge of my nose. "Mom, stop," I say. "Don't be so dramatic about it."

I don't say what I want to, what I wish I had the courage to remind her. *You're the one who left.*

Perhaps my mother isn't wrong—that I'm ashamed of her, that I might behave as though I'm superior. But those are such small lines pulled from our long and complicated story. So it's beyond irritating for her to distill our history down to something discrete and solid, something that makes our distance, both physical and emotional, seem like my fault, as though she hadn't made me feel unwanted for nearly my entire life, as though she hadn't moved out when I was ten, using her tips and salary as a hairdresser to rent a condo near the beach, almost an hour from the bungalow where we'd lived as a family, with no warning at all. I came home from school to find my father, who was far older than all my friend's fathers, red-eyed and stunned. "Mom left," he said. And everything he didn't say became clear to me over the weeks and months and years that followed: My mom had left. Not just left my father, but me, too.

She'd created a new life. One that didn't involve my dad at all. One that rarely involved me.

She was still young then—younger than all my friend's mothers. She was pretty and thin, and she liked to go out dancing with her "girls." She liked frozen cocktails, sunbathing, and painting her nails.

"When will Mom be home?" I remember asking my dad every night, and he'd shrug, tuck me in, pat the covers uncertainly.

"I don't think she was really ready to become a mom," he'd say apologetically, which seemed strange to me because she'd given it a go for ten years. Ten distracted and distant years. But I would have preferred eight more years like that, until I was off to college, than her disappearing entirely. And my dad did his best, but he never really caught on.

When I think about my mother's abandonment, it hurts my heart—the way she looked at me on my rare visits, like I was a kid stepsister she'd unfairly been asked to babysit. How she'd take me out for manicures, then sigh loudly about the cost and murmur that we should have just done them ourselves at home. How she'd answer calls from her friends and tell them, "I wish I could come, trust me, but Klara is here tonight," when I was mere feet away. She always said my name, never referred to me as "my daughter," as though a daughter was such a shameful thing to have. So I try not to think about it. I try not to think about her. I've always put my head down and focused on my schoolwork, and I wasn't the smartest student in my classes, perhaps not even in the top 20 percent. I couldn't control that. But I could work harder and longer than anyone else. I earned a scholarship to college in Maryland, then law school in DC, and things finally felt smooth for me. I was free. I was in control. I escaped Florida and I fled the mother who'd already fled me.

When I was twenty, and so many miles away from the place that had never felt like home, my father suffered a massive heart attack. Although I'm no longer a child, ever since he died, there are times when I feel like an orphan.

After all these years, when I think about or talk to my mother, I no longer feel such sharp pain. There's mostly rage, rage that simmers and hums like a white fluorescent bulb that might soon die, that probably isn't healthy, and probably should have dimmed by now, and is probably something I should discuss with a therapist.

I cannot stomach my mother playing the victim. And I absolutely refuse to contemplate or to allow myself—or *anyone*—to analyze how my relationship with my mother might affect my feelings about becoming a mother myself. Which is another reason why I don't want her to know about it. *You don't sound happy, Klara*, she'd say, glee so thinly concealed. Because it's trapped me, just the same way it trapped her. I know my options. I always have. But it's not so simple. Because there's you.

"I'm still your mom," my mother repeats, as though I hadn't spoken. Her voice wobbles.

"I know that." I sigh again. "Look, we'll plan a visit soon, okay? We'll get something on the books. Let me check my work calendar and check in with Troy. I'll text you." Saying this is easier than reminding my mother of her failings, than reminding her why I really don't want her to visit us or vice versa.

And maybe I like the fact that brushing her off this way will hurt her more—reminding her that I've built something. That I've built a life, in spite of and irrespective of her. I've built a life that's nothing like the one she walked out on. A life I so suddenly scarcely recognize.

I open my eyes. "Mom, I have to go," I continue. "Troy's calling me."

"Oh," she says. "Troy." She repeats your name, and it's almost impressive the amount of judgment she's imbued into that single syllable.

"I'll text you," I say again, and I end the call.

I won't text her. Still, our conversation will buy me some time. I'll be able to ignore her calls for a few weeks before I'll have to pick up the phone to have the exact same conversation again.

I wasn't lying to her about your call. I stare at the phone, your name glowing white across the black screen. I don't want to talk to you. I never do anymore, while you're at work and I'm not. I don't want to hear the hum of office background noise, voices rising and falling, the trill of a desk phone, the click of your mouse, the tap of your fingers across your keyboard.

I miss that. I miss my work. I miss talking to my colleagues. Heather's sharp wit. Gathering in the conference room to hash out case strategies over sandwiches from the deli around the corner. But I can't return to my firm. Not after the way I left things. And I don't feel well enough to perform with any competence.

How are you feeling? you'd ask, as you have every day of these past three weeks, ever since we moved into the house. I'm tired of telling you, *Not good.*

I shove the phone into my pocket.

As if on cue, the nausea grips me, clamping my insides. I shuffle into the powder room and kneel on the floor. I heave into the bowl, the coffee I shouldn't have drunk, the chalky orange-and-cranberry scone. You'd picked them up from a bakery near your office, presented them to me proudly that night when you got home, a kiss to the side of my neck. I didn't tell you that I don't like cranberries, yet I was simultaneously certain I've told you that before, could recall it with vivid specificity. I was afraid, somehow, that if I tossed the scones in the trash, you'd know. You'd open the can to see them there, a satisfied smile on your face, which would drop as you turned to me. "You could have just told me you didn't like them," you'd say, and when I insisted that I had before, you'd insist, even more convincingly, that I hadn't. Somehow it's better if I eat them.

I wipe my mouth with the hem of my T-shirt. My palms feel clammy, my forehead damp.

I think about calling Zoe. I'm surprised that I haven't heard from her since the day she came to visit—not even a text to check in. But I don't want to bother her during work hours, even though I know she'd answer.

I feel my phone vibrating in my pocket. You again, I'm sure. But I don't slide it out. Instead, I place my palms flat on my stomach. Beneath my shirt, beneath my flesh, is a bundle of cells. The size of a fig.

"It's just you and me," I whisper, and that's the first time I feel it—the love, the hope. And the surprise, the strength of it, nearly winds me.

34

It's been more than a decade since Troy has had a migraine. In fact, he's only ever had one in his entire life, and it began the second day of the bar exam. He sat in that room in the convention center for eight hours, typing his answers to the essay questions, feeling like someone was beating his skull with a hammer. He was certain he'd failed the exam.

When he got home that night, he vomited sticky and curdled white bread, the only thing he'd managed to eat. The next day, the pounding had dulled to a persistent but far less powerful knock, and the day after that, the pain was gone, just a slight tenderness in his brain, an instinct to flinch at bright lights and loud sounds. It was the stress, he assumed, from the most important test of his life, that had caused the migraine, and he'd not experienced the same intensity of pain since. As it turned out, he managed to pass the bar anyway.

It's back now—the unfamiliar but recognizable sensation, a thundering ache at the base of his skull, a twisting nausea in his gut. Brought about by stress again. This time, stress over his wife.

He wonders whether there's any feeling more unpleasant than nausea. He despises it. It's almost worse than pain. And he wonders whether this is how Klara feels all the time.

His car lurches forward with irritatingly periodic progress. All he wants to do is get home, press his forehead into his pillow, and sleep until the pain abates. According to the GPS app on his phone, he won't be home for another forty minutes.

"Call Klara," he tells his car. Then adds, "Call my wife," although the phone is already ringing, just because he likes to say the word, because it's still novel.

Klara doesn't seem to share his delight over their still-new roles as husband and wife. Something decidedly is wrong. There's been no sex for several weeks. At night, Klara curves away from him in their enormous bed, swallowed by the softness. He places a hand on her side, slides it down to her thigh. He listens to her breathing, slow and even and fake. In the morning, he asks her how she slept.

"Not good," she says. "The bed is so soft. My back, it hurts already. I'm not even big yet."

It's a warning. Things will only get worse, is what she means. Things will get harder, an excuse for her to pull away from him further.

The bed is so soft. The twenty-thousand-dollar bed and mattress and bedding. She'd sung its praises, this same bed, on their honeymoon. Now it's not right for her. She hates the bed. She hates the house. He can see it on her face.

Sometimes he thinks she hates him.

"What's wrong?" he asks her every morning and every night when he gets home from work.

"Nothing," she says, turning sharply as though he's startled her. "I'm just feeling awful."

She throws up every day. The nausea never subsides, she tells him. And her mind races. She has insomnia during the night. He'll awaken at one or two in the morning and reach for her before realizing she's not there, that her side of the bed is cool. He'll find her downstairs, pacing the hall in the dark, reading a baby book on her phone.

"Stomach cramps," she says. "Walking helps."

There's an accident ahead, three cars pulled onto the right shoulder of the highway. Traffic has slowed to a complete stop so that everyone can observe the smashed bumpers, the middle car with its airbags deployed. The three vehicles are bookended by police cars, their lights spinning blue and red.

Troy sighs. He's made no headway. In fact, his phone now tells him he won't be home for forty-four minutes. Like he's traveling backward.

He can't quite figure out where or how things have gone so wrong. The pregnancy has happened, just as he planned—the antibiotics he'd poured into the coffees he'd brought her for weeks had interfered with the effectiveness of her pill—and it was supposed to bring them closer. Klara was supposed to be so relieved that he was excited, that he'd already bought her a ring. She said yes, and she's gone through with everything. And yet she makes him feel like she's his prisoner. Like he's dragging her, forcing her into a life that everyone else would want.

It doesn't make sense.

Troy eases past the accident, then picks up speed to an almost reasonable pace. Until another snag builds and the taillights ahead of him flash red again.

But perhaps it's something chemical with Klara, Troy thinks. Something hormonal that she can't control. It's like postpartum depression, but it's hit her early. That could happen—he's not sure, but it sounds plausible. He should do some research. He should ask her new doctor.

She's hurting, his wife. This can't be his fault. He's suddenly desperate to tell her this—to say all the right things. That he forgives her for being so cold, so ungrateful. That he will help her get through this. He's desperate to hear her voice, to know that she is okay, to tell her that if she's not, she will be. He'll make sure of that.

He calls Klara again; it must be the fifth time today he's tried her. The phone rings and rings and rings, and Troy frowns, his nausea turning even more sour, the thunder in his head growing more deafening. She doesn't answer. She never answers.

Troy usually drives with a single wrist slung over the top of the wheel, guiding it deftly with the gentlest touch. But now his fingers curl tightly around it, knuckles whitening. After everything. How could she? How dare she?

35

"Hey there. I don't think we've met."

The wife seems to startle. She turns, the weed she'd just pulled dangling limply from her right hand.

"I live across the street," he continues. "Henry."

"Hello," the wife replies.

"Taking a break from your workday to destroy a few weeds?" Henry asks jovially. He feels white hot and alive because she's right here. She's said her name and it's perfect, pretty and classic, like she is, and she's smiling at him—uncertain, a hint of discomfort, of surprise, but still there.

The wife laughs gently. "Sorry," she says. "That was a perfectly reasonable question. It's just—not a lot of work getting done for me lately."

"Ah, well," says Henry. "I could say the same." He doesn't elaborate further. He can think of few things less appealing than discussing his employment troubles with the wife.

The gloss of her, the sheen. The slope of her nose, its straightness. Her eyes are wide, and there's a darkness there. A sadness, strongly steeped. Yet she seems to glitter beneath the high summer sun. Everything about her shines.

He fears this is it, the extent of their first interaction, but her eyes fall to the paperback tucked beneath his right arm, and she seems to brighten, to light from within.

"That," she says, nodding toward it, "is my favorite book."

"No way," he says, lifting it up. *The Cry of the Owl*, by Patricia Highsmith, worn and softened, and a bit on the nose, perhaps, but he's certain she hasn't noticed his interest in her these past few weeks. She hasn't caught him watching her. This is at least the third time he's read it. "It's not my favorite book, but it is my favorite Highsmith," he tells her. "I think most people would choose *The Talented Mr. Ripley*. Or *Strangers on a Train*."

"I like those, too," says the wife. "I like them all. You know, *A Suspension of Mercy* is a close second for me. And *Deep Water*. And *Strangers on a Train*, actually."

"I haven't read *A Suspension of Mercy*."

The wife laughs somewhat giddily, and Henry is elated. He created that, that joy, that audible bubble of happiness.

"It's—well, there's nothing like it," she says. "It's *insane*."

"One of the greatest suspense writers of all time," says Henry.

There's silence while they smile jubilantly at each other, and Henry is struck by how nice it is to have something in common with someone.

"I don't mean to hold you up from your weeding," says Henry, not sure how to propel the conversation forward, suspecting he should depart while he's ahead, before things take an awkward turn. "But we're on one of my favorite subjects. Books, reading. I could talk about books all day."

"So is that what you do for work, then?" she asks. "Something related to books?"

"Oh, no," he tells her. "I wish." He hoists his paperback higher into the air. "I was just taking a break. I was going to walk to that pond around the corner, sit there to read a few pages."

"That sounds nice," she says.

A pause. Henry smiles, his mind now entirely blank. "Anyway,

I just wanted to very belatedly introduce myself," he says, reciting his planned exit line. "I live over there." He gestures vaguely across the street. "I'll let you get back to your weeding, or whatever."

"Sure," says the wife, waving to him, smile faint, turning back toward her garden.

Henry salutes her charmingly, then turns away. He nearly floats up the street.

He could have asked her more questions, he realizes. He should have asked her how she's liking the neighborhood. He should have asked what she does for work. But that's how it always is. He only thinks of the right things to say once the opportunity to say them has passed.

But there will be other opportunities. They will speak again. It went well. She'd enjoyed talking to him, however brief it was.

He tries not to let himself think about the fact that it has gone well before. With Krista, for instance. She'd smiled at him, chatted superficially, laughed with him for weeks. She was in his master's program. Her eyes were an unusual navy, a little too far apart, which prevented her from being pretty. But there was something striking about her, her long, honey hair, the only blond in the entire cohort. Things were going well, he'd thought. Then he invited her out for a drink, and that friendly brightness dropped from her face.

"Oh," she said, startled. "Sorry, no. I have a boyfriend, actually."

She walked away before he could even attempt to save himself, to insist that he'd only been asking her as a friend, that the existence, or not, of her boyfriend was irrelevant.

He thought she was lying until he made his way into her private Instagram account and observed picture after picture of her striking face pressed against that of a man who appeared to be several years older, his brows unruly and low over crisp green eyes.

It didn't take Henry long to create a new account of his own, to fill its grid with predictable but believable images, to message Krista's boyfriend. Hey, man. Your girlfriend has been cheating on you. Sorry. Thought you should know. To attach the pictures he'd swiped from Krista's account, the ones she'd sent her boyfriend herself. But Henry had modified them slightly. It was quite impressive, actually, the way he'd been able to change the bend of her waist, the room behind her.

Krista couldn't have known what he'd done. He was too good. But he didn't hear her laugh again. They never spoke.

Henry doesn't actually want to walk to that pond—which is marred with goose shit—or sit beside it to read, but he has to now. He can't just go back inside his house in case the wife is still watching him. He hopes that she is.

Before Henry gets too far away, he glances over his shoulder. The wife isn't there, no longer pulling weeds. She must have gone back inside her house. It's as though she was out there waiting for him, waiting specifically for him.

Speaking to the wife has cheered him. He's no longer thinking of Krista—he's determined that this time will be different. And he's not thinking about Lacey's announcement, her new job, her promotion. He doesn't feel like a loser, like a friendless, involuntary celibate. He feels like a normal guy in his late twenties capable of making his beautiful neighbor laugh.

The pond is disgusting. Henry sits down beside it anyway, on the gentle crest of the hill. He rests his book on his lap and opens it. He turns the pages, but he doesn't read. He stares at the words, but they blur, and all he sees is the wife. He sees the high arches of her cheekbones, the swing of her light roast–colored hair.

And there was sadness in her eyes, the way it persisted even when she smiled and laughed, the darkness behind the light. The only time she truly brightened and that sadness lifted was when she was talking about his book.

He'd done that. Him. He's been right all these weeks. She isn't happy, and she needs him.

36

"Walk?" says Troy. He's standing beside the sofa in their family room, where Klara is reclining, a book propped on her chest. Her eyes lift ever so briefly before returning to the words on the page. But her gaze doesn't dart side to side. She stares blankly, merely pretending to read.

"I don't know," she murmurs. "It's so hot."

"It isn't that bad yet," he insists. "It'll make you feel better."

She has told him this, that walking helps the pains in her stomach, relieves the restlessness of her legs, stills her racing thoughts.

"Come on, Klara." Sterner than he'd like to be, but he needs her to do this. He needs to speak to her, and not in the house. In public, so that she can't escape.

She sighs, teenager-esque.

Klara makes a show of collecting her hair, pulling it taut and off her neck, then slipping a cap onto her head. She bends, ties her sneakers so slowly. He represses an urge to crouch beside her, slap her hands away, and tie them himself.

Finally, she's ready. They leave through the front door, and Klara sighs again, impatience saturating her breath as Troy pauses to lock the door behind them. And perhaps he is putting on a bit of a show, turning the dead bolt in place, testing the door. But he's noticed that she tends to leave the front door unlocked, and that irritates him. It's as though she's trying to tell him, to tell the world, that nothing inside is valuable or worth protecting, not even her. He's ordered the cameras, the video doorbell. They'll be here soon, and once they arrive, he'll call someone to install everything. He'll have to figure out a way to get Klara out of the house. He doesn't want her to know about the cameras, but they're for her own good. They'll keep her safe. They'll help him watch her.

They're silent as they ascend the hill toward the end of their street. Troy turns left just as Klara pulls right. He knows she's been walking occasionally while he's at work. He knows there's a route she typically follows. He knows everything.

He gives her this, corrects his path, goes right with her.

"I need to know, Klara," he says, shattering the thin glass of their silence. "What's wrong? If you don't tell me what's bothering you, I can't fix it."

"You can't fix it," she repeats, and he can't tell if she's scoffing, mocking, or telling him definitively that he cannot fix it.

He glances at her, face beneath the shadow of the brim of her cap, squinting straight ahead. The wrinkles around her eyes are more pronounced than when he met her.

"You've been so distant toward me since we moved in here," he presses. "I know you don't feel well, but you act like that's my fault. You act like you hate me."

A beat passes, heavy, telling. There is no rush to insist that she doesn't hate him.

"What did I do?" he asks. His anger is rising, but he doesn't allow it to breach his tone. This is why he decided to speak to her when they were out for a walk, in their neighborhood, people watching—so that he couldn't lose his temper, so that she couldn't run.

"I miss my job, Troy. I miss my condo. I miss the person I used to be. This isn't what I wanted. None of this." She sounds so weary, feeble, like she's already given up.

"I didn't make you quit your job. And I didn't realize that having every day to yourself, being able to do whatever you want, would be so awful for you."

"It's more than that, Troy. I've lost myself. I'm thirty-five and this is my life. Set in stone now. Suburbia, motherhood, exhaustion. I didn't want a baby. I told you that."

"Klara, I didn't make you keep the baby."

"But you were so happy," she insists. "You cried and you proposed."

"I was happy. I *am* happy. Should I have pretended not to be? Told you it was your problem and disappeared?"

"No, of course not."

"I mean, listen to yourself," he tells her. "You have a beautiful house. You have time to do what you want to do, to relax after so many years of working so hard. You have a baby on the way. And you have a husband who loves you more than anything in the world."

Loves or loved? He tries both on for size in his mind. But he knows. It's not a thing of the past. He still loves her. He just wants her to behave.

"But I didn't want this house. You bought it without even consulting with me. It's farther from my firm than I'd ever want to commute."

"Then find a job closer. There are law firms in the area." He's loath to suggest this. He'd rather she be home. But he doesn't see how he can get away with not doing so.

"Yeah," she says. "I'm eleven weeks pregnant. Who would want to hire me and give me maternity leave in six months or so?"

"It's not like you'd disclose you're pregnant in the interview. You don't even look pregnant yet."

"Well, I feel pregnant. I feel horrible. I feel sick and huge, like my body isn't mine. I'm not even capable of working competently right now."

Troy adjusts his own cap, uses the back of his hand to wipe sweat from his forehead. Klara wasn't wrong—it is too hot to be doing this.

"Then it's best that you just relax and focus on feeling well, and once you feel better, you can think about going back to work or whatever you want. Maybe in a few weeks the nausea will get better, and the fatigue. The doctor said that."

"Right." Clipped, dismissive. Like she wants it to persist. Like its improvement might threaten her martyrdom.

"And it's not as though you were so happy in your condo," he says. "You were lonely. We've talked about how lonely you were feeling."

"Because I'd just gotten out of a long-term relationship that ended very suddenly. I hadn't adjusted yet."

"So I was your rebound guy?" Troy asks. "Is that what you're saying? I was just a rebound but you accidentally married me and got pregnant, and I bought you a house, and now you're stuck with me?"

"Don't be ridiculous."

"Well, what is the problem, then, Klara? Because I don't understand."

He knows she sounds crazy—she knows. That's the point. Something feels wrong, yet she can't articulate what. She can't articulate anything he's done that's been truly bad. It's been all love and grand gestures, and she seems like a shrew for complaining.

He thinks of what she would tell Zoe, if she could contact Zoe. Or what might she tell a lawyer, if it came to that?

When I told him I was pregnant, he immediately proposed to me with a ring he already had. A two-carat stone. Even though we'd only been together for a few months. After our honeymoon, he surprised me with a big house in a nice neighborhood. He told me I could quit my job.

How dare he? What an asshole?

"Do you think you're depressed?" he continues when she doesn't answer. "Like it's something chemical?"

"I've told you before, no."

She has. Shut him down, dismissed him, acted like he knows nothing.

"Well, how do you know?" he presses. "You certainly seem depressed to me. I think you should be evaluated. Maybe your obstetrician can refer you to someone."

Another silence. The sidewalk ends and they step down, side by side, their bodies moving in tandem, even as Troy feels so far away from her, his wife. She isn't acting like the wife he's always wanted—it's as though their marriage broke her, a spell shattered when he slid the ring onto her finger—and he's livid. After all his careful plans, she isn't cooperating.

"I'm not depressed," Klara says at last. "And I don't want to talk about this anymore. It feels like you're cross-examining me."

Troy detects his fists closing, nails slicing into his palms. "Okay, Klara," he says, tight with anger. Because it's not. It's not okay at all.

The day passes stilted and separate. Troy fumes.

Klara doesn't feel like cooking—she never seems to feel like cooking anymore—so he picks up takeout and they eat in front of the television. She chose a bland noodle dish, grease seeping through the bottom of the cardboard container. He can see it glistening on her thighs.

He wishes she'd eat better. She wasn't wrong, what she said on their walk. She doesn't look pregnant yet; she just looks like she's getting fat.

Her gaze is blank, trained on the screen, avoiding his, avoiding him. The only time she looked at him was when they stood in the kitchen, sorting out their meals and utensils, and he poured himself a glass of red wine. She stared at him disdainfully, hand covering her mouth and nose. He watched her as he took a long, slow sip.

It's only eight when Klara tells him she's too tired and wants to go to bed. She's in the shower for what feels like an hour. Troy stays downstairs, hears the water rushing, wondering when she'll ever welcome him in again. He misses when they'd shower together, how he'd wash her body with his hands.

He doesn't understand. He's been so careful.

He watches the next episode of their current show, which will probably annoy her. She can add it to her list of absurd transgressions. Once he suspects she's fallen asleep—once she should be asleep, considering how tired she claimed to be—he ascends the stairs on whisper-soft feet. He slips into their bedroom, to Klara's side of the bed, the folds of white comforter around her, tucked beneath her chin.

He stands there and watches her for a long time, far longer than is necessary to ensure that she isn't awake. She's well practiced at pretending to be asleep, but this time he can tell that it's real. Her mouth is gaping open in a way that's more grotesque than he ever thought her capable of appearing, and she's snoring faintly. She's started snoring in the past few weeks. He suspects it's related to her pregnancy, and he hopes it will subside soon.

His side of the bed is still neatly made, his pillow resting on top, and he could pick it up, hold it over her face. He could press it down and count and wait. She probably wouldn't even put up much of a fight.

He doesn't want to do that, but he could, and this is a fact that gives him comfort.

Instead, he gently unplugs her phone from her charger, watching her the whole time. The screen lights, and he slides it into his pocket, then creeps away. She doesn't stir.

37

Henry has been waiting for the wife all day. He's desperate to see her, to speak to her again. She's all he's been able to think about ever since their first conversation.

He's been lingering in the living room, risking the judgment of his mother, risking her catching on to his plan, a plan that is still slightly unfocused, its edges blurred.

Finally, nearly noon, the unhappy couple's front door swings open. His lungs swell with relief.

The wife emerges, then seems to falter on her porch, perhaps stunned by the humidity, the heat of the day. He's ready, a paperback under his arm—*A Suspension of Mercy*, even though he finished it already—hoping it will spark a prolonged conversation. But she quickly steps off her porch, suddenly moving far too fast.

She's going out for a walk, he realizes. She moves down her driveway, dark ponytail brushing her upper back. He can't catch her.

The idea comes to him quite suddenly then. It might work, but he must time everything perfectly.

He retrieves his keys quickly, tosses his book onto the sofa, cuts through the yard to where his car is parked at the curb. He goes to the McDonald's drive-through, where he buys a Coke and a sweet tea, then tosses an empty Gatorade bottle onto the floor of his car to make room in the cupholder. The line of cars ahead is far too long, and it drags.

Henry taps his left foot anxiously while his right presses into the accelerator during his drive home. It's 12:17 when he turns to his street, and he's afraid he's too late. He's afraid he's missed her. He doesn't think she'd stay out too long, not in this heat, at this time of day.

But then he sees her up ahead. She's moving slowly up the hill, ponytail tumbling like his fizzing Coke, and Henry smiles.

He parks in his usual spot and leaves the car on, letting the air-conditioning blast his face while he watches the wife in his rearview mirror.

The beep of a car being unlocked, and his eyes fly to the wife's house, but it's not there. He can see in the mirror that his next-door neighbor is climbing into her car. It's an eyesore, a fifteen-year-old Honda Civic, faded gold, paint chipped almost completely off the roof and hood. She usually leaves it in the garage, but lately it's been in the driveway on occasion. Henry has noticed overflowing trash cans and recycling bins outside her house on collection days. One day last week, he saw an unmarked white truck come by and collect various boxes and bags resting at the curb, likely a donation pickup. She must be cleaning out the house, getting ready to list it. It's about time.

It's actually astonishing that she's lived there all these years.

Henry was young at the time of the murder. He vaguely remembers the screaming sirens, the yellow police tape, his parents' urgent whispers, Laurel's unrelenting curiosity and his mother's terse replies, hissed assurances.

The little Honda backs slowly out of the driveway. He watches the wife lift her hand in a wave as the car passes her.

Henry waits a few seconds more, until she's almost directly beside his car, then he turns off the engine, flings the door open, and steps out.

"I skipped my walk today," he says brightly, and the wife visibly startles. "Shit," he says quickly. "Sorry." His face is engulfed by flames, and he's mortified that he's fucking this up already.

"It's fine," she says, hand to her chest. "I just didn't notice anyone was in that car."

"Right," he says, disappointed that she wasn't looking for him or hoping to see him. Of course she wasn't. Henry feels a dark sort of hopelessness descending, settling around him, but he pushes through. He reaches into his car and removes the two fountain drinks.

"I was just out getting lunch and I picked these up on the way home," he says. "It's such a hot day. Would you like one?"

"Oh," she says, and she seems to recoil slightly, shoulders curling inward. "No, thank you." She glances behind her, toward her house.

"Are you sure?" he asks. "It's a Coke and a sweet tea. Take your pick."

"No, really," she says. Her shirt is white and sweat-damp, the outline of her bra straps drawing his attention. He forces himself to look into her face, to read her rising unease. She's still staring at the cups, and Henry suddenly realizes that she might have a rule never to accept an open drink from a stranger. But he's hardly a stranger. And it's not as though he would have drugged one of these drinks before offering it to her—not to say he's never drugged a drink before. He thinks of Ashley, who worked for the marketing company next to the IT firm where Henry was employed after graduating from his master's program. She wore her raven-black hair in a single braid. That night, it was rumpled, strands pulled loose from the elastic. She wasn't as beautiful as the others, but she was more willing.

He'd come so close—he was in her apartment—but then,

several drinks in, she still rejected him. Somehow he'd known that would happen, and her lids were already heavy, gaze unfocused. The feel of her skin, the sight of her bare breasts, the taste of her. It was what he, and she, deserved.

A few weeks later, Henry left that job in favor of his most recent company. He never saw Ashley again; she never accused him of anything. He was careful, and she was ashamed. And everything was going just fine until Lacey. Until she turned him down.

"Suit yourself," Henry tells the wife now, shrugging as though her refusal hasn't bothered him at all, as though he's not offended by her discomfort. He takes a long sip of the Coke just to show her that it's safe. "How's everything going?" he continues. "Read anything good since we talked?"

"I'm afraid I haven't." She looks behind her again, then takes a step away from him.

"I started reading *A Suspension of Mercy*," says Henry hopefully. "It's brilliant."

"Of course." The wife uses a finger, slides her sunglasses up her nose. "How far along are you?" she adds, although she sounds almost reluctant to ask.

He improvises quickly, tugging the most memorable scene from his reserves. "Sydney has just rolled up that area rug and taken it out of the house."

She laughs, sniffs. "It's crazy, isn't it?" But she doesn't give him time to reply. "Look, I've got to go, but thanks anyway." She nods toward the drinks in his hands, smiling tightly, taking another step away.

She turns quickly, barely giving him a chance to reply. "See you later," he calls out as she crosses the street, heading toward her house. He doesn't think she heard him.

He's frozen for a few seconds, until he realizes that if she notices him standing here, looking after her, she won't like it. He bumps his car door closed and locks it.

He returns to his own house, through the front door, because he doesn't want the wife to see him going around back to the basement. He's beyond disappointed. He's devastated, actually. He thought that offering her a drink after she returned from her walk would be such a considerate gesture. So why didn't she bite?

Twice she looked toward her house. She was thinking, Henry could tell, of her husband. He's not home, but his presence lingers. He's in the way.

That makes more sense—that she's afraid of her husband, rather than Henry. How could she be afraid of Henry? He's done nothing. And they're such an unhappy couple, the husband too possessive. He might be livid if he knew she was speaking to another man.

Inside, Henry doesn't see his mother, but he knows she's around. He goes straight to the basement and into his bedroom.

He tries not to let himself feel too defeated. He settles onto his bed, on its unmade, twisted sheets, and lets the air-conditioning swirl around him. It's only the beginning, he reminds himself. There's so much more he can do.

38

The weekend over, such a relief. To think how I used to look forward to Friday night, to Saturday and Sunday. My free time. Now I count down the hours to Monday, when I can again have the house I hate all to myself.

I'm still in bed when the doorbell rings. Not asleep, but I haven't yet steeled myself to commence the day.

It rings once. A pause. Then it rings again.

"What?" I ask no one, throwing the sheets off my body. My nausea roils, but I press it down, press a palm to my mouth.

I hurry along the hall, into one of the spare bedrooms where the windows overlook the front yard and driveway. I have no intention of answering the door, but I do want to know who would ring a person's doorbell at eight in the morning.

But when I look out the front windows and down, I see a familiar car in my driveway. My heart lifts.

I don't bother with changing into clothes, with finding a bra, because that's the beauty of being with your best friend.

I hurry down the stairs and pull the front door open just as she rings the doorbell again, and I'm smiling, but she's not.

"Klara," she says, arms out. She reaches for me and pulls me against her, and I can't comprehend the relief in her voice.

"What?" I ask as she releases me. "What happened?"

"What happened? I've been trying to text you and call you for a week. You haven't responded to anything, and my texts haven't gone through. I left you, like, fifteen voicemails."

"What?" I ask again, shaking my head.

"You didn't get them." She's laughing now, that giddy sort of laughter that accompanies a rush of relief.

"Come in," I tell her. "I'll make us a coffee, check my phone."

Zoe follows me into the kitchen, a gorgeous designer bag that looks crisp and new slung over her arm, orange pumps peeking out from the hems of her navy trousers.

"Are you going to work?" I ask her, reaching for mugs, for coffee pods. "My house isn't exactly on the way." Zoe has lived and worked in Northern Virginia ever since we graduated from college. She must have spent an hour and a half in her car this morning.

"Klara, I was so worried. I left my house early and came straight here. I'm supposed to be at work. I mean, I'll go after."

"I don't understand," I tell her. "I didn't have any missed calls from you. Or any texts."

"After I visited you, things got so crazy at work. And Daphne wasn't sleeping great. Then I had to go to New York for a few days. That's no excuse; I should have been checking in on you, but I wasn't."

"Zoe, it's fine," I tell her and tap the start button, hear the machine's first gulps. "I wasn't exactly checking in with you, either. I've been leaning in to my seclusion here, I guess." And I like how that makes everything sound so harmless, so voluntary.

"But then I did text you, last week. I asked you how you were feeling or something, but my text didn't go through. I tried calling and leaving a message. But you didn't reply. So I kept trying for days."

I open a drawer, remove a spoon. "I didn't get anything from you."

"I know," says Zoe soothingly. "I see that now. But for a day, I convinced myself you were mad at me and giving me the silent treatment. Then I thought there might be something wrong with your phone. I didn't have Troy's number, so I couldn't try him. I texted a few college friends, but none of them had heard from you. I worked myself into such a panic."

"I'm sorry," I say, bewildered. "I had no idea."

"I said to Garrett last night, if I don't hear from her by the morning, I'm just going over there. So I did. I couldn't take it anymore, Klara. I thought you were dead."

We blink at each other, the coffee machine hissing with finality.

"I emailed you," she adds insistently as I remove her a cup of coffee from the machine, pour cream.

"All right," I say. "Let me figure this out."

I leave her mug on the table and retrieve my phone from its overnight resting place, on my nightstand, plugged into the charger.

I look through my texts as I walk. Then my missed calls. My voicemail.

Zoe is sitting at my kitchen table, right leg tossed over the left, her left pump tapping against the hardwood floor.

"Seventeen new voicemails," I tell her, holding up the phone. "All from you. But I didn't get a notification. Not for any of them. I had no idea they were there."

Zoe shakes her head, extends her hand, silver bracelets coasting down her arm. Her chicness feels like an affront in the face of my sleep-rumpled hair, my wrinkled pajamas, cotton and striped.

"That doesn't make any sense," she says, fingers wiggling.

I pass my phone to her, then settle onto a chair across the

table from her. "No, it doesn't," I agree, even as my stomach sinks, a sloth-like creep.

A minute later, Zoe raises her eyes. "Klara," she says, tone accusatory, "you blocked me." She waves the screen toward me.

"I didn't block you," I say, automatically defensive. "Why would I block you?"

"See, these messages are in the voicemails from the blocked-numbers category. That's why you didn't get a notification. And that's why you didn't get my calls or texts." There's a divot between her brows. She taps at the screen, lips tugging downward, parentheses surrounding her mouth. "And all my emails are in spam."

She puts the phone on the table and slides it tentatively toward me, expression hurt now.

"I didn't do that," I promise her. "I don't understand."

But I do understand. It's textbook, really. I wish I could throw that in your face, how very unoriginal you are.

"Did you do it yourself, do you think? By accident?" Zoe asks hopefully. "You've never been very good with technology."

I feel my eyes narrowing, still staring at my phone, as rage simmers in my chest so hotly, threatening to scream.

Zoe lays a palm on my forearm. "Sorry," she says. "No offense. I just thought—"

"No," I say, cutting her off. "It's not that. I didn't do it by accident. I didn't do it at all."

Zoe lifts her hand, brushes hair away from her face, distractedly runs her fingers down a section of it. "Then what?" she asks. "What happened?"

"Something," I begin, my reluctance drawing my voice soft and low, "is very wrong with my relationship."

Her hand finds mine this time, across the table. She squeezes it, which tells me that whatever it is, I can tell her, and that she's sorry I haven't already. And I should have. I should have said more months ago, after I first told her about you, after she first met you, after she watched me try on my wedding dress. Instead, I've been marching along, pulled on a leash, obedient, listless. In peril.

I shake my head, words rattling. What I said, it wasn't quite right. "Something," I say, trying again, "is wrong with my husband."

39

Instead of the tea she'd planned on, Mary opts for a second glass of wine. She figures she's earned it. She cleaned out Owen's bedroom, made dinner, cleared the dishes, took out the trash, and started a load of laundry. Quite a productive day for anyone, she thinks, but particularly for her, her beaten-down, worn-thin self.

Hair still damp on the shoulders of her pajamas, she carries her wine to the family room sofa. The house is beginning to take on a desolate sort of feel, rooms gradually emptying of her things, of the possessions that have made up her life.

Her novel is resting on the end table. She picks it up, puts her wine down, then adjusts the heating pad and turns it up to high. It's warm in the house—she keeps the thermostat dialed up far higher than she'd like to save money—so she won't be able to manage the heat for too long. But for now, she needs it to soothe the pain shooting up her lower back, swirling around her tailbone.

Mary cracks her book and tries to read. From upstairs, she can hear the washing machine whirring. From downstairs, she can hear nothing. The words blur. She reads the same sentence three times.

Mary tosses the book aside.

It's understandable, she tells herself. This was bound to be a difficult day. Going through Owen's things, his clothes, his art, was always going to be upsetting for her. It was always going to stir up memories, to have them rise around her, suffocating and soft like dough. But it had to be done. It's not as though he could do it himself.

Across the room from the sofa where Mary is reclining is a bookshelf. It belonged to Mary's mother—she can picture it in the living room of the tiny rancher where she grew up—but it's still in good shape, staining slightly faded at the corners but wood solid. She already boxed up most of the books for donation, keeping only a few favorites she might like to reread. There simply won't be room for such a collection in the apartment. But she hasn't yet touched the bottom shelf. White albums lie on their sides, Mary's own writing smeared across the spines, delineating the years that they span.

She has studiously avoided these books for years, avoided them so much that she's never moved them from the shelf or the room.

"Why not?" she asks herself. She's already so irrevocably steeped in thoughts of her son. She might as well look through them now. There's no risk of sending herself into distraction, into sharp and tragic reminiscence. She's already there.

Mary retrieves the albums, two armloads of them, her back screaming, and sets them onto the coffee table. She adjusts her heating pad again, then takes a shaky breath before, with the most cautious finger, she opens the first book.

Owen. Newborn Owen. Eyes shut and mouth pursed yet slack. How she always remembers him as a baby, peaceful and golden, the sun itself in her arms. Ed would probably insist that he cried a normal amount, but Mary didn't think so. He almost never cried. Things were growing more difficult by then with Ed—his moods, his temper rising from the dark recesses where it had been hiding during the first few years of their relationship. Mary always had to do everything right, to land herself arrow straight through an ever-moving target. Perhaps Owen sensed that. He was always exactly what she needed.

The next page, Owen older, tomato sauce smeared across his cheeks and chest, fists full of spaghetti. Owen in one of the brown rubber baby swings at the park, tiny fists gripping rusting chains.

Owen clutching an ice cream, soft serve swirled, nearly as tall as his face, his grin wide. Owen in the backyard, a baseball glove on his hand, when he still found joy in playing catch, before Ed ruined it. Owen with a box of crayons, scribbling a knobby red one across the table, which Mary used to cover with butcher paper so that he wouldn't make a mess, one less thing for Ed to yell about. Every box of crayons, he always used up the red one first.

Owen on his first day of preschool, backpack stretching down to his knees, smile tentative, nerves flickering in his eyes. She remembers wanting to gather him up, tuck him into her, and travel back to the time when they were one. But he was growing up, and she didn't see, not then, how fortunate they both were for that.

Mary closes the album, reaches for the next.

She always thought that going through these pictures would defeat her. That it would make her sob and curl into herself. And Mary does cry. Of course she does. But—and she has to lift her fingers to her face, splay them across her cheeks to confirm—she also smiles.

Page after page, she turns, cheeks tugging. Tears stream, and she wipes them before they drop onto the plasticky pages. Her sweet boy, captured here. Only the best of memories maintained, pieces of a tragic life that appears, based on these alone, so joyous, so peaceful.

Then she nears the middle of the fifth book. Owen's fifteenth birthday, sitting behind an ice cream cake she'd made herself, tongue out because he'd refused to smile. Owen at the head of a hiking trail in Patapsco Valley State Park. That's where the pictures stop.

She remembers going on that hike with him. Saturday morning, the weekend before everything happened. There was a sudden, drenching rain shower when they were almost back to the car, and they ran the rest of the way to the parking lot, Owen slowing his pace to match his mother's. Sodden and laughing, they'd slammed the car doors.

"Well, if only we'd hiked a little faster," Mary said. "We could've avoided that."

On the way home, they stopped for sodas, burgers, and fries, clothes still damp, skin itching, but Mary wasn't ready for the outing to end, clinging to every last moment with her son. As though she knew that in just a few days, everything would change.

40

I don't confront you. I think about it for a long time. For days, it's all I can consider. *You went into my phone. You blocked my best friend.*

I ignore your calls—*just checking in, how are you feeling?* I observe you in the periphery while I eat my dinner, always takeout, always in the family room, in front of the television. In our bathroom mirror, it's your reflection I look at, not mine. *I know what you did.*

But I decide not to confront you. I hold it, for now. Something for myself. Something to use when the time is right.

Then, suddenly, I am twelve weeks pregnant. That's when the pain arrives.

I was twelve weeks pregnant.

There's pain, and then there's a clear liquid, a trickle, and I think that I've peed myself. The humiliation, the ways my body has failed me—I almost laugh. But the blood follows soon after, and it's not funny at all. The cramps that had been a minor annoyance all day suddenly scream at a much higher pitch, and their significance rings startlingly clear.

The bathroom, I think. I don't know where else to go, what else to do. But I can't make it to the primary bath, doubled over and staggering, wetness running down my legs, so I duck into the bathroom that's closer, the full bath on the second floor. *The kids' bathroom* is how you refer to it, which now seems thoughtless and cruel in addition to premature.

The pain is blinding, like a shot through my gut. It abates, and I can breathe for a few seconds. Then it's back again. I sit on the toilet, and I listen to the blood pour from my body.

I know what's happening, and it seems too late. I thought I was in the clear at this point. I'm so close to the second trimester.

The first few weeks after that positive test, I'm ashamed of how badly I wanted to feel these things—the pain in my stomach, the rush of blood. Natural and foretelling excuses to duck and run. I could get out of all of it without having to make a decision. But that didn't happen.

Not until now, when it's too late and my view has shifted. That first flicker of love has only grown. This baby, this bundle of cells, has been with me day in and day out. It has become my ally, the size of a plum now. And it always would be my ally, I thought. It would grow until I could feel the fizz of its hiccups inside me, until its limbs jutted against my lungs and ribs, until it emerged and I could feel the softness of its skin. Not just an ally, but a family. I am not my mother. I could be different. I could protect it. From everything. From you.

But that's not going to happen now, and it isn't fair.

My phone is on the countertop next to me. It had been in the side pocket of my drawstring joggers, which are now soaked with blood and fluid, a crumpled heap on the floor. I can reach it.

But I don't know who to call. My thoughts slog by, disjointed, confused. For a second, I consider calling for an ambulance. But I don't think this is a medical emergency, so far from viability. I consider calling my doctor, but I think the office closed at four. I'd need the after-hours number, which was printed boldly on fluorescent-orange paper and handed to me at my last appointment. I put that paper away somewhere. I can't remember where. I thought I wouldn't need it for many months, not until my due date was near.

Suddenly, for the first time in weeks, I feel the need, again, for you. In spite of everything you've done, I need you. I want to be taken care of, like the day I found out I hadn't made partner. I want you to rush home, to place your hand on my back, to hug me and hold me and tell me everything will be okay. I don't want to go through this alone.

It's Pavlovian, the need for you. It's how you've trained me.

You couldn't have blocked Zoe on my phone. You love me more than anything in the world. You wouldn't hurt me, would never hurt me.

I want so badly for these things to be true.

And I'm lying to myself. My vision is blurred by tears, but I brush them away, unlock the screen, and call you.

The rings trill. Another set of cramps grips me, and I fold over.

The call goes to voicemail. I try again.

41

Troy's phone rests on top of his desk beside his gray mouse pad, which is fraying at the edges. He's had the same mouse pad since he was a junior associate. And now, a partner. He's due for an upgrade.

The screen is alight, the vibration a faint rattle, and he stares at it.

After weeks of ignoring his calls, the nerve of her. His wife.

During his workday, a couple of hours before he typically leaves the office, she is calling him. Despite her coolness, the way she brushes away his concern. She's stopped saying she loves him. She's behaving as though she hates him. Yet she's turning to him now.

The past few days, he's caught her smiling faintly, caressing the gentle swell of her belly. Her love has been growing, finally, for the baby to be. But not for him. When she meets his eyes, her smile fades, slowly dropping away.

He's given her everything, and she's made him regret it.

Something must be wrong. It's the only explanation for her call. Something very wrong, and his chest hurts, a sudden pain, like something cracking in his heart, because he can think of only one thing that it might be.

And he thinks it's only fair that she be made to feel the way he has when she's ignored and rejected his calls, when he knows that she's at home, in the house he bought her, with nothing to do. She's done it countless times.

And he'll never admit this. Later, he will hold her and run his fingers down the length of her hair. He'll apologize and they'll cry together. He'll tell her he was in a client meeting and he didn't have his cell phone with him. She should have called his firm's receptionist and told her to pull him from the meeting. Why didn't she? She should have thought of that. His dependent, helpless wife. She's become quite inept, hasn't she? She really does need him. She needs him for everything.

Troy taps the red button. The vibrations stop. He switches the phone to silent, and he turns it face down.

42

The wife isn't home. Henry's father is at work, and his mother is out—lunch with a "girlfriend" again—so it's the perfect time. He's tired of watching, of waiting. He needs more.

He must be sure before he can determine precisely what he's going to do and how he will do it.

It's midday, sun high, the heat-index warning keeping the kids who don't have summer camp this week inside with their screens.

Henry goes around the back of the house as though he's supposed to be there, as though he's merely cutting between the yards. He's wearing khaki shorts, a polo tucked in. He doesn't look like a burglar, with his neat beard and the logo on his shirt.

He scans the back of the house for cameras, then moves across the patio, slipping a pair of gloves onto his hands—just in case. He tries the ground-level door first, which leads into the walk-out basement. Locked, so he steps onto the deck, tugs at the sliding door. It glides smoothly along its track.

The wife probably sat out here earlier, on the wicker armchair, put her coffee on the matching end table. She forgot to lock the door when she went inside.

He's in, and it's too easy.

The family room—a curving sectional, low glass coffee table, and flat-screen television across the room. Nothing on the coffee table except for a few coasters. He moves into the kitchen, its countertops gleaming, clutter minimal. There's a fruit bowl with a pair of bananas, three oranges. Two empty coffee mugs rest in the sink, along with a glass dish, remnants of a pasta dish. Henry's lip curls; the wife must have left in a hurry.

The foyer is tidy, like a house listed for sale. No shoes on a rack or littering the doormat, no family photographs. There's a swath of dove-gray wall clearly intended for a console table, but instead it's bare.

He must hurry because the wife won't be gone for long. She's never gone for long, only brief errands, garage door sliding closed behind her car before he can see her climb out, see the bags on her arms. Or an appointment, like the one he followed her to before—*Dr. Frances Singh & Associates, Obstetrics and Gynecology.* Wisps of unease bloom, but he pushes forward, into the living room. It's sparsely furnished, and there's a small aging table for four in the formal dining room, although the room could easily accommodate a setup for eight. There's a sense of deficiency about the furnishings, the lack thereof, like the couple just moved in here days ago and they've clearly relied on things they'd had in prior, smaller apartments.

He's taking too long, and he needs to get upstairs. The upstairs is most important. He takes them two at a time, hurtling upward.

Down the hall, he passes through double doors, and he's in the primary bedroom. The bed isn't made, comforter bundled and folded. There's a silken eye mask on her nightstand, a tube of hand cream. He squeezes a bead onto the soft spot inside one wrist, rubs them together gently as he scans the rest of the room.

Her closet—silky blouses, suits, heels he's never seen her wear. Her bathroom. Vanity cabinets open—makeup, glass bottles of serums and creams—then he shuts them. A home office with a feminine touch, floral swirls in the area rug. Her laptop, which he gets into easily. The other bedrooms, one nearly empty. The hall bathroom. Nothing, nothing.

Back downstairs. He hurries; it's time to go. He's seen enough. He's seen exactly what he needs to see.

He's certain now. He's been right about everything, all along.

Ours is a tale of murder.

He leaves the house, all stealth, all care, all speed. *Indeed*, he thinks, *it is*.

His shirt is drenched: the heat, the nerves, the thrill of what he did. It was bold, but what does he have to lose really? While what he has to gain is her—the wife—and his plan is becoming clearer.

Safely inside his own house, he goes straight into the basement. He drops his polo into the washing machine before entering his bedroom to retrieve a new shirt and slide the gloves into a dresser drawer.

His mother will almost certainly have to do laundry before he does. She does his father's laundry for him, too. She irons his work shirts while she watches old episodes of *Downton Abbey*. When Henry is down here, and he hears her footsteps, slow and steady on the stairs, he should probably offer to help her carry the laundry baskets down, then back up again when the laundry is done. He should probably even offer to do the laundry for her. That's what a good son would do. But he doesn't think she's a good mom, so why should she reap the benefits of a good son?

He's hoping she won't be home from lunch with her "girlfriend" for another half hour, so he takes advantage of being alone in the house to raid the fridge. But as he stands there, the frosty air swirling, he hears his mother clattering into the house. He's too far from the basement stairs, so there's no time to sneak down and avoid her, not unless she doesn't come into the kitchen straightaway.

But of course, she does. Henry can see immediately that she's tipsy. Her eyes droop downward at the corners. Her face is flushed.

He closes the fridge, and her buoyant expression seems to fall a few millimeters when she sees him standing there.

"Looks like lunch was a success," he says.

"What does that mean?" she asks. But her voice is mushy, words slurring together—*Wahdoeszatmean?*

"Jesus, Mom. Did you drive home like that?"

She turns to him, slams down the glass she just removed from a cabinet. "Don't be an asshole, Henry."

He's stunned. She has never spoken to him that way before.

"I had a nice lunch with my girlfriend," she adds primly, with deliberate annunciation. "I was perfectly fine to drive."

"Sure," he says. He steps around the island, moving past her, heading back toward the basement stairs.

"Any luck today?" she asks abruptly, shrilly.

"What?" He freezes, sighs warily, although he knows what she means. She's in a fighting mood now, but he's not. He just wants to shut himself back in his basement bedroom and close his eyes, to see the wife, the imprint of her face. He wants to think about what he just did, to languish in the success of it.

"Did you submit any more applications? Schedule any interviews?"

"Of course I did," he says patiently. "I do that every day."

"Then—why, Henry? Why aren't you having any luck?" There's a sadness in her voice now, a sudden weariness, her anger short lived, as though she's the one who's searching for work, as though she's the one who's failing.

"Trust me when I say that it's much more frustrating for me than it is for you," he says crisply.

His mother sniffs. Her arms are crossed in front of her chest, eyes watery. The glass still rests on the counter behind her, her need for a drink apparently forgotten.

"It just doesn't make sense, Henry. You're so smart. You always did well in school. You worked for years. The market isn't that bad right now."

He hates the way the compliments warm his chest. He can't help the tiny twinge, that he still craves his mother's approval.

"You didn't get laid off. Did you, Henry?"

But just like that, it's gone. He's ice cold, every part of him.

"I don't know what you're talking about," he says. He turns away again, takes another step toward the basement.

"Henry," she says tiredly. "I'm talking about Vivian Harris."

Another slur to her words, the name mush. Henry discerns it anyway. He freezes.

"Remember her? She was in the band with you in eighth grade. Played the clarinet."

Of course he remembers Vivian. She was the first.

He'd been a gifted trumpet player in middle and high school, always sat first chair. Directly in front of him was Vivian. Her hair was ink black, and it held the shine of the fluorescent lights that blazed so brightly above them.

"You used to follow her around. You put notes in her locker, and you never signed them, but someone saw you doing it. She wanted you to stop. She cried to her mom about it, and her mom called me."

He doesn't turn. Just stands there and listens to her words. He wills them to slide off his back.

"I had to talk to you about it. I told you to leave her alone. 'I just have a crush on her, Mom,' you said. And I told you not to. I told you to stop."

Vivian. There was no reason she shouldn't have liked him back. They could have held hands while they walked down the hall like the other eighth-grade couples. They could have experimented with kissing, with other things, behind the school's brick wall between the end of the last class and the start of band practice.

But she didn't like him. They never like him. That's why he makes them pay.

"You were so talented. You were so good at the trumpet. But I used to secretly wish you'd quit, just so that you wouldn't have to be around her anymore. It was hard for you, and for her."

He listens, stunned. She's never told him this much.

He waits for her to mention the last note he left in Vivian's locker—one final note. He was so young, and it was thrilling to insult her like that. She must have crumpled it and not told her mom. He was less bold back then, unsure how precisely to punish them.

"Next it was Sarah Davenport, in ninth grade," his mother continues, unstoppable now, as though hurtling down a hill. "Her mom called me, too. She was so condescending about it, like *she* felt bad for *me*. She said you were making her daughter uncomfortable. That you'd invited her to the homecoming dance, and she told you *no* but you were always looking at her. And you used to call her after school almost every day."

"And she answered," says Henry. He can't help but defend himself. "She talked to me."

She usually picked up after a few dozen calls. He called her landline because that phone number was in the school directory that was sent home with every family. Henry presumed she, like him, was the only one home at the time. After listening to the endless rings, she'd answer and, panic wavering in her voice, respond to his questions. She never asked him anything back or initiated any conversations, but he thought she was just shy. That was why she wouldn't speak to him at school. That was why she'd turned down his invitation to be his date for the homecoming dance. But he thought they were building something—those questions, those answers, phone hot against his ear.

"She was scared of you," his mom says gently, as though breaking bad news. As though it didn't happen fourteen years ago. "She was too nice to ask you to stop."

"Right." Finally, he turns to face her. He wants to make her look at him. He wants to see if she's going to bring up the dead squirrel.

The end of the school day, a stunning late-April day, students milling about outside. Sarah and her friends were doing gymnastics in the open field near where the lacrosse team practiced, showing off, their laughter shrill, their backpacks piled in a heap. The corpse was cold and stiff beneath his mother's hand towel, and Henry will never forget the smell. Swiftly, he unzipped Sarah's backpack, then dropped it inside. He looked up in time to watch her complete a roundoff, her shirt sliding down her bare stomach, arms reaching high, face resplendent. He waited just out of sight, up the hill, back pressed against the brick wall, to listen for her scream.

"The next one was Candace Watson."

"Wasson," he corrects automatically.

His mother sighs. "She went to the principal. You picked the wrong girl that time. She told the principal you were stalking her."

"I wasn't."

"You think that matters?" She's impatient, incredulous.

"Not according to you. Automatic guilt when it comes to your son. No due process. No presumption of innocence. If Laurel had been accused of something like that, you never would have believed it."

"That's not what I meant," she says. "I never meant that, Henry. Whether you were stalking her or not, of course the school was going to side with her."

Henry remembers her telling him that at the time, after she and his dad went to the school to meet with the principal. He stayed home, eating ramen noodles and watching MTV, waiting for them to return, to impose his punishment. She told him that he needed to stop. That the school wasn't suspending him or taking any disciplinary action, but that if it happened again, they would. Then it would be in his record. Colleges would find out about it.

Henry heard this loud and clear. Despite believing to his core that he'd done nothing wrong, that Candace had misinterpreted his affection, he understood that college was his best means for attaining independence. He had to get into the college of his choosing, preferably with a scholarship so that he wouldn't have to deal with student loans or asking his parents to make tuition payments he wasn't sure they could afford. He knew that Laurel had recently been accepted to a small private college in Pennsylvania, and that his parents had committed to covering the astronomical cost of that.

That was why he waited so patiently to impart Candace's punishment. The principal had been warned—he couldn't do anything too obvious, too immediate. By that point, people had social media accounts, and Henry's aptitude for computers and the web was emerging. It was simple for him to create the fake account, as untraceable as it could be, to message the school's principal, her pathetic and nearly friendless account heavy with photos of her cats, and let her know that Candace Wasson had cheated during her AP Biology exam—*look in the desk where she sat for the test, and you'll find an answer sheet she left behind.* Days later, he noticed Candace slip into Calculus class a few minutes late, face damp and punched-looking, and he smiled to himself. Her early admission to UPenn was rescinded, and Henry heard that she ended up attending community college for a year.

"I was so worried it would happen again," his mother continues before he can speak. "I held my breath for the rest of your years of high school, and the entire time you were away at college. And you never brought your girlfriends home, but I was so hopeful that you'd figured things out. I thought we were in the clear."

Henry feels like she's sliced straight through him, and there's a strange sort of peace in the pain.

"But then, when you told us you'd been laid off and said you had to move back home, I knew."

She stares at him, her eyes hard, and he studies her back, looking for some hint of love for him, for the person she created. But he sees nothing that looks anything like love, and she says nothing more. She doesn't bring up Kelly, the dog that went missing. Henry swallows. His mother's chest rises and falls rapidly, and she looks dead sober now.

"What did you do?" she continues. She's pleading, but he hears the flicker of self-righteousness. She's so sure.

Henry blinks at her. He lets her squirm. He lets her think he's considering telling her. But there's nothing to tell. It was fate. It was only fair, what happened to Lacey.

He shakes his head. "Nothing," he says, matching the ice in her tone. "You've always seen the worst in me. What kind of mother does that?"

She opens her mouth, closes it again, and Henry feels good. It feels good to hurt her, and this proves that he's right. He's right about her, and he's right about the wife.

He turns away again, and he steps onto the basement stairs. It's childish, but he slams the door behind him.

Henry shuts and locks his bedroom door, then lies down on his bed. He closes his eyes and listens to his heart thumping, the rage and adrenaline pounding with every beat, and the roar of blood in his ears.

He tries to conjure the wife's image to soothe himself. But he can't. She's become blurred and distant. He can't picture the slope of her nose. He can't see the shadow of her lashes against her cheeks. It's been too long since he's been close to her.

He didn't realize that his mother had been keeping a list. Vivian. Sarah. Candace. Someone at work.

Henry has a list of his own. Vivian. Sarah. Candace. Kelly. Krista. Esther. Ashley. Lacey.

He was more careful with Kelly—her copper hair; fair, freckled skin. His mother never found out about her, nor those who came after. How his punishments became bolder and more apt. How still he hasn't been caught.

The girls and the women he's wanted to love, and to be loved by.

And now, the unhappy wife.

But she doesn't belong there. That first time they spoke, she'd smiled at him. He made her laugh, and they talked about books.

There's the pull of that thread; they have so much in common. It's just her possessive husband, in the way. He's surer than ever.

43

My need for you disappears quickly. It was misplaced, it was habitual—something you've created, fashioning yourself as the solution to issues you've manufactured. It was shameful.

I wrap the baby in a washcloth—it's too small for even a hand towel—and I put the little bundle into a box. I don't know what to do with it. How can the loss of something so tiny be so staggeringly huge?

I've taken four Tylenol, and the pain in my stomach has begun to subside. I didn't have any pads, so my underwear is full of wadded toilet paper.

When you finally try returning my calls, my phone is switched off.

It's dark by the time you rush into the house. Your eyes are wide and wild, and I'm on the family room sofa, feet propped up, heating pad across my abdomen to ease the cramps that still occasionally crash over me. The toilet is flushed, the spatters of blood cleaned from the bowl and seat. The underwear and pants I was wearing are in the trash. I'll call my doctor in the morning, as soon as the office opens.

I buried our baby—a makeshift grave in the back garden. Overgrown with weeds now, mulch growing sparse. There was a smooth rock at the edge, and I placed that on top. Maybe that's wrong, but that's what I wanted to do.

I've taken care of everything. I didn't need you after all. I never have.

"Klara," you say, rushing toward me. "Why didn't you pick up? I'm so sorry, I was in a meeting. I didn't have my phone. I was so worried."

You crouch on the ground beside the sofa, drop your head to my lap. "What happened?" you repeat. "What happened?"

"The baby's gone," I say softly.

"What?" you ask. You lift your head, eyes searching mine. I stare straight into yours until you look away. I know you're lying to me, but again, I don't confront you. I'm gathering a little collection, like a toddler putting the most special rocks into his pocket. Things to hold. Things to use. I'm just not yet sure how.

"Are you sad?" you ask.

I look away. "Of course I'm sad. How could you say that?"

"You just seem so cold," you say, your fingers grasping for mine. Your head drops again, your cheek against our hands, and it's damp. You're crying, and I'm impressed.

"But you're in shock," you continue. "Of course you're in shock. And you had to go through it all by yourself. I'm so sorry."

I'm glad I can't see your face as you lie. You do it so convincingly. You always have.

My doctor's office squeezes me in the next morning. You don't go to work, instead buzzing around in the kitchen, bringing me a coffee, a bagel, far more deeply toasted than I like.

When it's time for my appointment, you drive, left hand on the wheel, the other on my thigh. I cross my arms and stare out the window. Already the nausea is lessening, slowing to a trickle I only notice when I'm searching for the sensation.

You park as close to the doors as possible, reach for the keys, your seat belt.

"You don't need to come in," I tell you. "This isn't an ultrasound. I'm not pregnant anymore." What I don't say: *This has nothing to do with you.*

You wouldn't accompany me to my annual pap smear, would you?

Your face darkens. I fling my car door open, and I'm out.

You're angry, and I don't care. There are things the doctor will say, and I don't want you to be there to hear them. We could have the fetus tested, to try to determine the cause of the miscarriage. My period should return within four to six weeks. We could start trying for another baby soon.

This is now, again, my body. You can wait in the car.

There's still tissue in my uterus, as I feared. I don't want to wait for it to pass, and I don't want to wait for the surgical procedure necessary to have it removed. The doctor sends a prescription to my local pharmacy. The nurse gives me a flyer with information about mental health services, about support groups for women and couples who have suffered from a miscarriage. I fold it again and again, a neat little square, and tuck it into the pocket of my shorts.

You've reigned in your anger, tightly controlled again, and your car coasts to a stop in front of the medical pavilion seconds after I step through the sliding doors.

"I was circling the parking lot," you explain once I've opened the door. "I ran out and got you a smoothie while I was waiting."

"Thanks," I murmur, accepting the cup, holding it between my palms.

"How—how did it go?" you ask, faltering, unsure.

"It was awful," I tell you; then I turn away, looking out the window again.

I camp out in our bedroom. The smart bassinet is still waiting near my side of the bed. Waiting for the baby who no longer exists.

"You can go to work," I tell you after the second time you come in to ask me if I need anything. "I'll probably just try to get some sleep."

"No," you say firmly, shaking your head.

"Oh." I'm looking at my phone. "I just got a text. My prescription is ready. Could you—"

"I'll get it," you say, nearly bounding out of the room. "I'll go and get it."

I wait until I can hear the squeak of the garage door as it drops closed behind your car, then I wait more.

I'm not sure what I'm doing, what I'm looking for, only that I don't have long to figure it out.

Your laptop is on the kitchen table, still open. You didn't go into work today, but that doesn't mean you haven't been working in between playing the role of grieving and doting husband.

You didn't lock the screen before you left—a rare act of carelessness—and not enough time has passed for it to have locked itself. A gentle graze of my fingers across the pad, and I'm in.

You have two different browsers downloaded, and I quickly discover which one you actually use. I pull up your search history, then scroll and scroll. I scroll back to the fall, when I first met you. That bar association event, my instincts. I pushed them aside. Handsome and perfect you. Foolish me.

And then I freeze, fingertips hovering. Because there it is: my name, nearly buried within your work-related searches.

You searched for me. And this wouldn't be disturbing—before I decided to go on a date with you, I searched for you, too—if it weren't for the date of the search. It was at least three weeks before the event when we met.

I continue scrolling. Your plan unfolds in the form of words you typed into a plain white box.

Klara Martin
Ann Taylor locations
Which medications interfere with birth control pill
How to get antibiotics online
How to buy liquid antibiotics online no prescription
Rifampin
Tetracycline
Ovulation tracker
How soon is a pregnancy detected
Tiffany & Co. locations
Top local real estate agents
Blocking a number on an iPhone
Tracking another person's iPhone activity

It's taking too long. I don't have time. It feels as though my stomach has dropped to the floor. This taste of stolen information—I'm starving for more. But I force myself to close the browser. I lock your laptop screen and watch it go dark.

I nearly have to crawl up the stairs, back into bed. My heart thunders, exhalations quick. I try to take a steadying breath. Now

I know. The coffees you were bringing me every day. Even when I didn't see you, when I needed space, you'd show up outside my office building, waxy cup in your hand, smiling that brilliant smile. My perfect boyfriend.

I pick up my phone, think of that term you'd recently searched—*Tracking another person's iPhone activity*—and drop it again.

You've been miles ahead of me this whole time, ever since we first met.

I always knew, didn't I? There is something wrong with you. Oil-slick and lurking. Dark and hidden, disguised and confusing for so long, but now, too late, I know for certain it's there.

You did this. You created this thing that I never wanted. That I grew to fiercely love. That I never should have had, that I never should have lost.

I am, I realize suddenly, alone again. I place a hand on my belly, know there's nothing there. Just remnants, tissue, nothing.

The garage door begins to creak upward again, a rumbling from below. You're back, and I want to scream.

I feel blinded by grief. For the baby I never wanted. For the baby that's gone. There is only one thing I can see, and I see it with startling clarity: It should have been you.

44

There's only one streetlamp on the entire street, and it's three houses up from Henry's.

He turns slightly, leans closer to the window, studies the house next door. He looks for motion-sensing lights or cameras. The woman who lives there is older, and she's probably not made any improvements to the house in years. Her aging gold car is parked outside, visible proof that money has been tight, that house projects haven't been feasible. Henry is almost positive she doesn't have a security system. She probably doesn't even lock her doors at night or when she goes out.

In that house, the danger was always inside.

He's looking at the lamp, trying to recall how far its brightness reaches, when his mother speaks to him for the first time in two days.

"Henry," she says, and he ignores her. He's been avoiding her ever since she brought up those girls. Vivian. Sarah. Candace. *You didn't get laid off. Did you, Henry?* He didn't appreciate that. Not at all.

But he had to come up for a bit of reconnaissance, looking for the wife, and here, instead, is his mother.

"Henry," his mother repeats. "What are you doing?"

He spins around. He didn't hear her approaching, and that bothers him. He likes to think he always knows when she's around, that he knows precisely what she knows.

Yet he should have expected her, watching, lurking, thinking the worst of him. Isn't that what she's always doing?

"Nothing, Mom," he says, and his voice cracks from lack of use. It's Friday morning, and Henry hasn't spoken aloud to anyone for at least a day.

"You're watching her, aren't you?" His mother tips her head toward the window, toward the unhappy couple's house.

Don't you dare, Henry wants to say. *Don't say her name.*

Even though she didn't.

"Watching her?" Henry sighs, a person who doesn't have time for such ridiculous accusations. "What are you talking about?"

"Like the others? *Henry.*" She's pleading with him. "We just talked about this."

Henry turns from her again. He looks at the wife's house, grand and unmoving. He looks at the streetlamp.

"I have absolutely no idea what you're talking about," he says, and then he looks straight through her. He ducks past her, and he's gone.

She thinks she knows, but she doesn't. She has no idea what he's doing.

It's not good. Not good at all. But it isn't what she thinks.

She's not like the others. He wouldn't hurt her—that isn't his plan at all.

He's going to save her.

45

After a few days, it's all gone. The tissue, the blood, the nausea. The fatigue is fading. The final vestiges of the life that is no longer a life, of a seemingly auspicious beginning, hopeful yet unwanted, inordinately complicated, are slipping away.

I'm desperate to tell Zoe, but all I can think about is what I saw in your search history. *Tracking another person's iPhone activity.*

I couldn't find anything on my phone, but that doesn't mean it's not there: an app that shares everything—my communications, my web browsing, my location—with you.

My body still feels excessively tired, excessively fleshy, the unfamiliar softness around my middle, the folds at the waistband of my shorts as I step into the room that was to be the baby's nursery.

I insisted, after two eggshell days in the house with you, that you return to work. *I need normalcy*, I pleaded. *Your hovering is making me feel weaker, like an invalid.*

You went. You aren't here. You took your laptop, your phone with you. But that doesn't mean there's nothing I can do with my time alone.

You'd been insisting to me lately that we order furniture for this room. A crib, a dresser, a rocking chair. *Order whatever you want*, you'd say. *Pay to have it assembled.*

Okay, I told you. *I will. I'll look.*

But I never did.

So there's nothing in the room but an area rug. It used to be in the living room in my condo, but you didn't like it. *How about upstairs, in your office?* you'd suggested when the van brought my things to the new house and we surveyed them, instructed the movers where to put everything.

But I already had an area rug that matched my turquoise desk. So, with nowhere else to put it, I unrolled it in the room we'd agreed would be the baby's nursery. At the time, you said nothing. You watched me do it, didn't help, walked away, off to see what the movers were unloading next.

But I see now, at some point and with no discussion, you rolled it back up. It stretches across the room like a fallen tree.

It's been weeks since I've been in this room. No reason to be here, or perhaps I've been avoiding it.

I bend, considering whether I should unroll the rug again, when I realize suddenly that the rug is no longer the only thing here.

There are two boxes pushed against the wall beneath the windows. They'd be clearly visible to someone walking by, glancing in, but I so rarely do that. They're open, flaps standing at attention.

I move closer, crawling toward them, disquiet rising, then use a finger to pull back one of the flaps.

Folds of pink and softness. A tiny pink onesie, newborn size. Footie pajamas, cream, with pink stripes or pink stars or tiny and inexplicable pink bumblebees. A pink dress, lace at the hem, matching leggings to go underneath. The next box has a little more variation, purples and yellows, but unmistakably, all of it, clothes meant for a baby girl. Clothes, if I did have a baby girl, I would never buy.

They are aggressively gendered, these clothes, purchased by

someone trying to make a point. Someone trying to communicate to his wife in such a quietly sinister way the very thing she didn't want to know.

But you did want to know. And you have access to my phone. To everything in it.

I am nearly always here, and I don't recall these boxes being delivered. I tilt a flap, check the shipping label.

Troy Weston, but beneath your name isn't our address—rather, that of your firm. You brought them in when I wasn't paying attention and put them here, waiting for me to find them.

I open my medical records app, log in. I tap breathlessly, locating the blood-test results my doctor told me not to review if I didn't want to know the sex of the baby.

And there it is. Female.

So you did know. You didn't just buy these clothes hopefully. Although perhaps that's what you'd claim if I confronted you. *Just manifesting*, because a girl is what you wanted. Perhaps if we hadn't lost the baby, finding these clothes would have prompted me to check, as I have just done. Anything to get what you want. I see that now, the way you got me.

The grief courses, slices a fresh wound through my gut. A baby, a girl. I press the heels of my hands to my eyes. I felt her, I saw her, I buried her.

The cruelty of it. I didn't want to know, and you couldn't give me that.

Your apologies always come quickly, profusely, but for deeply calculated cuts you inflicted on purpose. I feel those cuts now, the sting of them. I feel your grip, strong, as relentless as it is malignant, and I know that you will never release me.

Every move plotted in your beautiful head, behind your smiling lips, the crinkles beside your eyes. I catch you, confront you, and your excuses are impenetrable; you spit your pleas for my forgiveness, you highlight my lacking gratitude, you make me seem crazy. You make me *feel* crazy.

You'll push for another baby. Trying again. You'll make me feel broken and wrong for denying you, such a devoted husband, such a thoughtful provider.

I could leave. I could put my clothes in a suitcase, only what I really need. I could pack up the only possessions that mean anything to me—my laptop, my collection of books, my small box of mementos, nothing in there having to do with you. I could drive to Zoe's house. But I'm a lawyer, and so I know better than anyone how protracted the legal untangling of our lives could be. I'd have to wait for the requisite separation period. Then there'd be legal papers, with which you'd have to be served. Settlement discussions and court dates and delays. You wouldn't cooperate, wouldn't make any of it easy for me. My physical departure would only be the beginning.

And what I need is an ending.

I shove the baby clothes back into the boxes, fold the flaps over.

I've been lying in wait long enough.

Look through the house. That was my plan. I thought I needed to find proof of what you've done and some hint as to what you'll do next. I'd started with your laptop. Only the first step.

But I realize now, already, that's a futile exercise. Proof isn't going to help me. Your next steps don't matter. What matters are mine.

My hand dips into the side pocket of my leggings, and I remove my phone.

46

He wants to be there with her.

To be there for her, yes, but also to watch her. Yet his presence is so unwanted, so painful for her, and it was thus becoming too painful for him.

Besides, his work is not waiting just because Klara has lost their baby. There are hours to bill, clients whose hands he must hold. There is work to sell. His partnership with the firm is in its infancy, and so the pressure to sell is relentless. He should be doing far more—more networking events, golf with contacts on the weekends, dinner and drinks on him. But that would involve being away from Klara even more. It's not that she's been a terribly pleasant companion of late. In fact, she would probably prefer that he be away from the house more. And perhaps that's precisely why he won't do it. Particularly not now. She is no longer pregnant, the link between them, that tie that was meant to be permanent, suddenly gone. His perfect family abruptly dissolved into vapor, into nothing.

The blank space of Troy's document, open on one of his three computer screens, stares accusingly back at him. On another screen, the number of unread emails in his inbox gradually ticks higher. He rubs his face, turns his desk chair toward the windows, toward the city below.

He unlocks his cell phone.

Now he'll have to start over. And he's afraid Klara will double down. *I told you very early that I never wanted kids. The pregnancy, the miscarriage, hasn't changed that.* She could withhold sex—she's certainly been testing that already, citing her nausea, her exhaustion, turning away from him in their bed, tugging covers, pulling so close to the edge that it seems she'd rather fall off than risk his touch. He can only wait for so long. He's her *husband*. There are certain things she simply has to give him. There are certain things he's owed.

But what if she decides she doesn't want to be his wife anymore? She could leave. After everything he's done, she could leave. And that can't happen.

On his phone, he opens the appropriate folder, then the monitoring app he'd purchased several weeks ago, the icon revealing nothing of its purpose, which is one of the reasons he selected that particular app. He reviews Klara's recent phone activity—her texts, her calls, her emails, her searches. But there's nothing. She hasn't even reached out to her best friend about her miscarriage. Not that, if she did, her calls or texts would go through. That was why he'd set up the two-way block. With Zoe unreachable, she'd have to rely more on her husband. It was just another way of taking her in, of pulling her against him, curling himself around her, just the way he had on the plane, on their way to Grand Cayman, while she vomited into a paper bag.

He checks her location history next, and he's suddenly sitting quite straight, heart knocking, because Klara isn't at home.

The video doorbell he hadn't gotten around to setting up. The cameras still unhelpfully packed tightly in their boxes, concealed in the trunk of his car. He'd not yet managed to orchestrate Klara being away from the house so that he could have them installed. Now he wishes he'd made that more of a priority.

There's a faint tapping at the frame of his door, and he turns, irritated.

"Hi," says the young woman. Long and honeyed hair rests on her shoulders, frames of her glasses large and crystalline rose. "Do you have a second?"

She's Lily something—he's forgotten her last name—one of the newer associates. He staffed her on a project last week, although he can't recall at the moment which one.

"Sorry," he says quickly. "It's not a great time."

Her face falls, and she takes a step back. "Sure," she says too quickly, too timidly. She'll get eaten alive here if she doesn't grow a bigger pair of balls.

"I'll buzz you when I'm free. All right, Lily?" He flashes her a smile, observes the way her name in his mouth makes her flush.

"Thank you," she says, and she nearly curtsies.

"Shut that door on your way out, would you?" he calls out before turning back to his phone. Ordinarily, he might admire her ass as she walked away, but not this time. Not when his wife has left the house.

He hears his office door click closed, and he pinches his fingertips against his phone screen, enlarging the map to see where Klara has gone.

He feels some measure of relief, because she's not far from home. Not even two miles. He zooms in farther, sees that the small blue dot that represents Klara's cell phone is currently at their local library.

He looks for any previous activity, but there's none. She has, thus far, made only one stop.

Troy locks his phone again, places it down. Elbows resting on his desk, he laces his fingers together.

She's at the library. What could be more harmless? He knows

she enjoys reading, so it's not at all a suspicious place for her to go. She could be browsing for new books to read as she's resting at home, recuperating from the miscarriage.

But there's a sinking feeling still. He just can't quite articulate why.

47

Henry waits until the middle of the night. The single streetlamp is glowing dimly, and crickets hum. Nighttime in the summer is not actually quiet at all.

He doesn't close the back door completely. It sticks a little, and he doesn't want to pull it too firmly, to have it rattle the house. At least, not more than once.

It's warm, but he's wearing the same gloves he wore into the unhappy couple's house, black pants, and a black sweatshirt. The hood is up, drawstring pulled tight, so that only the features of his face are exposed. It's such a short distance from his back door to her front one. He doesn't even need to cross a driveway. He moves through the grass, and it's brittle and dry, which is good, he thinks. No dew to track inside. No footprints left behind.

Soon, his hand is on the knob of the door, and he's turning so gently, and there's not resistance like one might expect from a doorknob in the middle of the night—like there should be—but *give*.

Is being right the best feeling in the world?

Henry suspects that the feel of the wife will be better. The silk of her hair between the pads of his fingers. The softness of her cheek below the ridge of her bone, her breasts above the scrape of her ribs.

Stay focused. Push the door open. Slowly, slowly. Inhale, then freeze, then listen.

Henry hears nothing. No scream of an alarm, no countdown. There's no panel on the wall on which to enter a code. He pushes the door closed behind him.

Quickly, quickly. He knows exactly what he needs. No distractions. Twenty-two steps, and he's past two doors in the hall, both cracked, and into the kitchen, in front of the counter. Silver light spills in through the back sliding glass door. It's a full moon tonight. He locates the knife block easily, and he removes the largest one.

He holds it down, against his side. Silver and sleek, and the pearly light from the moon glints against it. His sneakers squeak once, but by then he's already in the foyer, then he's out the front door and he's closing it behind him. He's down the porch steps, across the lawn. Hood obscuring his peripheral vision, but it doesn't matter because he is fast, so fast, and then he's around the side of his house and back into the basement. This time, he has to close the door firmly behind him, but he does it so gingerly, so carefully, that the house doesn't rattle. He flips the dead bolt.

His heart is in his chest, and the roar of blood in his ears is the loudest thing he's ever heard, but it doesn't matter, because he's the only one who can hear it. He wraps the knife in a hand towel, then slips it beneath his mattress. He lies down, and he breathes until the roar dissipates, until his heartbeat slows, and he's never felt more alive.

48

When Troy gets home from work, the house is still and dark. There's a motionless feel, as though no one is home, its occupants out of town. But Klara's car is in the garage, and in his app, that little blue dot is hovering inside the box that represents their home.

Unease blooming, Troy flips switches, lighting his path.

He's far later than he wanted to be—a last-minute call from one of his most demanding clients, then accidents snarling and slowing his entire trip home—and he's starving. When he selected this neighborhood, this house, he knew he'd have to undertake a fairly lengthy commute, but that was necessary. He needed to pull Klara farther from her own office, to pull her into a less familiar county. But admittedly the traffic, and the length of his commute, have been worse than he'd expected. So wouldn't it be nice to have a meal warming on the stove when he finally made it home? A plate in the fridge? But the stove is bare, the fridge nearly empty. They've been subsisting on takeout, on easily prepared foods—Klara's pregnancy diet persisting, things bland and fried and beige. Often when he gets home from work, he hastily throws a sandwich together.

He climbs the stairs, listening for his wife, for anything.

He checks their room first, and she's there, an indistinguishable lump, the comforter twisted around her, glowing white in the thin blue light that streams in from the windows. He can see the top of her head but not her face; she's turned toward the wall.

"Klara?" he asks, and he's convinced she'll pretend to be asleep, as she so often does when he's around.

But she turns her head toward the sound, a baby bird searching, and he can tell that her face is wet.

It's nothing, the tiniest movement. But it's everything. It's an opening.

He goes to her. "Are you all right?" he asks, and her breath is shuddering.

"No." A whisper, defeated.

"What is it?" he asks. He crouches beside her, brushes comforter and hair from her face.

A pause. He waits.

"It's just hard. It's so hard."

"The baby?"

"It was just so sudden. I guess those things always are."

The pads of his fingers against her cheeks, she lets him blot away her tears.

"It's confusing. It wasn't what I wanted. You know that. But it was starting to be. I did want her."

Her.

Troy swallows, wonders whether she found the clothes, whether she checked her medical records after they lost the baby or whether she merely intuited the baby's sex, and correctly. But it's not the time to ask.

"I know," he says. "It's—a devastating thing."

"I'm so sorry," she says abruptly, watery. "I've been awful to you."

"It's fine, Klara." But he's buoyant, feels like he's floating beside the bed. This, precisely this, is what he's been waiting for.

And there's a part of him that's screaming that she doesn't mean this, couldn't possibly mean this. And if she doesn't—if this isn't real—why? She must have a reason. She's sharp, his wife. It's one of the traits that attracted him, but it's also made everything more difficult.

But there is one way he can test her.

"It's not fine," she's saying, but he leans forward and kisses her, and there's stiffness and salt, but then there's give. There's heat and warmth, and he doesn't want it to end, but he must test her.

He pulls back, strokes her cheek. "Let's just move forward, all right? We were happy. Let's find that again."

She blinks at him, then nods.

"I know it will take time. We're grieving."

"Yes," she says. A low whistle of a sigh, then she pushes herself upright, smooths her hair back, a sheepish smile. "I'm a mess."

"Not to me," he lies. "You're perfect."

Or perhaps it isn't a lie. After all, isn't this how he loves her most? Vulnerable and needing. Lost, alone, drenched from the rain, facing professional disappointment, or unexpectedly pregnant. When she's like this, that's when he thrives. He swoops in and shows her how she can't live without him.

"I can stay home again tomorrow," he suggests, even as he knows he can't. He has a closing that he can't move.

She shrugs, listless. "Whatever you have to do. I'll be okay."

"Maybe try getting out for a bit," he suggests gently. "A coffee or something."

She nods, fingers the ends of her hair.

"Did you do anything today?" he continues. "Did you get out at all? I was just thinking, I don't know—that might help."

Klara sighs again, wetly. "I tried, actually. I went to the library near us. I can't believe I hadn't checked it out yet. I was browsing the books, but then I happened to go past the children's area. There was a mother pushing her newborn in a stroller and holding her toddler's hand, and, Troy, I just couldn't. I had to get out of there."

"Of course you did," he tells her, stroking her hair. "Maybe just stay in, then. Order yourself a nice meal. Rest."

And she nods again, so agreeable she is, in this state, and his heart soars because she's passed the test. It's all checking out. That blue dot at the library. No other movement. He'll watch her closely, but he's hopeful.

At last, she's communicating with him. She's being honest. And in this moment, he loves her so much; he wishes he could just gather her up and tuck her inside of himself. He would hold her there, so tightly, so safely. He would never let her go.

49

Mary returns the photo albums to the shelf, switches her heating pad off, collects her empty wineglass. Outside, darkness has fallen, and tree branches whip in the wind; perhaps a storm is approaching.

Owen always loved thunderstorms. The wonder in his eyes. She'd let him watch them from the covered front porch sometimes, rain occasionally blowing against the house, soaking him. He didn't care.

In the kitchen, she contemplates a third glass of wine, fridge open, empty still in her hand. Quickly, before the temptation grows too strong, she nudges the fridge closed, then washes the glass and tucks it onto the drying rack. She can't afford what a third glass would do to her. She can't slog through tomorrow, headache pulsing. There's so much more to do in the house, the appointment with the Realtor inching closer. She must eliminate more of the clutter, more of the lived-in feel of it, before that.

Still, even if she cleans everything up, the Realtor will list off a litany of projects and repairs. She will have to be insistent. *As is.*

Mary turns the laundry over before she goes to bed, heaping it into the dryer.

She realizes she forgot her novel downstairs, so she opens her nightstand drawer. There, she keeps her comfort reads, as she thinks of them. Her favorite books of all time, in paperback form.

Usually, all it takes is a few pages from any of them before she's fighting sleep.

Mercifully, tonight is no different. The lull of the wine, the familiar words. She switches off the light and lets the book drop to the bed.

But there's nothing merciful about her sleep. Mary dreams of that night, of the killing. She sees the blood and feels the terror and the understanding, gripping and horrible, that nothing would ever be the same, despite that things hadn't been that good or happy before. Not with Ed.

How could she not dream of it? The hours in Owen's room, the photo albums, the memories.

Mary sits up, back against her headboard, and tries to catch her breath, palm to her heart, pressing, like she can slow it that way.

And then she hears it. A gentle creak, that particular board downstairs that always squeals when it's stepped on just so.

She sits up, reaches for the glass of water on the table beside her, and drains it, because she's suddenly devastatingly thirsty and can think of nothing else.

But once the glass is empty, she stills, listening. She hears nothing more.

She sighs, rolls the edge of the comforter in her hands. It's nothing, she tells herself. Or it's just him. Moving through his home while he thinks she's asleep. And she should be asleep. She should go back to sleep.

She turns onto her other side, adjusts her pillow. She closes her eyes. And as she tries to drift away again, she plays her favorite trick on herself, the one the therapist she saw briefly many years ago told her not to play.

She thinks of her boy. She pretends he's down the hall,

sleeping under rocket ship sheets. That he's still a boy, relatively untroubled. That none of it ever happened. That he'll wake up in the morning and he will run to her, just the way he used to. When he was so little, he always shone when he first woke.

Grinning, hurtling into her arms, so she could tuck her nose into the sleep-smell of his hair and neck. A bowling ball of heat and curls and smiles.

50

On Saturday evening, Henry finds his parents sitting in the living room. They seem surprised to see him. Henry's father's eyes track him as he crosses in front of the television and settles onto the sofa, at the opposite end from his mother, who's staring at him with surprise, with interest, as though he's the most popular kid in school, settling down at a lunch table of losers.

"Second inning, no score. Seems late for that," Henry says, looking at the screen.

His dad is watching the Orioles game, of course. He's watched nearly every game for Henry's entire life.

"They're in Chicago," his dad grunts. "An hour behind us."

He says nothing more. Henry knows where his father's loyalty lies. He knows that his mother has filled his father in on everything she thinks she knows. *He's doing it again, Bill, with the woman across the street. I've seen him watching her. Why won't he stop?*

She has no idea.

He won't stop. He can't. Not now. He's so close to her, his plan now firm and irrepressible.

Henry smiles and turns his attention back to the screen. He tries to pay attention. Once, the Orioles pitcher strikes someone out and Henry makes an appreciative noise.

"That was a nasty pitch," says his dad and takes a sip of beer.

He doesn't ask Henry if he wants one, but the vibe is not hostile. It isn't welcoming, but it's not uncompanionable, either.

His mother turns the pages of her book and sits with her legs crossed, angled away from her son. Every so often, in the periphery, Henry can see her watching him.

"Fifth inning," says Henry finally, announcing this for his parents' benefit. "I'm pretty tired. I'm going to head to bed."

"All right," his dad says.

"Night," says his mother softly, curiously. And he's certain now that they will recall this. *Fifth inning*. He said it aloud, imprinted it into their minds.

Importantly, his parents will remember all of this—the first evening in as long as any of them can remember that Henry sat with them. He watched the Orioles game with his dad. During the fifth inning, he went to bed. Later, that's what they'll tell the police.

No, they'll say. *None of us left the house at all that night. Henry went to bed, and we went to bed when the game was over. We didn't see anything. We don't know anything.*

Tonight might not even be the night, but Henry is hoping that it is. Either way, he's laid the groundwork. He's ready. But if all he manages is a little reconnaissance, so be it.

In his bedroom, Henry lies down, but on top of the covers, and he doesn't sleep. He waits. He waits until the sound of the television disappears. He waits until he can hear feet moving above him, then ascending the stairs. He waits long after the footsteps stop.

Once he has waited long enough, he changes into the same dark clothes he wore when he snuck into his next-door neighbor's house to steal the knife. He puts on gloves, too. They're black and too tight for him—he thinks they're his mother's—but they're the first pair he found. He slips the knife out from beneath his mattress; then he leaves his house with the stealth of a practiced assassin.

And a practiced assassin he is not—obviously. But he'll do his best.

51

For the first time since we moved into this house, I cook for you. Real cooking that requires perusing recipes and a special visit to the grocery store with a list of ingredients, things I wouldn't usually buy.

I went to Whole Foods earlier in the day, checking the two recipes I selected, flipping between them on my phone screen as I moved up and down the aisles. I loaded brimming paper bags into the back of my car; then, air-conditioning at full power, I sat in the front seat and sent you a text. What time do you think you'll be home tonight? I'm making you something.

I knew you knew where I was, the app on your phone informing you of my precise location. I pictured you reading my text, then checking that app, seeing that I was in the Whole Foods parking lot. I pictured you checking my phone activity, reviewing the recipes. A smile spreading as you replied.

You're late, later than usual, my awaiting surprise notwithstanding. Apparently, your clients or your partners or the traffic don't care about my plan.

It's dark outside, the cool white recessed lighting of our kitchen glowing above me as I hear the garage door rumbling upward, then back down. That inner door, the one between the garage and the hallway, always squeaks when it opens. Then your footsteps, past the laundry room, into the kitchen.

“It smells amazing,” you say, stepping toward me.

Your head dips, a kiss, and then I’m smiling tentatively back at you.

“What’s the occasion?” you ask, surveying the stove, every burner full. The stir-fry of shredded chicken, peppers, and bright snap peas in one pan; the rice; the two pots of sauce.

“My cravings for—real foods are coming back. The foods I used to love. I thought it might be fun to start trying out some new recipes.”

A hobby, domestic and insular and safe. You’ll love this idea. There’s been no talk of me returning to work, despite that I’m no longer pregnant.

“And look,” I tell you, picking up my phone. “I made this Szechuan peanut sauce, so it has peanut butter and sesame oil. It sounded so good. But this one doesn’t.” I show you the alternate recipe, allergy friendly, and point to the pot on the right. “For you.”

My game has been a long one, two weeks of kindness, of rekindling. Two weeks since I did my research at the local library. So you suspect nothing.

“Thank you so much,” you say, hand on my lower back. You press a kiss to the side of my head. “Let me just change out of my suit.”

And while I can hear your footsteps moving above, I find your final EpiPen in the front pocket of your work backpack and your phone on the edge of the island, and I fly outside, into your car. I hide them there, in the center console. You’d never leave them there. But they won’t know that.

I prepare my plate but let you make your own.

“The pot on the right,” I call out anxiously from my seat at the table.

"So you said," you say, laughing, amused by my caution.

Then you join me at the table, and I try not to stare as you fork up your first bite of food.

Immediately, your nose wrinkles, and my heart stills.

"You're sure?" you ask. "This smells like peanuts."

"I thought the same thing. But not compared to the other sauce," I say, then freeze. "You got it from the pot on the right?"

You're relaxed again, laughing at the concern on my face. "Yes, Klara. The pot on the right."

And then you're eating, and you're smiling at me, and I know what's behind that smile. Considering your next move, your next grab for control. Switching out my birth control pills, or secretly pumping me with some drug that will render the hormones ineffective. That worked before, why not try it again?

"How was your day?" I ask.

You touch your throat, shifting, uncomfortable.

I lift a finger. "Hold that thought. Bathroom," I say quickly, standing, grimacing as though I'm feeling unwell.

I take my time, washing my hands slowly. My phone is in my pocket, out of your reach. Your other EpiPens are hidden through the house, places you'd never leave them, but not implausible that you might have misplaced them, forgotten they were there.

As I open the bathroom door, I hear the rasp of your cry. I count to one hundred before I go to you.

You're on the floor, pawing at your backpack, searching for your EpiPen.

You see me, your face an explosion of red, the fear in your eyes. You're mouthing at me, *Pen, help, call.*

I don't move.

It's so tragic. I lose my baby and my husband in the span of a few weeks.

I told him which sauce to eat, but he had the wrong one while I was upstairs, finishing up a shower.

That's what I'll say. They'll believe me.

It's brutal to watch, more brutal than I'd expected, the gradual purpling of your face, the sounds you make. But I watch anyway.

I watch you take your final breath. I watch you die.

And I'm free.

Part II

NOW

52

Kate expels a breath harshly as she snaps her laptop closed on Klara and Troy. As though to punish. As though it's the computer's fault that the words have ceased to flow.

Three months. She's been stuck here for three months, rereading her own words over and over, walking endlessly, to nowhere, on their basement treadmill. When that didn't work, she started walking outside, white baseball cap shielding her face from the sun, moving slowly through the neighborhood streets, refraining from listening to music or audiobooks. She's forced silence on herself while doing meaningless chores around the house, freeing her mind to wander. She's tried gardening, too, but she'd let her flowers die, and she realized that she despises pulling weeds, that she's incapable of remembering to water.

She has been so diligently cultivating quiet, the blank canvas of her mind, hoping, waiting, for something to jiggle loose in her head so that the words will flow again.

Klara comes to understand Troy's grip, the controlling actions he's taken. She loses the baby, a fairly late miscarriage. She understands that she is alone, she is trapped. Enraged, calculated, she kills him in revenge, to regain her freedom. Kate had added that later—the plan, the murder—and it felt like a breakthrough at the time. She wasn't quite sure where she was going, but that had felt like the piece she'd been missing sliding into place. Except her final chapter isn't even a thousand words, and nothing more has come to her. She still has no idea what's next.

It feels like an ending, but if it is, she doesn't really have a book. It's not nearly long enough. It's only a short story, really—maybe a novella. And she's not sure she likes that ending for Klara. Is murder really the answer?

Her premise for the book was the arc of a couple's complicated relationship, one that was, unbeknownst to them both, abusive. For a while, Kate thought the wife would find happiness on her own, but as Kate wrote, Troy developed into too much of a villain to ever let Klara go, and Klara is intelligent enough to see that. With each week that's passed, with each progress-less week, Kate has become less sure that happiness is in the cards for either of her characters. So she turned to murder. And such a finality is murder. It's no wonder that she has nowhere left to go.

She sighs again, rubs her eyes. It's Saturday, and it's far too late to be sitting at one's desk. Ben has surely finished his workout by now. He must be out of the shower. He's probably poured himself a drink and settled onto the family room sofa with the remote, flicking through their various streaming services. Ben probably retrieved a glass for her, too, and it's sitting on the counter, both olive branch and silent invitation for her to pour the drink of her choosing. Because unlike her protagonist, Kate has never been pregnant. She only managed to give up alcohol for the first four months of them trying to conceive. Once she realized how difficult it was going to be, or that it might never happen at all, she resumed the occasional drink. She figures that everyone must do it.

And they've been trying for nearly fourteen months. It started long before they moved into this house. Long before she quit her high-pressure job to lower her stress, to improve her *fertility*, to focus on that novel that had been simmering in her brain, which is, apparently, not really a novel at all.

Kate leaves her office, trails downstairs, finds that she's both right and wrong. There is a glass on the island in the kitchen, empty and waiting for her. But there's no Ben. The television hanging on the wall in the family room is dark.

It's so late. She sat with her words, her open laptop, for much longer than she'd intended. She mixes herself a quick cocktail—always her preference over wine, especially red—then goes to look for her husband.

He's not in the living room, the sunroom, or the basement, always so chilly and dim. Her glass is cold between her fingertips, condensation dripping.

Kate peers through the windows of the door at the back of the house, and she can see his form, dark against the insensible pale-blue cushions of their outdoor sofa. They're still new, the cushions, but Kate and Ben haven't been vigilant enough about covering them, so it's only a matter of time before they're sun bleached and stained and worn.

Kate tugs the door open and steps outside onto the patio. She's greeted by more darkness—her husband didn't turn on all the outdoor lights, only the fairy lights that stretch above, from the side of the house to the edge of the deck—and by music. It's too loud, possibly disturbing to the neighbors at this hour.

"Ben," she says, tone scolding but playful. She's still feeling benevolent and affectionate toward him, the way she always feels after they've argued, then resolved things.

And they'd resolved things quite comprehensively—apologies and sex that was somehow both urgent and tender. When it was over, he'd tucked his face into the crevice between her shoulder and cheek. She could feel his breath against her collarbone as he whispered how much he loved her.

Now Ben doesn't stir.

"There you are," she adds belatedly, unnecessarily, because decidedly, he is there. Physically, he is there—there he is. Her husband.

But he still doesn't move, doesn't react to her voice, which is odd. So she moves closer.

"Ben," she says, and she's laughing now, wondering if he actually managed to fall asleep while he was waiting for her, until she realizes that his head is tipped forward at a strange angle, that something isn't right.

And as she moves around the sectional to stand in front of him, she can see his chest, and it all makes sense, just as it makes no sense at all.

Ben didn't move because he couldn't. He can't. He didn't hear her. He will never hear her again.

There are holes in his chest—wounds. They are oozing and deep and black in the darkness. The pale-blue cushions of the sofa are irrevocably stained.

The music swells, the chorus of the song, and the fairy lights twinkle, and Ben is dead.

53

Kate doesn't need to feel for a pulse. There's no point in that. She's far too late. He is right here, right in front of her, but he is so clearly gone.

She screams. At first, the sound scares her, but she doesn't stop. She screams her throat raw.

The police. Her phone. Where is her phone?

But then there are footsteps. A man running toward her, his own phone in his hand, its flashlight function engaged. His face is drawn tight in terror, obscuring its kind familiarity.

"What is it?" he asks, urgent and panicked, with a hint of *I don't want to know* lurking. "What's wrong?"

He's her neighbor. Dan or Dave or Dale. He lives next door with a wife and two teenage girls. His girls probably heard Kate scream, and his wife probably made him come. He has a pleasantly boring life.

This is a night he will never forget.

The neighbor's name is Dave. Kate finds that out later.

"Jesus," he says when he notices Ben's body. "Oh my God."

He steps closer to her husband.

"Don't touch him," hisses Kate. Her ferocity scares her.

Dave doesn't. He lifts his phone and calls 9-1-1.

While they wait for the police, Kate sits on the ground near Ben's body. He's still a little warm. She can't look at him.

Her knees are bent, the stones of the patio digging harshly into her tailbone. She wraps her arms around her legs, folding thighs and calves tight, and tucks her head down. She rocks, crying, keening, a child waiting for someone to scoop her up and fix it. To assure her that everything will be okay, even though she knows it won't.

Dave lingers nearby somewhere. Kate can't see him, but she senses his presence, shifting and uncertain. He has no idea what he's supposed to be doing, and neither does she.

When the police cars and ambulances arrive, uniformed people streaming into Kate's backyard, an EMT helps her stand and leads her to an ambulance, lights still flashing. They take her vitals, drape a heavy charcoal blanket across her shoulders. They treat her with sympathy, with care, and quickly decide that she's in shock but doesn't need to be taken to the hospital. Instead, the police help her into the back of a marked sedan, and Kate feels affronted that, on top of everything, they are making her feel like a criminal. She watches the EMTs wheel a stretcher out of the ambulance. There's a black body bag on top, waiting for her husband.

When she gets to the station, they're gentler with her. They bring her tea in a Styrofoam cup and water in a waxy paper one. Detectives Nia Scott and Frank Perkins sit down across from her, a wooden table and Kate's drinks between them. They tell her they're sorry for her loss, but it's very important that she speak with them, that she tell them everything she knows, everything she can remember. She should know that crime scene technicians are at her house, processing the scene. They will interview neighbors. They will not rest until they find out who killed her husband.

They study her face as they say this, searching for fear, and that's the first time Kate realizes they think that person, the one they are looking for, might be her.

All she wants to do is curl into herself, make herself silent and invisible and nothing, but they press on with their questions. How was her relationship with Ben? Marriage can be difficult. Were they fighting?

"No," she says coldly. She thinks of earlier that day—yesterday, by this point—sitting on the sofa with her husband. She remembers lowering her novel, stretching her legs out, asking him what he wanted to do about dinner.

Ben shrugged. "Whatever you want," he said. He crossed his legs, shifting slightly away so that her toes could no longer feel his warmth.

She flipped her book closed and pushed herself up, folding her legs onto the sofa, looking at her husband.

That morning, she had decided to take a break from trying to write, reminding herself of the tempting bit of advice that breaks were part of the process. It was too early to take a pregnancy test, her period not expected for another week, so there was a sense of futility surrounding the day. If Kate could have fast-forwarded, passed through it hurriedly, she would have.

She kept her notebook and laptop closed and gave herself time to read something else, thought that perhaps she'd go out to lunch or dinner with her husband, a quiet meal at a favorite local place. Later, she would review her notes and the rest of her words.

But Ben had been distant all day, offering no suggestions of a nice meal together, of a bowl of chips and fresh salsa to share, of frosty drinks or vibrant music. They had leftovers for lunch. Ben stared at his phone while they ate, occasionally raising his gaze to inspect her as though he had no idea who she was.

"What is with you?" she finally asked; he was there beside her on the sofa, yet he seemed blurred and obscure.

"It's just—" He shrugged listlessly. "Bored."

"You're bored," she echoed.

"Yeah." He unlocked his phone, scrolled through his screens of apps, locked it again.

"Well, do you want to go to dinner? Go for a walk? Watch something?" She suddenly felt quite motherly, supercilious, rattling off a practiced list of activities.

"Ethan texted me today," Ben said softly. "He said a bunch of them were going out to dinner. A new Indian place opened along the wharf."

"Okay," said Kate, the syllables sticky and slow. "So—do you want to go? You want to drive down to DC?" She could hear the incredulity in her tone. She was already calculating. Saturday-afternoon traffic. It would probably take them an hour and a half to get down there. Assuming Ben wanted to match their friends' drinking, she'd have to drive home. It had been so long, but she was pretty sure it was her turn.

"We never go anymore, Kate." His words were clipped, slicing into her thoughts. "We never see our friends."

"Well, we live up here now. And we've been trying for a baby."

"For fourteen months," said Ben, dropping his phone into his lap.

"In a few days, I can take a test," she said tentatively, which felt relevant, although she couldn't quite pinpoint why.

Ben didn't agree. "What does that have to do with anything, Kate? That's all you care about anymore. The days we can try. The days you can test. What about all the other days? These are our lives. And all of it feels so fucking futile."

Kate pulled her knees into her chest. Thoughts she'd had so many times before, but that he'd voiced them so casually gutted her.

"I feel like I barely know you anymore. You have this singular focus. You've changed so much."

"That isn't true." Chin resting on her knee, she watched him from the corner of her eye.

"It's all you care about. The baby that might never exist."

"You used to feel the same way," she urged. "Maybe I am a little obsessed, but that's normal. Who wouldn't be after we've been trying for so long? It's like the longer we try and can't get pregnant, the more I want it. That's normal."

"So I'm not normal? Me wanting to take a step back and try to enjoy all the other things in our lives, to do things with our friends like we used to, to consider that having a baby isn't everything, that it's not the only thing that matters, is unhealthy? Because that seems pretty healthy to me."

"I didn't say that." She didn't tell him, *no*. That it didn't seem normal. Not to her. "I've sacrificed a lot for this already, Ben. I left my job."

"I didn't make you do that."

She swallowed a gasp. Of course he hadn't. But it had been his idea—that she leave her high-pressure job to lower her stress, to see if that would help them conceive. She was hesitant. She'd worked so hard to be promoted to senior analyst, was one of only two women in the entire firm who had that title. A few more years of pushing, and she could be a member with equity and six weeks' vacation. The thought of giving that up, even temporarily, for the mere potentiality of something, something that still might never happen, something that might be painful and wrought and unnatural for her, felt insane. Yet she did it. She took that plunge. Because what if it was the stress that was preventing her from conceiving? She clung to a distant, broader view of the future, to that potentiality, to Ben, and to the wisps of the novel that had been rattling around in her brain and that had turned out to not be enough for a novel at all.

"I didn't say you forced me, Ben. But that doesn't mean it hasn't been hard. That doesn't mean it wasn't a sacrifice. So for you to tell me that I've changed since I left my job in finance and my sixty-hour workweeks—of-fucking-course. What did you expect?"

Her husband opened his mouth, closed it again. She thought her harshness had deflated him, that she'd shocked him into reality so that he could process the accusations he'd just made against his wife, but his eyes hardened, brows drawing low. "You are always home. You have so much less stress now, so much less work. But you're still constantly on your laptop. You're looking at your screen all the time."

"Oh, like you aren't constantly staring at your phone? Is that what we're fighting about now? Which one of us is more addicted to screen time?"

Ben pressed on, ignoring her. "I thought you must be almost finished by now, you have so much time to work on it."

Kate stared at him, at the creases in his forehead, wondering when they'd become so deep.

"You only have thirty-five thousand words. I looked up how many words a book should have. That's less than a half."

"You read my book," Kate said. She leaned away from him like he was burning hotly.

"It's not a book."

And, to her dismay, it was perhaps those words that sliced the deepest.

She wanted to defend herself. But he was right. It wasn't a book. Not even close.

"And the characters. Klara. She seems like you in some ways. And you gave her a mom like your mom."

"She's not like me," said Kate, then pressed her lips together, thinking better of finishing the thought: *She doesn't want a baby, and that's all I want.*

"Is Troy like me?" Ben pressed on. "Is that how you think of me? Am I that awful?"

"It's fiction," she snapped. "Troy is the villain. Don't be ridiculous."

Ben just shook his head.

"When did you read it?" she asked. She wasn't sure what else to say.

"This morning, while you were sleeping in."

He made it sound like a crime. *This morning, while you were cooking methamphetamine in the garage. This morning, while you were robbing Starbucks.*

"I can't believe you did that," she said, and she couldn't tell how she felt about it. She didn't know if she was hurt or angry, both or neither.

"It's good," he said, looking at his lap again. "You're a good writer. It's just short. I don't know why it took you so long to write that."

"It didn't. I mean, I've been stuck. I've been stuck for months."

"She kills him."

"Yeah," Kate said. "That's the only part I've added recently."

"Once you started wishing that you could kill me. Once you realized that you really couldn't get pregnant and started hating me for it."

Kate crossed her arms. "No," she told him. "We don't have a great life insurance policy on you."

Ben stared at her for a beat. The creases between his brows released, and he started to laugh.

Something shattered then. The sound of it—pure and stunned amusement. She began to laugh, too, and when was the last time they'd laughed together like that?

When Ben had finally collected himself, wiped his eyes, his face fell again, solemn.

"I wish it could've been easy, like it is for so many people," he told her. "If it had, if it had just happened, we'd be golden. We'd be great. The way we always were."

"We'd be happy," said Kate.

"We still can be, no matter if it happens," Ben said, and he sounded so sure, like it was so simple. "I'm still happy."

"Are you?"

He nodded, then tilted his head to the side, studying her, taking her in, his wife in her worn athletic shorts and one of his T-shirts, hair still glossy and sleek because it's the only thing she tended to every day.

"I love you, Kate. I love you so much."

"You do?"

His face cracked, crooked grin, lightness shining through. "Are you going to just keep questioning everything I say, or are you going to come over here?" He patted the cushion beside him.

She watched him, not sure that anything had really been resolved.

"Do you still love me?" he asked. And the fear in his voice—it made her chest ache.

"I do," she told him. And she did. "But I still don't feel like going to dinner at the wharf tonight," she added tentatively, not wanting to shatter the bridge between them.

Ben smiled gently, wryly. "Next time?" he asked. "I think it would be good for you. For us."

Kate wasn't sure, but she nodded. "Okay."

And just as quickly as it had started, the fight was over. They were good at that, at moving on. They always were.

"Come here," Ben said again. There was a softness in his eyes that Kate hadn't seen in weeks. He opened his arms.

So she went. So no, they weren't fighting.

So she doesn't tell the police about what they said to each other the day Ben died. And she doesn't tell them about her novel.

Now Kate sits in her living room, the curtains cracked so that she can see the road. The soaking rain that had begun at some point while she was being interviewed in the police station still hasn't stopped. Water streams down her driveway, coalescing with the runoff that rushes down the street, down the hill, toward the gaping mouth of the sewer at the base of the cul-de-sac.

She's expecting the police back at some point. They told her they would come by today to provide an update on their investigation. It had sounded like a threat.

They interviewed her for hours. They inspected her for blood spatter. She gave up her clothes, and she consented to them searching the house. She isn't trying to hide anything. She understands that she's the wife, and she was home. She's the most likely suspect for those reasons alone. She just wants them to hurry up and clear her so that they can actually figure out who killed Ben.

She hasn't been able to eat anything since before her husband died. She hasn't slept. When the officers dropped her off at home, it was nearly ten in the morning. Kate went upstairs to the bedroom she had shared with Ben. She showered numbly beneath scalding water, then dressed in one of Ben's T-shirts and her own shorts. She stood beside her bed and thought about pulling back the comforter. She thought about climbing inside. She thought about the fact that her cold feet would never again push through tangled sheets to find Ben's warm ones. She couldn't get in.

She sits on the sofa in her living room and watches the rain while she waits for the police.

Kate must have dozed off, because there's a knock on the door and she's pushing herself up from the sofa, her mind foggy, neck stiff. She rubs her eyes and goes to the door, darkness in her vision because she stood too quickly and she hasn't eaten, but she pushes forward, hand to the knob, and foolishly she flings the door open without looking out the side window to see who's on the porch.

Because she was dreaming of Ben. She dreamt that she couldn't find him anywhere in the house. She was looking in every room, calling his name, just as she'd looked for him last night. But she was looking in places he would never be—under their bed, in the hall linen closet—as though they were playing a game of hide-and-seek. In her dream, she was happy, and she was laughing. Then someone knocked on the door, and Kate went down to answer it, and there he was. Ben, standing on the front porch.

Of course, it isn't Ben on the porch, and it was the cruelest thing she could have dreamed.

"Come in," she tells the detectives. She leaves the door open and returns to her sofa. She's been expecting them, so she probably should have made coffee. She should offer them some, or some water. Is there a package of cookies in the pantry? The soft white-chocolate macadamia ones that Ben used to love? Kate won't eat them. He used to tease her for hating any dessert that had nuts or fruit.

"Are you okay, Mrs. Harvey?" asks Detective Scott, alarm in her voice. "Can I get you something?"

"Water, please," Kate says, relieved that she's not expected to play host in this scenario, too lost and dazed to ask the detective not to call her that.

"We just wanted to give you an update," says Detective Perkins as Detective Scott disappears into Kate's kitchen. "On where things stand."

"Perk, you want water?" Detective Scott calls from out of sight.

"No, thanks," he replies. He settles onto the armchair across from Kate. Ben had picked out the chair when they were in the furniture store together. They'd selected the sofa and two chairs and angled them around the fireplace. They were planning to put their Christmas tree in this room, in front of the windows so that its lights could greet them as they pulled their cars into the driveway. They were supposed to sit on the area rug while their kids unwrapped gifts.

"We spoke with Ben's brother," says Detective Perkins, and Kate feels her head swivel toward him.

"Ben isn't close with his brother," she says. That was why she'd not wanted to call him. She's not spoken with Chris in a year. She isn't sure if Ben had either. Ben's parents died during the first five years of their relationship, and Chris lived in South America. Perhaps that was why their bond became so close, so quickly. She was all he had.

"Well," Perkins says softly, "that's his family, aside from you. So we had to notify him."

Kate nods, looks down at her lap, hot tears pooling. A glass of water appears on the coffee table in front of her, and she takes it. She drinks until the dryness leaves her throat.

"What about Ethan?" she asks, horrified, glass sliding between her fingertips. "Who will call Ethan?"

The detectives glance at each other. "Who?" asks Scott.

"Ben's best friend. They're very close."

"We'll want to speak to him anyway," Scott tells her gently. "I'm sure he will find out very soon."

How? Kate wants to ask; then she realizes that her nightmare has only just begun. There will be a funeral to plan. She'll have to tell Ben's work. Media will hover around her, around her house. Drones have probably already snapped pictures from above to post on the news.

"As far as the investigation goes," Perkins says, "we're processing physical evidence. It's possible there is DNA of Ben's killer on his body. Under his nails, for instance. We'll get results in the next few days. The autopsy will be Tuesday."

Kate feels herself shaking her head sharply, as though that could clear the image of Ben in a silvery fridge drawer, the sound of a saw whirring as they cut through his bones.

"We're interviewing all of the neighbors and requesting security camera footage," Scott adds quickly.

"It's not really that sort of neighborhood," says Kate. She and Ben hadn't even considered getting a security system or cameras. Not even a video doorbell to look over their packages. She'd already told them this. They'd felt secure here. It was one of the reasons they'd left the city and chosen this quiet street.

"Some people may have them," says Perkins, almost defensively.

"So you don't have any idea who did it?" She can't bring herself to say it—what happened to her husband. "I mean, what if they come back?"

"Not yet, Mrs. Harvey. But it's not likely the person would come back. They'd surely be caught."

Kate watches him. *After he kills me, you mean? He won't get away with it twice?*

"Is there somewhere else you can go?" Detective Scott asks softly, and Kate's eyes tilt toward her face. She's comically pretty, model tall and thin, her blazer austere, blouse crisp, and Kate can see the gun winking at her hip. "If you don't feel safe here. And it would be a good idea if you could stay somewhere else. In the area."

Those last three words are decidedly colder. The detectives might still suspect she was involved even though there wasn't any physical evidence on her or in her house to indicate that she was.

Kate shakes her head. She doesn't feel safe here anymore, yet she doesn't feel capable of leaving.

"Or is there someone who can come stay with you?" Detective Scott continues.

Kate thinks of her mom. She hasn't called her yet. She wonders if her mom would get on a plane and fly up from South Carolina. Would she burn meals for Kate in her own kitchen? Smooth her daughter's hair and ask with indecorous interest how much money she has? Enough to get by? Would she smile to herself as she loaded dishes into Kate's dishwasher, thinking with misguided glee that Kate's grand and perfect life, the life she had always so resented, has crumbled and she needs her mommy after all?

"No," says Kate.

"A friend?" suggests Detective Scott.

"Ben is my best friend," Kate says plainly—a nonanswer, and that's when she starts to cry. Because Ben is gone, he is past tense, but mostly because she feels as though it's all her fault.

54

It's early afternoon on Sunday when Henry comes face-to-face with the detectives leading the investigation into the husband's murder. Henry still doesn't know his name.

The detectives, he finds out, are Nia Scott and Frank Perkins. Frank's hair is far sparser than Henry's, and Henry views this shared bit of misfortune as potentially helpful, that this man might see a bit of himself in Henry. He offers the detective a sympathetic smile, but still quite small and controlled, given the circumstances, as they settle onto chairs in the living room. His mother bustles around, offering coffee and tea. Although the detectives decline, she retrieves a tray with a crystal pitcher of water, four glasses, and a plate of homemade sugar cookies dusted with powdered sugar and places it on the coffee table, as though her girlfriend Carol has come to visit.

Henry wonders whether the detectives notice the disconnect—five people and only four water glasses. He wonders whether they know which person is not meant to have any water. He wonders whether they know it's him.

She's still upset with him; they haven't spoken much, nothing resolved, since the day she accused him of doing it again, her pleading tone: *Like the others? Henry.*

More likely, the detectives just think the underabundance of glasses is merely an oversight under these upsetting circumstances. Even more likely, they haven't noticed at all.

"Thank you," says Detective Perkins, glancing down at his notebook. "Mrs. Lawson."

"Janet, please," she says benevolently. "My husband, Bill, and our son. Henry."

Do they detect the way her eyes dart, the bare absence of pride, the way she wishes he wasn't here?

"Cara March, from across the street, told me what happened," his mother says in a whisper. "It's so awful. Apparently, her husband found…the body."

"Mmm," replies one of the detectives, noncommittal, and without opening his or her mouth. Henry isn't even sure which of them made the sound.

"Did you know your neighbor, Ben Harvey, well?" asks the woman. Detective Scott. She has a gentle tone and sympathetic eyes, wide and brown, but Henry has the sense it's inflated, the sympathy something she can turn on and off like a faucet.

"Not at all," Henry's mom says. "They stayed to themselves, ever since they moved in. I would have brought over a pie or something, you know, but the vibe was a little standoffish." She lifts her hands, palms facing out. "Not that I didn't like them," she continues hurriedly. "We just never shared more than brief pleasantries, just waving to them in passing. From a distance." There's a tremor in her voice that makes Henry uneasy.

"All right," says Detective Scott, looking to Henry's father. "What about you?"

"I never met them," he says, shrugging.

"Bill still works," Henry's mother says, leaning forward to adjust the pitcher slightly. "He commutes into the city, and he's out of the house a lot."

The detectives turn to Henry; his mother does, too, expectant. *He watches her. The wife.* He half expects her to say it.

"I met the wife," Henry admits. "We're not friends, certainly. We chatted a couple times in passing. We have similar taste in books. But I never met her husband."

He doesn't like to downplay his relationship with Kate, to behave as though it's nothing, but he understands that's what he should do.

"When did you meet Kate Harvey?" asks Detective Scott.

"Oh, I'm not sure exactly. A few weeks back, we were outside at the same time, and we greeted each other. We chatted about books a couple of times. As my mother mentioned, the vibe was a little standoffish."

"Could you explain further what you mean by that?" asks Detective Scott. She seems to be the leader of the pair, although she looks much younger than Perkins. Henry thinks of Lacey, of women and of snakes, and he has the urge to shake Perkins. He wants to warn him. *She could ruin your life.*

"Just that she wasn't very friendly. I'm not sure what more I can say."

There's much more, actually. There's Kate's novel. He found it on her laptop when he was in her house. He got past her password easily, and the document was already open. Those few little words, right there at the beginning: *Ours is a tale of murder.* He'd skimmed it, but there wasn't time to read. Not then. So he sent it to himself, deleted the sent email, erased the Trash, and then it was his, and it was like he'd never been there.

But later, at home, he read it all, every propulsive and vivid word. Her autobiography, he thought. At least the start of it. And it proved he was right. They weren't happy. The husband was possessive, controlling. He recalled following the wife to her doctor's appointment—perhaps she'd suffered a miscarriage at some point, just like her protagonist. She was looking for a way out.

She wanted her husband dead. All she needed was someone who'd become willing to go just that far, to take care of it for her.

But Henry says none of this to the detectives. If somehow he becomes a person of interest in the investigation, he may have to so that he can direct the police away from himself: *She asked me to read the book for her because I'm such a voracious reader. She thought I could help her finish it. And don't you think it's odd, Detective, that she wrote a novel about a woman who murders her husband, then her husband turns up dead? She was home at the time, wasn't she? Who else could it have been? She must have—she wrote his murder.*

"That's fine," says Perkins, accommodating, "if that's all you have to share." He reaches for a cookie, and Henry considers suggesting that his mother's cookies look much better than they taste.

"I'm sorry we couldn't be more helpful to you," his mother says, filling the silence that's fallen, only Perkins chewing, wiping crumbs from his dress pants.

"Just one more thing before we go," says Scott. "Could you each tell us where you were last night? From nine until this morning. If you don't mind."

"Well, they were watching the game," Henry's mother replies. "I was reading."

Reading. She says it reverentially, as though she were studying a first edition of James Joyce's *Ulysses* that night, rather than flipping through the worn Colleen Hoover paperback her girlfriend Carol had lent her weeks earlier.

"The game?" asks Scott.

"Orioles," his father grunts. "They won. Scored a pair in the top of the ninth."

"Right," Scott says as though she already knew this.

"So you watched the game, and that wrapped up around what time?" asks Perkins.

"Henry went to bed in the fifth inning," his mother says quickly.

"I did," says Henry. "I was too tired to stay up for the end." He shrugs sheepishly, feeling his mother's eyes on him. But she says nothing. They're all pretending that it's perfectly normal for Henry to sit with his parents on a Saturday evening, to watch part of an Orioles game.

"The game ended around ten forty, I think. Then we went up to bed," his father says.

"Yes, we always go to bed before eleven," says his mother.

"And none of you got up again after you went to bed? Did you need a drink, to use the bathroom during the night?" asks Scott. "Maybe you saw or heard something that seemed like nothing at the time?"

They all shake their heads, a dripping silence, and the detectives wait.

"I didn't get up until I heard all the commotion," his mother adds, the tiniest of wobbles in her voice. "Which was, you know, the emergency vehicles arriving. But that was midnight. And we had no idea what happened. I didn't find out until I talked to Cara March this morning."

The detectives stand. Henry notices Perkins place his cookie, only half eaten, onto a napkin. They thank the Lawson family and hand out cards, asking them to call if any of them thinks of anything that might be useful. They're rushing, and Henry can tell that, for now, he has framed himself as an innocent bystander, miles away from suspect.

The front door closes behind the detectives, and his mother turns to face him. And there's fear in her eyes, there's understanding—that which perhaps only a mother can have—and it doesn't bother Henry as much as it should. And he knows he should not be smiling, but he can't help it. She did well, his mother. She did exactly what she was supposed to do.

55

Another murder in Hawthorne Heights. Not in Mary's house this time, but across the street. The sight of those vehicles, their metal heft and flashing lights, and the people who departed them so quickly, so urgently and importantly, all of it took Mary back to that night nearly two decades ago.

Everyone is horrified that such a violent and gruesome death has happened so close to home, so near the place where they sleep and eat their meals, where they taught their children to ride a bike, where they bathed them after, rinsing scraped knees in sudsy water. But they are also relieved that it wasn't in their home, that it wasn't them. They're scared, yes, but not as much as they could be. Mary knows this better than most, and she shares these feelings this time. There is no blood on her hands. No blood in her house.

It's Sunday afternoon, and Mary has visitors. She never has visitors on a Sunday afternoon. She never has visitors.

"I'm very sorry for her," Mary tells the detectives who sit at her kitchen table. "It's such an awful thing. It's so shocking."

"Yes, it is," says the male detective. Mary has already forgotten his name. It was a generic name, and he's a generic-looking man. The woman detective is not. She's elegant and memorable, and she's watching Mary with cool eyes that, Mary senses, can convey a variety of emotions—whatever she chooses. And that she has chosen this expression of frosty distance, of interested suspicion, makes Mary very uncomfortable.

"Is she okay?" Mary asks. "His wife?"

The detectives exchange a glance, their eyes trailing sideways, finding each other's.

"I'm sorry," Mary says quickly. "Of course she isn't okay. Her husband was killed last night—that was a silly thing to say."

It was a strange thing to say. They're expecting her to be focused on her fear—a killer in the neighborhood, suspicious circumstances. But she's more interested in the people orbiting the man who died and what the living will have to face next. How can she not be, after what she went through?

She went back to bed after she saw the emergency vehicles outside, but she didn't sleep. She searched for news alerts with the name of her street, but nothing came up. Obviously. It was too early. But she'd continued to search, hoping that it was something insignificant—a petty break-in, a misunderstanding. Not murder. Surely not another murder. Finally, early this afternoon, there was something.

> Man found dead in his backyard in Hawthorne Heights neighborhood. Suspicious circumstances. Police are asking anyone with information to come forward. An anonymous tip line has been set up.

Neither the manner of death nor the man's name were listed in the article, but Mary could picture him, her neighbor. He had thick, dark hair, a trim build. She thought he was in his mid-thirties, born a few years before her son, perhaps. So much life left to live.

"And you don't have anyone in custody yet? No one saw who

did it?" And she suddenly does feel fearful, exposed, the way she's supposed to. Murder—so unfamiliar this time; distant yet still so close.

"Not yet."

Is Mary imagining it, the way the detectives' eyes flick toward the basement door?

"Were you home last night, Mrs. Irvin?" Detective Scott asks with a sense of finality. They're here to ask questions, not answer them.

"I was home all evening, and all night. The vehicles woke me up, but I stayed inside. It seemed like something awful had happened, but I didn't want to go out and interfere."

She saw them from her bedroom window—the neighbors in their pajamas and loungewear, creeping closer with gleeful horror.

"And were you acquainted with your neighbors, Ben and Kate Harvey?"

"I'm afraid not," Mary admits. "They only moved in, what, a few months ago? I saw them going out for walks on occasion. I think I noticed the woman planting flowers once. But I didn't stop by to introduce myself. Maybe that wasn't neighborly of me. But I really do keep to myself."

The detectives nod as though they don't doubt this.

Mary's hermetic existence makes perfect sense. Who would want to be neighborly with her, Mary Irvin? Who would ever ask her to bring in their mail or come by to feed their cat? Why does she still live here? You'd think she'd have moved out a long time ago, considering what happened in this house.

"What about your son, Mrs. Irvin?"

Perkins. The name comes to her as she stares at the man, at the shining patch of scalp on the top of his head.

"Was your son home at the time?"

Detective Perkins's tone is light and pleased. He wants Mary to understand that he knows. He knows about Owen. He knows what Owen did.

And how strange it is? How wonderful, in some ways, how awful, in others, to have this man, this detective, mention Owen? To make him real to her again, to prove that others know that he still exists.

How's your son? How's Owen? her colleagues used to ask her politely when they passed in the teachers' lounge at the school. It's been so long since she's heard his name aloud. It's been so long since she's seen him.

"Of course he was home," Mary tells the detective. "He was asleep, like I was."

"We'll have to talk to him, too," the detective continues. "You know that, don't you?"

Mary does.

"He's here, correct? He's supposed to be here, with you."

As though she does not know this—the conditions of his parole.

"He's here," Mary says softly. It's true, but it's also not. "He stays in the basement."

"Is he home?" asks Detective Scott. She's already rising, legs half bent as she pushes herself up.

"I believe so," says Mary, and the detective towers over her. "But you should know—he might not speak with you."

"He'll have to," says Detective Perkins. "Under the circumstances, he'll have to speak with us. We're interviewing everyone in the neighborhood. No one is exempt. And especially not him, considering his...history."

His vehemence is aggressive, and Mary feels herself flinch, just as she notices that Detective Scott is studying her silently, expression curious.

"What are you trying to say, Mrs. Irvin?" Detective Scott drops back onto her chair, as though she knows already that Mary's explanation won't be a simple one.

"It's not that he wouldn't want to help with the investigation," says Mary, and she hopes this conveys her confidence that her son did not kill that man. He had nothing to do with it. "It's that he doesn't speak at all. Not anymore."

"He doesn't speak?" Perkins asks, derisive. "That wasn't indicated anywhere in his case history."

"Well, I can't speak to what his parole officer has and hasn't put in her reports," says Mary, hoping that she isn't getting that young and lithe woman, with her perfunctory visits and gentle but hurried manner, into trouble. "But it started when he got home. He was sixteen when he was incarcerated in the adult facility. Can you imagine what he went through in there, being that young?" She closes her eyes. She can't imagine it—literally, cannot let herself do it. If she does, she won't be able to go on. "When his parole was granted, I picked him up to bring him back home. I was so relieved that he was out. I could keep him safe. But it was too late. He wouldn't speak. He wouldn't say a word."

"I—what do you mean? Has there been a diagnosis?" asks Detective Scott.

"How could there be? He won't leave. I brought him home, and he went down into the basement. He lives in the bedroom down there. I leave meals and other things he might need—toilet paper, cleaning supplies, shampoo, that sort of thing—on the stairs for him. Sometimes he comes up here to take other things that he needs. But not when I'm around. And he doesn't speak to me. He refuses to speak to anyone."

There's a silence, heavy and judgmental.

"That's...unexpected, Mrs. Irvin," says Detective Scott at last.

"Yes, well, it was for me, too. I've called doctors and I've done my own research. But it's clear to me that Owen doesn't want to deal with any of that. He just wants to be left alone for now. Maybe he needs to process everything that's happened. He's been through enough. I've decided to let him be for a while. I think he'll talk when he's ready. My sweet boy. What he's been through." Mary shakes her head tightly. She presses her lips together, as though she's holding her anger inside, letting it turn her lips white, deepening the lines that feather away from her mouth.

"Your 'sweet boy' is thirty-three years old, Mrs. Irvin. He's a murderer."

Mary turns to her. She expected such words from the male detective. Not her. Scott holds her gaze. She doesn't back down. Mary feels betrayed.

"You make it sound so simple, Detective. It's anything but."

Scott ignores her. "We'll need to speak to him. Now. Would you like to ask him to come up here or go down and let him know that we're coming?"

Mary suspects she's supposed to be grateful that the detective is at least offering her that much. But all she feels is betrayal. Of this detective, and of all the others before her. Of every cog in this massive and crushing wheel of a system that has so completely failed her child.

"I'll go down," Mary says. "I'll let him know what's going on."

There's motive, weight, behind each word. She's indicating to them now that Owen has no idea what's going on. Because he had nothing to do with that man's death.

She stands, and she moves away from the table. Her heart is in her throat because she has wanted to have a real and unselfish reason to intrude into her son's space, to see him, to come close, for so long, and now she has one, but it's possibly the worst reason she could have imagined. A murder, a stabbing, police here to see him.

Mary opens the door leading to the basement.

"Owen," she calls into the darkness. "I have to come down." She wants to give him a warning, but her voice is weak and it trembles. "I'm sorry," she adds because she is so sorry, for absolutely everything.

She takes a step forward, onto the top stair, the one where she has left meals and notes, gifts and clothes, over the last few years, all of it silently accepted. But nothing ever offered in return.

Mary descends the stairs slowly, somehow hopeless yet brimming with hope. She moves toward the darkness, toward the increasingly musty smell, toward the sound of nothing at all, toward her son.

56

The detectives have been gone for hours, or perhaps minutes, perhaps days. Kate still has not eaten and is sitting on the floor of the walk-in closet she and Ben used to share, legs bent and splayed to the side. Ben's dirty dress shirt is on her lap, and she is admittedly doing very poorly and probably, as the detectives suggested, should not be alone.

She lifts the shirt to her face and smells the collar, which holds the scent of Ben's aftershave, then the body of the shirt, which smells like his deodorant and so faintly of his sweat, and she will hold this shirt forever. She will sit here forever, pressing this shirt against her skin and inhaling, remembering what he looked like when he walked in the door on Friday evening wearing it.

"Hey," she said to him, and he dropped his backpack onto the floor and said it back. Then they ordered Thai food for delivery and watched three episodes of their latest docuseries on Max. If Kate had known that was the last night she'd have with her husband, she would have done things differently.

There was the clichéd suggestion that a person should live every day as though it was her last. But such a suggestion ignores life's necessary mundanities and unavoidable irritations. It ignores the fact that sometimes, one's husband will seem insufferable. Their stilted Friday night together, their argument on Saturday afternoon—that was marriage. And theirs was a good one, overall.

Not without cracks, but something solid, something on which she could lean.

Not anymore. Ben is dead. All that remains are memories and things. And the fact that if Kate had agreed to go down to DC for dinner with their friends, like Ben had wanted, maybe he would still be here.

Kate hears something then, and fear slices through her and pools in her gut. But it's nothing being shattered, nor is it the sharp knocks of the detectives at her front door. The sound is tinny, dull, metronomic—just her phone, vibrating, spinning itself dizzy on whatever surface she left it resting on. She doesn't know who's calling, and she doesn't care. There's no one she wants to talk to.

After the police left her house, they didn't climb into a sedan and drive away. They walked along the sidewalk, toward the house to the right of Kate's. Later, she noticed them crossing the street. She noticed other officers, uniformed, departing marked vehicles. She assumes they're still here, in her neighborhood.

She wonders whether they have interviewed Henry yet—the strange man across the street. She thinks of the way he so often appeared when she was leaving for a walk. On Friday, he was there when she returned, with an icy drink in his hand. She could tell that he thought it was a kind gesture. And that he was so oblivious to how frightening it was, how it made him seem like a hunter, a watcher, makes her wonder if he's not just a strange young man who loves to read, who still lives with his parents, who may not have a job, who never did tell her whether he does. He may be something far more dangerous. Something she should have raised with the police.

She'll do it. Next time they come, she'll tell them about him. She should have told them last night, his unsettling and persistent approach so proximate to Ben's death, but she isn't thinking clearly.

Nor has she told them about her manuscript. Her manuscript about a wife who murders her husband.

But Troy wasn't stabbed. And it's fiction. She wants to scream this at no one. At the same time, she doesn't want to think about her manuscript ever again. Despite everything, she feels a tiny cooling sense of relief, understanding that now she will scrap it. She will never finish that book. How could she, after what's happened? It has betrayed her, her book. Her own words. It was supposed to be fiction. Now look what she's done.

Kate likes it in the closet. It's windowless and mostly dark, light off, only a faint glow trickling in from the windows in the bathroom. Not too much, because the sky outside is still gray, rain still falling. Kate can hear it pelting the skylight in her bathroom.

She decides to put on Ben's shirt. It's silky against her bare forearms. She lowers herself down to the hard floor, grabbing a sweater, hers, that had fallen from a shelf, to tuck beneath her head. She buries her feet into a sweatshirt, Ben's, then curls her knees into her chest. She closes her eyes, and although she knows that she should be scared and alert and prepared, she feels safe. Safer than she has since the moment she discovered Ben on their patio, the seeping wounds in his chest. She doesn't know that after the detectives left, she failed to lock her front door. She doesn't know that, on Monday morning, this is how Henry will find her.

57

Mary hasn't seen her son since the day she picked him up from prison. That was three years ago. And it was the last day she spoke to him.

Rather, it was the last day he spoke to her. As she told the detectives, she continued to try for months after he got home.

"I can't talk about any of it," Owen told her once he was buckled into the front passenger seat of her aging Civic and the distance between him and the prison where he'd been for the past fifteen years slowly grew. "I'll stay in the basement. I need to be alone."

The comfort she'd felt because he was out of there, that detention center, had turned cooler as he'd failed to reply to her follow-up questions: *What do you mean, you'll stay in the basement? Do you want to move a bed down there? How will you eat?*

She didn't need his answers to those questions. But she did need something. His touch. His voice. Evidence that he was okay.

He wasn't okay. But they figured it out.

At first, Mary would knock on the basement door, then call down to her son. She went down to tell him about doctor's appointments she'd scheduled. On several occasions, she'd grown frustrated. She'd lost her temper and shouted at him. Other times, she cried. It didn't matter what she did; Owen ignored her. Or he shut himself in the bathroom and stayed there until she was gone.

They'd fallen into a bizarre and dysfunctional rhythm. Mary made meals for him and bought him the things he would need, leaving them on the stairs. She bought sketchbooks and colored pencils, drawing charcoal and watercolors with soft bristled brushes. She assumes he's been using these things, but she hasn't had the opportunity to see anything he's created.

A rhythm. Silent and strange, but Mary hoped that she was building trust with her son, that he would speak to her again soon. But money was growing tight. The house needed a new roof. The furnace and air-conditioning systems were nearing the end of their life expectancies. The hot-water heater acted up sometimes. Ed's savings were gone. Mary's pension from her years working as a public-school teacher wasn't enough to pay their living expenses and maintain the house. Mary knew she'd allowed things to fall into disrepair. She knew the gardens were overgrown, the branches of the cherry tree in the front yard bowed low to graze the ground, the shutters needed painting. The neighbors didn't like the disarray. They didn't like her. It was time to go.

She wrote a note to Owen explaining that she had to sell the house. She'd found an apartment they could rent, which would be easier. No upkeep, the landlord would take care of everything. It had a balcony and two bedrooms. He would come with her, of course. She would be cleaning out the house, getting it ready for photos and listing. She would leave the basement for last. They could move into the apartment before the house went on the market so that they didn't have to deal with people coming in.

She left the note on the top step with Owen's dinner one night. In the morning, his empty plate was there, and the note was gone. But she never got a reply.

Now her son is sitting at the elderly desk across the room. The screen of the tired, old desktop computer is alight. Mary had moved it down here when it became too slow, and she bought herself a new laptop from Costco. Perhaps Owen had found a way to clean up the computer, to suit his needs.

"I'm sorry, Owen," Mary says again, voice wobbling.

The room smells musty. It needs to be dusted and vacuumed. Mary wonders whether Owen has been cleaning the bathroom with the spray and brush she left for him.

Over the years, the basement became a place for their rejected furniture and things. They filled it slowly, as Ed approved replacements in the other parts of the house. The green leather sectional, worn in places, stretches across the room like a parenthesis, several rumpled pillows and blankets on top. Across from the sofa is a television that probably doesn't work, and the wheeled office chair, cracked black leather, is pressed against the desk. That is where her son sits, back still to her and tight with tension. His hair is long, gathered into a bun at the base of his skull. Her heart aches.

"There are two detectives here," Mary continues. "They need to speak to you."

Owen turns.

Her sweet boy. Pure gold. She hasn't seen his face in 1,092 days.

His skin is more lined than she'd remembered, around his eyes, across his forehead, and he has a dark beard. Razors. She's forgotten to buy him razors. He must be trimming it with something he found, because it's not long enough that he's been growing it out for years.

She feels tears coursing down her cheeks. "I'm sorry," she tells him again as she brushes them away.

He doesn't reply.

"They want to speak to you. A man across the street, he was

stabbed in his backyard last night." She studies Owen's face for something—anything—but he's looking at his lap.

Then he nods once. He knows. He must have heard the vehicles and commotion, too. He probably found the same article she did. Mary tells herself that must be it. That is how he knows. That's all.

"I have to let them come down," she says. "I don't have a choice."

She sounds defensive. Owen's gaze remains fixed on his thighs. His jeans are worn at the knees, and they seem too tight.

"I'll get them," she continues. "Sorry." She's saying it too much, but she can't say it enough. She should have left Ed. She thought staying was safer for Owen. She thought she could protect him that way. If she'd left, her son might have a job and a life. He might be married. Maybe he would even be a father himself, one who was nothing like Ed. She would see him at Christmas and for Mother's Day, the days other women saw their adult sons. When she held him, she would feel so small and she would remember when he fit perfectly into the crook of her arm. She would remember the way his scalp smelled and the petal softness of the backs of his hands. How she would stroke the pad of fat there as he drifted off, the quiet stillness in the perfection of his face as sleep took hold.

Instead, this.

Mary turns and goes back upstairs. The detectives are standing near the open doorway. They were listening. Of course they were listening. Perkins's arms are crossed, and Scott is studying something on the screen of her cell phone.

"Go ahead," Mary says icily. She wants it to be clear that her permission is not quite the same as consent.

Scott nods and slides her phone into the pocket of her blazer, which gapes open enough that Mary can see the gun on her belt. They disappear through the door, down the stairs.

The entire time the detectives are in the basement with her son, Mary paces. She knows they can hear her footsteps, the creak of the floors. She knows that she's revealing her nerves to them, but she can't stop moving. She listens to the hum of their voices, and she strains for the sound of her son's, but she doesn't hear him.

It's only ten minutes later, and their footsteps are heavy on the stairs again. Heavy with defeat and irritation.

"He will have to talk to us," Perkins says as he steps into the kitchen, eyes meeting Mary's, anger glaring.

Mary simply shrugs. She isn't sure what this man wants her to do. If she could get her son to speak, she would. Doesn't he understand that?

"We can bring him into the station," Perkins continues. "Put him in an interview room. Maybe the same one that they used the night he stabbed his dad."

Detective Scott places a palm on her partner's back.

"We'll be back," she tells Mary. She is calmer, more controlled, and this neatness, this precision and patience, worries Mary more than Perkins's palpable frustration.

The detectives leave. For now. But they will be back, just as they said. Although they didn't say when. This, Mary understands, was by design. They don't want her to know when, only that she should expect them, and that she should be scared.

58

The wife isn't answering the door, and Henry is concerned.

Any normal person would have gone to stay elsewhere under these circumstances. Who would remain in the house where her husband was murdered? Only a wife who wasn't terribly sad about the murder. A wife who hadn't been happy. Like her. And he saw her open the door to the detectives yesterday. He hasn't seen her leave since. He knows she's still here.

He rings the doorbell again, jamming his finger into the plastic button, which is brittle, a crack down the middle. His ear is pressed close to the door, and he hears nothing. It must be broken.

So maybe she's deep within the house and she cannot hear even his persistent knock. Maybe she's asleep, covers shielding her face. Maybe she's in the shower, water beading on her smooth skin, dripping from her hair, trailing down, down, down.

Henry reaches for the doorknob, twists his hand ever so gently. The door isn't locked.

He pushes it open, calling out, "Hello? Kate, it's me." If she can hear him, if she's even here, she would have no idea who "me" is, and she wouldn't recognize his voice, but he'd wanted to say it anyway. He wanted to know how those words would taste. *Kate, it's me*; the intimacy of them.

The house is too warm, and there's both an odor and a feel of dampness, but he closes the door behind him. Henry assumes that

Kate isn't in the kitchen or anywhere else on the first floor of the house. If she was, there would have been some reaction to his call. Still he hears nothing, so he takes his time, moving through the rooms.

The stairs are slick, hardwood, and Henry doesn't try to silence his steps.

"Kate," he calls out again from the landing, ready for her to know that he's here. "Are you home?"

Nothing.

The house is similar to his own, lacking his mother's dated touch of floral wallpaper trim, but with the same floor plan. And, of course, he's been inside before. Henry turns toward the primary bedroom, and while he can't yet see her, he senses that she's near. He takes the last few steps quickly, bursting into the room. But it's empty, and he's doubting everything until he hears a sharp intake of breath.

He looks to the bathroom.

"Are you here?" he calls out authoritatively. "Are you hurt?" He abandons his implication of closeness, instead behaving like the police might if they were looking for the wife, expecting her to be here, and she'd failed to answer the door.

In response to this call, finally, there is something. A terrified something—not quite a scream but holding the same level of fear that a scream does.

Henry is in the bathroom, then the closet, in only a second. The wife is there, sitting on the floor, face red and sleep creased, eyes hideously swollen, hair matted.

"What are you doing here?" she asks. She leans away from him, clutching her shirt around her chest as though he'd walked in on her naked, but she appears to be wearing quite a bit of clothing, like a homeless woman draped in everything she owns, despite the damp heat of the house.

He feels unexpectedly angry with her. She looks awful. She looks like a mess.

"Your front door was open," he lies. "I came by to express my condolences and saw that it wasn't shut all the way. I thought something was wrong." Something is wrong, clearly. She looks like she's been sleeping on this closet floor for days.

"It—what?" she asks. "So you just came in instead of calling the police?"

"What if you were hurt in here? Your husband was just killed. I didn't know how much time there was."

He's impressed by his quick thinking, although he does wonder whether she will report what he said about the door to the police. He doesn't want to be questioned about that, about coming to visit her.

"Can I...help you with something?" he asks quickly, trying to distract her. "Do you need me to get you some water? Or something to eat?"

Kate shakes her head and begins to climb to a standing position. She's moving stiffly, and the shirt, a white button-down, hangs to her knees, and Henry sees that it's not hers at all, but one of her dead husband's, and he does not like this.

"Please leave my house," she says, backing farther away.

Henry blinks at her, extends his offerings. "I brought you this," he says. The gift box he'd found in his parents' pantry—squares of chocolate and nut brittle, still wrapped in plastic, likely a holiday present his father had received as work. He must have brought it home and his mother hid it, for herself or simply so that his father wouldn't eat it. She was always worrying about her husband's weight. And that she kept it in the house, that she didn't dispose of it, despite that it's rife with nuts, shows Henry what sort of mother she is.

And on top of the box, a flower, clipped from his mother's front garden. Petals red and vibrant, not yet wilting.

The wife shakes her head sharply, and the way she's looking at the flower, at the box, as though they're weapons, unsettles him.

"Please," he says. "Take it. You'll be doing me a favor. I'm deathly allergic to nuts, so I really can't keep it."

He takes a step toward her, and she flinches. "*No*," she says. "Please, no."

Henry wants to insist again. He hesitates, opens his mouth.

"Please, just go," she says again, firmer, wild.

He stares, uncomprehending. After all that he's done for her? And he's here now with kindness, with gifts.

"You make me uncomfortable." She's almost shouting now. She's snapped, her fear uninhibited. "You are making me very uncomfortable." Each word a bite, crisp.

"I didn't do anything," Henry says, stunned. By her venom, by her terror. Her suspicion is palpable, and he understands that he must deflect. "It was the murderer, who lives in the house next to mine. It wasn't me."

He expects her to soften, to ask him for more details—to thank him. But the terror doesn't drain from her face.

"I didn't say it was," she says, so soft, and a touch bewildered, and he realized that he misread her suspicion, that he said too much.

She's pressed against the rack of clothes behind her now, as though she can disappear herself within them. "Please go," she says again. "You can't just let yourself into someone's house. Go and don't come back, or I will call the police. I swear."

He stares at her for another beat. He's nearly certain that she doesn't have her phone on her, that it's not concealed within the folds of her dead husband's shirt. But she could get to it later, and she could tell them that he refused to leave her house.

He doesn't want that. He doesn't want her to tell them about this at all. So, although his anger is roiling, a force that cannot be ignored, he goes. Back down the stairs, dropping the gift box, the flower onto the floor in the foyer because he can't bear to leave the house with them, then through the front door, and she's ruined it. She's ruined everything.

59

Henry is gone. Every door and window is locked—Kate checked after she heard the front door click closed behind him. The things he'd brought her—the box of gourmet treats, the flower—were lying on the ground, near the base of the stairs. The flower looked like it had been hastily cut from someone's garden. Not Kate's own—she hadn't managed to keep hers alive.

Kate left them there, on the floor. Now her hands tremble as she opens her laptop.

She can't shake the image of him there, in the doorway of her closet. *I didn't do anything.* Words that could have so many different meanings. But in the context of him inside her home, uninvited, of Ben's killing, they take on an alarmingly suspicious glow.

But she'll worry about that later—very soon. Now she's more focused on what Henry said next: *It was the murderer, who lives in the house next to mine.*

When the screen blinks to life, she ignores her manuscript, the seemingly benign file saved on her desktop. Instead, she opens her browser.

She types *murder* and *Hawthorne Heights* and adds *Maryland*, in case there are other neighborhoods in the world that share the same name and propensity for murder as hers.

Results flood the screen. Kate clicks on the first. She's still wearing Ben's shirt, and she shouldn't be—it's making her feel weaker, more disastrous. She should be taking a shower, washing her hair, calling her mom and her friends, checking her phone—where is her phone?—forcing herself to eat something. But first, this. For now, all she can do is read.

> In the sleepy neighborhood of Hawthorne Heights, Edward Irvin, age forty-five, died from injuries related to multiple stab wounds on Thursday night.
>
> Edward's wife, Mary Irvin, confessed to the murder but her confession was proven to be falsely made.

Kate's eyes volley across the screen, her fingertips scroll. She backs out of that article, opens another. She reads furiously, the way she used to swiftly skim pages of financial data, before taking a breath, looking more closely, digging deeper.

It was not Mary Irvin who, Kate calculates, is now sixty-one years old, who killed her husband Edward. It was Edward and Mary's son. His name was shielded in the earlier articles. He was simply referred to as "the son of the deceased, age 15." In later articles, after, Kate gathers, it was decided that the boy would be charged and tried as an adult, his name was revealed. Owen Irvin, who pled guilty to second-degree murder and was sentenced to twenty years in prison with the possibility of parole. After fifteen years, he was paroled. She read that part in the briefest of follow-up articles. Owen was believed to be released into the custody of his mother, who attended his parole hearings and expressed a willingness to take him in.

Kate's vision blurs. She snaps her laptop closed.

The bedroom Kate uses as an office overlooks the front yard, the street, the other houses beyond. She looks to Henry's house, then to the one to the left. She has seen the woman who lives there. She has seen her in plain colored T-shirts and long khaki shorts, carrying boxes and dragging trash cans to the curb, extra weight around her middle, graying blond hair brushing her shoulders. She has waved to her. The mother of a murderer.

Kate has wondered in passing whether she lives in that big house all alone. Soon, people will think the same of Kate.

And next to the mother and the murderer, Henry.

There is decidedly something off about him. At the same time, there's this obliviousness, a harmlessness—he makes her think of a washed-up magician who performs at kids' birthday parties and refers to the children as "fuckers" and "dickheads" as soon as he's in his car, heading back home.

She assumes Henry was lying to her. Her front door was not open. Unlocked—that, she could believe. She might have failed to lock it after the detectives left on Sunday. Even in the face of Ben's murder, old habits, distraction making her careless, and perhaps there's a part of her that would leave it unlocked on purpose. *Come in, finish the job.* There's a part of her that doesn't care what happens to her now.

But that the door was not even closed? That doesn't make sense.

Unless someone had opened it. Someone had been inside, looking for her.

Her suspicion of Henry suddenly shifting.

Owen Irvin.

Kate has never seen him. She tries to recall a man, about her age, outside the house across the street. But she can't.

Her phone. Kate needs to find her phone.

She moves gingerly through the house, still stiff from her night on the floor. Ben's dress shirt grazes her bare knees.

Her phone is resting on an end table in the living room, and she has dozens of missed calls, texts. She scrolls through them, messages from the police, from before their visit; from her friends; from Ben's best friend, Ethan, and his wife, Rosie. One from Chris, Ben's brother, which surprises Kate. She doesn't open any of them. There's nothing from her mother, so at least she hasn't heard the news. Kate will have to tell her soon. She will have to arrange a service—who else would do it? She will have to notify people and prepare a eulogy. *If we just could have had a baby*, she will say, *this wouldn't have happened*. She feels this in her chest, within the depths of her bones. If they'd had a baby, Ben wouldn't have been sitting out on that patio by himself. They would have been in their bedroom, asleep, the baby in its bassinet. Or perhaps they would have gone to dinner downtown like Ben had wanted, a rare night out, the nanny staying over to give them a break.

There's one text from a number Kate doesn't recognize. She opens it and discovers that it's from Ben's boss, expressing his condolences and letting her know that someone will come by to pick up Ben's laptop so that she doesn't have to worry about that. There's a startling coldness to the message, beneath the concern. Ben's work laptop hasn't been anywhere near her list of worries since her husband was murdered.

She doesn't want someone from Ben's work, someone she met at the last holiday party but whose name she's forgotten, to come to her house, to hug her, to bring her flowers that will smell like death. She'll ask the police if they will take the laptop.

Ben's backpack is still resting on the floor in the corner of the kitchen. He dropped it there on Friday evening and hadn't moved it since. Occasionally, he would work for a few hours on Saturdays, but he didn't on the day he died.

She unzips it, confirming that the laptop is still inside. She will leave it in the coat closet by the front door, out of sight, ready to be retrieved by whoever is willing to take it. But first, she flips through its contents, just to be certain there's nothing personal she might need. There's a notebook, a folder, pens littering the bottom of the bag, a case with a pair of earbuds. Kate leaves everything in there. She doesn't want it. She pauses, then, on a page that lacks the plain black print, the severity, of Ben's work-related things. It's glossy and vibrant and wedged behind the notebook, and she slides it out, the photo she'd found on her phone and printed last month. Her and Ben, the way he was looking at her, and it winds her, just as it had when she first saw it.

The morning she printed this picture, Ben had bent over the bed to kiss her hair before he left for work, and when he was gone, she felt hollow. Her empty day stretching ahead of her—its peacefulness, its possibility, so auspicious. Yet it felt too quiet, too vacant, too different from the way her days used to be, too similar to all the preceding unproductive days. It was neither a testing day nor a trying day. She didn't know what to write. She didn't know what to do.

She heard the garage door creak closed, and she couldn't go back to sleep.

Her aging cell phone was plugged into its charger on the nightstand beside her. She flipped through her screens of apps aimlessly, then opened her photo library and scrolled backward. She scrolled back nearly ten years, to when she and Ben first started dating. He wasn't in many of her pictures, and neither was she. Apparently, she was quite fond of taking photos of her meals and take-out coffee back then, foam hearts atop lattes. But there were a few of Ben, of Kate, of the two of them together. His hair was a little fuller, and hers was longer. Their eyes were brighter, faces thinner. This was before they were so worn, so broken down by the long hours they'd put into building their careers.

One picture stopped her. It was a candid shot of Kate and Ben at a bar. It must have been taken by a friend of Kate's, who'd sent it to her. Her hair was gathered into a low ponytail—she often wore it that way in her early twenties—and her shoulders were exposed, a black top tied at the base of her neck, skin golden. Her hands were up, slightly blurred. She was animated, speaking, gesturing. Beside her was Ben. He was smiling faintly, watching her and only her.

The look on his face—the very image of love, of worship. It made Kate ache. She touched her fingers to the screen, pinching, zooming in on her face, then on Ben's, and she believed that if she'd only had a quick glance at this image, a flash, then it was gone, she might not have recognized that it was of them.

She emailed the picture to herself, then slunk from the bed and into her office. She opened her laptop, then the photo, and she printed it, so large that it took up the entire eight-by-eleven paper. The page was damp and heavy with ink, and she carried it downstairs. She placed it on the kitchen table, in front of the chair where Ben always sat.

By the time Ben finally got home, it was after seven. Kate's laptop was shut, resting on the kitchen island, and dinner had been ready for a while. She'd been trying to keep it warm.

"Hey," he said as he stepped into the kitchen. He dropped his backpack onto a chair, heavily, but his expression brightened at the sight of her. "How was your day?"

"Look," she said, sliding the picture from the table, the paper fluttering as she stepped toward him. "Look at us," she said. "Look what I found."

He removed the still-flapping page from her fingers and looked at it, smile spreading until it had devoured his face.

"Weren't we so young and beautiful?" she asked as they stared at their own faces together.

Ben put the picture down, still grinning as he gathered her into his arms. "We still are, Kate," he said, his lips against her neck. "We still are."

Then they'd eaten dinner and talked about their days—his so busy, hers so not—and she'd forgotten about the picture, had lost track of it. Apparently, Ben hadn't. He'd put it in his work bag, something to look at while he was sliding his laptop out.

Now Kate smooths the picture flat, pressing her finger into Ben's cheek.

She's always hated decorating the house, unfurling area rugs, hanging photos and curtains, but in the living room, she'd carefully displayed a string of their wedding photos along the mantel. They married in Hawaii, just the two of them, feet in white sand, her in an eyelet sundress and Ben in a pale-blue polo and khaki shorts. She knows it will hurt; she wants to see them anyway. She wants more evidence of what they'd been.

But when she steps into the room and her eyes fall to the blocky white frames, she sees that the photos are gone. The frames are empty. Every last one.

60

One of Mary's only remaining joys in this, the sixty-second year of her life, is freshly baked cheddar-and-herb bread. On Saturday mornings, she buys it at the farmers' market held in the parking lot of the local library, before the library opens. It's only a seven-minute drive away, but people there don't think of her as the woman who raised a murderer. There, she is simply Mary, a regular.

She went this past Saturday, with a faded Orioles cap on her head. She knows that the bread contributes to the excess fat around her hips and middle, and that does bother her, but not enough to stop eating it.

She'd sliced the heel off the loaf when she got home, ate it at room temperature with cold butter. After that, she hasn't had any more. Her appetite died with the man across the street.

But now, again, she feels the beginnings of hunger burgeoning like spring's first blooms. She'll use the bread for sandwiches. One for herself, and one for her son. Owen, who now has a full beard and ponytail. In spite of everything, she finds herself smiling, thinking of him. Of his face. Of how close she'd been.

Until she considers that he still didn't speak to her, that he barely acknowledged her presence at all, and she thinks of the reason she went into the basement in the first place and understands that there has been no progress. That she has no reason to smile.

Her sweet boy. The detectives can't comprehend how she can still think of him this way. But they aren't mothers; they aren't his mother. Besides, what he did? It was for her.

Mary retrieves her supplies: the long wooden cutting board, the bread, turkey, lettuce, and cheese from the fridge. She moves to the knife block to get the bread knife, but it isn't there, still in the dishwasher from when she used it on Saturday morning. Her second choice of knife for cutting bread, long and slightly serrated, is also gone, which gives her pause. She can't recall using that one recently.

She checks the drying rack, the dishwasher. She checks the other slots in the knife block again, in case there are two knives in one slot. She's done that before. Not this time. She checks the utensil drawer, then all the other drawers. And if a man had not just been stabbed to death in the backyard of the house across the street, Mary would think nothing of the missing knife. She would assume that it had been misplaced, and that it would turn up eventually, when she wasn't looking for it, when she was looking for something else.

The missing knife is nothing. It must be nothing. But it's also, possibly, not nothing. It could be a problem. And the detectives could be back at any time. They could be on their way here right now, for all Mary knows. She doesn't have much time to think.

Owen will be getting hungry soon, wondering about lunch. But she must do this. She must do it now.

There's a box in the living room. She's been gradually filling it with items for donation. She's finished with the second floor of the house—Owen's old bedroom being the most difficult for her—and has been working through the first. Her appointment with the Realtor is next week. She wonders whether he will cancel, tell her they should wait a bit longer to list the house, what with the murder in the backyard of the house across the street, no arrest made yet. Mary wouldn't mind delaying the sale if money wasn't so tight.

She removes the knife block from the kitchen counter and places it in the box. She rearranges the contents a little so that the knives are concealed. She grabs a throw blanket from the sofa nearby, folds it haphazardly, and places it on top. She wasn't actually planning to get rid of that blanket, but she has others and she's desperate to finish this task before she has a chance to think too much and thinks herself out of it. Or thinks herself into doing something else.

Mary seals the box with a strip of tape and scrawls "Household goods" across the top flap in black Sharpie. She struggles getting the box outside and into her car, but somehow she manages. They may write that on her tombstone, in fact. *Mary Irvin: Somehow she managed.*

Usually, Mary would wait until she had at least a few boxes before making a run to Goodwill or setting up a collection at the curb, but she can't afford to do that now. So she takes the single box and she gives it away, and when she's back in her car, engine turning over, she can finally breathe. It's not until she's careening onto the highway that she remembers the bread knife still in her dishwasher. The block she had donated was missing two. She hopes that doesn't matter.

In Target, Mary selects a new block of knives. Her old block had eighteen; this one has only four. But does she really need more than four? Besides, she still has the bread knife, at home in her dishwasher, and she would rather have four of decent quality than a huge set of cheap ones. The larger sets are unjustifiably expensive.

The line for the self-checkout registers is longer than the lines for the two open cashiers, so Mary opts for the human, desperate to get home. She has a strange sense that the detectives will be there waiting for her, and they'll ask her where she was. She's terrified that if they do, she'll tell the truth.

"This is a nice set," says the cashier conversationally as she swipes it across the scanner. "I bought this same one for my boyfriend's sister when she got married last year, and she loves it."

Well, she wouldn't tell you if she hated it, would she? Mary thinks irritably, smiling tightly. She also has quite a strong opinion that a person over the age of forty shouldn't be using the word *boyfriend* to describe her significant other.

She's being cruel—only within her mind, but she feels shame stinging the back of her neck, her irritability evincing her fear.

"Perfect," she says instead of unleashing her misplaced vitriol. "I'm glad to hear I made a good choice."

She accepts the offer for a bag, needing it more for concealment than portability, and insists that she does not need a receipt, gift or otherwise.

Her heart hammers persistently against her rib cage the entire drive home. But for no imminent reason, because there's no police car in her driveway, nor parked along the street. They aren't here, and Mary did it. The knives are gone, and it's done. *Her cover-up*, she thinks. But that's absurd. It wasn't. It couldn't be. It was overkill. A mother's irrational melodrama. Because Owen has done nothing wrong. Not this time. And not when he killed Ed. And no one will ever convince Mary Irvin, who has somehow managed, otherwise.

61

The meeting with the detectives took longer than he expected.

Henry parks his car at the curb and climbs out. He beeps it locked, and he spares the wife's house only the briefest glance. He thinks of her in there, her mess, her grief. Her rejection of him the previous morning. The sting of her repudiation, after everything he did for her. The unfairness of it.

Still, he gave her a day. He waited for her to soften, to turn to him, to understand that he'd do anything for her. Perhaps she'd open the gift box, put the flower in a glass of water. To allow herself to be pulled, the tug of their connection, that invisible thread, dragging her across the street to Henry.

But that didn't happen. *You make me uncomfortable. Go and don't come back.* Her words still scream through him, and she ruined everything. She left him no choice.

She has no idea what he just did, what he told those detectives. Revenge really is sweet. And that's why, still watching her house, very slowly, he smiles.

When he steps into his own house, he can hear his mother's voice, the shrill grate of it, the deluded imperiousness.

"Have you told your work yet?"

"Not yet," comes his father's low murmur in reply.

Henry closes the front door softly, gently. He does not flip the dead bolt, nor does he move. He stands, back pressed against the door, and he listens.

"Well, when are you going to tell them? You have to give notice. Two weeks?"

"I'm not quitting, Jan. It's going to be longer than that."

Henry tries to swallow, but his throat is too dry. That's the only reason he came in through the front door—it was a more direct route to some water. He thought he'd be able to retrieve a glass in peace before stealing away, back into his basement lair.

"Once is a tragedy. Two is a pattern," Henry's mother says sharply.

"There was, what, twenty years between them?" Henry's father says. "It's not like they're connected. Like someone has been picking off the residents of Hawthorne Heights."

Henry'd brought a novel with him to the police station, in case he had to wait for the detectives. He shifts, sweat sticking the cover of the paperback to his forearm.

"You don't know that, Bill. You don't know who killed that man across the street."

"They'll catch him soon," says Henry's father, and Henry hears the rustle of paper. His dad is turning the page of his newspaper, or perhaps folding the sheet with the crossword puzzle.

Apparently, he took the day off from work again today. Henry wasn't surprised that his father didn't go to the office on Monday. His mother seemed frantic, rattled. Henry could sense her energy from two floors below. He hopes that she didn't notice his foray into the wife's house.

"Or maybe it was the wife," Henry's father continues. "It's usually the wife."

"It's usually the husband," his mother snaps.

"Not this time."

There's a brief silence, tight and tense.

Henry wraps his hand around the doorknob. He's going to

open it silently, then slip back out. He'll go around the back and head in through the basement. His thirst has become background noise, and he's certainly not going to stride into the kitchen and reveal to his parents that he's been standing in the foyer eavesdropping.

"We're getting out of here," his mother says. "Do what you have to do. But we're moving."

The knob spins under Henry's hand. He pulls the door open. The jam squeaks.

Footsteps, bare feet slapping against the tiled floors, then his mother is there. Henry assumes the sound had startled her, and she's come to investigate the source.

She appears in the opening at the end of the hall, blue-and-white cotton dress swinging against her knees, toenails aggressively pink, and he can tell that he's right. He scared her—the noise, the squeak of the door. And now she's seen—it's just him, her son. So the fear should drain away. But he looks into her face, and it doesn't. It's still there.

62

Mary can only assume that the police have become focused elsewhere. She's not heard from them since Sunday.

It should be a relief, although there remains a sense of peril in the air within her house. She tries to ignore it, to assure herself that if her boy has done nothing wrong, she has nothing to worry about, and that all she can do is focus on preparing the house for the sale and the move, for their fresh start, for their new life together, in a place where her son will sit at the same table while he eats the meals she makes and permit her a hug at bedtime, a kiss on the cheek before she leaves the house. She wishes she were naive enough to believe any of this in her core.

Her new knives are working out nicely. She has just finished cleaning out the family room, putting books and board games and DVDs no one has used for years into boxes, and is using the small paring knife to hull strawberries, preparing for a midmorning snack, when her doorbell rings.

She wonders whether Owen can hear it. She wonders whether he, like her, knows immediately who it is, feeling the peril grow heavier and more odorous, like smoke thickening.

"Come in," she wants to call merrily, welcoming, throwing them off guard, although she knows she bolted her front door. She's been trying to keep everything locked since Saturday night. She's been too lax with that in the past, but she'd always felt safe here, ever since Ed died. She had always assumed that her husband's death would be the only crime ever committed here on this quiet street.

Mary goes to the door and finds that it's just Detective Scott this time.

"Just a quick word, please," Scott says. "With you."

This relaxes Mary slightly, and she invites the detective inside.

"Coffee?" Mary asks. "It's still warm."

"Why not?" Scott settles herself at the kitchen table, in the same spot where she'd sat before, without waiting to be invited.

"Where's your partner?" Mary asks conversationally as she pours a cup for Scott. She pours a half cup for herself, too, even though she's had enough. She uses her favorite mug, one Owen painted for her when he was little, still unwashed from this morning, then joins Scott at the table.

"Chasing down other leads," Scott says flatly. Mary allows this to lift her slightly—that Owen is not their only interest. Although, of course, Scott could be lying.

"So," Scott continues, "we've arranged for an interview between your son and a psychiatrist for Thursday morning. Ten o' clock, at the station. Will you bring him?"

Mary takes a sip of the coffee, which is actually no longer warm, but she's only stalling. "Do I have a choice?" she asks.

"Of course," Scott replies, in a way that very much conveys *What do you think?*

"Owen won't talk to a psychiatrist. He won't say anything. It's a waste of time."

Scott shrugs and looks around the room.

"He doesn't trust police people. He won't speak to you or to a police psychiatrist. Not after everything he's been through. Who could blame him?"

Scott's eyes return to Mary with an abruptness that makes her startle. "Does he not trust you, Mrs. Irvin? It's my understanding he doesn't speak to you, either."

Mary swallows. "He's in pain." She's irritated now. Irritated that she invited Scott inside. Irritated that she offered her coffee, and in the Bethany Beach mug. She and Ed went there with Owen, when Owen was ten or so. One of the only family vacations they ever took. Mary remembers standing at the water's edge, clapping, watching Owen boogie board, crashing into the waves again and again. Ed sat in a folding beach chair behind them, cap low on his head, hands folded across his belly, and napped, sleeping off his hangovers.

"It's interesting, Mrs. Irvin, the way you seem to be in denial, even after all these years, about what your son did." Scott doesn't sound accusatory when she says this. Merely interested, perhaps a touch bewildered.

"Denial," Mary repeats. "I don't think so."

"He killed your husband. He stabbed him six times."

"My husband could have killed me that night, Detective. Owen saw that. He did it to protect me."

"Your husband slapped you, isn't that right, Mrs. Irvin? What Owen did, it wasn't self-defense or defense of another. Not in the eyes of the law. He did not use the least force necessary. He murdered him." Scott's tone is even, and her eyes bore into Mary's deep-brown pools that look bottomless.

"He was strangling me. That's why Owen stabbed him."

There's a pause. "That's what you told the police, after they didn't accept your confession, wasn't it? But there was no evidence of that. There was no physical evidence to support the claim that he strangled you."

Mary feels her fingertips reaching for her throat, grazing the skin there, which has become so thin. It's been so many years. The line between what really happened that night and what Mary believes has blurred.

She shakes her head. "It wasn't just a single incident of violence." She squeezes her eyes closed, trying not to see the images or hear the sounds of that night. But they rush in. She never has been able to stop them. Ed's raised voice. The sting of his palm against her cheek. Her own words, bold and foolish—*This is your fault.* Then his hands around her throat, the silence that followed. The rush of footsteps—Owen's. Although she couldn't make a sound, couldn't take a breath, he knew that she was screaming for help. He'd hurtled into the room, slid a knife from the block on the counter. He'd stabbed Ed twice in the upper back before Ed could even react. He'd been drinking, and his agility was inhibited, not that he was or ever had been an agile man.

"My husband, Owen's dad—it wasn't like he was a good person, that it came out of nowhere. He'd made things miserable for us for years. Owen snapped. It just as easily could have been me who'd done it."

"Is that why you confessed to the crime?" asks Scott. "Even though your husband's blood was all over your son. His prints were all over the knife. Yet when the officers arrived on the scene, you told them it was you who'd stabbed him."

Mary shrugs. She had, and her greatest regret is that they didn't believe her. No. Her greatest regret is that she didn't stab Ed. Before her son did, or after. The blood, it should have been on her hands as well.

She regrets the fight, too. But that's disordered thinking, she knows. It's the sort of thinking she'd been conditioned into over the years of her relationship with Ed. It was typical thinking in an abusive relationship, and that's what her relationship was, although she didn't realize that until years later. It wasn't violent, not until that night. It was so quietly, so subtly abusive that it was a secret from everyone. Even her.

Until Mary met Greg Behler.

He was a science teacher at the elementary school where Mary taught. He was three years younger and only two inches taller. He was wiry and bespectacled, in contrast to Ed's blond charm, his expansive shoulder span, the way he towered over her. Greg was divorced but childless. He was kind. He listened. When Mary spoke, he looked at her, and he laughed as though she was the funniest human in the world.

They never kissed. Mary thought that mattered. They never kissed, and they certainly never had sex. Mary had wanted to kiss him. At night, in bed beside Ed, she thought about kissing Greg. She imagined how different her life could be if she was married to Greg. She thought about packing up her things and Owen's, and moving them into Greg's three-bedroom townhome—which she'd never been to, but he'd described it to her in great detail—and then she'd shove those thoughts away and nudge Ed subtly, trying to get him to stop snoring without waking him.

There was no kiss, but there were letters. Letters that contemplated the things they would do if not for Ed. Letters that Mary did not hide well enough.

What Mary did was have an emotional affair. That's what Ed accused her of after he found the letters. Owen was in his room, presumably asleep. Mary had been at the school that evening. She'd stayed late to help clean up after Back to School Night. Greg had stayed late, too, and as much as Mary was enjoying being with him, the way their words couldn't stop flowing, the way he smiled shyly despite their closeness, gaze to the floor, she was eager to get home to Owen. She'd never liked it when Owen and Ed were at the house together without her.

Later, she discovered that Ed had spent the evening sitting in the family room, reading the letters he'd found and drinking beer. Mary had kept the letters in a shoebox in her classroom. But she'd had to bring the box home over the summer—she was moving to a new classroom in the fall and didn't want anyone finding them while school was out. She was planning to bring the box into her new classroom, but it was only the first week of the new school year, and she hadn't done it yet.

When Mary got home, blissfully oblivious to what was coming, cheeks still aching, face still flushed—she'd lingered with Greg for too long—Ed was waiting for her in the kitchen. In this very room, where she now sits with the detective. He was angrier than Mary had ever seen him.

He did slap her. Wrapping his hands around her throat, lifting her up into the air, her gasping futilely for a breath—that may not have happened. But when you tell other people and yourself the same thing for so many years, it can become your truth.

"Owen!" she screamed after Ed fell to the floor. She didn't know how many times Owen had stabbed Ed, only that Ed was no longer trying to get up.

Mary called 9-1-1. "My husband," she told the operator. "He's dying." Then she rattled off her name and address and listened to the woman's pleas that she remain on the line, that she provide more details. She ignored them. She hung up the phone, and they waited for the police to arrive. She held her son's hand, sticky with her husband's blood. She didn't gather any towels or press them against Ed's wounds.

"Your son didn't stop stabbing him, even after he'd fallen,"

Scott continues. "That he went for the knife so immediately, that he didn't stop—that's what made the crime so depraved."

Mary hates that word. They used it at the time—the police, the prosecution, the media.

"Yet you lied for him."

"You aren't a mother, are you, Detective?"

Scott does not reply, which Mary takes to mean that she's right.

"Then I wouldn't expect you to understand."

"You can bring him to the station," Scott says, ignoring Mary. "But you can't be in the room while he's speaking with the psychiatrist."

"Fine," Mary replies. She doesn't like it. She's not even sure Owen will get into the car with her and go to the station. And she's nearly certain he won't speak to the psychiatrist. But for now, she's not sure what else she can do but agree that they'll try.

She collects their mugs and carries them to the sink—which is rude, perhaps, because Scott may not have finished with hers, but Mary wants her to go now. "Is that all?" Mary asks.

Again, Scott doesn't reply, and Mary turns, curious about what has distracted the detective.

Her gaze is fixed beside Mary, to her left, to the cutting board resting on the counter, to the pile of strawberries, to the knife flat beside it. And just behind this array is the recently purchased knife block, glossy chestnut brown, blatantly new and too small for that place on the counter, between the toaster oven and the wire rack into which Mary slides her cutting boards. She didn't adjust the spacing of everything to account for it being so much smaller than her previous knife block.

"That's all," Scott says. "For now."

And then she stands up, thanks Mary for the coffee, and goes.

Off to tell her partner, Mary suspects, *She's hiding something. She's got new knives. She lied for her son before, and she'd do it again.*

Pointedly, Mary locks the door behind the detective, then returns to her place at the kitchen counter and resumes slicing the strawberries. Maybe she will prepare a bowl for Owen. He's always liked them. She remembers taking him fruit picking when he was a little boy. Blueberries and strawberries in the summer, apples in the fall. He always ate more than he put in his basket. "No," she'd tell him. "We have to pay for them first." And he'd grin up at her, face smeared red or purple, and she'd laugh, too full of love to truly be mad.

Ed never went with them. It was always just Mary and her boy.

63

“The news, Kate. My own son-in-law.”

Kate is quiet. This conversation, one of so many things she’s been dreading since she discovered her husband’s body on Saturday night, could be avoided no longer.

“That’s not right,” her mother continues. “You know it isn’t.”

Kate nods, although her mother can’t see her. Although there are so many things about this entire situation that aren’t right, and the way Kate’s mother learned about Ben’s death is the least of them. She wants to point out that her mother had barely known Ben—that she’d barely known Kate. That she’d always made Kate feel like there was something wrong with her for working so hard in school, for dreaming about having a successful career, for dreaming about moving away from the tiny swamp-like town where she was raised.

It was always just the two of them, growing up side by side in some ways. Yet there was never the closeness one might of expect of a young single mother and her sole daughter. There was a coldness. Kate always felt like the burden she knew she was. And no matter how hard she worked, no matter what she accomplished in her career, her mother never seemed proud. Only resentful, a misplaced and bizarre sort of envy seeping from her pores like the cheap perfume she’d always so aggressively worn on her neck and arms.

"It's such a shock, Mom," Kate says. "It still is. I couldn't—I couldn't talk to anyone about it. Not even you."

Especially not you.

"I should come up there and stay with you," her mother says, just as Kate feared she would. "I can help you."

Kate inhales sharply.

Two knocks at her front door, crisp like gunfire.

"Mom," Kate says firmly, "I have to go." She stands, looks through the front windows, and her relief at having a reason to end this call so quickly is extinguished. "The police are here."

She hangs up the phone.

It's two uniformed officers, standing on her porch. She stares through the windows before she flips the dead bolt, watching them, their marked car in her driveway, for several seconds, cautious and unsure, as though fearful they might dissolve into something else.

She assumes they're here to provide an update—an arrest, at least the zeroing-in on a single person. But they have no news, only a request that Kate get into their car and come to the police station with them because Detectives Perkins and Scott want to speak with her.

That's how they put it: "Speak with you," their expressions stern. They're both young, both male, both reeking of judgment and authority. Kate's unease, its stifling presence since she discovered Ben's body, roars in her ears.

Still, she says, "Okay. Let me just get my keys." What choice does she have? She must seem helpful. She must *be* helpful.

They step inside while she goes to retrieve her keys from the glass bowl on the kitchen counter. Ben's wallet is still in there, and her eyes burn as she pushes it aside. She always leaves her keys here—Ben has been known to misplace his, but never her.

"I—I can't find them," she half calls to the officers. She wants to search for them; she wants to understand. But the officers will think she's stalling, making excuses. They'll think she's scared, or guilty. She grabs Ben's keys instead, and her own wallet, and tucks them into her bag.

She rides to the station in the back seat of the marked vehicle. There's glass between her and the officers. She feels like a dog—one who's been a very bad girl.

Inside, she's led into a small windowless room, similar to the one they brought her to the night Ben was killed. In fact, it might be the same room. Kate can't be sure. It's all a blur, that night. Every moment since Ben was killed is dark, edges fuzzy, a charcoal drawing smeared with fingertips.

She doesn't wait long before Detectives Perkins and Scott enter with their notebooks and cell phones and importance.

When they relay her Miranda rights, pass the half sheet of paper across the table toward her, and ask her to initial and sign, Kate pauses. She's known all along—her status as wife, her presence at home—that she's a person of interest. But there's been no physical evidence, no reason she would've wanted to kill her husband. Something decidedly is going wrong.

Don't say anything, she tells herself. *Don't talk. Ask for a lawyer.* Everyone knows that—it's the only logical thing to do. But she didn't do anything wrong. She did not kill Ben.

Her mind filled with fog, she draws the paper closer to her with the tips of her fingers, as though it's white hot. She has lawyer friends. She should call one. But she's too curious, too desperate to know what these detectives have, to delay any longer. And she's an intelligent and competent person—she used to be. Can't she protect herself? *Too smart for your own good*, she thinks suddenly—the words her mother has said to her countless times, starting when Kate was just a little girl, perhaps more apropos than ever. She's still feeling rattled from the brief conversation with her mom. She'll have to speak with her again soon. Her mother won't give up.

Her thoughts race. She signs the paper, willing her hand steady, then shoves it back across the table.

"Why?" she asks, eyes flicking from the detectives to the cameras in the corners of the room, as a weariness, a numbness, a sense of removal, welcoming and dangerous, settles over her. "Why are you doing this?"

"Just some more questions for you," says Detective Scott lightly. Kate's rights, that half sheet of paper, gripped tightly between her fingers. She passes it to Perkins, who waves it vaguely, stands, and leaves the room.

"Obviously you have some new information," Kate presses, their fabricated nonchalance grating so sharply. "You still have no idea who's killed my husband, but you have something else on me. So what is it?"

Detective Perkins returns, a stack of papers in his hands. He slaps the stack onto the table, far enough from her that she must lean forward to read the lines of black across the page. The bottoming-out of her stomach when she does, and the pitiful size of the stack. It doesn't look like a book at all.

It might seem, as you read, that ours is a story of love.

It's not.

Ours is a tale of murder.

The reader's first words, but not the first words she wrote. She'd added those later, after Klara killed Troy.

And the police have them. They read them, printed them.

This knowledge makes her feel irrevocably exposed. It's too hot in the room, but she wraps her arms around herself, as though she can disappear within the bends of her elbows.

"Interesting, isn't it," Perkins says, "that you were working on a novel about a wife who killed her husband?"

"How did you get that?" she asks. She reaches ineffectually for the pages, noticing the tremor in her hand. "I don't understand."

The detectives exchange a look, unspoken words flying between them.

"Your neighbor sent it to us," Perkins says.

"My neighbor?" Kate leans back, aghast. "What neighbor? None of my neighbors know I'm writing a book."

Scott's head tilts, chin tipping, as though to say *Are you sure? Are you sure you want to deny this?*

Perkins removes a page from the bottom of the stack, slides it closer to her, and Kate can tell that it's an email. It's dated a couple weeks earlier. Here you go! reads the body of the message. There's one attachment, the file name: Untitled Manuscript by Kate Harvey.docx.

The recipient's email address is not one she'd known, but she does recognize the name. "Henry," she says. Her throat bobs dryly. "How did he do this?"

"You sent it to him," Perkins says firmly. "You were stuck, and you'd discussed books together. You were hoping another pair of eyes might help you, that he might have a suggestion for you to relieve your writer's block."

"Is that what he told you?" asks Kate. She thinks of Henry in the doorway of her closet. "He broke into my house and read it. He must have. He did that yesterday, too. I was asleep and he came in. He told me my front door was open, but it couldn't have been. He's—there's something wrong with him. He's been watching me and trying to run into me for months."

Another wordless glance.

"And you're just bringing this up now," Scott says. It's not a question.

"You should be talking to him," Kate insists, feeling frantic—sounding frantic. She can almost hear the clock ticking. Time, they are all running out of time. "Ask him about coming into my house yesterday. The pictures. He took pictures, I think, and my keys are missing." She reaches for the email again. "I'll check my credit card records. I must have been out running an errand and he went into my house. Or he somehow hacked into my laptop. On this date." She taps the page.

She sees now, too late, that he's not harmless at all. That she should have told them about what Henry was doing the first night they brought her here, as soon as she'd found Ben's body. That she should have, at least, called them yesterday after he'd let himself inside her house and found her in the closet. After she realized the pictures were missing. She has been so dangerously inert.

"Talk to him," she presses.

"We will," says Perkins, lifting a palm, dismissive. "But for now, I'm more interested in the fact that you wrote a novel about a woman who murdered her husband."

"That's not what the novel is about," says Kate, affronted by his gross simplification of the book's themes. "It's about a woman in an unhappy relationship. It's about how this woman finds herself in this relationship that feels intense but nice at times but that isn't healthy. It's actually abusive, but it takes her a while to see that."

"Is that like your relationship with Ben, then?" Scott asks. "Intense, unhealthy?"

Kate lifts her fingers to her forehead, feels the dampness there.

"Abusive?"

"Of course it wasn't," Kate says.

They watch her, nonplussed. They don't believe her.

"This is ridiculous," Kate snaps. "It's fiction. It has nothing to do with my life. No one is interrogating Stephen King about cannibalism," she insists, thinking of *Holly*, which she had recently devoured.

The detectives blink at her wordlessly, blankly, so she can't tell whether they don't understand her literary reference or are pretending not to.

Her head is swimming, throbbing, and she presses her fingertips into her eyebrows. The pain is the worst there.

"What time is it?" she asks wearily.

Scott glances at her watch. "It's eight forty," she says grudgingly, as though it's difficult for her to offer Kate even this, so little. There's been no tea this time. Only lukewarm water, the smallest sips of which turn Kate's stomach. She only ever drinks her water ice cold. Ben used to tease her, the way she'd fill her glass or water bottle with ice, going back for more once it had melted. "You're really only drinking melted ice," he used to say.

She's been here far too long, stuck in this room, while the person who killed Ben is out there.

"I didn't kill my husband," says Kate. She's looking at the camera as she speaks, the one across from her in the corner. "Clearly there isn't any physical evidence that I did. You're wasting your time." This, she tells the detectives.

Perkins seems to bristle, and she understands that if she makes him angry, if she prods at his misguided confidence and pride, he will only double down and hit her even harder.

And she cannot do this anymore. But she's not willing to confess.

"You are wasting your time with me," she says again. "Henry

has been watching me—stalking me. Breaking in. And there's a convicted murderer living across the street. I'd be focusing on them if I were you. And that is all I want to say. I'm asserting my right to an attorney. I don't need you to bring one in for me. I'll hire my own. And right now, I want to go home."

64

Mary doesn't know what to do, only that she must do something.

She wishes she had someone to talk to, someone she could ask for advice. But Ed never liked her having friends, and she quickly grew used to her solace.

When she started dating Ed, her old friendships evaporated, and the only friend she made while they were together was Greg Behler. She wishes she had never even spoken to him. She wishes that when they'd walked out of a staff meeting at the same time that day she had never glanced up, never caught his gaze behind those wire-rimmed glasses, his eyes intelligent and curious and awed.

But she did. And his smile took over his face. "Hi," he said. "I don't think I've met you yet. Greg."

He took her hand, squeezed it gently, and Mary felt thawed. He walked her back to her classroom, chatting the entire time. She'd never found it so easy to talk to anyone.

She wonders where he's living now. If he ever got married again. He gave up on her too easily. She couldn't have reached out to him, but if he'd tried again, more than just the once, she thinks she would have replied.

But now there's no one to call. She stands at her kitchen sink, pressing her fingers into the corners of her eyes. *Focus. The police.*

She can envision their next steps.

New knives. She's hiding something.

They'll pull her credit card records, see the charge at Target. They'll get the camera footage from the dump, from Goodwill, from other places in the area that accept donations of household items. They'll watch her drop off the box. They'll track down her old knife block, see that two are missing. They'll question her in a warm room with too bright lights. They'll question Owen. He might not speak, but what if they arrest him anyway? Will they have enough?

Can they arrest her? An accessory to murder. They'd threatened her with that before. They wanted her to testify against her son, and they were trying to scare her. They believed being charged with a crime would have been more horrifying to her than helping the state convict her child of murder.

But there was no need for that. Once it was decided that Owen would be charged and tried as an adult, the state offered a plea deal, and Owen took it.

Mary paid a lot for Owen's lawyer. He used to say that Owen would still be a young man when he was paroled. He'd have his whole life ahead of him. And Mary had clung to those words, that promise, not considering too deeply what sort of life it would be. A life as a convicted felon. A life of silence.

It's lunchtime, so Mary makes lunch. There's enough cheddar-and-herb bread for three slices. She uses two to make a sandwich for Owen, and she eats the third standing at the counter, dropping crumbs, staring at nothing. Her thoughts trail erratically, going nowhere useful. She can't tame them into order. She's too panicked, too afraid.

She adds a handful of pretzels to Owen's plate, like she's making a meal for a little boy, and this usually comforts her, a balm to her loss, but now it simply makes her feel intensely, irrevocably sad.

Mary leaves the plate on the counter for now and goes upstairs and into her bedroom. Her nightstand has a concealed drawer, above the more obvious drawer. It's meant, she assumes, for hiding important documents or expensive jewelry. Mary has neither.

The note she'd found when she was cleaning out Owen's closet is still there. She put it in her pocket after she found it, then moved it to this concealed drawer later that night, while she was getting ready for bed. She unfolds it, looks at the familiar but distant words.

Owen,

My love for you is the biggest thing in the world. Never forget that.

Love,
Mommy

Then she folds it up again and carries it downstairs.

She puts the plate with his lunch on the top step, and she rests the note beside it. She doesn't know why, but she just wants him to understand, no matter what comes next, that she loves him.

Mary shuts the basement door.

65

There are footsteps above, dull and low, much lighter than Ben's. She hears them on the stairs next, then Maya appears in the family room, her laptop tucked beneath her right arm, and the relief that floods into Kate's chest—at last, she can breathe.

When the police dropped Kate off at her house on Tuesday evening, there was a silvery electric coupe parked at the curb and a figure sitting on the front porch, something dark and boxy beside her, which might have been a suitcase, but Kate couldn't quite tell.

As Kate pushed the car door open, the figure rose, stepping into the glow offered by the light fixture affixed to the bricks between the garage doors, the one Kate and Ben never turned off.

It was Maya. She must have known, a deep and improbable sense that only a close friend could possess, that Kate needed her, more so than she needed anyone else.

"You okay?" asked one of the officers, staring at Maya curiously, hand hovering at the height of his weapon, and Kate realized that she was crying.

"I'm fine," she said, rushing across her driveway. "You can go."

Maya folded Kate into her arms, and Kate tried to remember when she'd last seen her. Maybe not since the small gathering she and Ben had hosted shortly after they'd moved into the suburban house that loomed beyond their embrace. It had been far too long, particularly considering how close they'd once been—sharing an apartment their last two years of college. Although, by her senior year, Kate was spending more nights at Ben's place than at hers and Maya's. But Ben was gone, and in that moment, her friend's arms pressed tightly against her own, for the first time since she found her husband's body, Kate understood that perhaps she was going to find a way to be okay.

Maya settles onto the sofa beside Kate. She grips the edge of her computer but doesn't lift the screen yet. "You won't speak to the police again," Maya says, watching Kate through narrowed eyes. "Not without me present."

"Yes." Kate rolls the edge of a throw blanket between her fingers. "You've mentioned that," she adds. Because Maya has, ever since she arrived. Ever since she recognized Kate and Ben's house on the news and her calls and texts went unanswered.

"I understand that, Kate. And I will keep reminding you every two minutes or so, just in case. It scares me that you went there with them last night."

"You mentioned that, too. But I didn't do anything wrong, so—"

"Innocent people get arrested all the time. They confess to things they didn't do."

"I know."

Maya's brows are arched, lips pressed tightly, as though there's much more she wants to say, but she's not letting herself.

She slides across the cushion, closer to Kate, her warmth, her scent, already filling the house. Kate is so relieved she's here, that she came without Kate asking, without Kate even realizing how badly she needed her. Kate texted her mother, after ignoring so many of her calls. My friend is staying with me for now. I don't have space for you. Not exactly true—there was plenty of physical space in the house—but it seemed to silence her. For now.

"You need to get out of here," Maya says. "I think we should leave in the morning, okay? You'll come stay with me."

It sounded like an invitation, a suggestion, but Kate knows better.

"I don't know if I'm allowed," she says, still pinching the edge of the blanket.

"It's Baltimore, not Nepal. They can get in their car and find you if they need to."

"Hmm," Kate murmurs. She swallows, guilt swelling within her, thinking that Maya might want Kate to come stay with her for other reasons, too. Last night, she told Kate that Emery had ended things and moved out three weeks ago. A two-year relationship suddenly dissolved, and Kate hadn't even known. She's been so out of touch, so singularly focused. That was what Ben had said on Saturday afternoon. She feels sick about it, his inconvenient lack of wrongness.

"And we need to talk about whether we can trust them," Maya says, ignoring Kate's prevarication.

"Who?"

"Can we trust that the police are really trying to figure out who did this? Or are they just trying to gather evidence against you?"

"I really don't know."

Maya sighs, then opens her computer. "This guy across the street. What's his name?"

"Which one?"

"Fair enough."

"Owen Irvin," says Kate. "The other man is Henry. I don't know his last name."

She watches as Maya opens a map, finds the addresses of the houses across the street from Kate's, then types those into the state's real property database. In less than a minute, they have a last name for Henry: Lawson.

Maya searches for Owen first, skimming the same articles Kate had found on Monday; then she turns to Henry. Her social media searches don't yield any results, but she finds a LinkedIn profile, a green band beneath his photo indicating that he's looking for work. Kate tilts her head back, lets herself enjoy the feeling of someone she can trust taking control, taking care of her.

That morning, Maya awakened before Kate. With her friend just on the other side of her bedroom wall, Kate finally slept. Maya made coffee, preparing a mug for Kate exactly the way she liked it, the way Ben used to make it for her, and ordered french toast with berries and whipped cream that had melted by the time the food was delivered, but its sticky sweetness lingered, and Maya looked on sternly until Kate had finished everything.

"He added an end date to his most recent employment, and it was eight months ago," Maya says, turning to Kate. "That's weird, right?"

"Maybe he's been working on a novel."

Maya rolls her eyes, fingertips skimming the mouse pad.

"I'm serious. He does like books. He stole mine."

"Or maybe something happened there. That's why he left."

When she closes her eyes, Kate sees Henry—standing in the street, those drinks in his hand, seemingly so friendly yet so threatening. She sees him in the frame of her closet door. The front door was open, he said. But it wasn't.

"I bet it did," she says.

Maya has already located the company website and is scrolling through the profiles of every staff member. "There's only one young-ish woman who works here," she says. "Janelle Granger. We could send her a message through your LinkedIn."

"What—I mean, what help would that be?"

"If we can find something else on him, that we can share with the police, we can get them to stop looking at you. You know you didn't do this."

This. Kate nods.

"And that means that someone else did. Wake up, Kate."

The harshness stings, yet Kate knows it's what she needs.

Maya's fingers fly across the keyboard. "Here, I'll use my LinkedIn. I'll just send her a message. I'm telling her that Henry is my client's neighbor and we have reason to believe he's dangerous. We're reaching out to people who might know him to see if they've had a similar experience."

"Eight months is a long time," Kate says. "Maybe there was an incident with someone who's no longer working there. Someone who left when he did."

"True. I'm not sure how I can narrow down the people who recently left that company. I could find former employees on here, but it would be pretty tedious to go through their employment end dates."

But only minutes later, Janelle has written back, as though she could sense their urgency, their need. Kate leans against Maya for a clearer view of the screen, the tidy, shrunken text.

> Hi. I actually think I was the replacement hire, so I didn't overlap with him. But something did happen. I heard it was awful. And that was why he left. But since I wasn't even there, I really don't feel comfortable telling you about it. Why don't you reach out to Lacey Albright? She would know and it's her story to tell. Sorry.

Kate has barely finished reading the message before Maya is closing her inbox, searching for Lacey's page, and sending her a similar note.

"I wish Janelle would just tell us," says Kate. "She clearly knows. It doesn't matter if she wasn't working there at the time."

"Maybe she will if I tell her it's related to a police investigation. Or maybe she'll agree to meet us for coffee. If we can get a meeting with her, we might be able to convince her to talk."

Maya sighs impatiently, then opens her work email, and Kate watches the number of unread messages tick upward in real time, feeling her guilt swell again.

"Do you need to go back to your office?" Kate asks.

"I can take a few days off. It's not a big deal." But she's opened a reply window and is typing furiously. Kate lets her eyes fall closed, until Maya gasps. "Lacey wrote back."

Kate sits up again, blood humming in her ears as she cranes her neck toward the screen.

I can't discuss him with you. Please don't contact me about this again.

"Well," says Maya. "That's not nothing, is it?"

"No," says Kate softly. "Not at all." They both stare at the words; silence thrums, intrigue rising.

"She said she *can't*, not that she doesn't want to." Maya is staring above the top of her screen, at the empty wall, at nothing.

"Does that matter?"

"I think so. I'm going to ask her if she has a lawyer. I'll tell her this is related to an active police investigation. And then we'll talk to the police and tell them what we've found."

The police—the thought of voluntarily bringing herself close to them makes Kate squirm. But they're already hovering, suspicious, even when she can't see them. That they've been quiet, out of sight, since Kate got home from the station doesn't mean that they've cleared her.

"Tell them what we've found," Kate echoes. "Which is what, exactly? All we know is that he had to leave his prior employment for some reason. That's a far cry from, from…" She stops.

"From murder," says Maya.

"And why Ben? Why my husband?"

Maya is staring ahead of her again, face blank. "I don't know."

Kate feels hopelessness descending anew. But then Maya is typing frantically, the clench of her jaw, her grit drawing Kate upward. "But we are going to find out."

Later, the sky darkening as they're still waiting to see if Janelle or Lacey will reply again, Maya is rinsing their take-out containers and muttering that they really do need to stop eating out. Kate moves around the house, checking that every window and door is locked. She's catching on, she thinks. She's being more careful; she's starting to look out for herself again. The shock is wearing thin, the fear beginning to scream, too loud to be ignored. Nor should she try to ignore it.

Maya is right. She's not safe here. She must go. Soon, she'll pack a bag, and in the morning, she'll follow Maya to her condo downtown. Farther from Owen Irvin, farther from Henry Lawson. Farther from this place where Ben's absence is too piercing a howl.

She can't remember checking the door on their screened porch, so she goes out there to ensure it's locked. She averts her eyes from the patio below, but what's not there is too glaring to avoid. The outdoor sofa is bare, wicker exposed, blood-soaked cushions gone. Ben's blood scrubbed from the stones. Like he was never there at all.

Once she's certain that everything is locked, Kate finds Maya upstairs, sitting cross-legged on the bed in the guest room, her computer resting on the comforter.

"Still nothing more from Janelle or Lacey," she says. "We'll give them a little more time. Maybe they have to sleep on it." She tips her head toward her laptop. "I'm just going to catch up on a few work things. You okay?"

Kate nods, although she's not sure if she is. "I'm going to bed."

"Already?" Maya asks.

Kate nods again and tries for a smile. But it feels wrong, and before she turns her back on Maya, she observes her friend's creased face, the furrow of her brows, her concern blatant, like a blinking neon sign.

Kate goes into her bedroom. She tries not to look at Ben's pillow in their unmade bed, his nightstand, the boat shoes resting on the floor in front of his dresser. In the bathroom, Kate reaches for her toothbrush, bracing herself for the sight of Ben's in the cup beside hers. But Kate's is the only one there. Ben's is gone, and Kate's hand shakes as she flips cabinets open, tugs drawers, searching. She tries to remember whether it was there this morning, whether she had even brushed her teeth, but her thoughts are mush.

She considers rushing down the hall, telling Maya. But telling her what? Ben's toothbrush is missing? Why would someone take a toothbrush?

It wasn't just a toothbrush, though, was it? It was the photos. It was her book. It was her husband.

And it was her keys. A means to silently enter her home—the significance of this suddenly squeezing her throat. *Wake up*, Maya had said.

Kate stares at the cup as though it might speak to her. As

though it might explain what's going on. But Kate already knows. She just doesn't know what, exactly, he wants. Or how far he'll go to get it.

"Maya!" she yells, her terror bare. "*Maya*!"

And she hears footsteps, light and panicked, as Maya runs.

66

Mary works in the garage for most of the afternoon. She's tired and distracted, disinterested in the chore, but she couldn't continue putting it off.

Owen took the note. She doesn't know what he did with it, whether he threw it away or simply tucked it into a drawer or pocket. She just knows that when she opened the door to retrieve his lunch dish, the note was gone. She paused at the top of the stairs, and he must have heard her there, must have sensed the door ajar. But he said nothing.

She does not want to look through these things, through Christmas decorations, lingering on memories, through things she never used, slow cookers and sleeping bags, through bins of toddler toys she should have donated years ago. She pushes boxes across the cracking cement floor, organizing them by category—donate or trash. She will call a junk-removal service next week to haul most of it away because she can't lift the boxes herself. Owen could help, theoretically, and she feels an uncommon flash of irritation toward him. She shouldn't have to clean up the contents of their lives alone. He was gone for so long. So often it still feels like he is.

At least he took the note. She hopes that means something.

At six, Mary goes inside to make dinner. She doesn't have the energy for anything more than a salad and a frozen pizza, although she shouldn't be eating pizza, age and weight that she is. But Owen always loved pizza. What little boy doesn't?

Of course, he's no longer a little boy, and Mary has no idea which foods he loves or which he hates. She knows so little about her son. No matter what she serves him via the basement stairs, he clears his plate. There isn't any gym equipment in the basement, yet she noticed on Sunday the way his shoulders strained at the seams of his shirt. He must be doing push-ups, using the weight of his own body to grow stronger and bigger even though he's safe now. When she picked him up from prison, she'd noticed how much stronger he looked. She assumed he needed to be, when he was in there, although she tried not to think about why.

Only twenty minutes later, the pizza is ready. She makes a side salad, too, with chopped cucumber and spinach. For posterity and nutrition. She doesn't feel like eating it.

Mary leaves Owen's dinner on the stairs. She stands in the doorway silently, waiting. She assumes that, again, he can hear her, that he knows she is standing there contemplating the state of things and that they have been largely the same ever since he got home. That they could eat together, could behave as mother and son again. That something is happening—another murder, the police circling, the appointment with the psychiatrist, about which Owen doesn't even know. That they need to weather this together, with honesty and communication. How else can she protect him? But Owen doesn't acknowledge any of this. There is only stillness and silence. He does not come. Mary closes the door.

She almost never watches television, but tonight she turns it on. She sits on the sofa to eat and finds herself absorbed in a reality show she's never seen before, fascinated by the young and beautiful people, their charmed lives and manufactured drama.

It's nearly two hours later that Mary finally retrieves Owen's dishes. When she sees what's on the top stair, her heart sinks. Disappointment courses through her, because there's a square of paper, aging and familiar, waiting for her beside his empty salad bowl and plate. He gave the note back.

Mary wants to cry out, to cry down to him. She is gutted that he couldn't give her even that—the impression, even a false one, that the note and its message still mean something to him.

Then she notices the writing on the paper. It's on the outside, exposed. At first, she thinks he folded the note the opposite way of the worn creases. Until she realizes that this is not her handwriting, and it's not in pen. It's faint-gray pencil, and she'd know this penmanship anywhere.

She reads what her son wrote.

67

Henry is trying to move on.

His understanding has settled, hardened. The wife is never going to like him. She is never going to love him. It doesn't matter that her husband is gone or that Henry was the one to do that for her, to free her from her unhappy marriage. She doesn't want to be with him. She doesn't even want to be his friend.

Please, she said. *Go. Leave.* The fear on her face.

It wasn't the husband in the way after all. The problem was her all along—why is it that every single one he picks turns out to be such a bitch?

Vivian. Sarah. Candace. Kelly. Krista. Esther. Ashley. Lacey.

Kate.

Move on.

This is what he tells himself on Wednesday evening as he stares through the front window, watching the wife's house.

Yesterday, he'd directed the police toward her. Later, he saw two officers arrive to pick her up. The detectives must have shown her the email. And she must have denied that she'd sent him her manuscript, but he's not sure that matters, not if they already see her as a liar. The detectives will be back to him soon. *She claims she didn't send this*, they'll say, and he'll double down. *She would say that, wouldn't she?*

He thinks he was pretty convincing. He told the detectives that he hadn't yet shared his feedback on the manuscript with her because the whole thing made him uncomfortable. It was so vivid, and it seemed autobiographical. He was sorry for not mentioning it the first time he spoke to them. He really did want to give her the benefit of the doubt, and it seemed silly to suggest that her manuscript could mean anything, but as the days passed and no other suspect emerged, he realized that he couldn't live with himself if he didn't tell them about it.

He doesn't regret it. It's what she deserved. And she will know, obviously, that she did not send that email to him. She will fear him even more. Her missing keys, the wedding photos, those reminders of her husband gone. He must have unsettled her, and still, she didn't turn to him. She saw him as the problem.

But that doesn't matter. It was over already. And now she's gone. He just watched her garage door rise, saw her hurriedly loading bags into her car, then slowly back out, following her friend's car out of the driveway, then up the street.

A man is dead. But that man isn't Henry. It's time to move on. He feels as though it's a loop, neatly closed—the husband dead, the wife under suspicion.

The unfairness of it, that his original plan failed, that she rejected him—rage suddenly grips him, white knuckled. He's trying to move on, but it's not that simple.

He turns from the window, gaze catching on a picture frame resting on the end table beside the sofa, almost exactly where his hand hangs. It's squat and gold, and Henry picks it up. Inside is a photo of Laurel, her baby resting on her chest. She's smiling sleepily and close-mouthed. This frame has been here forever, and Henry sits here often. He could have sworn it used to have a picture of him and Laurel when they were little. He thought it was one of them eating sno-balls on the front porch, sticky hands clutching Styrofoam cups, lips and chins stained red.

Henry studies the image for a second longer before he hurls the frame against the wall. It falls to the area rug with a dull thud; then a stunned silence rings out briefly, as though the house, the picture frame itself, cannot believe what Henry has done. Henry, too, is stunned. He's always so controlled, temper in check. He swallows anger like it's alcohol, lets it hum in his veins and change him until he's ready to act.

Then footsteps pound, devouring the silence, and his mother rushes into the room, eyes cartoonishly wide.

"What was that?" she asks when she sees him standing there, her gaze darting around the room until it lands on the picture frame resting on the floor, then travels up to the hole it made in the wall, the pale-sage paint chipping, shedding drywall dust.

"Jesus, Henry. I thought someone was breaking into the house."

"This early? Through the front?" Henry asks, cutting into her hyperbole, her melodramatic bullshit.

"What have you done?" She steps closer, so Henry backs away. She runs a finger along the crumbling line of drywall, only a few inches long, before picking up the picture frame and examining it. She doesn't put it back onto the table, just clutches it against her chest like it's a weapon she's afraid to use.

"We are going to list this house for sale soon, Henry. You should be helping us get it ready, not throwing things at the wall. You'll have to repair that."

"Okay," says Henry, but in a way that means, *Yeah, right.*

As if he'd even know how to repair drywall.

"A Realtor is coming on Friday morning," his mother presses. "Dad is still at the office. He's working on his retirement plans. We are going to leave, and I need you to help get the house ready."

He laughs—that she thinks she can direct him like this, like he's still a little boy.

Her face darkens.

"This is happening," she says, tight and clipped. "We are leaving this neighborhood. We are going to visit some condos near Laurel this weekend. And she found this adorable single-story place only a five-minute drive from her house. She started looking online for us as soon as I told her about the murder. She is so *worried.*"

She makes it sound like Laurel, with her worry and her baby, is a hero, like she solved the murder on her own. And wouldn't that be a twist?

"That's nice of her," Henry says placidly. His anger has drained as hers has intensified.

His calmness infuriates her.

"Why did you do that?" With one hand, she waves wildly toward the damaged wall, still holding the picture frame against her with the other. "What do you have to be so angry about?"

He refuses to answer.

"You act like you are so affronted all the time, Henry." She spits the words. She's sparking, rabid with anger now, like he's never seen her before. A switch flipped, a mask drawn down. "Like you are a victim, like nothing is your responsibility and it's all so unfair. But what is so unfair about your life? We have given you everything."

He stares at her.

"Why?" she demands again. "Why are you like this?"

She wants so badly for him to speak, so he won't. He won't tell her what he did for Kate. That he watched her for weeks, for months. That he plotted and inserted himself into her life and that even after everything, she doesn't want him. She never did. He won't tell her that it wasn't fair the way all the others treated him. That Lacey ruined his life simply because she had the power to do so. He wouldn't have hurt her. He wouldn't have hurt any of them. He won't tell her that her disappointment makes him feel hollow, like he is nothing. Like she, his own mother, doesn't love him.

He watches her, and he does not speak, and she can't help but let her fury drive her words.

"We are moving out of this house," she says, voice like a rubber band pulled taut. "So you need to start thinking about that. You need to start making plans. You need to figure out where you'll go."

Moving. Leaving this house, this neighborhood, behind. Leaving Kate, leaving the murder investigation, for a new city. A new home.

A new group of women to choose from.

Her eyes flicker over him, fearful. "Where are you going to go?" she presses, desperate now.

A shame to waste it, everything he's done. But perhaps that's not the way to look at things. He's proved what he's capable of—that he's a person who can kill. Not just that. He's a person who can get away with it.

Henry lets the silence ripple and rise, until his mother's frustration is near to overflowing. Then he shrugs. "I'll go with you," he tells her. "Make sure the new place has a bedroom for me."

The look on her face—at last, he feels his own anger, over the wife, over everything, releasing. He thought he was just saying it to piss her off. But her horror has turned him righteous, and he thinks, why not? Why not go with them? He will share a small condo or single-story house with his parents, if that's what he has to do to get out of here.

Someplace new. A fresh start.

68

Mom, I know something.

Will she keep it forever? Tuck it onto a shelf in her closet? Her son's first words to her in so many years, nearly as precious as when he first said "Mama," when he was thirteen months old, with plush cheeks and corn-silk hair, quick to smile, chubby hands always reaching for her.

Mary clutches the paper between her fingertips as she tentatively descends the stairs. The note is an invitation, yet she still feels like she's intruding. She has respected his desire for silence, solace, with great diligence, and she would have preferred that he went upstairs to her.

But it's clear that Owen is expecting her. He's not sitting at the desk, back to her, but on the sofa, waiting for her to join him.

As soon as she sits, he speaks.

"This is difficult." His voice is raw, cracked like something used too much rather than the opposite.

Immediately, Mary begins to cry. Her son hasn't spoken to her for three years.

"I'm sorry," she says, wiping her eyes and nose furiously with her sleeve. "Please go ahead."

"The night before the man was killed, someone was in the house." Soft, rushed, no time wasted. She can tell he doesn't want to do this; he wants it to be over.

Mary stares at him, trying to digest his words while she's still so stuck on the fact that he's speaking at all. And he's so near. Not close enough that she can feel his warmth, but close enough that if she just lifted an arm, extended it toward him, she could.

"Who?" she asks, the weight finally registering, settling heavily into her mind. *Someone in the house.*

"I don't know."

"What did he look like? What did he do in the house?"

"It was dark, but I could tell that he had a beard. He was average height and build. I think he was wearing a hood, or maybe it was a hat. He came in through the front door. I don't know how he got in."

Mary feels her cheeks flush, but she simply shakes her head. She doesn't admit her propensity for failing to lock the doors. She'd open the front one to retrieve a package or to go out to the mailbox, then forget to lock it behind her when she returned. It could be unlocked for days, sometimes, until the next time she left. She'd only become more careful about that since Saturday night.

She feels violated—someone in their house while she was upstairs asleep and oblivious. Someone who could have hurt her, or her son.

"He took a knife."

Mary nods—of course he took a knife. The missing knife that never did turn up. Mary had disposed of the rest of the set, thinking—what? That Owen had used the missing one to kill the man across the street? She never really thought that. She'd thought very little. She'd acted instinctively, protectively. As it turned out, she'd been protecting a stranger.

"He took a knife, then left," says Mary, fitting the pieces together. "He used it to kill the man across the street. I wonder if he was trying to…frame you." She feels ridiculous saying it.

"Would he have even known I was here?" Owen's gaze flicks away from her face to the nothingness behind her, as though her eye contact is too much.

"No," says Mary firmly, but she knows that's not true.

She has tried to conceal Owen's presence in the house, but when he was released on parole, there was a blurb in the news. The neighbors knew, and they didn't like it. Those who were here at the time hated that there was a murder on their quiet street, and they'd seemed to hate it more when he returned.

"A man with a beard," she says thoughtfully. Average height and build. That could be almost anyone.

"I was in the doorway of the basement stairs when I heard the front door open. I was coming up for some food. I was in the dark, and I stood there and watched. Then, when he left, I went to the front windows. He was rushing around the back of the house next door."

There's a gray hair in Owen's beard and a smattering at his temples, so improbable, so difficult for her to accept.

"Henry," she says. "The boy next door."

Although Henry is no longer a boy, either. He is—maybe—five years younger than Owen? His family had moved to the house when he was just a toddler, he and Owen too far apart in age to play together. Henry had an older sister, but Mary never saw her playing outside with the other neighborhood kids. She seemed to be a more introspective child, like Owen.

She knows almost nothing about Henry. Only that he'd moved out of the house for college, disappearing with the car his parents bought him, returning home during the holidays. At some point, he'd returned for good, with a different, more expensive car which he parked at the curb out front. She assumed he'd fallen upon relationship or job problems, or both, and was trying to put himself back together. And for some reason, he had killed the man across the street. He'd used Mary's knife to do it.

He'd always seemed like a quiet boy, polite and inoffensive. She wonders what drove him to murder. Mary knows better than most people that everyone is capable of it. Everyone has a breaking point. She was so close to her own, but Owen reached his first.

"Why didn't you tell the police this?" she asks.

Owen still isn't looking at her. His right hand is squeezing the left. There's a scar running along his wrist, raised, pale, and unfamiliar. Mary wants to lean over and kiss it, the way she had his skinned knees and scraped elbows when he was small.

"I don't want to talk to the police."

Mary presses her lips together. She should tell him about the appointment with the psychiatrist tomorrow morning—she must tell him—but that would feel like a betrayal. It might make him shut down again, and she doesn't want him to stop talking.

"So don't tell them," she says. "You don't have to speak with them. You don't have to do anything you don't want to do. You've done nothing wrong."

She's thinking of her neighbor now. Not Henry, but his mother. They never were friends—Mary didn't have friends—but Janet was one of the more accepting people in the neighborhood. She was quiet about everything after Owen was paroled, and that was exactly what Mary had wanted.

The week after Owen got home, Mary was getting her mail when Janet was out front watering her pansies. Janet didn't look at her with hatred, with disgust, with blame—*you raised a murderer*. There was sympathy in her eyes. Mary recognized it immediately, although she saw it so infrequently.

"All right, Mary?" Janet had asked, and Mary wasn't, but she'd nodded.

And that was that. Two words, almost nothing, between mothers. Yet it was more kindness than anyone else in the neighborhood had offered her.

She is thinking, now, that if Owen reveals what he saw, people will be looking at Janet the way people have, for almost two decades, looked at Mary. Because it's always the mother's fault, isn't it? It crosses everyone's mind when they hear about a horrible man doing a horrible thing. At some point or another, they will think that his mother must have done something wrong.

And Mary doesn't want another mother to face that. She doesn't want another mother to lose her son. Not Janet.

There's been enough loss, has there not? Stop the bleeding.

And Mary doesn't want to help the police. She wants nothing to do with the system that insisted her boy needed to be tried as an adult and that so badly failed him. Owen needed help, not prison. They both needed help.

"Innocent people sometimes do get arrested," Mary continues, thinking out loud. "And, of course, if the police had real reason to suspect you were involved, you would have to tell them what you saw. But for now, they don't, do they? They can't make you talk at all."

Owen is looking at her now, finally, the unfamiliarity of his adult face so wrong.

"They might not even believe you." She hates to admit this, but she fears it's true. The police had always seemed to be against them. "Is that what you want?" she continues. "To stay silent? Or do you want to tell them what you saw?"

She must let him decide anyway. It's not her information to hold or to share.

He blinks at her once, twice, then shakes his head. To anyone else, perhaps it wouldn't be clear what he means, but Mary is his mother, and so she knows.

"You've done nothing wrong," she says again, and she hopes he understands that she means that broadly. "I'm just so happy that you spoke to me."

Owen shrugs, looking at his hands. Mary is desperate to press him. They talked, and what does that mean? Does it mean he will keep speaking to her? Has he made an exception, out of necessity? Or is this the start of a new normal?

She does not allow herself to question him. She has always believed that he would come to her when he was ready. As it turns out, she was right. She knows that he will continue to give her more as he's capable.

And her heart—Mary knew it broke that night. She's known ever since that it was broken. And she feels it now, more acutely than ever before. The crack, the blood, the spill.

"I couldn't tell you, Mom," he says abruptly, a mere whisper, and she's clinging to that word, its gravity—*Mom*. "I couldn't tell you about everything that happened in there. So I couldn't talk at all. It was easiest that way."

"You don't have to tell me a thing," she says firmly. Is that a gift to him or to herself? Because would she want to know? Any of it?

"I love you so much, Owen," she says, instead of all the questions hammering at her mind.

One corner of Owen's mouth tips upward. "I know that, Mom. I never doubted that."

His acceptance, his trust, his forgiveness—all of it winds her.

"I made so many mistakes," she says. "I know that I did. Things were hard when you were a kid, and I know it was worse, living here. The other families in this neighborhood weren't like ours. But I hope you know that I was always doing what I thought was best for you. Sometimes I was wrong. But everything I did was out of love. It's—" Mary swallows, wetness spilling down her cheeks.

She tries to take a breath, but it's choppy and sodden, and she can't continue. She can't say anything more.

"It's the biggest thing in the world," Owen says, finishing for her. "Right?" he adds.

Mary uses the backs of her hands to blot her face. Then she smiles. Her sweet boy, pure gold. "Right," she tells him. "You're absolutely right."

69

When Henry was four, he stepped on a baby bird.

It was May 13, a Friday, which later seemed apropos. Janet was tired of his unrelenting neediness. She was tired. She had recently started him in preschool on Tuesdays and Thursdays and was becoming increasingly wistful on the remaining days of the week, which racked her with guilt and only made her more irritable toward him. He had stopped napping and didn't play independently as often as she thought he should. She remembered Laurel sitting peacefully on the floor for hours at that age, flipping through picture books, rocking her baby doll, pretending to feed her bottles.

"Mommy, I want to go outside," said Henry, tugging at Janet's shirt. It was nearly three, and Janet was pouring marinade over a dish of chicken breasts. In a half hour, they would have to walk down to the bus stop to meet Laurel.

"Two more minutes," said Janet, although she needed at least five.

"Now," shrieked Henry.

"Just go," Janet nearly shrieked back at him. "Just go out the back and be careful on the stairs. I'll be right out."

She knew it was wrong, but the tiny thrill that ripped through her when the back door slammed closed behind her son was too delicious to pass up.

Janet rubbed the marinade into the chicken. She chopped a squash so that it would be ready for later, after Bill returned from work. She and Henry had picked up fresh rolls that morning, and she'd benevolently purchased him a butterscotch-chip cookie, which had bought her ten minutes of peace as he gingerly ate, studying his treasure between bites as though he could not believe his good fortune, in a way that made her heart swell with affection.

There was laundry in the dryer, so Janet went down the basement to pull it into the hamper. She was already pushing it, so she left the folding for later. She went outside, through the back door in the basement, and found Henry on the patio. He was holding the yellow wiffle bat and searching for his ball.

"I can't find it," he said upon seeing his mother. His tiny voice wavered with frustration.

"Okay," she said. "Just calm down, Henry."

Then she took another step closer to him, and she froze. Her hands flew to her mouth. She closed her eyes so that everything would go dark, but it didn't work. With her eyes shut, she could see it there, imprinted like an after image, the downy gray feathers like fur, beak open but flat, crimson guts spilling.

Janet opened her eyes, looked up. There was a nest on one of the beams above. For weeks, Janet had watched the parents build it from nothing. She knew there were eggs but didn't realize they'd hatched. Perhaps only one had been viable. A single fledgling.

"Oh," said Henry, his own gaze on the bird.

"What happened?" she asked. She was horrified, too upset to try not to be. She was the mother. She couldn't cry. It was her job to keep it together, to handle this. But all she could think about was the mother bird she'd been watching for weeks looking down at her dead baby.

Until Henry spoke.

"I stepped on it," he said, sounding surprised by the admission.

"Henry," she said, inhaling sharply.

Her son looked up at her, reading her expression, those dark and analytical eyes. "I'm sorry, Mommy. I didn't see it. But I felt something soft under my foot so I must have stepped on it."

Janet tried to feel relieved. It wasn't sadism, but an accident. He hadn't seen the bird. He had apologized.

But the coolness in his gaze, the adamant disinterest, that moment of calculation, before he told her what happened. The flatness of his tone. She didn't believe him.

"Let's go inside," she said harshly, grabbing his arm, pulling him toward the door.

"But I want to hit balls," he wailed.

"No," she said. She pulled harder. She just needed to get him into the house. She would put something on television for him, then go fold her laundry. After they got home with Laurel, they would have to play in the front yard or inside. Bill would have to deal with the bird when he got home because Janet simply couldn't.

She has never looked at her son the same way since. And that baby bird, which Janet can still, more than two decades later, see so clearly when she closes her eyes, isn't the reason. Not really. That was only the beginning.

Janet Lawson has never, in her entire life, been to a police station.

She tells the man seated behind the desk in the reception area that she wants to speak to the detectives leading the investigation into the murder that happened in Hawthorne Heights. She cannot bring herself to say the victim's name.

She sits on an uncomfortable gray chair and waits until Detective Scott appears.

"Mrs. Lawson," she says. "Thank you for coming in." There's interest in her eyes, but she doesn't ask Janet why she's here. Not yet.

Janet stands and follows the detective. Her pants are impossibly black, with a thick weave, an expensive-looking gloss. Janet wishes she had a pair. She wishes she had someplace to wear them.

She grips the straps of her purse, has a sudden fear that someone will ask to search it. But no one does. Scott leads her into the bowels of the station, her heels tapping on the cheap, laminate tile.

Janet declines the detective's offer of water, coffee, or soda. Her heart is in her throat; she just wants to get this over with.

"What can I help you with?" Scott asks once they're both seated in a private interview room. She throws one long leg across the thigh of her other.

"Before I say anything," Janet says, "I want to make sure that I can't get into trouble for it."

Scott's eyes narrow. "Well, I can't promise you that, Mrs. Lawson. Not without more information. For instance, if you're going to confess to murdering Ben Harvey, I can't promise you immunity."

Janet's purse is heavy on her lap. She clutches it, arms grasping tight, as though it's her baby.

She thinks of Henry as a baby, red-faced; he always seemed to be crying. But when he wasn't, when he fell asleep at her breast and his face went slack, he was the most gorgeous thing she'd ever seen. The weight of him against her. She could cry, the weight of the love too much. The euphoria of his sleep was perhaps the sweetest thing she'd ever tasted.

But that was before. That was long before.

"What if it wasn't me?" Janet asks now, fingers digging into worn leather. "But I know who it was?"

There's a charged pause. It feels like neither of them is breathing.

"That would be different."

Janet wants to be sure, but she understands that she will have to share what she has before they promise her immunity. She doesn't think it's likely that they'd charge her with a crime. It's completely understandable that it took her so long to say anything. In fact, she will probably be lauded as a hero for coming forward at all. For being restless and unsettled—the way Henry had sat with her and Bill when he never did—and unable to fall asleep on Saturday night. For hearing the slam of the basement door, the way it rattled the house, past midnight. For listening for more, curious, perhaps a little fearful, then hearing the rush of water through the pipes, the way it sounded when the washing machine was running, and seconds later, more water, still distant—the basement shower. For creeping down two flights of stairs with practiced silence, the way she used to when Henry was an infant and she'd finally got him to sleep. For pausing the machine, for lifting the lid. The smell of blood, the clothes black.

What had he done?

The woman across the street, she thought. The one he'd been watching.

The shower was still running.

He'd get rid of the clothes after he washed them. Burn them, throw them in a neighbor's bin? She wasn't sure, but she knew he wouldn't keep them. He was too smart to keep them. She also knew she couldn't take them. Yet something as insistent and sure as only a mother's instincts could be was telling her to do something.

On the shelf above the machines, behind the detergent, she found an empty plastic bag. A pair of scissors. She carefully made a cut in the shirt, then tore across the hem. She shoved the trail of fabric into the plastic bag, tied the handles in a knot.

She rushed upstairs into the powder room. There was a smear

of blood on her fingers. Janet vomited into the toilet before she washed the blood away.

Then she returned to bed, slipped onto the mattress beside Bill who was still snoring obliviously. He'd always been oblivious when it came to Henry.

It was the most difficult thing she'd ever done. Until now.

Janet has no idea what her next-door neighbor knows; she knows nothing of the sacrifice Mary is trying to make for her, protecting Henry.

She unzips her purse. Scott's eyes flick toward the source of the sound.

Janet thinks of him. Henry. He believes he's going to come to Pennsylvania with them. He has no idea she's here. But the move is supposed to be Janet's fresh start. She's going to live near Laurel and help with the baby. Maybe she'll even be able to see her grandson every day. Henry will not ruin that for her. He's ruined enough.

She's been a mother for thirty-two years. And now she's a grandmother to a perfect, full-cheeked baby. To whom, she wonders, does she owe most? Her daughter, or her daughter's son? Her own son, who's failed her so? To what does she owe herself? Is she, a mother, worth anything at all, independent of them?

She reaches into her purse, grips the filmy, thin plastic.

"This is a piece of my son's shirt," says Janet, shoving the bag across the table. "The one he wore the night he killed our neighbor."

EPILOGUE

Tonight, Mary tries a new recipe. For the first time in her life, she's been finding joy in cooking. She spent too many of her early years working in cheap restaurants, so close to the heat, the sweat, the hurried mess of the business of food preparation. She spent too many years cooking for an unappreciative Ed, then too many years alone.

Now she spends idle minutes browsing recipes on her phone. Instead of a weekly haul of groceries, she goes out every few days, picking up just what she needs. And although she no longer needs it, because she brings home so much less with each trip, she has help now bringing the bags inside and unloading them.

The pan is fragrant, heat on her face, tingling the inside of her nose. She shakes it gently, food turning, then pushes it away from the burner. She removes two plates from the cabinet, but she doesn't dish out the food. She doesn't have to.

Mary takes a step, then the ding of her phone, which is propped on the counter, her recipe still lighting the screen, stops her. She picks it up, feels herself flush as she reads the message and taps out her reply. She doesn't hold his words and wait until she's decided on the perfect response. They'd never needed to behave that way. Each of them, whatever they had to say, was always exactly right, unflinchingly accepted.

She'd never been a social media person, but—the new

apartment, the fresh start, her courage soaring—she'd joined Facebook with a single purpose. It wasn't difficult to find Greg. He never had remarried.

Still smiling, she puts her phone down and leaves the kitchen, warm and bright, a hundred times smaller than the kitchen in her old house. But, at least as far as she knows, no one ever died here.

Mary goes down the hall, the hall lined with art, some of it framed, some bare canvases hanging from hooks—the damage-free sort since she's only renting. Some of the art is old, and some of it new. In the corner of each piece, the same initials: *OLI.*

She passes her bedroom, door gaping open, and approaches the next. The door is shut, and she moves silently, tentatively—old habits. But once she's there, just outside it, her boy on the other, the relief, the golden hum of relief, and she's brimming with it, she's smiling, as she taps lightly on the frame.

"Owen," she calls, and she wonders if he can hear the relief—can he feel it? Her delight, her surprise. "Dinner's ready."

There's a pause, a pulse of silence. A rustle of paper. Then he speaks.

"Okay, Mom. I'll be right there."

Kate sits at the desk pressed against the window in the spare bedroom of her new two-bedroom condo. The glare from her laptop screen lights her face, a siren screams in the distance, and voices and laughter rise from the sidewalk. Everything is bright and boisterous, and Kate feels safe here in the city. Surrounded, even when she's still alone.

She checks the clock in the corner of her laptop screen. Still an hour before she has to leave, a late lunch with a woman who just started working at Kate's new company in this city where she still doesn't know many people. The woman is in her early thirties, childless, and perhaps a little too exuberant for Kate's taste, a little too eager to make plans. But Kate is trying. Maya has insisted on it. "You need more friends in this city than just me," she's always saying, nudging Kate's shoulder and grinning, so that Kate can't be offended. And she is right. Kate needs more friends who aren't part of a couple, who aren't used to Ben being there, who don't look at her tentatively, fearfully, as though the misfortune and violence might be contagious.

If this were a movie, or maybe a book, once the police cleared her and arrested the man across the street, the one whose mother had turned him in, which had rendered Kate and Maya's plan unnecessary, Kate would have found out she was pregnant. She would have learned that she was carrying Ben's child, and she'd have a successful pregnancy. She'd give birth to a boy who would grow to look just like Ben, and although it would be difficult, raising him on her own, she'd have that piece of her husband forever.

But this is her life, and so her period had started five days after Ben died, which was almost precisely when she was expecting it. And the pain of it, the expected, the highly probable blood, hurt so sharply. She felt lost. She felt like nothing.

Because Ben wasn't wrong. And she can only admit that now, months later, steeped in the irrevocability of Ben's goneness. She can acknowledge that she had become obsessed, singularly focused. That she had lost all the parts of herself that she'd once known and cultivated and felt pride in. That she'd been wishing away her days, clinging to the premise that she would be happy once she was pregnant. When, not if. She'd come to believe that she and Ben needed to be parents. That a future with children was a precondition to their present happiness, to their life together. Yet Ben knew better. After all, for all those years, they'd almost never spoken about children. They had things in common. They went to brunch and hiked trails identified as strenuous. They talked about adopting a dog. They had birthday dinners. They cleaned their bathroom together on Sunday mornings. As the moments that comprised their early thirties ticked by, and that singular focus took hold, Kate became lost. And Ben, patient and supportive Ben, had been trying to find her.

But Ben is gone, so very gone, and so it's easier now to admit that he wasn't wrong. And she misses him. The lack of him, the hole where he'd once been, screams in her ear, echoing and vibrating her core, even here in this condo he never set foot in, in this city they only very occasionally visited.

She's pretty sure that she's going to walk to the local animal shelter tomorrow to look at the cats. She's pretty sure that will help. And tonight, she'll meet Maya and a friend from Maya's law firm outside the American Visionary Art Museum, their bikes in tow. They'll ride to Fort McHenry, and Kate will feel her heart pumping; she'll feel alive. She'll think of Ben, and doing so won't make her unable to breathe. Not anymore. She'll be home before dusk, as the city's smog sits low around the bellies of the high-rise buildings. Before it gets too dark, she'll go inside. She'll turn on every light in the condo. She'll play music, and she'll feel something close to content.

And she's lucky, really, that their plan didn't pan out. That Henry was arrested instead—justice in the more ordinary sense. It's not lost on her that she should feel lucky to have her freedom. Even though there are still moments when she believes she might've preferred revenge.

Before closing her laptop, Kate scrolls to the beginning of her document and adds two blank pages. On the first, in all caps, she types the title: OURS IS A TALE OF MURDER.

On the next page, she writes the dedication. This is probably premature and presumptuous because only published novels have dedications, and this is merely the beginnings of a manuscript. But she doesn't care.

For Ben, she writes.

She'd thought she was finished writing for the day, but suddenly, she's scrolling downward furiously, fingertips to mouse pad. She's trying to be gentle with herself. No pressure. No word-count goals. Yet she realizes that she wants to keep going. For the first time in so long, there's so much she wants to say. She's been waiting for the words to flow. Here, at last, they come.

She continues to type. No more Klara or Troy. Instead, she's telling their story, hers and Ben's. A tale of murder. But not always. First, it was a tale of love.

The police and their questions kept her there for hours.

Janet told them that she didn't want to see her son. She didn't want to be home when they arrived to take him away. So she waited in the interview room until they'd secured the warrant for his arrest and transported him to the station.

Detective Scott had rapped sharply on the interview room door. "We've brought him in," she said softly, sympathy in her voice.

Janet collected her purse and stood. Her legs felt weak. Henry was there, which meant she could go.

She'd have to tell Bill what she did—what Henry did. Janet wondered if her husband also knew precisely what their son was. She wondered if he'd be upset with her, or would he, beneath the heaviness of the shame and the disappointment, taste just the sweetest hint of relief? The sense that with time, that taste would only grow stronger?

As she swung her car into the driveway, she reached up to press a finger into the garage door opener. She noticed something resting on the front porch and suspected it was a package. Something Bill or Henry ordered, because Janet herself still preferred going to a store when there was something she wanted or needed, and she knew that made her unusual and perhaps a bit old-fashioned. She thought about the detectives arriving and pounding on her front door, of Henry answering with his calm confidence. Did they use handcuffs? Did he resist?

She shook her head. It was done now. It was over.

Once parked in the garage, Janet climbed out of her car, trying to release the stiffness from her bones, trying to stretch the humming ache out of her lower back. The chair in the police station interview room was terribly uncomfortable, and she felt dirty and stale, like the odor, the very essence of all the bad people who had ever passed through the station's doors, had permeated her skin and clothes. She would shower and change into something fresh, and then she'd speak to Bill.

But first, she moved to the front porch to retrieve the package, which, she saw now that she was closer, wasn't a package at all. Rather, it was a round tin, red, as though intended to store Christmas cookies, but new-looking, as though purchased for the purpose of being left on Janet's front porch, for the purpose of being gifted to Janet.

She picked up the tin, turning it in her hands, looking for a note, but there was none, only a piece of tape fluttering forsakenly, half stuck to the lid, indicating that there may have been a note at some point but the wind took it away.

The front door was locked, and Janet didn't bother with digging through her purse for her keys. Despite that she only just dropped them inside a minute earlier, her bag had almost certainly devoured them, and to find them would require some digging and some patience. At the moment, Janet was fresh out. She stepped off the porch, returning to the garage, and entered the house that way.

In the kitchen, Janet eased a finger beneath the rim of the lid and popped it open, and she was met with warm and welcoming scents, odors of nostalgia, of banana, like the bread her mother used to make, of cinnamon and sugar. And something else, but she couldn't quite identify it.

Janet removed a muffin from the tin and peeled away the paper wrapper. She was in the police station for so long, and she was starving. She accepted their third, or maybe it was the fourth, offer of something to drink, but they never gave her anything to eat.

She'd taken a bite of the muffin, then another, before it occurred to her that she shouldn't be eating it at all. Food that had mysteriously appeared on her front porch, no note—it might not be safe.

She dropped the muffin back into the tin and wandered into the living room, looking out at the house across the street. The home of the man who her son killed. They couldn't be from the wife. That wouldn't make sense at all.

She wondered whether they were from Mary, a thank-you for turning in her own son. But would a thank-you be appropriate? Janet knew Owen had been under suspicion, but that wasn't why Janet did what she did. Besides, Mary couldn't yet know.

Peanut butter, she realized suddenly, bringing her fingertips, still lightly crumbed, to her nose and inhaling. That was what she could smell when she opened the tin, what she could still taste on her tongue.

And she no longer thought the muffins might be poisoned. Not for her. Not for most.

But Henry. Well, a bite could have killed him.

READING GROUP GUIDE

1. The story opens with a short section revealing a line that will be repeated throughout: "Ours is a tale of murder." How did this opening inform the way you viewed the events of the story, and what about this line becomes central to the mystery?

2. Throughout the story, the narration style changes. Klara's perspective is told from the first person, whereas the other characters are told in third. Why do you think that is, and how did it affect your reading experience? Do you think it added a component to the mystery?

3. Klara's feelings toward Troy progressively become more hesitant, and though she agrees to marry him, she seems to know something isn't right in their relationship. What are some of the things that make Klara question her husband, and why do you think Klara stayed with him if she knew there was something off?

4. What are some of the actions that Troy takes to bring him and Klara "closer," and how did he justify himself? Were you particularly surprised by anything that he did? How might this story be reflective of the way emotionally abusive and manipulative relationships are formed?

5. For most of the novel, Mary's story is seemingly unconnected from the rest of the events playing out. How does her piece of the puzzle come to fit with the rest of the plot? Did you see this coming, and if not, what did you think was going to happen?

6. What similarities were you able to draw between Troy and Henry, specifically in their thoughts and actions toward women? What might this say about the themes of possession and obsession that weave through the novel?

7. We know from the beginning that this is a tale of murder. As you read, who did you think the murder victim was going to be? Were you right, and if so, how did you know?

8. A major theme woven into the story is the effect our relationships can have on us. Besides Klara and Troy's romantic relationship, what other kinds of relationships are explored in the novel?

9. Part II begins with a twist that dismantles everything you might have thought was happening in the novel. How did this particular twist change your view of the events that occurred throughout? Did you see it coming? Then, think about your reading habits in general. Do you like big twists, or do you prefer novels that don't catch you off guard?

10. The last line of the novel throws another wrench in the story, leaving us with an open-ended twist. Who do you think sent the peanut butter muffins to Janet's doorstep?

11. There is a metafictional component to this novel. How did this aid in the mystery and, ultimately, change the course of the narrative? Have you ever read a novel that used these storytelling techniques before, and if so, how did it compare?

A CONVERSATION WITH THE AUTHOR

This is such an inventive and twisty novel that we couldn't put down! What was the inspiration behind the story?

The idea for this novel began with Klara and Troy—a professional couple whose relationship was not quite right. But I hit a wall when writing their story and couldn't figure out where it was going. That block gave me the idea—what if they were characters in a novel written by another character who, like me, was not sure where the story was going? What if the reader did not know this? Once I had that idea, I came up with the characters to fill out the neighborhood. Mary, with her tragic past and mysterious family member living in her basement. Henry, who the reader thinks is observing Klara, and his misguided and ultimately murderous plans. These characters really guided the rest of the plot and helped me find Klara and Troy's path as it converged with the author (Kate) who'd created them.

This novel is told from a few different perspectives, all of which are incredibly different from one another. Did you have a certain character you particularly enjoyed writing or, alternatively, one you found to be challenging?

I enjoyed writing Klara the most. Her thoughts and actions reflect the societal pressures sometimes placed on women her age, and it was fun to write her voice in a different point of view from the other characters, her chapters sort of like letters to Troy. It was most challenging to write Henry's chapters and Troy's. To delve into the minds of these wholly unapologetic and entitled men and try to understand their thinking—to convey that they saw no issues with their own behavior—was a difficult exercise.

Though this is a fun and fast-paced thriller, it also explores many complex themes, namely the effects of abusive relationships. What do you hope readers will take away from your story?

I hope readers will empathize with Klara's confusion about her relationship with Troy. What at times felt to Klara and seemed to others like intensity and devotion was actually emotional abuse and manipulation. Even though she is highly intelligent and educated, it took Klara a while to understand what was happening in her own relationship. Her actions were also influenced by other outside pressures: her age, her career stalling a bit. I hope readers understand that even a strong and independent person like Klara could be a victim of abuse in a way that doesn't look quite like what we might think of as an abusive relationship.

There are many twists in this novel, but there's a huge one that is sure to shock readers! How did you come up with this twist, and how might it have changed the way you had to go about writing?

It was my own writer's block when writing Klara and Troy's story that led me to come up with this twist. I wondered if I could write a "book-within-a-book" element to their story, where the reader did not realize they were characters in another character's book. Could I trick the reader into believing Klara and Troy were living in the same world as the other characters, Mary and Henry? It was challenging but a lot of fun to try to make this work and to play with the fact that Troy and Klara aren't "real" to develop that twist. Although, none of the characters are real—the reader confronts that in a way we often don't when we become lost in a novel. When writing, I had to be very careful to fit what was happening to Klara and Troy in with what Henry and Mary were encountering in their neighborhood, living across the street from Kate and Ben.

ACKNOWLEDGMENTS

First, I must thank my readers. I'm so grateful to be in the position to sit down and draft acknowledgments for my third novel. There are so many amazing books on the physical and digital shelves, and I'm incredibly grateful that you chose this one.

Thank you to my brilliant agent, Sarah Landis. I truly feel so lucky to work with you, and your early enthusiasm for and notes on this manuscript were entirely transformative. It would not be the book it is without you.

Thank you to Shana Drehs and her team, to everyone at Sourcebooks Landmark. For your thoughtful suggestions, professionalism, excitement, and everything you've done to shepherd this book along. It's been a dream to work with all of you.

Thank you to my early readers for reviewing and sharing this book. Your time and consideration mean so much.

To my parents, for fostering my love of reading and learning, and for everything else.

To my husband, for your endless support and encouragement, for believing in me most, particularly when my belief in myself has wavered. Writing and publishing books can be emotionally exhausting, with the highest highs and the lowest, loneliest of lows. Thank you for being there with me through them all.

Finally, a note to our boys. While I was writing this book, it felt like something different from my prior manuscripts, a unique way to play with timelines and with various points of view. Then, as the plot took shape, as the holes filled, it became clear. *You're writing about motherhood*, I thought. *Again.* Consuming, crushing, hideous, beautiful motherhood. A book full of bad men—a mother's worst nightmare, particularly a mother to three sons, like me. I suppose that when I wrote this, as always, I was thinking about my sons. I was thinking about being a mother. So that's what this book, like everything, is about. And that's what this book, like everything, is for—you, my sweet boys. The tentative, proud smiles when you hold my books, when you see your mom's photo in the back. Here's another one for you. Thanks to you, my sons, I do this. I create and I feel and I process this strange and cruel world. And you are my suns, pure gold and perfect, the everything around which I am so lucky and grateful to orbit. And my love for you really is the biggest thing in the world.

ABOUT THE AUTHOR

© CRYSTAL TSENG

Nora Murphy is the author of *The Favor* and *The New Mother*. A practicing attorney, Nora resides in Maryland with her husband, three sons, and four rescue pets.